PRAISE FOR

The Geographer's Map to Romance

"A funny, cozy romantasy with a splash of Indiana Jones. I can't wait for the next installment!"

—Julia Quinn,
#1 *New York Times* bestselling author of the Bridgerton series

"Charts a trajectory from first dances to second chances, equal parts earnest and tongue in cheek, and entirely, madly charming. Holton has done it again with her trademark frothy, joyous storytelling, this time celebrating love and landscape (often sublime; sometimes explosive). Her writing positively sparkles with magic."

—Brigitte Knightley,
author of *The Irresistible Urge to Fall for Your Enemy*

"India Holton's books are unlike anything else in romance right now—and that's very much a compliment!" —Paste

"Effervescent. . . . Holton ratchets up the whimsy in her worldbuilding and her characters leap off the page, especially taciturn Gabriel, who manages to imbue myriad meanings into a simple 'Hm.' The result is a delicious, feel-good romp." —*Publishers Weekly*

"Holton layers on detail and frothy jokes like a pastry chef with an eye for fabulous icing roses, covering every inch of the story with sugared delights. Beneath this is an unfolding reconciliation between Elodie and Gabriel that becomes more satisfying as the book advances." —*Library Journal*

The Ornithologist's Field Guide to Love

"India Holton infuses the story with wry wit and meta inside jokes. Every sentence is positively vibrating with the kind of charm that will have you pressing your lips together with laughter. And yet amid all the outrageous and camp fun, Holton also succeeds in building a genuine love story—between two people who have kept the world at a distance for years but somehow find a home within each other. And if that doesn't sell you, then you should at least know this book has one of the funniest twists on the 'one bed' trope I've read in a long time."

—NPR

"Holton continues to be the world's leading engineer of the *romp*. . . . Positively confectionary: a sweetly earnest love story wrapped in layers of sharp wordplay, deadly magical birds, and cheeky narrative awareness."

—Alix E. Harrow,
New York Times bestselling author of *Starling House*

"Holton's prose winks and sparkles with wit and magic, flitting expertly between laugh-out-loud hijinks, swoonworthy romance, and adventure filled with fowl play. . . . Pure, rollicking fun—and will set your heart aflutter."

—Allison Saft,
New York Times bestselling author of *A Fragile Enchantment*

"No one writes banter and charm like India Holton. Beth and Devon's love story isn't just entertaining and educational—it's swoonworthy. . . . An unputdownable academic adventure."

—Raquel Vasquez Gilliland,
USA Today bestselling author of *Witch of Wild Things*

"By Jove! . . . A delightfully madcap rivals-to-lovers romp featuring India Holton's trademark wit, genteel ladies who enjoy tea with their fisticuffs—and of course, oodles of magical murder birds. I was charmed from beginning to end!"

—Jenna Levine,
USA Today bestselling author of *My Roommate Is a Vampire*

"I adored India Holton's latest historical fantasy romance! My heart must be a bird, because Professors Beth Pickering and Devon Lockley have captured it. Holton writes with wit and whimsy, building a tender and sensual romance while sending her characters on a madcap adventure dotted with exotic birds, ruthless ornithologists, and a gaggle of very concerned French fishermen. The story is charming, swoonworthy, and delightfully nerdy, and Holton's prose sparkles with both sly humor and gorgeously rendered descriptions. This is a magically romantic delight."

—Sarah Hawley,
author of *A Witch's Guide to Fake Dating a Demon*

"India Holton's writing is not only the most vibrantly unique I've ever read, but also the tears-in-your-eyes funniest. Her characters—from the rivaling heroes to their colorful supporting cast—all sparkle with pure wit, swoonworthy charisma, and magical warmth. I want to dive headfirst into *The Ornithologist's Field Guide to Love* and live forever among the feathered creatures and charming academia."

—Kate Golden,
USA Today bestselling author of *A Dawn of Onyx*

"Few things are as delightful as an India Holton book, and every time I get the chance to read one, it feels like Christmas morning. Clever wordplay, gorgeous prose, adventure, and romance that made my heart happy-sigh over and over—*The Ornithologist's Field Guide to Love* has *everything* that I want in a novel, and the reading experience was like sitting in a magic cauldron, bubbling over with joy."

—Sarah Hogle, author of *Old Flames and New Fortunes*

The Secret Service of Tea and Treason

"Everything I wanted and everything I didn't know I needed. No. one writes like India Holton—and I have never met a more immersive read! This Victorian rom-com absolutely sparkles! It was tenderly strong, hilariously romantic, and deliciously steamy. A pitch-perfect addition to this fantastical series!"

—Sarah Adams, author of *The Cheat Sheet*

"Oh my giddy heart! . . . Brilliantly bonkers, romping fun—sleuthing shenanigans, explosive action, and most of all, radiant, romantic joy. I adored every page."

—Chloe Liese, author of *Two Wrongs Make a Right*

"With moments of high comedy and incredible sweetness, a gazillion more uniquely Holton-esque shenanigans, and a wonderful neurodivergent heroine to boot, *The Secret Service of Tea and Treason* is joyous, marvelous fun."

—Sangu Mandanna,
author of *The Very Secret Society of Irregular Witches*

"Following up *The League of Gentlewomen Witches*, one of my favorite romances of all time, was no easy feat, but Holton manages to match its perfection with this exemplary undercover romance."

—BuzzFeed

"Holton's trademark wit and prose are present throughout . . . and there is no shortage of sparks between Alice and Bixby. You'll find yourself laughing out loud and swooning at numerous parts of the story."

—Paste

The League of Gentlewomen Witches

"A brilliant mix of adventure, romance, and Oscar Wilde–esque absurdity—one of the wittiest, most original rom-coms I have read all year."

—Evie Dunmore,
USA Today bestselling author of *Bringing Down the Duke*

"There's no literary experience quite like reading an India Holton book. . . . A wild, rollicking, delicious carnival ride of a story, filled with rakish pirates, chaotic witches, flying houses (and bicycles, and pumpkins), delightful banter, and some serious steam. You've never read Victorian romance like this before . . . and it'll ruin you for everything else."

—Lana Harper,
New York Times bestselling author of *Payback's a Witch*

"Sexy, funny, and utterly charming. . . . Like a deliciously over-caffeinated historical-romance novel. Not only does Holton treat us to a fiery feminist witch as our heroine and a dashing pirate as our leading man, but she also gives us lyrical prose and crackling banter to enjoy on the side. Buckle up, readers, because this is a ride you won't want to miss."   —Lynn Painter, author of *Mr. Wrong Number*

"What happens when a prim and proper witch crosses paths with a dashing pirate? Flaming chaos and delicious debauchery, of course. . . . Another wickedly funny romp through this glorious world created by India Holton."

—Harper St. George, author of *The Devil and the Heiress*

"When a prickly witch meets her match in a dangerously endearing pirate . . . the match bursts into flames! India Holton's joyous, swoony, genre-exploding novel is a marvel, bristling with wit (and weaponry!) and brimming with love. . . . Will steal your heart, fly it to the moon, and return it to your chest, sparking with magic and just in time for tea."

—Joanna Lowell, author of *The Runaway Duchess*

The Wisteria Society of Lady Scoundrels

"Holton is having as much fun as the English language will permit—the prose shifts constantly from silly to sublime and back, sometimes in the course of a single sentence. And somehow in all the melodrama and jokes and hilariously mangled literary references, there are moments of emotion that cut to the quick—the way a profound traumatic experience can overcome you years later."

—*The New York Times Book Review*

"This melds the Victorian wit of Sherlock Holmes with the brash adventuring of Indiana Jones. . . . A sprightly feminist tale that offers everything from an atmospheric Gothic abbey to secret societies."

—*Entertainment Weekly*

"Easily the most delightfully bonkers historical-fantasy romance of 2021! Featuring lady pirates in flying houses and gentlemen assassins with far too many names, I enjoyed every absorbing moment."

—Jen DeLuca, author of *Well Played*

"The most charming, clever, and laugh-out-loud funny book I've read all year—it is impossible to read *The Wisteria Society of Lady Scoundrels* and not fall in love with its lady pirates, flying houses, and swoonworthy romance. India Holton's utterly delightful debut is pure joy from start to finish."

—Martha Waters, author of *To Have and to Hoax*

"With a piratical heroine who would rather be reading and a hero whose many disguises hide a (slightly tarnished) heart of gold, *The Wisteria Society of Lady Scoundrels* is the perfect diversion for a rainy afternoon with a cup of tea. What fun!"

—Manda Collins,
author of *A Lady's Guide to Mischief and Mayhem*

ABOUT THE AUTHOR

India Holton resides in New Zealand, where she has enjoyed the typical Kiwi lifestyle of wandering around forests, living on wild islands and messing about in boats. Her writing is fueled by tea and thunderstorms.

TITLES BY INDIA HOLTON

DANGEROUS DAMSELS

The Wisteria Society of Lady Scoundrels

The League of Gentlewomen Witches

The Secret Service of Tea and Treason

LOVE'S ACADEMIC

The Ornithologist's Field Guide to Love

The Geographer's Map to Romance

The Antiquarian's Object of Desire

THE
ANTIQUARIAN'S
OBJECT OF DESIRE

INDIA HOLTON

PENGUIN BOOKS

PENGUIN BOOKS

UK | USA | Canada | Ireland | Australia
India | New Zealand | South Africa

Penguin Books is part of the Penguin Random House group of companies
whose addresses can be found at global.penguinrandomhouse.com

Penguin Random House UK,
One Embassy Gardens, 8 Viaduct Gardens, London SW11 7BW

penguin.co.uk

Penguin
Random House
UK

First published in the United States of America by Berkley,
an imprint of Penguin Random House LLC 2026
First published in Great Britain by Penguin Books 2026
001

Book design by Katy Riegel
Printed and bound in Great Britain by Clays Ltd, Elcograf S.p.A.

The authorized representative in the EEA is Penguin Random House Ireland,
Morrison Chambers, 32 Nassau Street, Dublin D02 YH68

A CIP catalogue record for this book is available from the British Library

ISBN: 978–1–405–97261–1

Penguin Random House is committed to a sustainable future
for our business, our readers and our planet. This book is made from
Forest Stewardship Council® certified paper.

MIX
Paper | Supporting
responsible forestry
FSC® C018179

For Dale and Steph, with love

TABLE OF
SIGNIFICANT CHARACTERS

IN ORDER OF APPEARANCE

AMELIA TARRANT . . . would rather be reading

CALEB STERLING . . . had a character description but accidentally blew it up

MR. DUMMERSBY . . . opinionated

VARIOUS ACADEMICS

CORNELIUS OTTERSOCK . . . at the end of his tether and all out of knots

VANITY TUNNICLIFFE . . . liable to commit charades at any moment

JACK SHEFFIELD . . . a man of few words and even fewer facial expressions

MAVIS AND HILDA . . . ladies of a rural persuasion

BASIL THROCKMORTON . . . a villain, although his mustache is too bushy to twirl

GRIMSHAW . . . an expertly dolorous butler

SIR NIGEL HARROWAY . . . curious

LADY RUPERTA HARROWAY . . . lady of the manor

ASSORTED SERVANTS

MRS. CUDDLE . . . a grim housekeeper

CHAPTER ONE

In history, there is no single point of beginning.
I, on the Past, Cornelius Ottersock

IT HAD JUST gone six o'clock in the evening and nothing had exploded yet. This was good news for the staff of the Minervaeum, London's premier club for academics, where arguments and experiments all too often detonated into chaos. They dared not relax, however, for the night was still young and the library full of historians. No one is more dangerous than people who have little interest in the future.

Some fifty gentlemen cluttered the somber, book-lined chamber, enjoying sherry, nibbles, and a haze of pipe smoke. A few dozed in leather armchairs, for they had been up since the twelfth century, academically speaking, to prepare for a symposium that commenced the next morning.

Only one woman was present, alone at a table in a corner. Several books lay open before her, and she consulted them as she wrote page after page of notes. Lamplight dappled with rain shadows from a nearby window flickered over her tightly bound dark hair and black dress, making her seem evanescent, like a ghost trying to research a way back into life.

"Who is that charming creature?" asked Mr. Beaulieu, a junior professor who had come over from Paris for the symposium. Studying the woman's quiet poise as she sipped from a dainty porcelain cup, and noting in particular the lack of a wedding ring, he felt something stir in his heart where before there had been only midterm breaks and Brie cheese.

"That's Amelia Tarrant," Mr. Dummersby of the British Museum told him. It sounded rather the same as *that's a Viking ship coming toward us*.

Beaulieu's eyes widened. "The antiquarian professor from Oxford University?"

Dummersby nodded solemnly. "Correct."

"Mon Dieu!" Beaulieu reared back, crossing himself. "In France we call her La Terrifiante Erudite."

"In England we try not to call her anything, in case she hears us."

They regarded the woman from behind the safety of their pipes. She set down her tea to stir it before laying the teaspoon on a napkin and taking another sip. Her eyes closed at the taste.

"She looks so genteel," Beaulieu remarked rather wistfully.

"Looks can be deceiving," Dummersby warned. "I once paid her a compliment and she's refused to work with me ever since."

"No!"

"Yes. I ask you, what kind of woman doesn't like being told by a colleague that she has beautiful lips? And last week she argued with Professor Sterling over a magical candlestick, causing a fire that nearly burned down the Ashmolean Museum."

"Mon Dieu!"

Dummersby gave a shrug that said quite plainly, *it's all you can expect from antiquarians.* They were forever causing drama with magical antiques instead of just quietly reading about drama like proper historians.

"Sterling," Beaulieu mused. "Isn't he the one who found Jane Seymour's lost ghost in a jewelry box?"

"That's him. He and Tarrant are fierce enemies."

"Fascinating," Beaulieu murmured, eyeing Amelia once again. Then the library door swung open, admitting bright light from the corridor beyond and dazzling his attention. Beaulieu turned to see a man enter, reading a book as he walked.

Beaulieu gasped, for the newcomer was scandalously close to being naked. Clad in nothing more than trousers and an open-collared shirt, he had no pomade in his blond hair, not even the merest hint of a mustache anywhere about him, and worse, his fingernails were polished with a red tint. Beaulieu had never seen the like before, and was uncomfortably interested.

The man looked up from his book and, discovering a crowd of historians staring at him, blinked with surprise. "Good heavens," he remarked mildly. "What have you done to the kitchen?"

"It's next floor down," someone called out.

"Oh." He paused, seemingly hoping that the library might transform itself into a kitchen if he but waited a moment. Then he caught sight of the buffet table and, with a shrug, headed for it. Historians scattered from his path.

"Who is he?" Beaulieu whispered rather trepidatiously.

"That," Dummersby intoned, "is Professor Caleb Sterling."
Clink.

At the small, sharp sound, both historians jolted. Amelia Tarrant had set her cup down in its saucer. She stared across the room at Sterling.

THUD.

Now the entire gathering jolted as Sterling slammed his book shut. He stared back at Amelia.

Beaulieu had considered himself an expert on the Black Death until this moment, seeing the expression in Sterling's eyes. Amelia, for her part, did not even blink.

"Oh dear," Dummersby murmured. "Here we go again . . ."

AMELIA WATCHED COOLLY as Caleb approached. He took his time, pausing now and again to chat with people in the crowd, but he flashed her dark glances just to prove himself an absolute villain. She frowned in reply.

She'd not seen him since the Ashmolean incident. After the flames had been extinguished and the museum's curators settled with tea and biscuits, she'd been summoned by Professor Ottersock, head of Oxford's Material History faculty, and she'd made her attitude clear to him.

"I hate the man," she declared (albeit in the polite, gently modulated tones of a well-brought-up lady for whom hatred was something expressed only in strictest privacy). "I certainly did not intend to meet him in the museum at night. We argued, which is how the candlestick got dropped. It won't happen again, I can assure you."

In response, Ottersock just *looked* at her over the glass of laudanum he was about to drink for his sudden migraine.

"Sterling is a scoundrel," Amelia added for good measure. And then, worried that she'd gone too far—"He's also an excellent historian and valued colleague, of course."

"Sit down, Tarrant," Ottersock said wearily, gesturing at a

chair in front of his desk. "Talk to me about what's going on for you."

Good God. Amelia had not become an expert antiquarian and professor at the age of twenty-six by *having conversations*. "I'm fine," she said, which was as emphatic an end to the matter as any British person could provide.

Ottersock sighed and scratched at his bushy gray sideburns. "Let me put it another way. I want to know what on earth you were thinking, young lady! Mishandling a thaumaturgic candlestick and causing a fire is one thing, but a girl should not be working alone in a museum after dark, let alone bantering with a male colleague!"

"Arguing," Amelia corrected him.

"Engaging in private intercourse," he corrected her right back, with all the authority of a faculty head and older white male.

Amelia was so alarmed by this definition she nearly gasped aloud. She'd barely escaped losing her position at Oxford earlier this year due to Caleb Sterling. Although they had been friends since they met as eight-year-olds in boarding school, the moment Professor Throckmorton from Medieval Studies caught them hugging, that became impossible.

Throckmorton, caring not that Caleb had merely been consoling her after she received news of her grandfather's death, had spread such malicious gossip that Amelia was officially told to either marry Caleb or quit her professorship. After all, just because women had been admitted to tertiary education after Queen Charlotte demanded it a hundred years earlier didn't mean they were free to *act like men*. Heavens, if female academics started touching their male colleagues willy-nilly (so to speak), what would come next? Trousers on ladies?!

She'd survived the scandal, unmarried and employed, because no one would call Caleb and her friends these days. Indeed, they were the very model of foes. And yet still she felt her job in peril.

"I'm afraid I have no time to discuss the matter," she told Ottersock. "I'm going to Hereford to follow up on a clue about treasure in the cathedral there." Actually, she'd planned her departure for tomorrow, but getting out of town fast seemed the only way to avoid this talk. "My train leaves in two hours."

Ottersock choked on his laudanum. "What? You can't just run off! We haven't finished our discussion! Sit down!"

Driven to desperate measures, Amelia looked at her wristwatch, then raised big, imploring eyes to the faculty head. Alarm that she might start crying blazed across Ottersock's face.

"Fine," he grumped. "Go! And for God's sake, don't blow anything up!"

She'd gone, only returning this afternoon in time for the symposium—and with *absolutely no awareness whatsoever* that Caleb also was staying at the Minervaeum. Indeed, when Professor Jemeson from Cambridge University's Classics faculty waylaid her in a corridor to inform her of this ("Now, don't go burning down the club, little lady, ha ha ... Say, want to come to dinner with me?"), Amelia had expressed complete surprise.

Unfortunately, Jemeson had not told her about the presymposium drinks being held in the library, and now here Caleb was, walking toward her through a crowd of people trained to tell stories. Amelia looked up to the ceiling's painted heaven, but its frolicking cherubs offered no inspiration. When she looked down again, Caleb was standing on the other side of the table, as if he'd magically folded space and time to reach her.

"Good evening, Mr. Sterling," she said in a prim voice.

"Miss Tarrant," he drawled. "Sitting alone in a corner, I see."

"Hoping to avoid unpleasant company," she replied pointedly.

He smirked. She stared. The atmosphere grew almost unbearably tense (perhaps because everyone in the library was holding their breath).

Then Caleb gave a dramatic sigh. Dropping into the chair opposite Amelia, he leaned forward, elbows on the table and chin set atop his linked fingers. His blue-eyed gaze seemed to twinkle behind wayward strands of hair. "Hello, Meely."

Amelia glanced at the historians behind him, who hastily looked away as if they possessed no interest whatsoever in the conversation. "Please leave, Mr. Sterling," she replied. "I'm trying to work."

"You needn't call me Mr. Sterling when we're alone." He grinned with appallingly winsome charm. "*Professor* will do fine."

How anyone could make such a respectable title sound indecent, Amelia did not know. "We aren't alone," she pointed out. "There are fifty other people in the room."

"When I'm with you, it feels as if the rest of the world vanishes."

Amelia rolled her eyes.

"Speaking of vanishing," he continued, "you fled after the Ashmolean fire—"

"I went to Hereford," she corrected him.

"I've been worried."

"Nonsense. You've been sleeping half the day and reading"— she angled her head to see the title of his book, and her nose wrinkled—"Byron."

"Of course I've been reading Byron," he retorted, as if it were obvious. "My best friend disappeared into the ether!"

"Sh!" Amelia glanced again at the crowd, but they had

given up hope of scandal and returned to their conversations. "I only went out of town for a few days. That's hardly a good reason to succumb to Romantic poetry."

"Was it because I got my eyebrows shaped and you were overwhelmed by their beauty?" he asked with apparent sincerity.

Amelia *tsk*ed. "No, I—" She paused, looking at his eyebrows, and he grinned. She speared him with a frown, although only briefly, in case she hurt him for real. "Scoundrel. No, Professor Ottersock started asking too many questions, and I needed an excuse to get away. You know that if he realized the truth about us not actually being enemies, he'd immediately fire me. He hasn't budged from his notion that a male and female professor being bosom friends would bring Oxford into disrepute."

"Well if you're going to use a phrase like 'bosom friends' I can't say I blame him," Caleb said, then smiled again as her frown reappeared. "So when you sent me a note to meet here tonight, you weren't planning to tell me goodbye forever? And in public, where I couldn't make a scene?"

Amelia suppressed a laugh. "As if being in public ever deterred you from making a scene. No, I'm not planning to say goodbye. I wouldn't leave Oxford." She paused for the slightest of moments, then added, "My aunt Mary would get too lonely."

"Ah yes, poor Aunt Mary, with only her husband, your brother, your cousin, his wife, and your parents for company." He chuckled, and a dozen heads in the crowd whipped around to see what was happening and whether it signaled an imminent explosion.

"You are a pest!" Amelia declared at once in a strident voice.

Caleb straightened, shaking back his hair. "And you are poison!"

Murmuring, the crowd turned away again. Amelia and Caleb exchanged a look that mingled amusement, exasperation, and old remembrances—the kind of look only possible when you have known someone most of your life. *No*, Amelia corrected herself, *"known" skimped on the truth*. She didn't just know Caleb. He was deep inside her heart, the truest friend she'd ever had, her most favorite person in all the world.

He was not supposed to be. Society, faced with the minefield of co-ed schools, tolerated the opposite sexes being friends only so long as they never touched, never went anywhere alone together, and never progressed beyond the most polite of conversations.

Because of that, she and Caleb had, since adolescence, kept the richness of their friendship scrupulously hidden behind a facade of "just chums." But one slip had been all it took . . . one hug in a supposedly empty lane . . . to ruin everything. When Throckmorton went on his gossipmongering spree, their academic peers (generally speaking, a group of bookish old men who themselves had never been hugged, except that one time Mama was a bit drunk and feeling sentimental), were immediately ready with charges of seduction! misconduct! and making everyone else feel all hot and bothered!

Only a show of outright enmity had been able to stop the virulent rumors and ensure Amelia kept her reputation and her job, and Caleb kept his lifestyle as a wild, carefree bachelor (which mostly involved sleeping in late and adding bacon to every meal).

They'd become rather good at it; indeed, Caleb seemed to be having so much fun coming up with novel insults for her that Amelia didn't quite know whether to be entertained or offended. And the madcap scheme was actually working. Professor

Ottersock complained daily about their antagonism, but he never guessed that Amelia and Caleb might be doing worse things than arguing; i.e., lounging next to each other on a sofa, drinking tea, and discussing their favorite types of biscuit.

Amelia could only suppose that society's fear of men and women being close friends originated with historical events, such as when Isabella of France chummied up to Roger Mortimer and together they invaded England, overthrowing the king, her husband. Otherwise, the whole nonsense was beyond her. Fortunately, she was an antiquarian, not a psychiatrist, because she found people utterly inexplicable.

Caleb leaned back in his chair, propping his feet up on the table, ankles crossed. Amelia stiffened, imagining the germs that were no doubt leaping from his shoes to populate her books. "What are you writing?" he asked.

"My speech for the symposium tomorrow."

"Is it about the amazing treasure you found in Hereford Cathedral?"

She raised an eyebrow. "How do you know I found anything?"

"Because I know you."

All of a sudden Amelia's interior twinkled, as if her cells had turned to stars. "It's just a trinket, nothing important," she said. (It was extraordinary.) "Not even worth discussing." (If she didn't win this year's Petrarch Award for Excellence in Historical Research, King Henry VIII was an exemplary husband.)

"Can I see it?" Caleb craned his head as if he might be able to read her notes from a distance, upside down.

Amelia laid a hand over the page. It contained a rough draft, and not even Caleb was allowed to see her grammatical errors. "You'll learn about it tomorrow."

Caleb's eyes widened with genuine astonishment. "You don't think I'm actually going to attend the symposium? Good God, there's nothing more tedious than listening to a gaggle of historians droning on."

"*You're* a historian."

"I'm an antiquarian. Haven't you heard, that's—"

"Entirely different," they chorused, and shared a brief, sardonic smile—then hastily erased it in case anyone was watching. "So . . ." Caleb said, rocking his feet side to side. "Does your treasure do anything interesting? Would it turn Ottersock into a frog? Please say yes."

"*Caleb,*" she murmured chidingly.

"Sorry," he lied. "Come on, bella luna, show me."

Amelia drew breath to chide him for using the nickname, which he'd come up with years ago in a moment of random poeticism and which she'd never been able to talk him out of. It was a very pretty endearment—just not when used in a room full of their colleagues. Then she froze, noticing a nearby historian straining to overhear them. It was Dummersby from the British Museum, second only to Professor Throckmorton as academia's worst tattler. Immediately she glared at Caleb.

"Do not even think about touching that teaspoon!"

She flicked her gaze meaningfully toward Dummersby, and in a flash Caleb's feet were down and he was leaning forward, snatching her teaspoon from where it had been lying on a napkin beside her cup.

"Stop!" Amelia commanded, but he was already leaning back in the chair again.

"This?" he said, staring incredulously at the teaspoon. "This is your amazing treasure? Really? What does it do, turn tea into wine?"

Well, really! Even though they were pretending, Amelia felt a stab of offense. Getting to her feet, she rounded the table with a determination she'd learned from studying Queen Isabella, the She-Wolf of France. Caleb stood, his chair scraping against the floor, his grin twisting into a wary grimace.

"You are an unprincipled miscreant," Amelia told him.

"Mm-hm," he agreed, nodding.

"Give. It. Back."

He held out the teaspoon. "Show me what it does. I dare you."

"Oh well, if you *dare* me," Amelia retorted sarcastically. She did not reach for the teaspoon—she'd known him far too long to fall for a trap like that—and he stepped forward, coming so close she could see the flecks of gold in his eyes. The other historians had begun setting down their drinks, stuffing canapes into their pockets, and edging for the door, but Amelia didn't notice. Caleb's gaze was intense in its focus. He'd changed his brand of cologne while she'd been away, and the woodsy freshness infused her breath like a summer's morning. The warmth of his smile pressed against her lips, although they weren't touching.

"I *double* dare you," he said, his voice deep and shadowy.

Little flutters of sensation went through Amelia's stomach. *I must have bound my corset too tight,* she thought. After all, she wouldn't flutter for Caleb. Their relationship was entirely platonic, their touches innocent—for example, when she brushed a crumb from his sleeve, beneath which his arms had grown so muscular over the years; or when he reached for one of the ginger candies she kept in her skirt pocket and accidentally stroked her thigh through layers of cotton and lace . . .

"Is it getting hot in here or is it just me?" Beaulieu asked, fanning himself.

We're only friends, Amelia reiterated to herself. Friends who were fake hating to protect her reputation.

Flutter flutter, her stomach replied.

She glowered even more fiercely at Caleb, and he glowered right back. "Someone go fetch the building's fire warden, hurry!" a professor exhorted in a loud whisper.

Without taking his eyes off her, Caleb lifted the teaspoon and drew the tip of his tongue slowly up it.

Alarmed that her evidently shrinking corset might crush her, Amelia snatched the spoon from him. "For heaven's sake," she grumbled. "This is a very sensitive and dangerous item."

"It tastes like sugar," he said. "You stirred your tea with it." He cocked his head, smiling with fascination at her, and Amelia flushed, imagining him smiling like that before he kissed a woman.

"It's thaumaturgic silver," she said. "In the Siege of Hereford during the civil war, a vicar hid it inside the cathedral's crypt, to be used as a final defense should the building be stormed. He left a vague mention of this in his journal, which I deciphered."

"Okay," Caleb said, still smiling.

The teaspoon began to feel warm in Amelia's hand as she clutched it even tighter. "It's *magical.*"

"Prove it."

Nearby, a lamp crackled.

"Please," he added, fluttering his eyelashes. And while Amelia was trying to decide whether he'd darkened them with cosmetics, he reached out to grab the teaspoon again. She automatically slapped his hand away. He slapped hers back.

At which point, both remembered they were standing in full view of their peers, and proceeded to act accordingly.

In other words, a hand-slapping match broke out. Within seconds the teaspoon dropped to the floor, ignored.

"Ruffian!" Amelia exclaimed.

"Pernickitator," Caleb retorted.

"That's not a real word!"

"See what I mean?"

Tiny blue flames of magic began to flicker along the spoon's handle. In response, books tumbled from shelves, and the lamp's glass shade melted.

"You are outrageous!" Amelia declared. She almost skidded on the teaspoon, and Caleb caught her by one elbow to steady her. "You are obnoxious!" she added, pulling from his grip. *"You are overly opinionated!"*

"And you've clearly spent ages consulting a thesaurus to describe me. It's highly suggestive." He raised his eyebrows, but when Amelia lowered hers in a frown, he retreated. In doing so, he accidentally kicked the teaspoon. It went skittering across the floor, trailing sparks and making historians leap from its path.

"Being suggestive is the *purpose* of a thesaurus," Amelia said.

"You should try poetry instead."

The teaspoon clattered. Sausage rolls began levitating off the buffet table.

"You are a beetle-headed, flap-ear'd knave!" Amelia shouted, driven to the Shakespearean level of insults.

Thud thud thud. More books fell off their shelves or flew across the room, pages flapping, to slam against a wall. Historians ducked behind armchairs or cowered beneath desks. Beaulieu emitted a high-pitched scream and fainted into Dummersby's arms.

"Better that than a stinging wasp!" Caleb retorted.

Amelia blasted him with her fiercest stare, the one she usually reserved for students who claimed three grandmothers' funerals in one year. The usual pretense at enmity was escalating out of control, just as it had in the Ashmolean when a curator came upon them standing close together while they inspected the candlestick. She could not understand why, any more than she could stop it. Arguing with Caleb was beginning to have the same effect on her that the divine right of kings had on England's Parliament, and she couldn't seem to restore her calm head.

Suddenly the teaspoon leaped up, spinning as if it were stirring the air. Flares of blue light and fire burst from it. The historians began to shout and push one another as they made a dash for the exit. Finally noticing, Amelia turned to stare at the spoon with trepidation. Beside her, Caleb did the same.

"What's its power?" he asked from the side of his mouth.

"Intense combustion in response to environmental discord," Amelia said.

They glanced at each other with a silent *oh, damn* . . .

As THE EXPLOSION boomed through the Minervaeum, its staff sighed wearily and went to fetch the ever-present water buckets.

CHAPTER TWO

There are two sides to every story.
And usually, they're both wrong.

I, on the Past, Cornelius Ottersock

"IT WAS ALL my fault," Caleb confessed to Professor Ottersock with an apologetic smile, two days later in Oxford. "Miss Tarrant is entirely innocent. Indeed, she is a victim of my bad behavior and should not be included in any blame."

He spoke easily—as well he should, considering he'd been making that exact statement for years, whenever anyone in charge inquired about What the Hell Happened. Which was often. But look, he couldn't help it if he possessed a dazzling genius that disdained ordinary rules of both society and science, and that consequently saw him being summoned to headmasters' offices more times than he could count. It came as no surprise to find himself in one again now.

This office, inside Balliol College at the heart of Oxford University, looked the same as all the others—dark wood walls, dusty floor, a clutter of books, and a rather dingy portrait of Queen Victoria—as if there were only one head's office in all of Britain and its various tenants jumped through space and time to occupy it. In fact, it was Ottersock's personal office, forced into use as the Material History faculty headquarters since the previous one was wrecked by a poltergeist who escaped from an old textbook. As a consequence, Caleb could see through a half-open door the professor's unmade bed, presided over by a battered toy giraffe.

His smile quirked. Beside him, without so much as a glance, Amelia swatted his thigh with the back of her hand. The woman possessed an uncanny awareness of whenever he was being inattentive. Caleb obediently focused on Ottersock across the man's large, untidy desk and strove not to fidget, sigh, or outright leave the room while the professor gathered his thought.

Just one thought; Caleb was sure of it. Ottersock had never enjoyed great breadth of mind, especially when it came to them.

On the desk lay the Hereford teaspoon, unscathed by its eruption of magic, despite the damage it had done to the Minervaeum Club. Amelia was staring at it fixedly, as if the little old spoon were in fact a sword Ottersock would use to sever any hope she carried for tenure. Her eyes were narrowed, her posture even more scrupulous than usual, and the book she held was being hugged to within an inch of its life. (Mary Wollstonecraft's life, to be precise, from what Caleb could see of the cover.) She appeared on the verge of an extreme reaction, such as chewing her thumbnail.

Personally, Caleb doubted Ottersock would fire her. After all, last year at a Windsor Castle garden party for lady academics, she'd identified a teapot as being enchanted mere seconds before a servant poured thaumaturgic magma from it into Queen Victoria's cup. But then again, the faculty head truly had been furious back in April when he heard from Throckmorton about the two of them embracing, and not even the sight of Her Majesty's thank-you card to Amelia, which he kept framed on his office wall, had calmed him. He might not have ousted her had it really come to it, but he could easily have demoted her, and Caleb knew that, belonging as she did to a family bristling with brilliant, ambitious academics, Amelia would have considered this just as awful.

There also existed a good chance that, were it not for swearing they'd become estranged, the two of them would right now be married. Which would be most disturbing indeed.

Wanting to offer Amelia reassurance without ruining their guise, Caleb knocked the side of his foot against hers. She frowned.

Sigh, Caleb thought with, indeed, a noiseless sigh. Lately, Amelia had seemed all too convincing when it came to feigning hatred. Could she have grown weary of their friendship? No, that was impossible—he was a delight. She must have secretly taken acting lessons. Mind you, it didn't help that he'd been feeling a little off these days himself. Every time he looked at Amelia, an odd frazzlement possessed his body. Caleb didn't understand what had befallen him (probably because his idea of self-reflection involved checking his hair in the mirror before he went out), but he suspected that he'd picked up a stomach ailment somewhere.

"Idiotic!" Ottersock exclaimed.

Amelia stiffened even further, but Caleb only shrugged his mouth and nodded. When a man escapes a childhood in the Bethnal Green slum through academic scholarships and goes on to earn a professorship before the age of twenty-six, he feels unmoved by being called an idiot. Besides, Ottersock wasn't entirely wrong. The conversation with Amelia in the Minervaeum Club's library had affected Caleb in much the same way Parliamentarians affected King Charles I—i.e., made him lose his head.

"A thaumaturgic explosion!" Ottersock went on, taking a jar of willow-bark headache powder from his desk drawer. "Professors engaging in physical violence! A symposium canceled! And don't think I didn't hear about what happened on the train you took back to Oxford yesterday!" He frowned at them as he sprinkled some of the willow bark into a glass of water with practiced efficiency.

"The train incident wasn't our fault," Caleb said, brushing a tiny speck of fluff from his suit jacket to illustrate how unconcerned he was. "If Madame Kharensky didn't want to be exposed to robust language, she shouldn't have entered a carriage with antiquarians. After all, it's in our job description: we say it like it is."

Amelia cleared her throat, which Caleb understood to be the polite-lady version of muttering viciously under her breath. He knew she had Opinions about proper behavior on a train, but it had been an emergency situation. Madame Kharensky, Oxford's premium source of private news, had appeared in the carriage just as Caleb was helping Amelia with her luggage. The only possible reaction had been for him to shout *"Stop bloody dawdling, Tarrant!"* and drop the suitcase. Amelia in turn had denounced him as a dratted miscreant—which had made him laugh, her blush, and Madame Kharensky call upon the conductor to evict them from the train forthwith. Altogether it had been embarrassing, but at least the madame wouldn't spread nasty stories about Professor Sterling being solicitous toward Professor Tarrant—in other words, seducing her via luggage.

"I apologized at the time," Amelia told Ottersock, "and

evaluated the lady's Rundell garnet brooch for her, after which she was mollified."

"Hm," Ottersock said meaningfully, eyeing her from beneath arched eyebrows that were almost as bushy as his sideburns and mustache. Really, the man's face was a veritable thicket of whiskers, as if all the hair on his head had shed onto it, then stuck, leaving an entirely bald dome. When his eyebrows arched, it was like a Pomeranian dog pricking up its fluffy ears. Amelia stared into the middle distance, but she grew so rigid that Caleb feared they might have to place her on a trolley and wheel her out once the meeting was over.

And yet, she didn't have *complete* control of herself. One fine dark brown strand of hair had escaped her tight bun, defying half a dozen pins. It slipped down her bodice, stroking her breast, and Caleb . . .

". . . shattered!"

Blinking, he realized Ottersock was mid-complaint about the Minervaeum's library ceiling. "It was only *slightly* shattered," he assured the man. "Only two cherubs and half a cloud."

Ottersock gave him a long, grim stare. For a moment, the air seemed taut with potential shouting. Lamps flickered, and on the cabinet behind the professor, a stack of unread essays began to rustle ominously. Caleb and Amelia glanced sidelong at each other, then at the teaspoon. But it had not moved.

Ottersock shook more willow-bark powder into the glass. "Do you not care *at all* that they had to cancel the Two Hundred and Seventh Symposium of Historical Martial Enterprises Undertaken in the British Territories Including France?"

That he managed to say this all within one breath was impressive (and evidence of a lifetime of lecturing students whose attention span barely lasted five minutes). Caleb, however, was unfazed. "There's always next year."

"Which will make it the two hundred and seventh symposium in two hundred and *eight* years!" Ottersock shouted. "Completely out of kilter! Oxford will never live this down!" He swallowed his powdered drink in one gulp, grimacing at the taste.

"There really was no need to cancel," Caleb said.

"Professor Murkle's mustache turned pink!" Water droplets spat from Ottersock's lips, causing both Caleb and Amelia to take a step back. The essays behind the professor began to rise, page by page, from their stack. Ottersock continued on, oblivious. "Professor Taumalolo is under the delusion he's a kangaroo and was last seen hopping down the Mall. And I've had Cambridge's vice chancellor on the telephone, complaining that half his historians are speaking Middle English! And *not* just to show off! That teaspoon has damned powerful psychoconjunctive magic."

"Uh-huh," Caleb agreed, watching the essays fold themselves into darts and attack the portrait of Queen Victoria.

"Er, Professor . . ." Amelia began, reaching for the teaspoon.

"That's enough!" Ottersock shouted, slamming down the empty glass, and Amelia snatched back her hand. "I'm at my wit's end with you both!"

"But—" Caleb attempted, as a bust of King Henry VII suddenly breathed fire at a potted fern, thus putting it out of its miserable and withered existence.

"But—" Amelia also said, as several essays transformed into large moths that began flapping wildly, emitting blue sparks.

"Silence!" Ottersock roared. "The pair of you are leaving!"

At once, their attention snapped to him. "Leaving?" they chorused.

"Are you firing us?" Amelia added, her face blanching. Even Caleb felt disturbed. He'd spent his entire life aiming to become an Oxford professor. Without the job, he didn't know who he might become, but memories of grimy streets, thin gruel, and his father's death from cholera still haunted him with what he might have been.

Ottersock snatched up the jar of willow bark and began shaking powder directly into his cupped palm. "I'm not firing you. Yet. I'm sending you to the countryside."

"The what?" Aghast, Caleb was sure he must have misheard. A large moth landed atop Ottersock's head, but damned if he was going to say anything about it. Even Amelia remained silent, her brain no doubt stuck at the "yet" part of the conversation.

"Countryside," Ottersock repeated. "The big green place with lots of trees and hardly any students."

Caleb and Amelia looked at each other, wide-eyed, a silent conversation whipping back and forth between them. Then realizing that Ottersock was watching with roused suspicion, Caleb immediately frowned. "This is all your fault!" he grumbled at Amelia.

She gasped with credible outrage in reply. "Mine? If you weren't such a—a *rapscallion*—"

"Ooh," he gibed. "Never have I been so insulted."

Her eyes flashed. On the desk, the Hereford teaspoon began to tremble.

"Ahem." Ottersock cleared his throat with such vehemence, he must have strained his tonsils. "Can't you two stop with the enmity for just one hour?"

They murmured apologies. Ottersock tipped his handful of headache powder into his mouth, swallowing it unhappily. Wiping his lips with the back of his hand, he scowled at the door behind them. "You can come in now, Miss Tunnicliffe."

Caleb and Amelia looked back to see a young woman enter the office. She was attractively plump, with her black hair in a fashionably tall knot, and she wore a striped dress suit that didn't just say *I mean business* but practically gave a podium speech about it.

"Professor," she greeted Ottersock. "Professor, Professor," she added, nodding to Caleb and Amelia. Her tone was crisp, and yet the tightness with which her lace-gloved fingers clutched her reticule suggested nervous excitement behind the poise. She glanced at the moths and the fire-breathing statue, and her eyes widened.

"This is Miss Vanity Tunnicliffe," Ottersock introduced her. "She is a curator from the British Museum, and has a job for you."

"Actually, I'm just a receptionist," Miss Tunnicliffe said bashfully. "All the museum's curators were at the Minervaeum Club when some *dreadful* person let off a magic bomb. They're in various states of enchantment, so I was dispatched instead."

Ottersock's jaw twitched. Amelia stepped forward hastily, holding out her hand to the young woman in polite welcome.

"How do you do, Miss Tunnicliffe?"

"I am very well, Professor Tarrant," Miss Tunnicliffe replied, shaking the hand daintily. She spoke like a woman who wielded the Queen's English in the same conscious manner one wore an especially fashionable hat. "And you?"

Caleb rolled his eyes. They'd be here all day at this rate, and he had important work to enjoy ignoring. "What's this about?" he interrupted.

Miss Tunnicliffe turned to him, her expression brightening as she took in his remarkably good looks (or so Caleb assumed, disregarding the influence of the lamp behind him). "Professor Sterling, it's an honor. I attended your talk on the Big Bang last year."

Well perhaps they could spare a few minutes for small talk. "Ah yes, the explosion of Alfred the Great's statue in Southwark," he said, smiling with instinctive flirtatiousness. "I hope you found it interesting."

"Oh, yes, it was stellar!" Miss Tunnicliffe very nearly tittered but caught herself in time. "I'm here because Sir Nigel Harroway, a private collector of antiques, is donating a substantial portion of that collection to the British Museum. He suspects several of the items are made from thaumaturgic materials, so the museum requests that Oxford University loan us some specialists who can identify and organize the items before they're transported."

"Nobody is more specialist than us," Caleb assured her with a grin.

"Nobody is more annoying than you," Ottersock muttered. Miss Tunnicliffe glanced at him uncertainly, and he huffed in weary resignation. "They're really very good," he conceded.

"The senior curator did recommend Professor Glebe from Cambridge University—"

"No, no!" Ottersock held up his hands as if he could physically repel that very idea. "Tarrant and Sterling are the best. You want to take them, honestly. And keep them for as long as you wish. I promise they'll do excellent work!" He gave Caleb and Amelia a warning stare. "Not even these two can get into trouble in Cumbria."

"*Cumbria?!*" Caleb echoed in horror.

"But—but—" Amelia was apparently too dazed to form a proper sentence.

"But it's rural," Caleb supplied, unable to repress a shiver.

"And hours away," Amelia added.

"And rural," Caleb repeated, justifiably so.

Ottersock frowned with bewilderment. "How did you not realize 'the countryside' would be rural?"

"I assumed you were talking about somewhere like Greenwich. I can't go to *Cumbria*. I'm a great indoorsman; too much fresh air upsets my digestive system."

"Besides, term starts in a few days," Amelia said. "I have lectures to present."

"Me too," Caleb said, although in fact his plan for this term's lectures currently involved presenting a table clock that wasn't actually an antique, he just hoped his students would fix it for him, and taking a field trip to Jabbercoffee café to "study its old windows" while he drank a cappuccino.

"Pish!" Ottersock interjected. "Associate Professor Capping will take over both your lecture schedules. She can easily do so in addition to presenting her own lectures, holding tutorials, providing pastoral care to students, keeping up with her administrative duties, and captaining our faculty badminton team."

"Be reasonable, man," Caleb urged. "It's far too much to put on anyone, expecting them to go to *Cumbria*."

But Ottersock had long ago sacrificed being reasonable on the altar of faculty management. "It's decided, Sterling." He jammed the lid on the willow-bark jar like an exhausted student putting a full stop at the end of a dissertation. "Miss Tunnicliffe will accompany you to the Harroways' estate in her capacity as a . . . well, a receptionist, I suppose . . . and as a chaperone, since obviously a man cannot travel with a woman to whom he's not married."

"But traveling with two of them is acceptable?" Caleb asked wryly.

Ottersock ignored that. "Go home. Pack your bags. You leave today, eleven o'clock sharp!"

This dramatic announcement inspired a moment of stunned silence. (That is, apart from the papery rustle of the moth that was industriously spinning a cocoon in his hair.) Then Amelia said, "That gives us only an hour to prepare."

"And leave how?" Caleb asked suspiciously. Knowing Oxford University's approach to budgeting, he expected to be walking part of the distance.

"I'm supposed to be attending a family dinner this weekend," Amelia said.

"I don't have suitable shoes for the countryside," Caleb added.

Ottersock exhaled forcefully. The willow bark was causing his pupils to constrict, but this did not prevent him from scowling at both professors. "Your train departs at eleven o'-clock. On—" He jabbed the desktop with his pointer finger. "The—" *Jab*. "Dot." *Jab*. "Be on it or your jobs will be history!"

"Er . . ." Caleb said. "Strictly speaking, our jobs already are hist—"

"Go! Now!"

Being as they were not *complete* idiots, they went.

As AMELIA EMERGED from Ottersock's office into Balliol's Garden Quadrangle, she angled a hand over her eyes, shielding them against the morning light and hiding her frown. Cumbria! In autumn! With barely any warning! For an undetermined period of time! Just as term was beginning! And various other concerns that were comparatively minor but nevertheless also warranted exclamation marks!

Never before had she been so frazzled—and that was saying something, considering her job involved such things as time-warping clocks, ghost swarms, and undergraduate students. She faced catastrophe on a weekly basis. Usually a bit of glue fixed it. But there was no fixing this. Once again, Ottersock had overturned her life.

I should have accepted that offer from Heidelberg University, she told herself dourly, ignoring the fact that not only could she barely speak a word of German, but her mother had threatened to suffer a nervous collapse should she move to "that backwater"—i.e., Europe. And yet, she really couldn't bear to leave Caleb, who'd been her dearest friend since their early days at boarding school, when he found her crying in the dank shadows behind the dormitory and told her jokes until she laughed. The idea of life without him was a bleak one, and made the sacrifice of her gentility for their fake-hating scheme worthwhile. Albeit only just.

He came up alongside her, having paused to greet a random cat. His hands were in the pockets of his black plaid trousers, an improper habit from his childhood that no one had been able to break in him. A breeze tousled his hair into a state of uncontrived gorgeousness. Any passersby glancing at him would see only casual ease, but Amelia recognized the shadow in his eyes as he stared across the Quad, where cold sunlight gleamed on the rustling autumnal trees and immaculate lawns. She knew what he was thinking: that this represented the exact amount of nature he wanted in his life, thank you. Her own thoughts turned to a pair of new students loitering on the path. They were holding maps but nevertheless looking around with help-less bewilderment, and Amelia had to hold herself back from going to direct them. Getting lost at the start of term was essential to ultimately finding oneself by the end.

"Cumbria," Caleb grumbled. "This whole situation is—"

"Infuriating," she chorused with him in an identical tone of aggravation. They began walking side by side toward the Library Passage. As they went, Amelia felt inordinately conscious of Caleb's masculine presence beside her, and of the way students glanced at them—perhaps wondering if they were a couple? (Or perhaps, judging from the wary looks, aware of their explosive reputation.) Indeed, she had to press her hand against her stomach, for the flutters had commenced again.

So ridiculous! She'd walked beside Caleb a thousand times before. She'd stood beside him as head girl and head boy in secondary school, and shared a stage to present joint lectures. He'd been this much taller than her for years. This much stronger. There existed no good reason for her to suddenly realize he was strong enough to toss a woman over his shoulder and carry her away . . .

Hm, her body murmured.

"Ottersock is being completely unfair," Caleb said. "You do realize that it's autumn, yes? There's going to be mud. And rain."

"This is England," Amelia reminded him. "There's always rain. Make sure you pack the mackintosh I bought you last winter."

"And breezes," he went on. "I'll get bronchitis or—oh God—a red nose."

Amelia rolled her eyes at this whining. "You ought to have

considered the possible consequences before behaving so atrociously at the Minervaeum Club."

Caleb shot her an aggrieved look. "Come on, bella luna, you know *everyone* behaves atrociously at the Min. That's the third time this year the library ceiling has been broken."

She sighed. "True." In glum silence they crossed the Front Quad and, nodding to the porter, exited onto Broad Street. A chill breeze swept past them, musky with the smell of decaying leaves. Beyond the dreaming spires and solemn stone rooftops of the city, dark clouds were gathering.

"Well at least we're leaving before that storm gets here," Caleb said.

Amelia smiled at him. "I know you need your sunshine."

"That's what you're for," he answered frivolously.

Amelia felt a throb of emotion. Caleb was always saying such things, and yet it made a different impression on her heart this time. *He* was different, although she couldn't quite put her finger on how.

Something in her must have taken that to be a literal instruction, for she found herself touching a finger against Caleb's forearm, as if that would solve the mystery. Alas, however, it only left her with a great deal more questions. Questions that Caleb turned into an outright interrogation by reaching out to tuck a loose strand of her hair behind her ear. Amelia suddenly felt as if she'd been strapped to a vibrating machine and electrified.

At precisely that moment, a group of sophomores emerged from a bookstore across the street. Amelia took a hasty step back. "Mind your manners, Professor Sterling," she scolded, lest anyone had noticed their intimacy. *Wait, no!* she thought, blushing. *Not intimacy, proximity!* Just proximity. There was nothing intimate about him fixing her hair, his fingers stroking the sensitive, delicate shell of her ear, making her feel—

"I must go," she said abruptly, turning away so Caleb did not see her red face. "I'll meet you at the train station in forty-five minutes."

Without another word, she strode off in a fine display of dignified nonchalance for all of three seconds before Caleb called out.

"Your house is in the other direction."

Damn. "I am taking a stroll," she lied.

"Don't be silly." Following her, he grasped her wrist.

Amelia repressed a gasp as an electric sensation shot right through her. Immediately, Caleb let go, as if he'd experienced it too. They stared at each other like she was English, he French, and the space between them a vast battlefield in Agincourt. The air felt affrighted, and Amelia realized she was breathing too fast when Caleb's gaze dropped to watch the effect of it on her bosom. Half a second later he caught himself and looked up again, his eyes silvery beneath their lashes, his own breath stilled.

Amelia opened her mouth to say something—anything—

Then she turned and fled.

CHAPTER THREE

History infuses our present the same way
tea infuses water (although it rarely tastes as good).
I, on the Past, Cornelius Ottersock

B Y THE TIME Amelia arrived at the Oxford train station, she had Made A Decision. The sort of decision that requires capital letters and a brisk nod of the head. As she entered the platform with a suitcase in one hand, gray coat flapping and beret threatening to become stylishly askew at any moment in the darkening wind, she stated this decision firmly (but silently, since talking aloud to oneself in public was undignified).

No longer would she be rattled by Caleb.

After all, they had been friends for two decades. There existed no good reason for her to suddenly go all fluttery in his presence. It was bad for her cardiovascular health (to say nothing of museum galleries and library ceilings). Furthermore, *fluttery* was worryingly close to slang. A Tarrant never used slang when any number of erudite, multisyllabic words were available instead, even if no one else understood what they meant. Henceforth, she would be sensible and self-controlled.

"You're late."

Amelia jolted as Caleb appeared at her side as if from

nowhere. Dressed in a black suit and matching coat whose wool had clearly been shorn from very expensive sheep, he looked like he'd stepped out of one of the dramatic poems he was forever reading. Amelia's Decision instantaneously shredded within the storm of her pulse. In its place arose a memory of the crescent moon tattoo on Caleb's left bicep. He'd shown it to her soon after he got it, unbuttoning his shirt, drawing the fabric aside . . .

"You're wrong," she snapped before she could stop herself. "I am here three minutes before eleven."

Caleb grinned boyishly. "It's *two* minutes before, actually," he said as he took her suitcase easily, never mind the large case in his other hand and the bag slung over his shoulder. "But that's fine; the train will be late of course."

Of course it would. This was England. Silently lecturing herself to calm down, Amelia wrapped her thin coat around her as they walked along the platform in search of Miss Tunnicliffe. A small crowd awaited the train, dressed in somber colors as if to match the weather. Around their feet skittered old leaves and torn newspaper pages, and Amelia wondered if there was time to ask the station manager for a broom before the train arrived.

"You're cold," Caleb accused her, frowning at her wind-blanched face. "Why are you wearing such flimsy gloves and a cheap coat?"

Because I earn less than you, thanks to our different genitals, Amelia thought darkly. And because she'd not been raised in poverty like he had, and therefore didn't feel a great desire to spend most of those earnings on fancy clothes and other outward shows of success. But a busy train station was hardly the place for such deep conversation, so she answered with a lesser truth instead. "Because I visited the bookstore before the clothier. Where is Miss Tunnicliffe?"

"I don't know, I got here after you."

Amelia gave him an incredulous look. Just then, someone called out, "Yoo-hoo! Professors!"

They half turned to see Vanity Tunnicliffe waving to them from beside a stack of pink luggage. She looked far more keen about the journey ahead than any intelligent person had the right to be.

"Oh God, don't make me," Caleb grumbled under his breath. "Meely, sweetheart, tell them I caught tuberculosis and had to go home to bed."

"Sh," Amelia whispered, striding forward so he would have to follow.

As they approached Vanity, the girl's grin expanded beyond all hitherto known laws of physics. "I was worried you weren't going to come," she said in her pseudo-rich accent. "Are we excited? I'm excited! It's very exciting!"

"Indeed," Amelia lied politely. Beside her, Caleb set down both their suitcases and began removing one of his fur-lined leather gloves.

"So exciting," Vanity reiterated. Leaning forward, she confided, "This is my first field trip."

"Really?" Amelia said, affecting surprise. Caleb took her right hand and began pulling his glove onto it, directly over the black kid glove already there, muttering all the while about her dying of pneumonia and thus abandoning him in the un-tamed wilds of Cumbria. "We're pleased to have you with us," she told Vanity, smiling.

"Oh! Oh!" Vanity responded delightedly. "We're going to have so much fun! Let me introduce the other member of our team."

She gestured at a large, dour-faced man standing to attention a few steps away. He appeared to be in his forties and possessed more hair above his lip than anywhere else on his head. If he knew the concept of "fun," he clearly did not like it.

"This is Sergeant Jack Sheffield," Vanity said. "He's been seconded from the army to provide security for our assignment."

"Good morning, Sergeant," Amelia said.

"Hello," Caleb said.

Sheffield nodded in response.

"So are we all ready?" Vanity asked. "Packed warm underwear? Updated your wills?"

"I beg your pardon?" Caleb paused in wrangling his second glove onto Amelia's left hand to stare at the girl suspiciously. "Our wills? Why?"

"We'll be dealing with *magical antiques*," Vanity explained slowly, as if they'd never taken a history class before. "Magic is dangerous!"

"Only rarely," Amelia assured her. "And not so much with manufactured items. Even if something is constructed from a metal or animal material containing a significant amount of thaumaturgic conjures, that energy invariably dissipates at an exponential rate."

Vanity digested this silently. But just as Amelia was drawing in breath to offer a more high school–level version of the explanation, the girl said, "So it's like a rich man on a first date: all flash and no follow-through."

Caleb appeared to choke on his saliva. Amelia, however, managed to keep a straight face. "Hm, yes, that's a good analogy.

Magic seldom lasts long in artifacts, which is why we don't generally have people running around with weapons made from enchanted candlesticks. Sometimes it *does* last, though, and in that case our job is to study it, then ensure the item is secured before the wrong person takes it to sell on the black market. All manner of villains are willing to pay a fortune to get their hands on magic, which they'll use for nefarious reasons—"

"Such as publishing a report about it before we can," Caleb said, grinning.

Amelia cast him a brief frown. "Such as assassinating the Queen by use of a thaumaturgic iron poker—"

"Even though a regular iron poker would be just as effective," Caleb interjected.

Amelia's frown darkened. Giving up her explanation before Caleb turned it completely into a game, she tried a new angle. "Of course, in the natural world things can be more dangerous, such as with magical birds—"

Now Vanity was the one to interrupt. "Ooh, did you see that contest for Birder of the Year? So exciting! Professor Lockley is just dreamy."

Amelia said nothing, very carefully. She could only too well imagine Vanity's response upon learning that Devon Lockley was her cousin. The girl might well perish from an overload of enthusiasm.

"According to Mr. Hunt," Vanity said, "magical antiques can cause damage to the very fabric of time, killing us all instantly—and slowly—and a hundred years in the future. Because, you know—"

"—the fabric of time is damaged," Caleb supplied, and Vanity grinned, her head bobbing, as if she rather hoped such an entertaining event would come to pass.

"Mr. Hunt," Amelia mused. "I don't know that name. Is he a thaumaturgic analyst?"

"No, he runs the museum's shop," Vanity said. "But he's read *The Necromancer's Clock*."

Amelia and Caleb were briefly silent. Then—"Isn't that a gothic novel?" Caleb asked uncertainly.

"A *bestselling* gothic novel," Vanity corrected him. "Unfortunately its author is a recluse, refusing all social and media attention, or else I'd have asked her to join our team."

"Oh dear," Amelia said over Caleb's sudden amused cough. "Well, we Oxford professors shall try to do our best for you."

"And that's saying quite a bit," Caleb added as he released Amelia's hand, which was now so thoroughly gloved she could barely move her fingers. "I really am rather clever," he assured Vanity with a dazzling smile, "and Miss Tarrant manages to keep up. Don't worry, love, we'll save time from being destroyed *and* catalog your antiques for you."

Vanity's expression swooned all over her face. Amelia, abruptly irritated by the whole conversation, considered explaining that, when it came to temporal matters, the worst a thaumaturgic object ever did was transform old energy waves into what people thought of as ghosts. But the train arrived before she could commit education.

Vanity handed out their tickets, and Amelia bade everyone a pleasant journey. Taking up her suitcase, she strode along the platform until coming upon an empty compartment that looked decently clean. A quick brush of the seat and she was able to sit in comfort, laying her suitcase beside her and exhaling a contented sigh. The next several hours stretched ahead of her in a pleasantly unsociable vision of reading, gazing out at the countryside, and enjoying the marmite sandwiches she'd had just enough time to prepare.

"Shift over."

She looked up to see Caleb enter the compartment. Her wits didn't have enough opportunity to respond before he was tossing his luggage onto the overhead rack, then hers after it. He plonked himself down beside her, the woodsy scent of his expensive new cologne wafting through her personal space. Amelia *tsk*ed but was unable to move aside without her skirt bunching uncomfortably beneath her.

Without any apology, Caleb leaned back at an uncouth angle, stretching out his legs and crossing his ankles as if he were in his home instead of a public train compartment. Or, rather, what Amelia had intended to be *her private compartment*. Friendship was all well and good until it came to train travel, at which point every reasonable person ought to behave like a stranger.

She drew breath to request that he exit at once—

"I do so love a train ride!" Vanity sang as she entered the compartment, Sergeant Sheffield following closely with her three suitcases and his own rucksack.

"Uh . . ." Amelia said.

"Isn't this cozy?" The girl settled directly opposite Amelia, arranging the rustling, striped billow of her skirts, clattering the bracelets on both her wrists, and generally assailing Amelia with a number of small stimuli that altogether felt like a circus show.

"Cozy indeed," she managed to say. From the corner of her eye, she saw Caleb tip his head onto his right shoulder and look at her through a fringe of eyelashes, wry humor sparkling in his gaze. He of course knew exactly which of her nerves Vanity got on, having himself honed them to sharpness over the years. Amelia refrained from smacking him only because that was what had got her into this blasted situation in the first place. Instead, she smiled politely at the young receptionist.

Vanity giggled in reply.

Giggled. Amelia hadn't heard anyone do that since her undergraduate days at Balliol College, when the other girls at the dining table chatted around her while she read. *Why couldn't Sir Nigel's antiques have destroyed time* before *I got this assignment?* she wondered gloomily. Then, realizing they might have, she became suddenly excited by the idea. Never mind her book, she would spend the journey's hours thinking about chronological—

"I have some exercises to help us break the ice as we travel!" Vanity announced with glee.

A frisson of horror struck Amelia. "Exercises?" she repeated. "You mean push-ups and jogging on the spot?"

"She means charades," Caleb said, his tone so dry it could have beached Noah's ark.

"Yes!" Vanity exclaimed, pointing at him. "And I thought we could go around in a circle"—now the finger spun to them all in turn—"saying our names and three things we love about ourselves."

"Charming," Caleb drawled, which Amelia silently translated to *kill me now.* Sergeant Sheffield, sitting beside Vanity in a widespread pose that made it obvious he was more used to being seated on a horse, emitted a very quiet puff of breath that might have been dark humor, irritation, or the consequence of stuffy nasal passages. Other than that, he stared at nothing, his face expressionless, his eyes darker than the night before the Battle of Hastings.

As the train departed the station, Vanity rubbed her lace-gloved hands together briskly. "We'll start with Mr. Sterling! Although I must confess, sir," she added with a coy smile, "I've heard enough about you to feel that I already know you."

"Oh?" Caleb asked, nonchalant. "Such as?"

"You like fine wine, fine women, and fast carriages."

Caleb laughed. Amelia set the back of her fingers against her mouth, coughing discreetly. Vanity needed better sources, for Caleb suffered motion sickness in any horse-drawn carriage traveling faster than four miles per hour, and his preferred women were "fine" only insofar as they had to pay a fine if they were caught soliciting their services, since he considered actual romantic relationships far too much hassle.

"What have you heard about Miss Tarrant?" he asked, and blithely ignored the sharp look Amelia threw him.

"Enough that I was quite frightened asking for her to join our team!" Vanity giggled. "I must say, though, Miss Tarrant, you don't *look* like an antisocial harridan."

There followed a taut silence as Vanity beamed and Amelia strove in vain to dislodge several words lodged in her throat.

"Coffee!" Caleb declared suddenly. Getting to his feet, he grasped Amelia by the wrist and pulled her up also. Surprised, disoriented, she swayed, putting a hand on his chest to steady herself. "Come on," he said as he yanked open the compartment door. "Let's go get drinks for everyone. And maybe they have some cake!"

Amelia followed him by necessity into the train's corridor. "God save me from people," he muttered as he towed her through a vestibule into the dining car. It was unoccupied, and Caleb pulled out a chair at one of the white-clothed tables. "Sit," he directed her.

"I thought we were just ordering coff—"

"Sit."

With a fussy little sigh, Amelia did as bid, and he pushed the chair in for her. She removed the gloves he'd given her and laid them neatly upon the table while Caleb dropped into a chair opposite.

"We need a plan," he said.

Amelia looked up from aligning the gloves one atop the other, her eyebrows arching in surprise. "I don't think I've ever before heard those words from your lips."

Even as she spoke, her brain desperately tried to stop her but to no avail. *Your lips, your lips,* echoed through her thoughts with a hot, sibilant whisper. All at once she could see nothing but those same lips gliding into a smile, could feel nothing but the electrification of each fine hair along her arms as if merely speaking about Caleb's mouth was equivalent to having it kiss a slow, gentle path from her elbow to her wrist.

Oh for goodness' sake, she thought testily, even as she blushed all over. She was *not* attracted to Caleb. She was just . . . thirsty. Er, for tea, that is! A perfectly normal, utterly chaste thirst for tea.

"Tea," she told herself with severe emphasis, then blinked as she realized she'd spoken aloud.

"Tea should always be at the top of any plan," Caleb said, blessedly ignorant of the chaos unraveling her mind. "Although considering you've gone from looking cold to looking hot, perhaps we should make it iced lemon tea, yes?"

"This is a disaster," Amelia murmured—for just as the sobering thought of tea had begun calming her flutters, Caleb's insertion of *looking hot* brought them right back. She was at a loss to understand herself. A properly behaved woman doesn't just go to Hereford for a few days and return with a spontaneous attraction for her best friend!

Although, if she were being honest, it wasn't *entirely* spontaneous. There had been that night in the Ashmolean when they'd stood together inspecting the thaumaturgic candlestick, and Caleb's fingers had brushed hers, inspiring a thrill that she'd supposed at the time to have been the candlestick's magic. And a few weeks before that, when she'd glanced up from a stack of papers to find him leaning on the frame of her office's open doorway, watching her, the warm, intimate smile on his face sending tingles through her entire nervous system . . .

And then there had been the first time she set eyes on him, two decades ago behind the school dormitory—a pretty, fair-haired boy offering her his rather shabby handkerchief so she might dry her tears.

She'd been sent to school for being an impossibly wayward child. A Tarrant ought to be sober-minded, as her father had explained while chastising her for having come in from the garden with daisies adorning her hair. (*"If you must bring nature indoors, my dear, it should be for the purpose of conducting scientific experiments."*) They must also put away childish things when they reach the age of reason, as her mother had informed her when, at seven, she cried upon watching her toys being packed up and sent to a local orphanage. (*"We simply cannot be having with these hysterics, darling."*) When Amelia proved incapable of controlling her emotions by eight years old, it was concluded that boarding school, with its healthful regime of cold baths, bullying, and desperate loneliness, would cure her of such instability. And indeed it had in fairly short order, but they'd kept her on at the school for the rest of her childhood anyway, out of sheer habit.

Caleb, on the other hand, was there after being raised up out of a missionary Ragged School and given a scholarship on account of his ~~charming the teachers~~ intelligence.

Despite their differences, the pair of them had become inseparable, to the degree that now Amelia was inclined to believe them two halves of the same soul—a sentiment that would almost certainly horrify both Ottersock, who'd probably drag her and Caleb down the nearest church's aisle on the basis of it, and her parents, who'd never believe in souls unless given proof via a double-blind study.

In truth, Amelia's small, shy heart had fallen instantly in love with Caleb's prettiness and his gorgeous, kind smile. But almost as instantly she'd repressed that emotion in favor of friendship. After all, the reason she'd been crying was because she'd been condemned to boarding school for the crime of being too silly. And nothing was more silly than love.

"Completely," Caleb agreed rather disorientatingly, and Amelia hastened to recall their place in the conversation. "Mud, fresh air, and now a giggly museum receptionist as well. I haven't known such a disaster since—well, since two days ago, when we nearly blew up the Min. Still, it could be worse."

Amelia looked at him dazedly. "How?" she asked both him and, secretly, herself. "How could it *possibly* be worse?"

Caleb shrugged. "We could be helping with the party Ottersock always gives during freshers week to welcome new students."

The awfulness of that thought broke Amelia out of herself. "Yes, that would be worse."

"Novelty paper hats," Caleb went on. "Professor Staples reciting naughty limericks."

She laughed. "Stop, I'm going to have nightmares."

He did stop, and he smiled at her fondly. He'd noticed her turmoil and had made her laugh on purpose, as a diversion, just as he had that very first day. Goodness, how she adored him. He resided at the very center of her heart, alongside her brother Gabriel, her cousin Devon, and Aunt Mary's triple chocolate cake. Romantic attraction would imperil their friendship (since *of course* he wouldn't feel the same), and Amelia could not bear that. There existed only one safe conclusion: she was wrong, this wasn't attraction, it was something far less frightening, such as a brain derangement.

There, fixed.

While Amelia exhaled in relief, Caleb leaned forward in his chair, elbows on the table and cheek resting against his linked hands. The window beside them glimmered with rain. The fields beyond were a turbulence of shadows, as if remembering ancient battles. But Amelia saw only Caleb. And he in turn regarded her with a contemplative steadiness that almost set her fluttering again. "Don't be upset about what Miss Tunnicliffe said," he told her. "It was nonsense."

"That's easy for you to say," Amelia replied. "I absolutely reserve the right to be upset about having to play icebreaker games."

Caleb grinned. "Oh, Meely, you do inspire me."

Amelia raised an eyebrow, instinctively suspicious. And sure enough: "We should get some ice from the train's kitchen," he went on, "and something with which to break it . . ."

All her emotional tumult forgotten, Amelia gave him a teacherish look. "You shouldn't say such things in public. There are no doubt students and faculty members on this train. What if they heard you being so irreverent?"

"Then they'd know for certain it was me," he answered

easily. "But I wouldn't want to worry you, love." Reaching into his coat pocket, he brought out a small cone-shaped candle snuffer. Placing it on the table, he tapped it with a finger. Thaumaturgic blue light emerged, expanding until it enclosed them in a faint glow that took on the shape of the snuffer before fading to translucence. Now, even had someone walked right up to the table, they would hear nothing, the magic having created, as it were, a cone of silence.

Caleb leaned back in his chair. "We smash up the ice and 'accidentally' spill it all over Miss Tunnicliffe's lap," he said. "What do you think?"

Amelia shook her head, exasperated. "That's the Walsingham candle snuffer from the Ashmolean, isn't it?"

"Uh-huh."

"You stole it." (As an antiquarian, Amelia had been taught that stealing was not automatically a crime—it all depended on whether the theft was against one person [bad!] or an entire culture [please do present your stolen items at an international conference!], but she personally did not approve of it either way.)

Caleb waved a hand, unconcerned. "I covertly borrowed it for an undefined period of time. So you think we need a better plan than showering the girl with ice?"

"Why do we need a plan at all?" Amelia asked.

"So we're prepared if Miss Tunnicliffe suggests charades or tries sharing stupid gossip again."

Amelia went abruptly still, for she suddenly understood what all this was about, and her heart felt like—well, shattered ice, actually. After a long moment of taut silence, Caleb sighed.

"Talk to me, Amelia."

"I am," she answered, frowning. "We're having intercourse right now."

"Hm. If that were true, I think I'd have noticed. Miss Tunnicliffe is—"

"Excitable, that's all. She means no harm."

"She harmed me," Caleb argued, abruptly serious. "I was offended on your behalf."

Suddenly Amelia became alert to the vital fact that the gloves were not lying exactly straight. As she remedied this, she felt Caleb watching her with exasperation. "You're not a harridan, Meely," he said. "No doubt Miss Tunnicliffe has been talking to that feebleminded sleaze Dummersby at the museum."

"No doubt," she agreed steadily, although she dared not look up from the gloves. "Now, what variety of coffee do—"

"Your students love you," Caleb talked over her. "The people who manage the soup kitchen where you volunteer love you. And I"—he paused for the merest fraction of a second, really no time at all; in fact, Amelia decided she'd imagined it—"think you're all right enough, I suppose. Not as amazing as me, but not too bad."

"Goodness, such high praise," Amelia drawled. The gloves were now aligned to exactitude, one atop the other, so she began smoothing their fur trim.

Caleb shrugged. "I had to say something nice or you'd bully me until I did."

"Ha ha."

He leaned forward again, pulling the gloves away from her. Amelia scowled at him, he grinned back, and the air sparkled with magic—which was, of course, due to the cone of silence and nothing else whatsoever.

A waiter approached their table, and Caleb hastily pocketed the candle snuffer. They ordered tea and coffee to be brought to their compartment, along with cake (at Caleb's request) and fruit (at Amelia's).

"Right," he said, pushing his chair back. "Are you ready to face the excitable girl again, bella luna?"

Amelia frowned. "I do wish you would address me correctly in public."

Caleb's expression became wounded, although his eyes continued to twinkle. "Surely I've earned the privilege of calling you by an endearment? After all, we've kissed—"

"We were eleven!" Amelia retorted, aghast. She could still recall the moment vividly. She'd been hiding behind a curtain during a game of catch-and-kiss at Fortuna Andrews's birthday party . . . Caleb had found her and asked if he could claim his kiss . . . She'd snootily agreed since it was after all the rule. The sensation of his quick peck on her mouth lingered these many years later, like a stubborn ghost.

She rose, as much to escape the memory as anything. At once, Caleb was on his feet. Irreverent and lazy he might be, but he'd also been drilled in essential good manners over the years by teachers determined to show school benefactors that their pet Disadvantaged Child was worth the investment.

"One more thing," Amelia said. "On this assignment we'll be representing Oxford University, so we ought to behave properly." She cast him a glance that made it clear she meant he alone.

"Sure, love," Caleb agreed.

"And you should stop with the 'love,'" she added severely.

He gave her a long look. Then, stepping toward her, he leaned in so as to speak in a low, warm voice that, like his manners, had been polished over the years but still occasionally glided through slum strength and educated softness. It rounded vowels here and there, doing Things to Amelia's nerve endings.

"I'm never giving up my 'love,'" he said. Then he walked on, the backs of his fingers deliberately brushing against her skirt as he went.

Well, really! Amelia stiffened with ~~titillation~~ *outrage!* But she had to quickly unstiffen and follow him or else she'd be forced to run to catch up.

They arrived back at the carriage in time to hear Vanity say, "Heavens, Sergeant Sheffield, I'm *sure* you can guess what I spy with my little eye!" The sergeant made no reply, but his silence spoke volumes. Indeed, it was practically a thousand-page Russian novel.

"Miss Tunnicliffe," Caleb said with a cheerful smile as he sat down, "would you like to see my antique candle snuffer?"

Vanity's eyes widened. "Ooh, yes, please!"

Caleb took the snuffer from his coat pocket, tapping its side as he did so, and . . .

"Oops!" he said as he dropped it. His foot jerked, kicking the snuffer beneath one of the bench seats. A faint blue glow drifted across the floor.

And thus they were able to enjoy the next few hours in blessed silence.

♡

CHAPTER FOUR

*Those who fail to learn from history are doomed to repeat
the class if they want to earn their degree.*
I, on the Past, Cornelius Ottersock

A COLD WIND SWEPT over the fells surrounding Staveley,
dragging shadows like a warning of the night to come. The
village's lights glimmered pale and fragile within a cocoon of
chimney smoke, but not even that uncertain comfort was to be
found along the narrow lane leading up to Ravenscroft Manor,
home of the baronet Sir Nigel Harroway. This was old land,
land like a strange wild dream, and walking it required heart
as well as muscle.

"I'm going to perish from exhaustion," Caleb complained,
pressing his hand against his brow. "If pneumonia doesn't get
me first, that is. I can't believe Ottersock would force us to
walk such a terrible road!"

He didn't have to even glance in Amelia's direction to know
she was regarding him with a cool steadiness. "You haven't
walked it yet," she pointed out. "You are in fact sitting in a pub,
enjoying tea. There's no reason to be quite so dramatic."

"I'm preparing myself," he retorted. "One glance at Miss
Tunnicliffe's map told me all I need to know."

Amelia remained unimpressed. "It's just over a mile."

"A mile *uphill*," he specified, jabbing his ham sandwich at her. "I'm an antiquarian; I'm not made for physical labor."

"You play rugby on the weekends."

"That's different. Besides, I heard thunder before. We're going to be caught in a storm and become lost forever in the wilds."

"The farmlands," Amelia corrected him.

"The grimdark hills," he shot back.

"Ahem." Vanity cleared her throat with loud impatience. All her cheerfulness was gone, the seven-hour journey from Oxford having eroded it to the degree that she now made Bloody Queen Mary seem jovial. Even her topknot was beginning to droop. "Sergeant Sheffield should be back any moment with a rented carriage or horses," she said, and glared at the pub's door as if she could will him into returning. "Any. Minute."

"I'm not so sure," Caleb argued. "Sheffield seems like a sensible chap. After spending all day being threatened with charades, chitchat, that brown water the railway company thinks is coffee, and now a long—*long*—hike uphill"—he flung a pointed look at Amelia—"he's probably fled back to the safety of the army."

"You're ridiculous," Amelia said, frowning mildly over the rim of her teacup.

"Ridiculous for you, Professor Tarrant," he replied with a hand on his heart.

Amelia raised her eyes toward the ceiling, on which someone had painted the poet Wordsworth wandering among clouds. But in fact, Caleb had been speaking unironically. She looked tired, her face even paler than usual, her eyes limned with shadows. The least he could do was annoy her into alertness until they were able to rest for the night.

"Anyway, you can't talk," he went on. "You're wearing the most appallingly sensible shoes I've ever seen. You probably could have walked here from Oxford without developing a single blister. But these are Crockett and Jones calf leather Derbys, Amelia. The worst they should encounter is a threadbare rug."

Amelia did not even glance at the beautifully shod foot he angled out from beneath the table. Vanity, however, muttered under her breath about what she'd like to do with a calf leather Derby in relation to his head. But before violence could be committed, an elderly woman who had been dining with another at a neighboring table approached them.

"Excuse me," she said, her voice pitched low, her expression nervous. "May I ask, are you poets?"

"No, ma'am," Amelia told her politely. "We're antiquarians."

The woman's anxiety deepened to wariness. "Is that some kind of religion?"

Caleb laughed. "In a manner of speaking."

"It's a branch of history study," Amelia explained. "We're university professors."

"Oh dear, really?" The woman gave them a pitying once-over. "I overheard that you were planning to visit Ravenscroft Manor and just assumed . . ." She paused, glancing around as if anticipating danger. Suddenly a flash of lightning illuminated her face with stark brightness against the shadows of the pub's interior. But her eyes were impenetrably dark as she reached out to grasp Amelia's shoulder. "I beg you, don't do it. Don't go out to that manor."

Caleb's interest immediately perked up at this dire advice. "How intriguing," he said, and winked at Amelia, who had gone rigid at the woman's touch. "Let me guess, strange and dreadful things happen there?"

Thunder crashed overhead, and the pub's lights briefly flickered, scattering shards of darkness through the room. The old woman cackled.

"No, the roads are in a poor state from recent bad weather. Mavis and I"—she indicated a fellow octogenarian at her table—"went for a ramble out that way yesterday but had to turn back after only five miles."

Amelia gave Caleb an eloquent look, but the woman had not finished. "It would be a terrible shame if a fine gentleman such as yourself ruined his elegant shoes."

"Aha!" Caleb declared, pointing triumphantly at Amelia. "I told you so. A discerning lady recognizes elegance when she sees it."

Amelia smiled placidly, as if she knew a secret she was not telling him. Caleb found himself thinking, not for the first time in their long acquaintance, just how lovely her eyes were, soft and dark, with lashes so long they rightfully belonged on a morally gray hero. Really, it was altogether fortunate he'd settled years ago for being no more than friends with her, otherwise he'd fall in love every time he gazed into those beautiful, deep—

"Professor!" Vanity exclaimed. "You're coming undone!"

Caleb's pulse jolted him out of his reverie into a wild, confused moment before he realized that Vanity was referring to his sandwich. It had begun drooping in his hand; already he'd lost a slice of tomato and was at immediate risk of losing the ham too. But they did not have far to fall: Amelia had lifted his plate while he'd been ~~mooning~~ casually looking at her eyes, and she held it in position to catch the sandwich bits.

"Oops," he said, and let the rest of the sandwich drop. "How far is—" he began to ask the elderly woman, but looking around did not see her. "Where did she go?" he asked, surprised. Had she been a ghost? Supernatural encounters were common in his line of work, but rarely did they seem so realistic. "She just vanished!"

"Actually she said goodbye, then walked away while you were staring at Miss Tarrant," Vanity told him rather sourly.

Caleb was saved from blushing by the timely arrival of Sergeant Sheffield. The man approached their table then stopped, hands behind his back, gaze fixed upon the middle distance.

"You procured a carriage?" Vanity asked, perking up at the hopeful possibility.

Sheffield nodded, once.

"Marvelous!" Immediately the girl was on her feet. "Shall we go?" She clapped her hands and rubbed them together as if that might accelerate time.

Caleb rose, gathering his coat from the back of his chair and putting it on. Amelia followed more slowly, tidying her used dishes as she did so. "Sergeant," she said, "would you be kind enough to help us with our luggage?"

Sheffield sprang into action, gathering up both Amelia's and Caleb's suitcases, Caleb's extra bag, and two pieces of Vanity's luggage, in a feat of strength that Caleb could only describe as *showing off like a bloody wanker*, especially considering the impressed look on Amelia's face. He attempted to offer some help, but Sheffield was already moving for the exit, leaving Caleb with only a few remnants of chivalry.

But upon extending his arm to Amelia, he got a confused frown in return. True, the last time he'd done so was some three years ago, when she wanted to get an antique brass bird down from where it had flown to an upper shelf in the British

Museum. Nevertheless, he felt inexplicably annoyed. Pivoting on his heel, he smiled at Vanity instead.

"Miss Tunnicliffe," he said, "may I offer you my assistance?"

Vanity giggled and lifted her hand to place it on his forearm—but at that moment Caleb saw Amelia roll her eyes, and he turned back to her, causing Vanity's hand to drop awkwardly through empty space.

"What was that look for?" he demanded.

Amelia's expression, however, was now entirely genteel. "Nothing," she said, so calm and so obviously meaning *something* that Caleb wanted to take her in his ~~embrace~~ grip and shake her—although why, exactly, he could not say. They stared at each other, unspoken words spiking the air between them. Vanity took a nervous step away.

"We should be going," Amelia said.

"I was *trying* to go," Caleb pointed out, "but you stalled me with a look."

"I'm not looking at you," she said, although in fact she continued to fix him within her gaze.

Why not? he wanted to demand. But being a mature adult (despite all evidence to the contrary), he said instead, "Alas for you, missing out on this ravishing beauty."

"There is no need to be like that," Amelia replied, imperturbable.

"Like what?" He could feel his eyes darkening with a genuine intensity of emotion, and the stiffness of Amelia's expression confirmed it. Turning back to Vanity so abruptly the girl jolted, he smiled at her again. "What do you think I'm like?" he asked, earnest and charming while his subconscious shot darts at Amelia behind him.

"Uh—" Vanity began hesitantly.

Caleb flung his stare back at Amelia. "People who make accusations should do so unambiguously."

Amelia replied with a slow blink, the kind that reduced misbehaving students to tremorous wrecks requiring the support of the nearest chair. Caleb himself was made of sterner stuff, however, and remained upright (although it must be acknowledged that, as he watched the glide of her eyelashes, he became more upright than was strictly comfortable under the circumstances).

"Maybe we should just go . . ." Vanity attempted. But she might as well have been a professor lecturing last thing on a Friday afternoon for all that they listened to her.

"I should think your behavior is clear to everyone without me needing to describe it," Amelia said.

"Just admit that you left your thesaurus at home," Caleb answered tartly.

Three plates on the table exploded.

Caleb and Amelia ducked with the speed of people well used to tableware being more dynamic than is the norm. Alarmed shouts echoed through the room. *Oh my God!* Vanity cried out, stumbling backward. Cutlery began to levitate, flashing with a blue tint of light along their silver handles.

Straightening, Caleb and Amelia looked at each other, irritation replaced by professional excitement.

"An eructation of perceivable thaumaturgic energy," Amelia said. "Do you have a thaumometer at hand?"

"Why would I need it?" Caleb said. "I can *see* the magic."

"Hm," Amelia responded, as if one's senses were an inadequate source of information, regardless of the teacup hovering right before her eyes. "This building must stand on a deposit of thaumaturgic minerals."

"Or something in the room is enchanted," Caleb suggested.

Amelia shook her head. "Unlikely. An object of such potency would be too valuable to be sitting in a third-rate pub."

"Hey!" exclaimed a nearby waitress with indignation.

Amelia turned to apologize but stopped abruptly upon seeing a dessert trolley begin to glide across the room. No one was pushing it, but this was of minor concern compared to the fact that it glided two feet above the ground.

"Well, that takes the cake," Caleb drawled.

Amelia gave him a look so unamused she might have been mistaken in that moment for Queen Victoria.

"I see my joke landed as flat as a pancake," Caleb said. "By God, Professor Tarrant, you're a tough cookie to break."

"For goodness' sake," she muttered. "If you don't—"

Thwack.

A large custard pie, having leaped up from the trolley, slammed itself against a framed portrait of the prime minister. It would have incited roars of laughter had the pub been a pantomime theatre or the House of Commons; as it was, horrified cries rang out.

And then the chaos really began.

Pastries began shooting off the trolley, pelting diners and, in some cases, bursting into flames midair. People clambered from their chairs and ran for the door, screaming, shoving tables and each other. A pavlova detonated, bombs of cream flinging through the room.

Caleb felt someone clutch him from behind and looked around to discover Vanity huddling wide-eyed against him. Disengaging her gently, he grasped her shoulders, shaking them a little to focus her attention. "Miss Tunnicliffe!" he shouted over the cacophony. "You need to evacuate the room."

"Are you sh-sh-sure?" she asked, all her vivacity turned to custard. (Caleb spared a second to congratulate himself on yet another excellent pun.)

"Absolutely," he said in the firm professorial tone he rarely bothered to use. "Go on ahead. Miss Tarrant and I will deal with this kerfuffle."

Nodding, Vanity picked up her remaining suitcase, and clutching it like a shield, she joined the guests and staff in dashing outside. Caleb watched to be certain she was safe, then turned back to Amelia, who had plucked her cup out of the air and was sipping tea placidly as she contemplated the situation. Caleb smiled at the sight.

"What?" she said. "I can think of no good reason why you should be smiling. This is all your fault."

Caleb stuttered a laugh. "I beg your pardon?"

"You must have an unsecured thaumaturgic object upon you," Amelia said, gesturing at him with her teacup. "You had the candle snuffer; what else is in your pockets?"

"Nothing," he said, trying to repress a surge of indignation. "Besides, my coat's pockets are lined with cloth of gold to"— he paused, ducking as a plate of sandwiches whizzed past him—"repress the energy emissions of any thaumaturgic objects in them," he said as he straightened again. He stared fiercely through a fall of his hair at Amelia. "What's in *your* pockets?"

She bristled. "Nothing, of course!" She set down her cup on the tabletop, so offended that she completely ignored its saucer. "*I* don't walk around casually with invaluable magical items upon me."

One of the plates on their table began spinning furiously, sausage rolls flinging off it with the speed of bullets.

"Are you sure?" Caleb asked dryly.

"I most certainly am!" Frowning at him, she patted the pockets of her skirt in emphasis.

Her frown went abruptly still. She winced.

"Oops?" Caleb suggested.

Reaching into one pocket, she drew out a teaspoon and held it up, still wincing.

Caleb laughed. "That's the Hereford teaspoon, isn't it?"

"Maybe," Amelia murmured.

"The teaspoon that broke a hole in the Min's library ceiling."

They both looked up at the painted fresco overhead, then back down at each other again.

"I put it in my pocket when I left Ottersock's office," Amelia said, "but was in such a hurry to catch the train I obviously—"

"Forgot it was there." Caleb finished the sentence before she did. "It happens to the best of us. I mean, not to me, but . . ." He shrugged, and Amelia's eyes flared. The spoon began to vibrate, blue sparks shooting from its bowl. Immediately Caleb grabbed it from Amelia's hand and dropped it onto the table.

"There was no need to snatch," Amelia grouched.

"Excuse me for caring about your fingers," Caleb snapped in reply.

Flames burst from the spoon. They whirled into the orbit of the spinning plate, rapidly becoming a fiery tornado that smelled of grease and dubious meats.

"Er, perhaps we should stop creating environmental discord," Caleb said.

"It might be too late for that."

They looked around at the magical chaos. Tableware dancing, food flying: it was more hectic than even an aristocrat's party.

"Ottersock is going to kill us," Amelia said.

"Or fire us," Caleb countered.

"That's worse."

"Don't worry, we'll just blame it on the weather. He's sure to believe us; we're pretty effective liars by now. But we should probably try to contain the spoon's magic." He paused, frowning. "That really does sound ridiculous. Couldn't you have found a magical dagger or ring instead?"

Amelia ignored the question. "I have a lead-lined container in my suitcase; it's just the right size to secure the spoon and block its magic." She turned to reach for the suitcase before remembering that Sheffield had already taken their luggage away. "What about putting it in your coat pocket?" she suggested instead.

"Worth a try." Caleb reached for the teaspoon, but the merest brush of his fingers against its handle sent a painful shock through him. "Aah!" he shouted, snatching back his hand.

"Just deal with the pain for a few seconds," Amelia said testily.

Caleb gave her an outraged look. "These are the fingers of an artist and pianist! I'm not risking them."

"Rude sketches in textbooks don't count as art." She gazed at him for a long moment, but Caleb knew she wasn't really seeing him. There were practically cogs of thought spinning in her expression. "Since the energy is triggered by discord, why don't we do the opposite?" she suggested. "Show accord. Friendliness."

"All right." Caleb extended his hand, Amelia took it, and they exchanged a firm handshake, smiling at each other rather foolishly.

A bacon and egg pie on a neighboring table erupted in a cloud of chicken feathers and flew away, squawking.

"Perhaps a hug?" Amelia ventured.

Caleb dutifully wrapped his arms around her and she embraced him in return, as they'd done several times throughout their history: on graduation days; when he won the Henry Beauclerc Award; when she won it the following year; and most fatefully, upon news of her grandfather's death. Caleb had always loved hugging her. She smelled of lilac and new books; she held him as if she really wanted to; and altogether she felt like his dream of a home. But the feeling now was like he'd entered that home, taken off his clothes and all his defenses, and tucked himself into bed with her.

Flakes from the ceiling showered over them like painted rain.

"Not working," Caleb said, pulling away from Amelia before his body began to react the same way his heart had. "We've obviously grown too expert at arguing."

"It's becoming a habit," Amelia agreed worriedly. "A bad habit. I don't like it."

"Yes, but it's better than transferring to Cambridge University," Caleb contended. "Their football team is rubbish."

"But the campus is pretty."

"In that case, I'd fit right in," Caleb said. He smiled crookedly at her. "And you too, of course."

They looked around the room hopefully, but this spot of banter had not fixed anything.

"We need something more," Amelia murmured.

Their eyes met with silent understanding. Caleb's stomach suddenly felt like a pub turned to chaos by magic.

"We've kissed before," Amelia said with a calmness that wasn't entirely convincing.

"We were eleven," Caleb reminded her.

Blue smoke began to billow overhead. They looked up at it worriedly; then their eyes met again. This time, the understanding was even more potent. But just as silent—because Caleb for one had no idea how he could ever put into words what he knew in that moment. Well, the words were actually simple. *I want to kiss you.* But the reasons were a tangle he could not even begin to unravel.

"What's one kiss between friends?" Amelia said, reasonable as ever. "And we are friends," she added more loudly, addressing the magic surrounding them. "We love each other."

"We do," Caleb said. And cupping one hand against her jaw, ignoring the wild leap of his heart, he closed his eyes and kissed her.

CHAPTER FIVE

If history is "a cyclic poem written by time,"
as Shelley says, then some episodes of it can only
be described as limericks.

I, on the Past, Cornelius Ottersock

A KISS IS ALMOST never just a kiss. All through the ages it has been the sealing of a contract, a moment of letting go, the proof of devotion, a betrayal—and a thousand other profundities that can be pecked onto a cheek or applied to someone's lips, occasionally with the tongue serving as an exclamation mark.

For Amelia, however, kissing Caleb *was* just a kiss, and no amount of opinion from the lower galleries of her body could change her mind. After all, she had been kissed two or three times before (alas, the fact that she couldn't be specific about the number indicated their quality), and this experience allowed her to be entirely cool now.

Or, rather, she felt hot, so hot she'd like to strip off all her clothes, but she was *rhetorically* cool. Which was the important thing.

Caleb demonstrated a skill greatly improved upon that he'd shown at Fortuna Andrews's party when they were children. His lips pressed gently, and yet it were as if a tremendous weight of emotion was being pressed against Amelia's very soul. She didn't care about this, mind you. Nor did she care that his bare hand was cradling her jaw, tilting it as he pleased, with a slightly domineering attitude that, under normal circumstances, would incite a frown or scoff of laughter from her, rather than the tingle happening in her stomach (or a place in that general vicinity).

A flaming teapot hurled across the room, on direct course to smash against them. Without breaking the kiss, Caleb put an arm around Amelia's waist and pulled her against him, turning them out of the teapot's path. His hand moved from her jaw to cup the back of her head protectively.

As a natural consequence of this, the kiss deepened, just at the point where Amelia gasped with surprise at being abruptly cuddled against a man's strong, broad chest. Thus due to physics, and with no intention *at all* on either of their parts, the tidy connection of mouths transformed into something more dynamic, lips sliding, clasping, growing heated. It was everything Amelia had imagined a kiss from Caleb would be (not that she'd ever imagined such a thing, merely speculated one or two dozen times, as an intellectual exercise). And yet it was also strange, beautifully strange, as if she'd stumbled into a dreamworld. All her sense of the familiar, and of the innocent friendship between them, was dissolving like sugar against Caleb's mouth. He tasted of something wilder, darker, and altogether dangerous—a delicious poison, or strong black tea. His fingers tightened on her hair. Amelia leaned into him. The tingle became a throb.

Abruptly her mind slammed up a high, spiked barricade against the desire swelling up from her heart. It stuck reminders like heads on the spikes: if word of this kiss reached Ottersock, she would be forced down to the level of teaching at a community college, all her parents' dreams for her career destroyed.

The teapot fell with a crash to the polished floor, pretty much at the same moment Amelia's heart crashed also. She began to stiffen in Caleb's hold. As she did so, he began to soften. In unison, they broke the kiss. At once, they looked around—to check the magic, you understand, and not at all to avoid looking each other in the eye.

A dazed silence hung limp and miserable over the ruined pub. Tea and beer dripped from fallen cups onto the floor. A bouquet of flowers was on fire. And the bacon and egg pie roamed beneath tables, clucking as it pecked at crumbs. Otherwise, nothing stirred.

"Well, that worked," Caleb said in a completely ordinary tone, as if he'd not just unraveled Amelia's nerves so completely, she wasn't certain of her ability to stand upright. Fortunately he was still embracing her.

Unfortunately, however, *he was still embracing her.* The throbbing grew so insistent, it was as if she had a clockwork model of a heart in her underwear, pulsing in time with her own.

The ridiculous image restored Amelia to her better senses. "Um," she said awkwardly.

At once, Caleb released her, stepping back. He pushed a hand through his hair, shifting it off his forehead. Instantly long strands began to fall again, tangling with his eyelashes. "We should probably get out of here before—"

"—the spoon causes more trouble," Amelia inserted.

"—someone clicks that we're to blame for the mess," he said at the same time. He flashed a grin, the usual Caleb-type grin to warm her heart and remind her that he was her friend. *Just* her friend, Amelia added sternly to herself.

Although it wasn't really a matter of *just*, of course. It was almost everything to her. He was. At the same time, however, he was *not* someone to get all soppy over, merely due to a kiss (despite the evidence of actual soppiness occurring within her at that very moment). Nor was she thinking *God, please let him kiss me again, with or without the involvement of magic.*

Or, rather, she was thinking it, but only *to prove that she wasn't thinking it.* And she did *not* feel attracted to Caleb. Anyone would go a little daft after being kissed so efficiently, to say nothing of the flaming teapot.

"We shouldn't have done that," she said, striving not to touch her mouth.

"It was effective," Caleb pointed out—and if he was gazing at her mouth as though he also wanted to touch it, Amelia felt sure it was just a figment of her now overwrought imagination.

"Perhaps," she answered briskly. "But what if Miss Tunnicliffe saw and mentioned it to Ottersock or Throckmorton?"

Caleb frowned bewilderedly. "Does she even know Throckmorton?"

"Probably . . . maybe . . . I'm not sure, but . . . possibly," Amelia muttered. Sympathy crossed Caleb's face. He moved as if to hug her, and Amelia took a prudent step back. Snatching up the now-inert Hereford teaspoon from the table, she gave him a brisk, sensible nod. "Let us proceed with all haste."

"Flee the scene of the crime," Caleb translated wickedly. "That's my girl."

"I am not your girl, I am my own woman," Amelia replied in a pedantic tone to counter the flutters that his words inspired.

"I beg your pardon," Caleb apologized, and the flutters disappe—

He set a hand against her lower back. *Flutterflutterflutter.* A veritable typhoon filled Amelia's interior. This did not suggest attraction, however, merely that . . . that . . .

"Be careful where you step," Caleb said with helpful timing.

Amelia ignored the implication that she needed guidance to walk across a room (and furthermore that she'd most likely caused this whole debacle by feeling jealous when Caleb offered such guidance to Vanity). They made a cautious path through the mess of broken plates, glasses, and food. Emerging into the dreary, overcast late afternoon, they discovered a small crowd of diners, pub staff, and random passersby murmuring together on the footpath. They appeared to be the typical population one found in rural England: plainly dressed, eyes darkened by instinctive suspicion, and at least one pitchfork held up among them. Silence descended as everyone turned to stare at the historians.

"All fixed," Caleb announced with a cheerful smile.

"What happened?" a waitress asked, twisting her apron anxiously. "Was it a ghost?"

"No," Amelia reassured her. "There's—"

"Are you certain?" The woman's large-eyed gaze shifted to the door Caleb had closed behind them as if she expected a diabolical spirit from the netherworld to smash through it at any moment.

"Absolutely certain," Amelia said. "The—"

"Because the Eagle and Child pub down the road has a ghost, and they get so many customers they can't fit them all in."

"Oh did you say *ghost*?" Caleb interjected smoothly. He stepped forward, his hand gliding across Amelia's back as he went. "Yes, it was a ghost." The crowd gasped excitedly. "Big fellow, dressed like a Viking." Rather disappointed murmurs sounded. "I mean, *king*. Like a king." The murmurs increased in pitch and enthusiasm. Amelia saw Caleb's eyes light up in the way they always did when he got an opportunity to tell stories.

"Now, I'm no expert," he said, then paused to look endearingly through his eyelashes, making it clear he was so expert he could afford to be modest about it. Amelia estimated two women and an elderly gentlemen fell in love with him on the spot. "I just have a doctorate in history—"

"Ooh," the crowd said. Amelia amended her count to *four* women, one gentleman.

"—and I think what you have here, fine people, is the ghost of King Edward . . ."

He paused again, and as one the crowd leaned toward him, breathless with enthrallment. Caleb gave them his most wickedly gorgeous smile.

". . . the third."

"Aaah!" The crowd exhaled with delight. Why England's beloved warrior king should be haunting a rather dingy pub in a remote part of the realm went unexplained. If there was among the villagers even half a heart now not lost to Caleb, it would amaze Amelia.

"We have subdued the royal ghost and sent him back to the other world—" Dissatisfaction rippled through the crowd, and Caleb immediately changed tack. "But he may return at any time! However, I must warn you." His face became somber, and the crowd stilled, their attention fixed upon him as if he himself were royal. "King Edward did leave just the tiniest bit of mess. As the French could tell you, that's an unfortunate habit of his. But he did say he'd never seen a more charming pub"—Caleb aimed his smile at the waitress, who twisted her apron so forcefully she nearly yanked it off—"in the most beautiful village of all England!"

Cheers arose from the crowd. Caleb grasped Amelia's elbow, tugging her forward. "Let's go," he urged in a low voice.

"Wait," Amelia said, tugging back. Reaching into her coat's inner pocket, she took out a card and presented it to the waitress. "Our apologies. Please send the bill to this address and you will be paid in full."

The waitress regarded the card with confusion. "The bill? For a tiny mess?"

"Is that Ottersock's card?" Caleb asked, surprised.

"I always carry them in case of such moments," Amelia said. "I have several printed off."

Caleb raised an eyebrow, recognizing the sentence was incomplete. That was the problem with lifelong friends. (Well, that and them becoming suddenly, achingly attractive.) Amelia winced. "Every term," she admitted.

Caleb laughed. Then the waitress, suspicion growing on her face, drew breath to ask another question—

"Must dash!" Caleb declared, and pulled Amelia away. They wove a path through the crowd, smiling, nodding, and ignoring all questions with the adroitness of teachers. As they emerged, Amelia saw Sergeant Sheffield on the far side of the street, standing to attention beside a—

"Good heavens," she said. "What is that?"

"That," Caleb answered in a disbelieving tone, "is a dogcart."

They eyed the horse-drawn vehicle warily. Dilapidated and clearly never having suffered from being washed, its four-seater body balanced in precarious fashion between two large thin wheels, seemingly reliant on dubious physics and a great deal of wishing from Vanity Tunnicliffe, who sat in one of the backward-facing seats, surrounded by piles of luggage. Its horse put Amelia in mind of the Hereford teaspoon—ancient, gray, and looking like it too had recently been unearthed from a crypt.

"I'm starting to think Ottersock hired these people to torture us slowly and painfully," Caleb muttered.

"Oh my God!"

At the sudden shocked cry, they glanced back to see the waitress had opened the pub's door and discovered Caleb's interpretation of "the tiniest bit of mess."

"Hurry," Caleb hissed, yanking Amelia so abruptly she stumbled. He half dragged her across the road and, before she could chide him, set his hands on her waist and lifted her unceremoniously onto the cart's rear footplate. Amelia rearranged luggage until she was able to sit beside Vanity with a suitcase on her lap and another beneath her feet.

The young woman giggled. "Isn't this a fun adventure?"

"Hm," Amelia said so tonelessly, her family would have been proud.

Caleb was clambering into the seat behind Amelia, facing forward. "Go, go, go!" he urged Sheffield. The sergeant made no reply, mounting his own seat and taking up the horse's reins at such a calm, measured pace Amelia could practically feel Caleb's nerves vibrating. Flicking the reins expertly, Sheffield set the horse into a trudging walk.

"Stop those people!" came a furious shout from the waitress.

"Go!" Caleb reiterated to Sheffield, pointing along the street as if this would in some way help. In response, Sheffield flicked the reins again. The horse walked 0.05 percent of a mile faster.

Caleb leaned back against Amelia with a pathetic moan. "I'm going to get sick," he complained.

"Cheer up," she told him as lightning flashed through the dimming light. "You're soon going to be too rain soaked to care. If, that is, the townsfolk don't kill you first."

Indeed, two waiters and an elderly lady were rushing toward them, brandishing fists and, in the case of the latter, a handbag.

"Remind me why I didn't take up a quiet career, such as geography," Caleb asked, looking over both his and Amelia's shoulders at the pursuers.

"Because you don't like getting dirty shoes," she said.

He sighed, leaning back against her once more. "No, it's because you were doing history. Which makes this all your fault, I believe."

Amelia sensed Vanity staring at her wide-eyed and gave the girl an apologetic smile for Caleb's nonsense. Then she held up a warding hand to the pursuers, who were nearly upon them.

"Gentlemen! Madam! Stop, please! Your behavior is unbecoming."

Immediately, the waiters flushed, stumbling in their haste to obey her. The elderly lady, bringing up the rear, halted so abruptly her ruffled hat nearly flew off. She turned on a sensible heel and strolled off, chin high, as if she'd merely been taking exercise and was quite finished now.

"I told you that Oxford University would cover all costs," Amelia lectured the men. "It is most unseemly of you to harass us in this fashion."

"Er," said one waiter.

"Um," said the other.

Amelia raised her voice slightly as the dogcart continued to carry her inch by inch away from them. "I want you to write three pages on the importance of paying attention, and furthermore straighten your neckties."

Automatically they reached for their collars.

"You may go now."

Both men nodded to her thankfully, murmured apologies, and scurried away like schoolboys having been caught smoking behind the bicycle shed.

"Gosh!" Vanity exclaimed with delight. "That was remarkable, Professor! I can see why people call you—"

BOOM!

The universe proved its benevolence at that moment by sending a large clap of thunder. Vanity squeaked. Closing her eyes, Amelia lifted her face to the cold, somber wind. She felt a single raindrop like a kiss. She felt Caleb's finger stroke the edge of her hand.

Flutter flutter went the whole world.

CHAPTER SIX

They say history is written by the winners, but that's not true.
It's written by journalists, historians, and conspiracy theorists.
I, on the Past, Cornelius Ottersock

IT WAS GOING to be a dark and stormy night. Well, of course
dark, since that was the definition of night, but a storm could
also be reliably predicted. Amelia need not be a geographer to
do that. Turbulent clouds, rumbling with thunder, blotted the
sky above the low hills. To the north and east, the horizon was
lavender like . . . er . . . lavender flowers (Amelia's teachers had
never gone in for poetic metaphors, considering them too Amer-
ican for decency), but to the west the last of a bitter red sunset
seeped through the clouds, casting beams of old light that illuminated autumnal groves here and there, making them seem to
catch fire.

From her seat at the back of the dogcart, Amelia gazed
around her with wonder. She'd had no time to research the
history of this region before coming here and so, instead of
enjoying it intellectually, was forced to fall back on emotion.
The expansive panorama filled her heart with a great and desperate yearning, such as she'd felt when a Tudor goblet came

up for auction at a price higher than she could afford. As the wind blew loose strands of hair over her face, she imagined herself to be a Saxon princess on her way to marry a great king. He'd ride out to meet her, his noble brow shining in the late light, his hair golden like his crown, and as he knelt on the dirt road to welcome her with all honor, he would declare—

"Uuurghh," Caleb moaned at her side.

"Upon my word," Vanity declared from where she sat in what had been Caleb's seat until his nausea had forced an exchange. "I've never seen a fully grown man be so affected by the smell of horse . . . er . . ."

"Excrement," Amelia supplied complacently, and upon hearing Vanity's gasped response, she winked at Caleb. He gave her a big-eyed, mournful look in turn.

"Poor boy," she murmured, and patted his knee. "Look at the beautiful sky."

"I'd rather look at you," he said. "It's less nauseating."

"Always one with the charming compliments."

"You deserve it," he said, and smiled beautifully. Glimmering raindrops began to appear, as if the sky were falling in love with him.

"Eek!" Vanity squealed. "We're going to be drenched!" She flapped her hand at Sergeant Sheffield. "Make the horse move faster!"

Caleb's eyes grew even larger, pleading silently with Amelia. "Professor Sterling and I will walk," she announced. "That will ease the horse's load. Besides, I'm sure the manor isn't far now."

Vanity did not even make a show of polite refusal. And the look on Sheffield's face was so disinterested, so utterly incurious, it could have been framed and hung on a gallery wall as a fine piece of postmodern art. Amelia and Caleb climbed down and stood in the middle of the lane watching the dogcart advance until it disappeared around a bend. When the dust it had kicked up settled again, they began to walk. The cold breeze moaned like a dirge around them, shedding a few more raindrops.

"How cruel of you to make me hike in this downpour," Caleb said mildly.

"I'm a harridan," Amelia reminded him in a matching tone. Taking from her skirt pocket one of the tissue-wrapped ginger candies she kept for moments like this, she passed it to him.

"You're a darling," he countered, unwrapping the sweet. "At least this weather is appropriate for our journey to a place called Ravenscroft Manor."

"What do you mean?"

Caleb cocked his head to smile at her with mild astonishment. "Have you never read *The Mysteries of Udolpho*?"

"No."

"*The House of the Seven Gables*? *Wuthering Heights*? I know— you've surely read *Jane Eyre*."

Amelia frowned slightly. "Eyre. Is she related to Truelove the Eyr, who fought at the Battle of Hastings?"

A laugh burst from Caleb's throat and lit his eyes. "Sweetheart, tell me you read fiction. Any fiction."

"I've read Shakespeare," Amelia replied a little snootily. Then, after a moment's uncomfortable silence, she was forced by honesty to add, "Although only because we had to at school. Can't say I much liked it."

Caleb almost tripped on a pebble, so great was his astonishment. "How can you not like Shakespeare? You're English!"

Amelia shrugged. "There's too much historical inaccuracy."

"But every time I turn around you either have your nose in a book or are hugging one. In fact, there's one in your pocket right now, isn't there?"

What a foolish question. "Of course there is."

"But you don't read novels." He clearly could not comprehend this.

"I read biographies. National histories. The occasional annotated diary." After all, what need had she for fiction when the annals of history provided a great, sprawling tale of turmoil, comedy, and romance?

Staring blankly along the lane, Caleb shook his head. "I can't believe I didn't know this about you."

"There's a lot you don't know about me," Amelia answered rather darkly.

They entered the heavy shadow of trees shrouding the road's slow curve. The world grew mysterious, almost sinister in the gloom. Leaves rustled with ominous secrets, and whisper-fine ribbons of blue light drifted and faded, suggesting sorcery lurked in the shadows. Amelia and Caleb slowed their pace, looking around with a natural caution behooving professors of thaumaturgic phenomena ("Magicians," Caleb liked to say, to which Amelia would just shake her head)—she scanning for an old gravestone or roadside marker that might be enchanted, he for signs that a ghost or werewolf might suddenly pounce on them. But nothing was evident. As they emerged from the darkness, however, they stopped abruptly.

"Good heavens," Caleb exclaimed.

They stared out at small hills stitched roughly with stone walls, patched here and there with clusters of dark, shabby pine trees that bled red-tainted shadows in the dying sunset. A little farther ahead, the dogcart carrying Vanity and Sergeant

Sheffield had turned onto a long driveway leading to a manor house set deep within the view. Built in the late medieval era, it carried its age like a grudge. Vines crept over its moldering stone. Diamond-paned windows stared out at the cold and murky evening, unlit, secretive. Monstrous gargoyles perching atop the gables roared without sound.

As they watched, the manor's great front door opened, revealing a faint luminance that grew stronger as the dogcart drove closer to the house—no doubt servants igniting lamps, preparing for the guests.

Suddenly lightning crackled across the sky. Several of the manor's windows winked internally with an uncanny sapphire glow that transformed the darkness into a ghost of itself. Sparks leaped along the windows' lead grilles before vanishing.

Caleb leaned a little toward Amelia.

"I say, those flowers all along the driveway are daffodils, right?"

"Yes," Amelia answered.

"And would you call that blossom on those trees over there?"

"I would."

"Blossom. In autumn." Caleb glanced back over his shoulder. "Did we accidentally take a wrong turn and end up in the southern hemisphere?"

Crossing her arms, Amelia frowned at the view in much the same way a doctor frowns at a mysteriously ill patient—somber, yet not unexcited by the challenge. "Magic," she said. "That blue light is a sure sign of it."

"Strong magic," Caleb added, "considering lambs are frolicking in that field."

"A fey line must run through here," Amelia mused as she began walking again. Her brother Gabriel, a geography professor, had once shown her a map delineating the various seams of thaumaturgic minerals that crossed Britain and that very occasionally flared up to cause magical disorder. (Which is to say, she'd snuck into his bedroom when he wasn't home and peeked at the highly classified document, since she had a theory about historic events and zones of earth magic). "If that's the case, and Sir Nigel does have thaumaturgic antiques in his collection, we may be facing an interesting situation."

"I wouldn't call it interesting," Caleb grumbled, pulling up the collar of his coat protectively. "It's eerie."

Amelia gave him an amused look. "It's lambs and flowers."

"Exactly. It should be wind-torn trees and desperate women escaping ravishment from their cruel landlords."

Amelia blinked at him, utterly confused. "What?"

"You'd understand if you read books," he said, grinning mischievously.

"I read b—" She stopped, frowning, although mostly at herself for taking his bait. Caleb chuckled, and when Amelia smacked his arm it became an outright laugh.

"You are a fiend," she told him.

"But a pretty one," he argued.

They turned into the driveway. A gust of wind swept past them, setting their coats billowing. White blossom petals scattered through the dim air like sorrows. A lamb cried out plaintively for a mother that was nowhere to be seen.

Amelia shivered, and Caleb looked at her sharply. "You're cold again," he accused her.

"I'm fine," she lied.

"Come here, I'll give you my coat."

"You can't," she said, walking a little faster as he began to slip the garment off his shoulders. "It's not safe. Ottersock will surely have mentioned to Miss Tunnicliffe that we're enemies."

"Why would he?" Caleb reasoned. "In fact, considering she might have thought it a problem, and given the job to Cambridge Uni instead, he more than likely kept it secret. And there's no one here from Oxford—no Madame Kharensky, no Throckmorton—to tell her about it. We're safe, Meely."

Safe. Amelia felt a warm sigh go through her. Safe to smile and talk freely without damaging their reputations, let alone their careers. Gladness swelled her heart, and for a moment she thought she might actually cry from it. Pretending to squabble and feel angry had been so hard, these past few months.

But gladness was a short hop to the perilous chaos of joy. Retreating at once into self-restraining calm, she said a brusque "Hm."

Caleb understood this to be acceptance, however, for he removed his coat and practically tossed it onto her back. Then, walking backward as Amelia continued to march along the driveway, he began to wrangle her arms into the sleeves, grumbling all the while about her apparent determination to ruin his life by dying of a chill. Once he had her sufficiently clothed, he turned to walk beside her, and he rubbed her upper back as was his habit whenever he disrupted her nerves with his behavior.

Disrupted, however, was an understatement. Amelia felt like one of the blossom trees, buffeted, shaken, and coming apart. And actually not entirely *safe* after all. Caleb fussing with her clothes was nothing new; indeed, they had been doing it to each other forever—him shifting her hat to a more fashionable angle, her straightening his tie, him fixing her unbuttoned cuff, her straightening his tie (again) or jacket. But now, appallingly, she imagined him removing her clothes instead . . .

A clap of thunder made her jolt. The drizzling rain intensified, as if the clouds had shattered.

"Run!" Caleb shouted. He grasped Amelia's hand, and they raced together along the driveway toward the castle. His coat, too big for her, slapped against her legs . . . the wind snatched her beret . . . hairpins dislodged, sending strands of hair tumbling down to whip across her face. Now everything about her was in disarray. She felt as if she might unravel all the way out of her sensibleness into a wild and silent ghost that would wander the fells in search of its lecture schedule.

The thought should have left her aghast. No Tarrant ever tolerated unravelment. It was practically the family motto: Tidy, Organized, and Keeping a Stiff Upper Lip to Such a Degree That Stress Is Too Scared to Approach You. (Or, as was formally printed on their stationery, *Stabilitas Perpetuus*.) But perhaps whatever magic surrounding Ravenscroft Manor that had made daffodils flourish in mid-autumn also revived a remnant of the happy child she'd once been, for all of a sudden she found herself laughing. Caleb glanced back at her, and at the sight of his delighted grin, Amelia knew she would indeed become a ghost after she died, never mind science or sensibleness, for she would never leave him.

"All right?" he asked through the loud thrum of the rain.

"No," Amelia answered, the word broken into pieces by laughter. Caleb's eyes glinted, and his smile grew so wide it seemed like he'd just come across a secret trove of ancient magical gold. "Be careful!" she warned him.

"It's getting harder to be," he answered strangely, his smile fading . . .

"I mean, watch out!" With her free hand, Amelia pointed ahead, and Caleb looked forward just in time to see they were about to crash into a hedge. Hastily he corrected their path, laughing now too. Thus they ran, in much the same way they had in the old days of their childhood, sparkling with appreciation for each other's company, along the final stretch into the courtyard of Ravenscroft Manor.

Several footmen holding large black umbrellas were assisting Sheffield with unloading the dogcart. Vanity stood at the manor's large open doorway, talking to a man obscured by the shadows inside. Amelia, slowing her pace, misjudged a step and stumbled against Caleb. He put his arms around her, and together they dissolved into gasping, laughing breaths. Almost at once, a servant was upon them with an umbrella. They were efficiently hustled toward the door. Vanity smiled and waved in greeting.

"Professors! You'll never guess who I just found here!"

Amelia, still huddled against Caleb (only to keep them both under the umbrella's protection, you understand), and still light with heady silliness, answered with a smile—"Who?"

"He says he's a friend of yours!" Vanity turned behind her with an encouraging gesture. A large, brown-bearded man stepped forward, arms crossed, eyebrows raised above an expression of smirking satisfaction that must have been second only to that of the Scots when their king inherited the rule of England.

Instantly, Amelia stopped smiling; indeed, she stopped breathing altogether. Beside her, Caleb straightened, moving away from her, relinquishing the shelter of the umbrella. Icy wind howled through the space between them.

"Well, well," said the man. "If it isn't the two worst enemies in Oxford's entire faculty."

Amelia raised herself to the full height of her Tarrant dignity, pushed aside the wet tangle of hair from her face, and looked up at him with every appearance of serenity.

"Hello," she said, "Professor Throckmorton."

Chapter Seven

History is the consequence of psychology.
I, on the Past, Cornelius Ottersock

STEPPING INTO THE entrance hall of Ravenscroft Manor was like traveling through time. High oak walls, black ceiling beams, and worn flagstones presented a somber grandeur that had persevered for hundreds of years. At least, so Caleb supposed, despite seeing only glimpses of it behind a jumble of artwork, embroidered hangings, and shelves cluttered with objets d'art. A veritable battalion of marble statues lined the hall, alongside Georgian chairs, medieval stools, Carolingian tables, and what might have been a particularly fine example of a Jacobean sideboard were it not so piled up with random knickknacks that it looked positively Victorian. Dust drifted on wispy light from old-fashioned oil lamps, and shadows lurked resentfully behind the ceiling beams, threatening to produce ghosts at any moment.

Altogether it overwhelmed the eyes, confounded the brain, and aggravated the nasal passages. Caleb half expected a curator to appear demanding they pay a fee to tour the exhibits.

"So charming!" Vanity enthused. "Professor Tarrant, isn't it charming? Truly quaint and charming!"

"Indeed," Amelia answered in the gracious tone that Caleb knew all too well meant *actually it's dreadful, but I would never offend you by saying so.* She was looking around the hall with polite tranquility, but Caleb could see in her eyes the same wearying awareness he himself felt: it was going to take *weeks* to sort through the objects here. And almost certainly by the end of it his sinuses would be destroyed, considering all the dust and the cold drafts. Perhaps he should just resign now as a history professor and flee down to London, where he could take up work as a . . . a . . .

Actually, never mind. He couldn't think of any other occupation that allowed a man to lie around half the day reading exciting tales of the past and call it "work." He'd just have to get through this assignment the best he could, despite the weather and lambs and Professor Throckmorton.

Who was standing nearby, a sneer cutting through his bushy beard as he watched Amelia smooth back her wet hair.

Caleb felt a flash of anger. Despite never having been a violent man (except that one time he wrestled a junior professor for possession of the last cream doughnut in the faculty lounge), the only reason Throckmorton did not experience an unfortunate accident of the fist-meets-jaw variety was because Caleb stood too far away to excuse it as a mishap.

Besides, at six foot three and with a robust girth, the professor of Medieval Studies towered over him. Caleb's own height of five foot eleven might have been more reasonable, but it also suggested that a cautious response to Throckmorton's sneering would be wiser.

"What are you doing here, Basil?" he asked.

"Mansion!" the man bellowed, making Vanity peep with

startlement. "Brilliant! Fifteenth century! A must-see! Arrived an hour ago. Pure coincidence!"

This explanation was accompanied by a decidedly more articulate glance that took in both Caleb and Amelia and that made it clear Throckmorton's definition of *coincidence* was *something that happens after you hear two people you suspect of misdeeds are going to be working together in Cumbria, and you rush to get there before them so you can make their lives even more miserable than you already have.*

Caleb again felt himself tempted toward violence. Amelia, however, was looking straight through the man with such equanimity, one might mistake her for yet another statue in the room were it not for how her nose had turned red from cold. Indeed, she gave no indication of even having heard him. Drawing from her example, Caleb took a slow, settling breath.

"I'm surprised we didn't see you on the train," he said. In truth, though, considering Throckmorton's tweed suit, pipe, and slight odor of a recently devoured steak and kidney pie, he was practically indistinguishable from half the faculty at Oxford University. It was how he managed to be such an effective gossip.

"Manchester route?" Throckmorton asked. When Caleb nodded, the sneer slithered back into place. "Went by Wolverhampton."

Before they could fall, with inexorable English habit, into debating train routes and timetables, a sudden chilling noise echoed through the entrance hall like thunder, only quieter and emerging from a human voice box.

"Ahem."

Everyone went deathly still. An elderly gentleman had

appeared among them as if by sorcery. Dressed in a funereal black suit, with a few thin strands of hair clinging to existence across the otherwise bald dome of his head, he stood a little crookedly, his shoulders stooped as if the weight of the entire world rested upon them. And yet he exuded an authority such that he could only have been a king or a butler. His white gloves and fob watch suggested the latter, but the look in his small dark eyes was profoundly regal.

Which, again, suggested he was a butler.

"Welcome to Ravenscroft Manor," he said in a dolorous voice. "May I presume that you are the experts sent to evaluate Sir Nigel's antiques collection?"

"We are, indeed," Amelia replied. "Good evening. I am Professor Tarrant and these are my colleagues, Professor Sterling, Miss Tunnicliffe, and Sergeant Sheffield. I believe you have already met Professor Throckmorton."

She spoke with impeccable manners, not a single vowel out of place, and yet Throckmorton reddened as if she'd denounced him outright as a villain. *That's my girl,* Caleb thought proudly. Then he was the one to redden as the words echoed in his heart. *My girl, my girl . . . mine.*

Good God, was he becoming delirious as an early symptom of pneumonia?!

"I see you are rather wet," the butler noted in a manner other people used when saying *I see you have the plague.* "And you must be exhausted after your long journey. We will establish you in bedrooms, where you can dry off before having the honor of meeting Sir Nigel and Lady Ruperta at dinner."

Ah, so it was going to be like that. The people with doctorates awarded after years of mastering complex skills were to be graciously allowed—probably just this once, as a special treat—into the august presence of those whose superiority rested on their blue blood and weak chins.

"Cheers," Caleb said, careful to keep bitterness from his voice.

"Thank you," Amelia added nicely.

"Oh!" Vanity exclaimed, hands fluttering. "Oh!"

Everyone stared at her in bemusement, but she did not notice, instead pointing dramatically up the staircase that led to the second floor. "A ghost!"

As one, the historians turned to look. A figure in diaphanous white swept away from the landing, disappearing into the shadows. Glancing at Amelia, Caleb raised one eyebrow; she shrugged in reply.

"Dinner is at seven," the butler intoned, as if this distraction had not occurred. He went to leave, but Vanity cried out, stalling him.

"But wait, Mr.—Mr.—"

"Grimshaw, ma'am," he supplied.

"There was a ghost, Grimshaw!" she reiterated, gesturing again to the upper landing with such vigor, her bracelets clattered.

"Do not be late for dinner," the butler replied. "Lady Ruperta would be most displeased."

Chilling the atmosphere again with those last two words, the miniature winter that was Grimshaw shuffled away, and the footmen promptly swooped in. Taking charge of all the suitcases, they led everyone upstairs, where the landing proved haunted now by nothing worse than a taxidermied elk's head on the wall, its horns thick with dust. Throckmorton, Sheffield, and Vanity were guided to the left, down a long, creaking corridor lined on either side with stacks of books. Caleb and Amelia went right.

For a wild, pulsing moment, Caleb imagined there had been a miscommunication, resulting in them being given one room that contained only one bed. But to his absolute, definite relief, two rooms were provided, directly opposite each other. A footman accompanied Caleb into one, deposited his luggage on the floor, provided directions to the nearby water closet, then loitered in meaningful silence.

Caleb got the hint. "Much obliged," he said, and grabbing a random number of coins from his trouser pocket, he tipped the fellow what proved to be ten shillings, by which time it was too late to take it back. With effusive thanks, the footman literally bowed out, closing the door behind him. Excited murmurs could be heard from the corridor, where he was no doubt telling his colleague what a fabulously generous chap the handsome professor was.

Sighing wearily, Caleb brushed back his sodden hair and turned to inspect the room.

Ten seconds later, he was knocking on Amelia's door.

"Meely," he whispered through the wood paneling. Then noticing that the two footmen walking away down the corridor were glancing back at him curiously, he smiled and waved with a show of blithe innocence. The moment they disappeared around the corner to the stairs, he knocked again. *"Meely."*

The door cracked open and Amelia appeared in the narrow space, her expression so beautifully serene Caleb knew he'd irritated her. "Yes?" she asked.

"My room is creepy," he complained.

"Spiderwebs? Rotting floorboards?"

"Orange and pink wallpaper," he said. "And there's a cushion made to look like a hedgehog."

"Poor boy," she sympathized, but alas did not offer to console him with a hug. "My room appears to have a ghost."

Instantly, cute cushions were forgotten as professional excitement rushed into Caleb's heart. (After all, he might be good-looking, witty, debonair, and modest, but he was also a brilliant academic.) "Really? Can I see?"

Amelia held up a small copper device that appeared in all aspects to be a compass. It was, however, a thaumometer, a specialist gauge designed to measure the degree of magical energy within a room. While not as powerful as the version used by geographers, it nevertheless excelled in capturing delicate spectral vibrations. Caleb watched its tiny needle tremble near the height of its range. He found himself distracted, however, by the sight of Amelia watching it. She was pale-faced, shadow-eyed, and now completely dispossessed of hair clips. Caleb hadn't seen her hair down in years and was oddly enthralled by the fact that it wasn't as long as he'd imagined, falling like dark silk to not quite halfway down her back. With unusual self-restraint, he did not reach out to caress it.

"So let me get this right," he said. "The moment you entered your room, with wet clothes, soaked shoes, and on the verge of hypothermia, you got straight to work."

"No," she corrected him calmly. "I tipped the footman and waited until he left. And then I got to work. It's important to acquire a base-level reading of conjures before the space becomes disturbed."

Amused by such adorable prudence, Caleb set one arm up

against the doorframe and leaned in closer. "You are incorrigible," he told her. And if his voice was low, a little husky, this was merely due to the cold weather.

"Nonsense," Amelia replied briskly. "I am professional. Several medieval coins are framed on the wall, and I suspect one of them is expressing its thaumaturgic energy in a spectral form. Do you think they'd miss me if I absented myself from dinner? I want to investigate this further."

"Yes, they'd miss you," he said, although he doubted this was true. *He* would miss her, however, and that justified the lie.

"You could tell them I was tired after our journey." She was back to watching the thaumometer, and if its gauge hadn't been so clearly active, Caleb would have suspected her of merely trying to get out of socializing. Dinner parties were to Amelia what being stretched on the rack was to Protestants in the reign of Queen Mary Tudor: a constant threat in the background of life, promising misery.

"Meely," he said, trying to regain her attention, and when that didn't work he set a finger and thumb beneath her chin, tilting it up gently so that she saw him instead of ghosts in her machine. She blinked in surprise, her gorgeous lashes sweeping down, then fluttering slightly as they rose again. Gratification sparked deep in Caleb's body as he realized he'd put her just a little into disarray. Not so much that she slipped out of herself and became unhappy, which would have made him unhappy too, but just enough to be like the gentlest kiss on her wrist—an act he'd never dare to attempt in reality, although suddenly, quite desperately, he wished that he would.

The thought alarmed him. Amelia was the calm center of his life. His best friend. Romantic attraction would imperil that friendship (since of course she wouldn't feel the same), and

Caleb's pulse thundered at the very idea. Releasing her chin, he let his hand fall to his side, where its fingers stretched and curled as something like magic tingled within them. "What are we going to do?" he asked, although it felt futile.

"Well, to begin with," Amelia said sedately (although her eyes were doing that coppery-gleaming thing they always did whenever she felt stirred by some secret emotion), "we are going to track the occult signature. Then upon locating its—"

"I mean," Caleb interrupted, "what are we going to do about Throckmorton being here?"

It wasn't really what he'd meant, but he was willing to deceive them both.

"The same as we've been doing for the past five months," Amelia answered. "Pretend enmity."

Caleb crooked the arm propped against the doorframe so he could rub his thumb knuckle against his brow. "Bloody hell, this is exhausting. Can't we just lock him in the attic for the duration?"

Humor tugged fleetingly at one corner of Amelia's mouth. But she countered it with a gently stern frown, such as Caleb had seen her direct at her brother often enough. Because, of course, that's what he himself was to her—a kind of brother.

"Goodness, what a pitiful sigh," she remarked. "Don't worry, Professor Throckmorton is unlikely to stay for long once he finds out this house doesn't even have gas lighting. Now, you should go and dress for dinner." She tapped the thaumometer against his chest. "You worry about me getting sick, but you're just as wet."

That was true. He was a drippy mess. And as he looked at her now, and looked, and could not seem to stop looking, he felt himself melting even more. So he pushed himself away from the doorframe with a wry grin. "Very well. As you wish. Prepare to be dazzled."

Amelia rolled her eyes. She closed the door, but before it clicked into place she abruptly opened it again. Caleb's heart staggered, hoping for—what exactly, he did not understand. Just hoping, longing.

"Remember," she admonished. "We hate each other."

"Absol—" he began.

But she'd already shut the door.

THUNDER SHOOK THE last light from the sky, and the shadows in Ravenscroft Manor crept down from the ceiling beams to swarm through its halls, whispering with cold drafts. Amelia stood quietly within them, staring at a bone white shaft of light that fell through the half-open door of the dining chamber. She would never admit to fear, but a substantial amount of trepidation certainly gripped her heart.

A few years ago, she had traveled to Paris and the Musée de l'Histoire de France to make a presentation about a singing hat believed to have belonged to Napoléon. The audience of two hundred gentlemen historians smirked as she walked onto the stage, patently anticipating that she'd prove women had no place in academia. Upon arriving at the lectern, she discovered that, instead of her lecture notes, she'd accidentally brought a letter from her mother advising her to pluck her eyebrows and wear a tighter corset. It had been a chilling moment.

This one was worse.

From the other side of the door came the sounds of women laughing, interspersed with jocular booms from Professor Throckmorton. They might as well have been the sounds of guns and cannons. Amelia never quailed from lecturing groups of people, but making small talk with them was a whole different matter. It felt rather akin to having conquered half of France but not knowing how to manage one's own turbulent archbishop. At least with that presentation for the singing hat she'd been able to call upon her well-trained memory and thus proceed in a state of such calm grace that the audience found themselves both thoroughly educated and terrified by her intelligence. Here, now, however, she had no skills to summon.

It wasn't that she was antisocial. It was just that she had a dislike for society. Growing up in a boarding school tended to do that to a person.

"Excuse me," came a meek little voice, and Amelia turned to find a gentleman standing beside her. Short and rather scrawny, wearing a brown jacket that had seen better centuries, he looked rather like an accountant that had taken a wrong turn in Manchester and somehow ended up in the damp, windswept farmlands of east Cumbria. As he peered up at Amelia through small, round spectacles, he gave her a sympathetic smile.

"Don't want to go in?" he asked, twitching a finger toward the dining room's door. His voice was paper-thin and the finger trembled slightly, as if he were barely holding on to this present moment, although he couldn't have been more than sixty.

"Oh," Amelia said, a little startled by such a frank inquiry. "Just taking a deep breath first."

The man nodded. "I have to do that too." He leaned a little closer to confide, "I don't know why I was summoned to this; usually I'm not required to come down. Honestly, I'd rather be left alone to my work."

She smiled. "Well, I'm glad you're here. It's very nice to meet you."

He appeared surprised by this basic courtesy. "How kind! I hear they've brought antiquarians up from Oxford. Are you one of them?"

"Yes." She held out a hand. "Amelia Tarr—"

Suddenly a sharp voice flew out of the dining room, slicing through their conversation. *"Nigel!"*

The gentleman flinched. "See you in there," he said rather grimly, taking Amelia's hand and patting it with flimsy encouragement before hurrying away into the room. Amelia blinked at his departing figure, bemused.

That was Sir Nigel? She'd been expecting someone more . . . *more.*

"Hello there."

Encompassed by cologne and a sense of comfort, Amelia did not need to look around to know Caleb had arrived. As he came to stand alongside her, he tapped her arm with the back of his hand. "I see you're late again."

She arched an eyebrow. "You really ought not say that when you arrive after me."

"Oh, but I'm *fashionably* late," he answered with a grin, tugging on the satin lapels of his dinner jacket. Indeed, he looked insanely handsome, his blond hair swept back in a style that made its dampness seem a deliberate choice all the boys would soon be copying, whereas Amelia's own hair, pulled into a bun, was merely, hopelessly wet. There existed no sign that he'd endured a long day of travel, rambunctious magic, and miserable childhood memories involving horse dung, to say nothing of the kissing (which Amelia could only hope he didn't rank as equal with the dung). Of course, his smart clothes and soft pink eye shadow helped, but mostly it was just Caleb and his exquisite genes. Amelia didn't know whether to be jealous or in love.

Well, not *in love*, but . . . but . . .

Thankfully, at that moment she noticed his bow tie was slightly askew. Unable to resist the lure to tidy it, she set her hands on his arms and turned him toward her. "Really, at your age you should be able to arrange your neckwear properly," she grumbled as she straightened the offending bow. Caleb glanced at the dining room door, but Amelia had already ensured no one could see them. (Two footmen stood nearby, watching the whole scene avidly, but they did not count.)

"Perhaps I leave it crooked just to give you the pleasure of fixing it," he said smilingly.

Tingles danced in Amelia's stomach. She wished she wasn't intelligent and sensible, so that she might pretend they were caused by some digestive ailment, rather than by hearing Caleb's husky voice speak the words *to give you pleasure*. She could feel him looking down at her and she stared determinedly at the tie, which she'd somehow rearranged to a state even more askew than before. Biting her lip, focusing on the little pain, she got the bow straight and stepped back.

Caleb stepped with her. He caught her hand, which was a good thing since Amelia felt alarmingly off-balance. His smile was wicked, but in his eyes she could see sympathy. He, of course, understood her hesitation at the threshold. He'd had to prod or cajole or sometimes half drag her into faculty parties and award ceremony dinners more often than she cared to remember. "Come on, bella luna," he said. "Let's go meet the enemy together."

The words snapped her back into good sense. Tugging her hand free, she frowned at him. "I do not require assistance from an adversary such as you, Professor Sterling," she said pointedly.

"Oops," he answered, and leaning close, he whispered, "Sorry. Looking at you in your evening attire, I completely forgot I'm supposed to hate you." And he slid a wry gaze down her white-collared but otherwise simple black dress and gray cardigan.

Well, really! How rude! And outrageous! And oddly thrilling! Feeling herself on a shoreline with a great red tidal wave of blushing heading rapidly her way, Amelia lifted her chin, threw Caleb a vicious glare, then marched into the dining room. As she did so, she caught the flash of a smile on his face and realized that he'd played her so she would forget her nerves. Charmed, she felt herself begin to smile also.

And then she looked around the room, and the smile collapsed as her mouth fell ajar in astonishment.

Chapter Eight

IT WAS AS if she'd stepped into a dream. A sensible, sober dream of dark oak paneling, a dark oak floor, and books lining every wall. By the light of numerous candles, their gilt-worked spines glinted. The smell of their old pages filled the air with an intoxicating mustiness. Some people sat around a large dining table, but Amelia dismissed them from her attention. Was that a complete set of Gibbon's *The History of the Decline and Fall of the Roman Empire* she spied? And that oil painting of Lord Nelson above the hearth looked at first glance to be authentic! She swayed a little with dizziness, for her mouth remained ajar, having abandoned any interest in breathing. After all, what was oxygen compared to a really good private library?

"Professor!"

Vanity's high-pitched voice yanked her back into her proper senses. The girl was waving from the far side of the table, and Amelia shut her mouth in order to smile politely in return. Only now did she notice the particulars of the dining setup. A table of the same heavy, dark oak as the walls was laden with so much crystalware, gold-rimmed dinnerware, and silver cutlery that it looked like a display at a home decor exhibition. A centerpiece of two swans facing each other with their wings extended charmed her until she realized with a lurch in her stomach that they were actual swans, and indeed part of the dinner. Spontaneously converting to vegetarianism, she looked away, driven at last to regard the people present.

Other than Vanity, only four others occupied the room. (And an uncounted number of servants.) Sheffield sat rigid at the table's end with an attitude suggesting it would be a dereliction of his duty to consume anything. Throckmorton was opposite Vanity, drinking deeply from a wineglass—an action that looked rather like how Amelia felt. Sir Nigel sat hunched beside him. And presiding at the head of the table was a woman so ferociously dignified that Amelia initially wondered if a duchess had come to call. Her voluptuous silver-haired coiffure gave the impression of being crowned with a tiara, although it was not. Her black taffeta dress was so old-fashioned it rebounded into vintage magnificence. She peered at Amelia through a lorgnette while simultaneously snapping her fingers at Sir Nigel.

"Sit up straight," she muttered to him through the teeth revealed by her elegant smile. "Welcome," she told Amelia, lowering the lorgnette with a brisk little sniff that told Amelia she'd been classified as Uninteresting and Badly Dressed. "I am Lady Ruperta Harroway, and you must be the antiquarian girl who's come to look at Nigel's knickknacks. We've just been hearing *all* about you from Mr. Throckmorton."

Recollecting how laughter had emerged from the room, Amelia dreaded to think what the medieval studies professor had been telling these people. And although she was no coward (after all, she'd chosen to become an antiquarian despite the very real risk of being killed by a fifteenth-century ashtray—and worse, her parents' disapproval), she did wish rather fervently that she could retreat to her bedroom, where a comprehensive biography of Mary Wollstonecraft awaited her. But the only way she could imagine that happening was if something exploded, and not even she wanted to see that befall such an excellent library.

"I am sorry if we're late," she said, resisting an urge to curtsy to the formidable Lady Ruperta.

"We're not sticklers for time here," Sir Nigel spoke up in his thin voice, gesturing to a longcase clock across the room. Lady Ruperta sniffed in a manner that made it clear time was very definitely stickled, no matter what her husband might think, but Amelia had once again discarded any interest in the woman's existence. The clock was walnut . . . seventeenth century . . . probably a Cabrier, considering the fine details on its front panel. A subtle blue light tinted the air around it, suggesting the presence of thaumaturgic energy. There was also the minor clue of its minute hand moving backward.

Ooh! Amelia thought (a professional term meaning *I formally acknowledge this to be something worthy of my expert consideration*). An enchanted Cabrier clock far surpassed anything she'd seen in the manor's entrance hall. Even if it represented the only item of value in Sir Nigel's collection, the British Museum would nevertheless be pleased indeed.

"And you must be Mr. Sterling," Lady Ruperta was saying while Amelia mused whether she ought to run back upstairs and get her thaumometer. The hostess applied her lorgnette once more to the task of inspection.

"Hello," Caleb said in the languid, smiling way he employed

whenever he wanted to charm the greatest number of people possible in the shortest amount of time. And indeed, Lady Ruperta blushed. Vanity fanned herself with both a hand and her eyelashes. Throckmorton reached for the nearest wine carafe to refill his glass. "It's an honor to visit your lovely home," Caleb continued—at which even Sir Nigel began to look a little bewitched.

"Yes, it is," Lady Ruperta replied. Recovering her wits, she showed a skill possessed only by aristocrats and high school teachers: looking down her nose at him while still peering through her lorgnette. "I trust, Mr. Sterling, that you and your assistant understand antiques."

"Associate," Caleb corrected her, still smiling.

"*Girlfriend,*" Throckmorton interjected, poorly disguising the word as a cough.

Caleb's expression did not falter, but judging from the manner in which he blinked, Amelia knew he was dissecting the medieval studies professor with an imaginary butter knife. "Allow me to answer that question," he said to Lady Ruperta, "by telling you that the cameo at your throat is a fine example of a late-eighteenth-century Tassie."

"Oh!" The lorgnette slipped from Lady Ruperta's hand as she reached up to touch the cameo under discussion. "How clever of you to notice! Sir Nigel gifted it to me for my last birthday. 'A treasure for my treasure,' he said. *Didn't you, Nigel?*" she added, her voice cracking like a whip and jolting Sir Nigel from an apparent doze.

"Yes, dear," he replied automatically.

"I say," Vanity spoke up. "Isn't a Tassie rather com—"

"Complex in its craftsmanship, yes," Caleb spoke over her smoothly.

"Please, do sit down," Lady Ruperta urged Amelia and Caleb, all graciousness now as she gestured to the remaining vacant chairs. Amelia was impressed. She hadn't witnessed Caleb disarm a foe so swiftly in years.

Footmen moved forward then to aid in seating them. Caleb was placed next to Vanity, and Amelia into the seat beside Throckmorton, who gave her a sardonic glance. But she did not mind, for she was now in possession of an excellent view of the clock. The last time she'd felt this excited about an antique was when she found Richard III's flame-breathing codpiece in a stable yard in Leicester. While the footmen began serving the meal, she tilted from side to side to see around them.

There followed an onslaught of pleasant conversation about the weather (ghastly), the journey north (hideous), and the accommodations ("I decorated those bedrooms myself," said Lady Ruperta, which almost certainly meant she told hired tradesmen how to decorate them). Amelia inserted a word or smile now and again when prompted by her subconscious— although to be fair, this was all she'd have done even were she not absorbed in clock gazing. People *did* interest her, but usually only after they'd been dead a hundred years.

While noting the clock's silver hands and trying to decide if its spandrels were genuine gold or just painted, she heard Throckmorton say, "Professor Sterling is a great adventure sportsman."

"Then we shall have to arrange for some hunting and hiking, and perhaps some fly-fishing in the river," Lady Ruperta replied.

Caleb's coughing fit made it difficult for Amelia to listen for a whine of kinetic thaumaturgic energy emitting from the clock, but she surmised it was probably negligible since none of the wineglasses had shattered. While theorizing that the finial would be its discharge point, she saw Vanity pat Caleb's forearm and murmur something that must have been amusing, judging from the delighted grin he gave in reply. Her pulse stammered—for yes, a blue spark did leap from the top of the finial, proving her right!

Counting the seconds it took for a minute to unwind (forty-two), she absentmindedly ate a few spoonsful of mushroom soup. In the background, Lady Ruperta was describing the extent of her husband's antiques collection. A few words breached Amelia's concentration: "several rooms . . . basement . . ." and what sounded disconcertingly like "higgledy-piggledy." Amelia translated that as *at least three weeks spent away from home* and would have felt quite morose about it had not, at that moment, the clock chimed five.

Despite the hour hand being aimed at seven.

Quite electrified, Amelia set down her spoon—missing both the soup bowl and the table, and not at all noticing as it clattered to the floor. Everyone turned to look at her, and Lady Ruperta sniffed contemptuously.

"I see you're interested in Nigel's old clock. It's quite valuable, you know. It cost what we would have paid for a holiday to Brighton."

"It's broken," Nigel murmured regretfully.

"It's enchanted," Amelia told him.

Caleb looked over his shoulder at the clock and said, "Hm," with mild surprise. The minute hand had begun to spin rapidly around the dial. "That doesn't seem very safe."

"Goodness me!" Vanity exclaimed with a nervous laugh.

"It's stood there for three years," Lady Ruperta said. "I can't see why it would suddenly become dangerous." She narrowed her eyes, as if suspecting Amelia or Caleb had crept into the room before dinner to sabotage the clock for some nefarious purpose. After all, university academics were about as trustworthy as snake oil salesmen, the way they went on about the value of getting an education. What would the world come to if everyone listened to them? Well-informed lower classes? But then nobody would want to clean her chamber pot!

"Sometimes the act of recognition can trigger latent magic in an object," Amelia explained. "We still don't fully understand why. I shouldn't worry, though. From what I can see, the clock's magic is unstable but appears weak. We're quite—"

"Egad!" Lady Ruperta interjected with a horror that would have been assuaged had she only allowed Amelia to continue. "Nigel! Why did you allow into our house people who can recognize magic and therefore put us in danger?"

"Because you said I have too many antiques," her husband answered. "You insisted I winnow the collection."

Lady Ruperta stared what would have been daggers were she not so refined, and that therefore were the salad knife equivalent of angry marital looks. Sir Nigel merely went on eating his soup. The atmosphere grew so tense, it needed no magic to make it feel perilous. Swallowing dryly, Amelia looked across the table to Caleb, but he was smiling with steady reassurance at Vanity, whose eyes had widened anxiously. Even Throckmorton appeared uncomfortable, although that could have been due to the empty wine carafe in front of him.

"Grimshaw!" Lady Ruperta snapped, making everyone jolt. "Carve the swans!"

Oh God, Amelia thought, and looked instinctively around for an emergency exit.

Suddenly, out of the blue (literally: an azure haze of visible thaumaturgic energy), the clock began ticking so excessively it sounded like a room full of disapproving aunties clicking their tongues. Everyone stared at it nervously.

"Has that happened before?" Caleb asked.

"Never," Nigel said, his face becoming animated with excitement.

"Will it destroy the fabric of time?" Vanity cried out.

Caleb smiled. "Not with us here to protect you."

"Oh," she breathed dreamily, her eyes shining as she gazed upon him. Caleb rose from his chair and, hands in trouser pockets, strolled over to the clock. He nudged it with the toe of his shoe, and when that did not cause an explosion devastating the house and surrounding region, he angled his head, inspecting the dial more closely.

"Looks seventeenth century."

"I think it's a Cabrier," Amelia said.

"Yes, here's his name engraved on the cartouche." Pausing, he frowned slightly as he searched his thoughts. "Wasn't it a Cabrier clock that malfunctioned at Windsor Castle, briefly turning Prince Albert into a Christmas tree?"

"Eep!" Vanity squeaked in alarm.

"Don't worry," Caleb told her. "This one is making a lot of noise, but I don't think it has enough magic in it to do something like that."

"How can you tell?" the girl asked.

"Well, partly because you don't have any tinsel garlands and sparkly painted balls hanging off you," he said, making her giggle, "but also due to several more subtle indicators, such as the particular blue shade of the thaumaturgic emissions. The sound of the tick."

"Whether there's a bitter smell in the air," Amelia added. "And most of all—"

"Just a *feeling* one gets," she and Caleb chorused.

"A feeling," Lady Ruperta scoffed. "I certainly hope my plumber doesn't fix the pipes because of a *feeling*."

"Perhaps it's better to call it an instinct developed after inspecting hundreds of enchanted antiques over the years," Caleb said.

Lady Ruperta exhaled a sharp, sardonic little breath. "You don't look old enough to have inspected hundreds of anything."

He grinned. "I'm a boy wonder. As for this clock, my feeling is that there's no concern."

"I concur," Amelia said. "It appears to be a non-incendiary, low-amplitude device."

"Low amplitude?" Lady Ruperta asked.

"Only emitting a small amount of energy," Caleb explained. "I'd say ten thaumaturgic conjures at most."

"So not much tick for its tock," Vanity said, and returned to her soup with an air of disappointment.

Sir Nigel, on the other hand, seemed surprisingly anxious for a man who possessed a house full of potentially dangerous antiques. "You're sure it's not going to explode, then?" he peeped.

"Quite sure," Amelia reassured him.

Sir Nigel looked to Caleb.

"Professor Tarrant is correct," Caleb said with just enough emphasis on Amelia's title to thrill her, since he could hardly lecture their host on the evils of male chauvinism (although, she mused, that would be one way to get them back to Oxford quickly). "The clock is unstable but weak. Even if it did explode, the most that would happen would be us all feeling a vague sense of déjà vu. And that's not very scary—trust me, I've experienced it before. We're quite safe."

A breath of relief went through the room. Throckmorton leaned across the table to take the full carafe of wine that was set in front of Sergeant Sheffield. Grimshaw stepped toward the swan display, carving knife at the ready. Amelia looked away, all her horrified anticipation of that procedure rushing up again. Suddenly, a flash of silver light sparked at the edge of her vision. Then another. The air seemed to throb with a soundless force that reverberated along her every nerve.

Jumping up so fast her chair crashed to the floor, she gestured urgently to the diners. "Everyone out! At once!"

Astonishment stunned the company. But no British person was capable of defying a command made in such a stern, teacherly voice by a woman wearing a knitted gray cardigan, and so mumbling in fright (Vanity and Sir Nigel), annoyance (Lady Ruperta), and frustration at not being able to finish the soup (Throckmorton), they promptly quit their seats and made for the exit. As he lumbered through the doorway, Throckmorton sneered at Amelia. "Only here an hour and already making quite the fuss, Tarrant."

She ignored him, beckoning to Sergeant Sheffield so the man would move faster than a steady march. Within less than a minute, the room was cleared, even Caleb obeying her without question. Amelia paused in the doorway, watching the books begin to stir on their shelves as the candlelight, trembling, flushed blue with magic.

"Come on, you," Caleb said from behind her. Grasping her arm, he pulled her over the threshold and slammed the door shut.

BOOM.

Chapter Nine

Beggars and kings alike bow to the power of magic.
I, on the Past, Cornelius Ottersock

"WELL, THIS IS unexpected," Amelia said as she and Caleb stood in the dining room five minutes later. From out in the hallway, where they had insisted the others remain, Lady Ruperta called through the closed door, "Is everything all right?"

Amelia and Caleb exchanged a taut glance. Amelia tilted her head toward the door . . . Caleb shook his . . . She frowned . . . He gave a much-put-upon sigh and trudged across the room and opened the door a crack.

"Everything's just fine," he lied. "But best you stay out for a little longer. Maybe go have some brandy while you wait?"

Amelia heard only a murmur of replies, shot through with one sharp *Nigel!* Then Caleb closed the door and turned back to the room.

"What the hell are we going to do about this?" he asked bemusedly.

"I don't know," Amelia admitted.

They stared in troubled silence at the scene. Everything seemed exactly as it had been before the percussive disturbance.

The dinner was undisturbed on the table, the books neatly lined up on their shelves. The clock continued to tick backward, no trace of blue-tinted enchantment about it now. Amelia felt frazzlement encroach upon her nerves yet again, for there was only one thing worse than magic exploding during your first evening on assignment: it *not* exploding, when you made everyone run out of the room because you thought that it would.

"I could have sworn there was a sonic detonation," she said, "but perhaps I misheard."

"You didn't," Caleb told her. "And you know what it was."

She looked at him with some surprise, for only rarely had she heard that tone of voice from him: light, friendly, but with an unyielding quality that explained why his students were always successful despite his apparently lackadaisical approach to teaching them. "No, I don't know," she said. "The clock—"

"Is not responsible. Tell me, Meely, what you were thinking just before things went boom."

"Sonic detonation," she corrected him.

"Whatever."

Amelia frowned, trying to remember what her thoughts had been. "I admit, I was annoyed about Sir Nigel not taking my professional word, but that was hardly enough— Wait. The butler was about to carve the swans, and I couldn't stand the thought of watching them being—" She shuddered, unable to finish that sentence.

Thwack.

They turned to see a book lying on the floor.

Thwack. Another flung itself from its shelf to join the first.

Caleb turned back to Amelia, brows raised. Apparently she was supposed to divine some meaning from this expression.

"It is *not* my fault," she retorted, for indeed she'd always been able to read Caleb's face.

He contrived to lift his brows even higher.

"Well, really," Amelia huffed. "There's no need to be rude. Are you suggesting I have some kind of telekinetic power, as if I were a Saxon brooch or—or—?" Feeling her temper grow hot, she stopped, taking a deep, calming breath. How well this worked can be evidenced by the way half the candles in the room suddenly flickered and went out. Shadows wavered across Caleb's face like a *told you so*.

"If you'll excuse me, please," she said with an attitude she'd have liked to call serene but that was actually closer to stony. "I want to locate the *real* source of the thaumaturgic emissions."

But before she could turn away, Caleb stepped toward her. His silence was intent, holding her rooted to the spot, and Amelia watched with some trepidation as he took another step. He drew so close she could see old London darkness in his sky blue eyes, reminding her that he'd been raised among criminals and that a few sharp fragments of their unscrupulous teachings remained at the back of his psyche. He set one hand against her hip and began to glide it slowly downward.

Such a force of frazzlement erupted in Amelia's stomach that she felt like a thaumaturgically charged wedding ring in the court of Henry VIII. Then Caleb found what he was looking for: the pocket in her skirt. As he slipped his hand inside, he smiled crookedly.

You are a fiend!—is what Amelia would have told him had she been able to speak. But dry throated and half-deaf from the thudding roar of her own pulse, she could only stare at him furiously while he rummaged in that secret place. Behind him, a saltcellar (*circa early eighteenth century, trifooted, sterling silver*, Amelia's brain noted automatically) began rising from the dining table, salt flying out of it in a slow, glittering eruption of thaumaturgic energy. The crystals twinkled like stars in the gilded shadows. Caleb's fingers moving against her thigh made Amelia feel like she had a similar constellation of salt and sorcery inside her own body. And from the expression in Caleb's eyes, he knew it.

"Fiend," she managed to whisper at last.

"If you say so, darling," he answered, his voice soft yet gritty, making that internal constellation swirl. Slowly, he withdrew his hand and held it up to reveal what he'd taken from the pocket.

Amelia flickered a glance at it. She would not have been a Tarrant if her facial expression altered when it found an alteration of her understanding, but it must be said that her eyelashes became a tempest. "Oops," she said succinctly.

Caleb flipped the Hereford teaspoon around his fingers. "One would have thought you'd have put this in a safe bag as soon as you got the opportunity," he remarked.

"Yes, well, I meant to," Amelia said with an arch dignity she did not actually feel in that moment. "But I was in a hurry to change for dinner."

"I note you did change. That's a different dress you're wearing. Yet somehow the teaspoon ended up transferred to its pocket instead of a safe bag."

"There must be a confoundment aspect to its magic," Amelia said. The thought immediately excited her, and she reached for the teaspoon so she might inspect it for some evidence of this theory. But Caleb held it up, out of her reach.

"Perhaps you're enchanted and don't know it," he said.

Amelia's eyes narrowed as she regarded him. "Perhaps you are mistaken in a belief that you can condescend to me."

She spoke in a markedly polite tone that warned him to either apologize or face the consequences, and in response, Caleb did what any friend would under these circumstances: stepping back until he met the edge of the dining table, he held the teaspoon behind him.

Amelia's eyes grew wide with incredulity. "You're stealing my artifact!"

"Your artifact has developed a thaumaturgic connection to your emotions," Caleb replied calmly. "I'll take it upstairs and put it in one of my safe bags."

This was actually a good plan, reasonable, professional, and *utterly unacceptable*. "It's mine," Amelia said, stepping into the gap Caleb had created between them.

"Is it precious to you?" he asked with a touch of sardonic humor.

"What?" She gave him a bewildered look. "No. I'm in the middle of studying it, that's all. By the way, have you noticed the saltcellar hovering behind you, sending out magic like darts?"

"Don't try to change the subject."

"I'm more concerned about the cellar's magic changing *you*." She took another step forward, and Caleb promptly climbed onto a chair. Good heavens, did he think himself eight years old again?

No, scratch that. The last time he climbed on furniture was *three months ago*, jumping atop a desk to cajole his students into admiring a gold statuette of Anubis. (*"Carpe dius!"*)

"Get down," Amelia ordered him, sounding so bossy Mr. Dummersby from the British Museum would have felt vindicated in his ~~fear~~ manly mistrust of her.

"Nope," Caleb said, shaking his head. "I'm worried you've been ensorcelled by this spoon, Meely."

"You're the one refusing to let it go," Amelia pointed out. "I don't care anymore. That saltcellar is a far greater worry." Hoisting her skirts, she climbed onto the chair next to his.

Boom!

Thaumaturgic energy burst from the saltcellar, making Amelia sway on the chair. She stretched out her arms to balance herself.

"Please do be careful," Caleb said mildly.

"Never mind me," she replied, flapping a hand at him. "Grab the cellar!"

Muttering under his breath about the peace and quiet of the city he could be enjoying right now, Caleb clambered onto the tabletop. Carefully avoiding plates and glasses, he reached for the little silver dish.

It promptly leaped higher.

"*Tsk*," Amelia said, climbing onto the table alongside him. "Why are you not taller?"

Caleb steadied her as she nudged aside a bowl of fruit to clear a space in which to stand. "I'm tall enough for the important things," he said, and bent some five inches to kiss her forehead.

"That's very charming," Amelia told him dryly, "but please concentrate on the matter at hand. Or, more accurately, *not* at hand."

They looked up at the saltcellar where it floated just beyond reach, a tiny moon within a drift of salt stars.

"Pretty," Caleb said.

"Dangerous," Amelia countered.

He shrugged.

Suddenly, tiny beams of magic shot out from the cellar, stabbing one of the books on the shelves. A cloud of typeset letters burst forth and began flapping around the room in a broken, scattered manner, like modern poetry.

Amelia frowned. "We need to—"

"Waltz beneath the salty starlight?" Caleb suggested.

"Constrain the saltcellar," she told him chidingly.

"I'll hit it with the teaspoon."

Amelia clicked her tongue. "You will not. There's a good chance the cellar isn't especially magical in itself but is absorbing the teaspoon's energy, just as the clock did. Bringing the two into contact could be disastrous."

Caleb's eyes twinkled with luminous, salted magic. "We could always try what we did in the Staveley pub to stop the enchantment."

Amelia blinked dispassionately in response to this, even as her nervous system got together to throw a raucous surprise party for the memory of The Staveley Pub Kiss. *There is no call for capital letters,* she told herself austerely, to which came an instant, adamant reply: *THE KISS.*

As a teacher, however, she was used to people being adamant about things that were actually nonsense, and therefore ignored herself. "Or we could use a silver candlestick to knock it down," she proposed instead.

"Well if you want to be *boring*," Caleb said.

Amelia sighed with exasperation but nevertheless couldn't hold back a faint smile of her own. "You're such a pest," she told him fondly.

"I do my best."

Her smile deepened. His gaze grew heavy. The saltcellar began to spin, but neither of them noticed. An intense, silent conversation passed between them . . . *We really need to focus—You're right, as always—So will you focus?—What do* you *think, darling?—I think you'll go on being silly—See, always right.* It was the same conversation they'd been having most of their lives, and for which they no longer required actual words. Had Ottersock witnessed that deep, intimate look, he'd have suffered an apoplexy. They should have stopped; should have focused on work as Amelia suggested. But they kept on just gazing at each other, their faces sparkling with constellations of magic.

And perhaps that magic affected them, or perhaps some strange kind of gravity. For Caleb blinked, swaying just a fraction closer to Amelia, and at the same time she drifted toward him, lifting her face. He bent his head, angling it, moving as slowly as she. Their lips parted; their breath faded away. They kis—

Click.

The tiny sound pinched at the edge of their awareness. Without moving, Caleb looked up through his eyelashes, over Amelia's shoulder . . .

And then, abruptly, he was moving very fast, straightening away from her, his expression darkening into a scowl.

"You are infuriating!" he snapped.

Amelia gasped with outrage. "And you are unbearable!"

Caleb's eyes flashed with an anger that looked hot, so hot, Amelia felt a similar flash beneath her heart, alighting her pulse into a firestorm. "I hate you!" she averred, clamping her hands against her hips.

"I hate you too," he said, and Amelia was amazed the air between them didn't go up in smoke.

"Fighting *again?*" Throckmorton boomed with disbelieving indignation from the door, which he'd stealthily opened while they were intent upon each other. He stormed into the room, thrusting his pipe at them as if he stood in a classroom, chastising two naughty students. "Delinquent! Unprofessional!"

Amelia barely heard him. "Everything is your fault!" she told Caleb, and held her breath excitedly, awaiting his reply . . .

"Only in your imagination!" he retorted, causing her breath to release in a trembling rush. Indeed, her whole interior seemed to be trembling. Still glaring at Caleb, she thrust out one arm, pointing to farther down the table. "Professor Throckmorton, bring me a candlestick!"

"Going to smack Sterling with it?" Throckmorton asked hopefully.

"Ooh, yes please," Caleb said, bouncing his eyebrows at Amelia.

She frowned in response, and her excitement transformed into something for which she had no name, never having experienced it before. It felt simultaneously like the electrifying tension of a tightly clenched fist and the exhilaration of letting go. "What nonsense," she said, and snapped her fingers to hurry Throckmorton. "Candlestick!"

"Unsure if a good idea," the professor said as he handed one up to her. "Considering the Ashmolean fire."

"That's true," Caleb said as he continued to stare at Amelia. "Miss Tarrant is good at setting things aflame."

She hefted the candlestick, and his smile quirked. Then he took it from her, and unbuttoning his suit jacket with one hand, he reached up high, his white linen shirt straining against a chest that suggested he was not as indolent as he gave the impression of being. He whacked the saltcellar with the candlestick.

Clank went silver against silver.

Twang went Amelia's heart.

Immediately, the little bowl plummeted to the table.

And that was when things went *really* wrong.

"AND SO, IN conclusion," Caleb told Sir Nigel and Lady Ruperta as they stared open-mouthed at him from their separate brown leather sofas in the drawing room, "dining on the floor is the norm in many countries, and indeed is considered good for your physical well-being."

Brandy splashed in Lady Ruperta's glass as she half rose. But immediately she dropped back again, as if realizing one could not claim righteous superiority if one threw brandy in a man's face—not even if that man had just destroyed her dining table. Sir Nigel puffed fretfully on a cigar.

"We are very sorry about the broken table . . . and the ruined meal . . . and, er, the two shattered chairs," Amelia told them. "You can at least be reassured that we have the antique responsible contained securely, so it can do no further damage."

She held up the linen napkin fashioned as a sack, into which she and Caleb had wrangled the saltcellar after recovering it from the food-spattered wreckage of the dining table. Blue-tinted steam was exuding from the cloth as the antique's thaumaturgic energy cooled. Lady Ruperta frowned at the sight, but Vanity, perched uncomfortably on one of the dozen antique chairs crammed into the room, was staring at Amelia with amusement. Amelia did not much like this but could understand it nevertheless. She looked ridiculous. Getting caught in the middle of an exploding five-course meal does not benefit one's coiffure, unless swan feathers and cold mushroom soup should ever become fashionable headwear. And the less said about what stained her cardigan, the better. *Definitely becoming vegetarian*, she promised herself.

The only positive aspect of the whole shambles was that Throckmorton had retreated to his bedroom, declaring that, once he'd got all the oak splinters and fish bones out of his beard, he'd be packing to leave the "Disaster! Zone!" and catching the morning train back to Oxford, where no doubt the university's entire teaching body would be awaiting his report. He'd given Amelia and Caleb the gist of it as they dragged themselves up from the floor where the saltcellar's thaumaturgic blast had thrown them: "Incorrigible! Reckless!" and other Adjectives! that Amelia had tuned out as she'd hunted for some water, or even better, wine, to wash away the taste of salt. Her back ached, her spirit was mortified—and yet, had she known that an explosion of magic was all it took to get rid of the reprehensible medieval studies professor, she'd have organized one far earlier.

"Do you wish to include the saltcellar in your donation to the British Museum?" she asked Sir Nigel. For although she remained quite certain that the item contained only a slight thaumaturgic signature, and that the Hereford teaspoon's influence had compounded it, she was not going to ~~admit it had been all her fault~~ deprive the museum of such a charming antique.

Sir Nigel nodded rather mournfully in agreement, and Amelia and Caleb were then given permission to withdraw for the evening. "I shall have servants bring you hot water and towels," Lady Ruperta said, less with genteel consideration and more with an eye to her carpets. "And whatever supper can be contrived, since we are bereft of our proper dinner."

Amelia drew breath to offer another apology—

"Thank you," Caleb said, and turned to Amelia with a stern look. "After you, Professor Tarrant," he said, gesturing toward the door. As a result, she was obliged to leave without demeaning herself in the name of politeness.

"Well, that was fun," Caleb said sardonically as they trudged upstairs in the company of a footman carrying two lanterns to illuminate the way.

"Do you mean the explosion part?" Amelia asked. "Or the part where Lady Ruperta looked at us as if she wished we'd gone the way of the roasted swans?"

"The part where my favorite suit got splattered with God, what even is this?" He delicately lifted one of his jacket's lapels and sniffed. Disgust writhed across his face.

"Best not to ask," Amelia advised.

"That teaspoon is a menace."

"It did find the thaumaturgic objects in the room, however," Amelia reminded him. "Think of how easy it could make our job here."

"By causing explosions of magic left, right, and center," Caleb said. "I'm all for making things easy, but I'd rather not sacrifice another bespoke Henry Poole and Co. suit." He brushed futilely at his jacket, then gave a tragic sigh.

Amelia took pity on him. "Pass the jacket to me. I'll soak it in the vinegar solution I use for my hair. That should get the stains out."

Caleb eyed her hair musingly, then must have decided it was in good condition despite the feathers and the soup, for he began removing his jacket. "You have a fix for everything, don't you?" he said, smiling at her in a friendly manner that made their hot, sensual moment in the dining room seem like nothing more than a magic-ignited fever dream. Which of course it had been. Not real at all.

"Yes, I do," she said briskly. Taking the jacket, she draped it over her arm. "I'll get onto this right away, and then I'll write up a record of the evening and a detailed description of the saltcellar for the museum curation team. And then I'll—"

"You'll rest," Caleb interrupted.

"But—"

"We've had an abhorrently long day, Meely. You're allowed to rest now."

"Hm," Amelia said, unconvinced. A Tarrant never rested if they could help it. Deep inside her heart she harbored a small, ridiculous fear that, if she ever truly relaxed, she'd be carted back to boarding school. But there was no point in arguing with Caleb . . . mainly because she intended to discard his advice the moment she was alone in her room.

"Don't forget to put the teaspoon in a safe bag," she admonished him.

"I won't," he said.

"And don't forget to scrub your fingernails thoroughly. If enchanted salt got under—"

"I know, Meely. Do you want to bathe me yourself, to ensure I get washed behind my ears?"

"Ahem," coughed the footman a few steps ahead, belatedly reminding them of his presence. Amelia gave Caleb a vehement but silent lecture about the Conventions of Decent Conversation in Public, and in response to the rapid movement of her lips, he just grinned.

Reaching the top of the stairs, they proceeded wearily along the corridor, Caleb trailing his hand absentmindedly over the cluttered sideboards at its edges, and Amelia, coming behind him, straightening the vases, framed miniatures, and statuettes he knocked askew. Upon arriving at their bedrooms, the footman opened Amelia's door and hung one of the lanterns on a wall hook just inside the room. He then paused expectantly, and Caleb rummaged in the jacket hanging over Amelia's arm until he found a coin to tip the man.

"I don't suppose this is an all-expenses-paid trip?" he murmured to Amelia, who huffed a laugh. "Yes, that's rather what I thought." He looked into her room. "No ghosts or monsters. But— Eurgh!" His nose scrunched as he surveyed the red-and-pink floral wallpaper and matching bedclothes. "Are those supposed to be roses or cow's hearts? Actually, never mind, I don't want to know. Rest," he commanded, waggling a finger at Amelia. "Eat. Sleep. Dream of me."

"That wouldn't be very restful," Amelia quipped in reply— then flushed the same colors as the walls, realizing how her joke might be construed. But Caleb was already leaving, inspecting his tie for stains as he went. The footman, professionally blank-faced, closed the door, and at last Amelia was left in peace.

For approximately ten seconds.

"*Merde!*"

A man's furious shout whipped the quiet, shadowy air behind her. Amelia whirled, raising the saltcellar in its napkin like a weapon—

Then stopped abruptly, her fright falling away into annoyance. "What are *you* doing here?" she asked wearily.

"*Comment oses-tu me parler ainsi!*" yelled Bad King John of England, his eyes blazing with ire beneath the faded, glimmering memory of his medieval crown.

Chapter Ten

The sands of time are constantly getting
into people's underwear.

I, on the Past, Cornelius Ottersock

At first, Amelia tried to ignore the ghost. This was a
rather strange tactic considering, as a historian, she knew
perfectly well ignoring King John of England while he was
alive had done no one any good, and was unlikely to do so now
that he was inexplicably haunting her bedroom. And indeed,
with every move she made—packing away the enchanted saltcellar, taking off her shoes and stockings, plucking swan feathers from her hair—he shouted *"Merde!"* and waved his sword
with a dangerous majesty.

Whether the king was swearing at someone in his memory
or reexperiencing his death from dysentery, considering *merde*'s
scatological translation, Amelia knew not and cared less. She
was in the process of hunting down whatever antique was responsible for his apparition when servants appeared with hot
water to fill the copper tub in one corner of the bedroom.

"Thank you," Amelia said, watching them walk through
the Plantagenet king's specter without blinking. "I say, do you

feel a chill or anything unusual?" she asked the young house-maid who laid a tray of food on the bedside table.

"No, miss," the girl replied with the extreme politeness of someone whose workday had started fifteen hours ago and who suspected Amelia was now going to have her haul up fire-wood and set a fire in the hearth.

"Hm, interesting," Amelia murmured. No doubt her own awareness of the supernatural activity was due to a superior—

"Unless you mean the ghost," the girl added before Amelia's ego embarrassed itself further. "The house is jam-packed with 'em. They even wander the hills, begging to be let inside. You get used to it after a while."

There really must be a fey line here if the ghosts are outdoors too, Amelia mused. She smiled absentmindedly at the maid, who responded with a direct look, such as the footman had employed earlier. Amelia felt herself thus convinced to tip the girl a penny. Then the two servants who'd brought the water also required the same, and after they all departed she could only be glad she'd not asked for someone to make up the hearth fire, considering what it might have cost.

She bathed rather hurriedly in her chemise, since although King John had died six hundred and seventy-five years ago, she still didn't want him ogling her. She set Caleb's jacket to soak. Then, dressed in a white cotton nightgown, she sat on the bed, drying her hair and eating a cold supper while the ghost ranted. Rest was impossible under the circumstances; instead, she brought out her assignment journal to document the evening's magical events.

But even in King John's quieter moments, rain beat vehemently against the windows, flashing now and again with lightning, and drafts whined beneath the door, making the lantern's light flicker. *How am I supposed to focus on academia in such a dark ambience?* Amelia thought irritably.

"Sometimes history ought to remain secret," she snapped at the ghost.

"Tu sens comme une latrine sale!" he replied, shaking his sword yet again.

Being informed that she stank like a dirty toilet was the final straw. Logically, she understood King John could not in fact smell her. Emotionally, she'd had enough. Taking up the lantern and the biography of Mary Wollstonecraft she'd not yet been able to read, she left her bedroom, crossing the dark, cold hall to scratch against Caleb's door. The floorboards groaned beneath her bare feet, as if to mourn this decision. The night beyond her lantern's light watched her with malice. She thought that she heard hushed voices, and paused, heart in her throat . . . but it must have been the draft that was stirring her nightgown's hem, even if it sounded eerily like women talking inside the walls.

"Caleb," she whispered as loudly as she dared, considering that Throckmorton was accommodated nearby and that she, dressed only in a nightgown, with not a scrap of professorial tweed anywhere about her, was barely decent. Knocking on the door was out of the question, lest a servant suddenly appear to open it in return for a cash reward. And trying to send a message through the psychic power of thought achieved no success beyond mortifying her intelligence. *"Caleb,"* she whispered once more.

Finally, the door creaked ajar. Caleb peered out through a narrow gap, his hair tousled, his face spectral in the lantern's light.

"Oh, it's you," he said. "I thought you were a—"

"Ghost?"

"Vampire bat," he corrected her, and she laughed. Immediately pressing her lips together to curtail the sound, she gave him a wide-eyed, incredulous look.

"Vampire bat," she repeated in a whisper. "They don't even live in the UK."

"You'd know that they do if you'd read even one penny dreadful novel." He took her arm and pulled her into the dimly lit room, closing the door behind her.

"Caleb!" she protested. She'd wanted to get into his bedroom, but she'd not imagined manhandling would be involved. (At least, that was her story, and she was sticking to it.)

"You don't want to be seen skulking outside my door," he said. "What's up?"

The question entered Amelia's brain and promptly cowered in fright as it was met by a barrage of thoughts all shouting at once, for Caleb was clad in nothing more than a pair of long underpants. They clung so tightly to his thighs, Amelia would have dropped the lantern except that one part of her brain was steadier than the rest and had absolutely *no* intention of depriving her of that light source.

Trying to be a proper lady and respectful friend, she directed her vision toward Caleb's face. But it was impossible not to be drawn back to his well-honed nakedness, and she found herself almost going cross-eyed with the effort to both look and not look. His crescent moon tattoo seemed to smirk knowingly at her.

"I—I—uh—" She blushed as equanimity failed her. And Caleb, who himself was not the blushing kind . . . unless you counted how he made others redden, be it from coyness (undergraduate students), desire (women—and a few men), or blustering outrage (Professor Ottersock) . . . made no effort to remedy the situation. Clearly he was aware of her reaction to his body, and he didn't dislike it.

I dare you to say what you're really thinking, his shadowed gaze urged.

But Amelia knew she could not play this game with Caleb. He would absolutely win, and she didn't think either of them was prepared for the consequences of that. They'd almost lost their jobs because of a single hug. She'd almost lost her entire wherewithal because of the kiss in Staveley. Pulling herself together, she lifted her chin and looked him steadily in the eye.

Or at least tried to. But she discovered with a shock that his own gaze had slipped down to her nightgown, and suddenly she apprehended that its thin cotton was less protective than it had seemed in the privacy of her own bedroom. She resisted an urge to ~~flee hysterically~~ . . . ~~become a nun!~~ . . . ~~throw all caution to the wind and kiss the man~~ cross an arm over her bosom. No one had seen beneath her clothing since she was nineteen, when James Bowfooter got her bodice almost entirely off before good sense reasserted itself in the nick of time. She wasn't prudish, per se; she was simply like all other girls in nineteenth-century England: aware of the dangerous limitations to contraceptive practices.

The thought of those practices took what remained of her inherent tranquility and threw it violently into a storm of frazzlement. "King!" she blurted.

Caleb's eyebrows sauntered up. "Really, 'Professor' is adequate."

Amelia was rolling her eyes even before her brain caught up with her. When it did, thankfully it brought a restoration of rationality. So Caleb was mostly undressed? *Uninteresting.* So he was a more intriguing specimen of manhood than she had imagined? *Irrelevant.* So she wanted to pull down his long johns and gain a full appreciation of that manhood? *Oh my God, Mother Mary, and all the saints.* As thunder shook the blustering night outside and shadows caressed Caleb's torso, Amelia's good sense vanished once again, forcing her to seek desperate refuge in religion.

"I thought you were supposed to be resting," Caleb said, looking stern.

"Ghost," she said. "King John. Can't sleep." She sounded like Throckmorton, but it could not be helped. Any use of a pronoun might just spin her into an overwhelming jumble of *me, you, us . . .*

Caleb did not immediately answer. His gaze became analytical, as if she were an ancient text he needed to translate. Then he took pity on her, and reaching out to a shirt tossed over a nearby chair, he put it on. This did not exactly help matters, however, since the sight of his long fingers working the buttons created a swirl of hot sensation deep in Amelia's stomach.

"Do you want to sleep in here tonight?" he asked.

Amelia nodded. Then frowned confusedly, shaking her head. This was not going as she expected. It hadn't occurred to her that not only might Caleb be undressed for sleeping but that she'd be such a fluttery idiot. "No," she said, "I shouldn't."

"No one would know. We'll bar the door and make sure you're back to your room first thing in the morning."

He spoke as if he proposed sharing a train carriage, not a bedroom. And so he should. After all, they'd been close forever. They'd lain side by side on a school rooftop, gazing up at the stars, and sat leaning against each other backstage at a conference, their fingers playing together idly as they awaited their turn to address the audience. Sleeping in the same bedroom represented nothing more than a convenience on this wild and haunted night.

"I mean, I can't ask you to sleep on the floor," Amelia said.

Caleb laughed. "Yeah, I'm not doing that even for you, darling. The bed's large enough for us both."

"Oh." Her pulse raced, and not just because of this scandalous suggestion. Caleb was *rolling up his shirtsleeves*. Staring at his forearms with their shapely muscles and fine dusting of blond hair, she felt her blush return with a vengeance. True, the man had moments before been half-naked, but somehow this smaller revelation of bare skin was even more alluring.

"Hello?" he said, and she looked up to see his head lowered, angled, as he tried to catch her gaze. A patient but slightly quizzical smile was on his lips. *Stop thinking about his lips!* Amelia's brain shouted at her, even as her body throbbed with panic. What had he been saying? Something about pillows?

"Tired," she said. "Long day."

His smile deepened, so warm and fond that Amelia bid farewell to her melting heart. "Poor thing," he said. Taking the lantern from her, he held out his free hand. "Come with me."

In a daze, Amelia placed her hand in his and found herself being led toward the bed. She glanced over her shoulder, looking without success for the ghost of the calm, capable woman she'd been before entering this room. Really, she ought to have just put up with King John stabbing her. At least that would have been educational.

I imagine there are many interesting lessons Caleb could teach you tonight, came a wicked voice from the back of her mind, where she stored her unorthodox theories about Anne Boleyn, opinions of Professor Ottersock, and secret liking for malt whiskey. Hearing it, Amelia tripped over what was probably a snag in the carpet but felt altogether too much like her scruples. Her book dropped to the floor.

"Oops," Caleb said, releasing her hand so as to put a steadying arm around her. This in fact proved to be as far from steadying as it was possible to get without resorting to a salacious metaphor, but Amelia thanked him nonetheless. He set down the lantern on a small table beside the bed, then retrieved her book.

"Mary Wollstonecraft," he said, reading the title. "Interesting choice. Peter Wilmot and I visited her grave once." Pulling back the bed's counterpane and sheet, he gestured grandly. "Tuck yourself in. I'll go bar the door."

As he moved away, Amelia took a deep breath, trying to calm herself. There was still time to leave . . .

But no, leaving would be silly. *We are just friends,* she reminded herself. And two friends—two professional, adult colleagues—can share a bed without it being anything more than a good night's sleep. After all, she'd shared one with Professor Anne Tremblay from Edinburgh University when they were undertaking a joint study of carnivorous bagpipes, and nothing untoward had occurred beyond the sharing of chocolates and gossip. The same would be the case with her and Caleb, she was sure of it.

Climbing into the bed, she rearranged the counterpane tidily over herself, smoothing every wrinkle. Caleb was wedging a hard-backed chair beneath the door handle, and from her position, Amelia had an extremely edifying view of his posterior encased in the long johns. *I wonder what would happen if I started a fight with him?* she mused.

The thought was languid, silkily warm, sliding against her consciousness. The memory of their argument in the dining room sizzled. Increasingly, this pretense at enmity was playing havoc with her body, leaving her breathless and yet hard-pulsing at the same time. Caleb had transformed from her easygoing friend to a man deliberately trying to create sparks in her, and he proved very good at it. Even the adversarial way he looked at her was incendiary. And now here she was in his bed. She managed to convince herself that she'd arrived here solely due to escaping a mad ghost. Her motivations were innocent.

Alas, if only the same could be said for her imagination.

Caleb turned, brushing back his hair, and looked at her through the sultry lantern light. Amelia looked back at him. *You're safe with me,* his eyes said.

I know, hers answered.

Damn, the silence between them sighed.

He approached the bed. But he didn't walk; nothing so simple. He prowled, or so it seemed as she watched him, his every step lithe and slow and purposeful. His gaze never leaving her. The storm howled; the shadows danced liked worshippers of the wild god Pan, intoxicated by their unruly, sacred lust. Amelia's self-pretense fell away, revealing the raw and naked tumult of her pulse. She did not have enough time to even choose between *oh my God* and *I am in so much trouble* before Caleb reached the bed and, drawing back the covers, crawled in, his mouth curving like a tiger's claw, his eyes a promise of the storm . . .

And then he flopped back against the pillows. Kicking the bedding so as to get his legs under it, he squirmed, and muttered about lumps in the mattress, and pulled the covers up over himself with reckless abandon. Settling at last, he crossed his arms at the same time Amelia did.

They sat side by side, facing forward.

"Thank you for letting me stay," Amelia replied in a stiff little tone that would have made her mother proud (providing her mother didn't know she was using it while in bed with a man to whom she wasn't married).

"You're always welcome, Meely," Caleb answered. He glanced at their legs stretched out in parallel beneath the counterpane. "Gosh, I haven't shared a bed with someone since back in Bethnal Green."

A shadow skittered through his gaze, the way it always did when he mentioned his childhood in the bleak rookery of East London, even all these years later. But he was smiling, and so very pretty in the gloss of lantern light, it was as if nothing foul had ever sullied him.

"Really?" Amelia asked. "Never? What about when you—er—"

He looked at her sidelong, his smile arched crookedly. "You sure you want me to answer that?"

"Maybe not," she murmured. Distracting herself from the uncomfortable line of thought, she leaned forward to pull the counterpane up over him more, tucking and smoothing efficiently. "In the morning, I want to find the source of the ghost in my room. I'm assuming it's a coin or—"

"Amelia." Caleb caught her hand rather tightly in both of his and moved it to lie on her lap, even as he drew up his knees. "It's late at night. I insist that you relax."

Sighing, she relented at last, leaning against him, her head in the crook of his shoulder. He tilted his own head so it rested on hers, and sighing too, he slipped his arm around her back to hug her.

"I thought the countryside would be more peaceful than town," she said, fiddling drowsily with lacework on the counterpane.

"I can't imagine why. The place is full of demon dogs, murderous ghosts, highwaymen, and mysterious strangers on enormous black horses . . ."

Amelia smiled. "Only in novels."

"And populist newspapers." Caleb joined her in tracing the holes of the lacework, and their fingers gently tangled and twisted together, the way they had so often over the years.

"Ah, well, if you are going to cite such *excellent* sources," Amelia remarked wryly, "what can I do but submit to you?"

Caleb went still, fingers and breath and even, it seemed, his very pulse. Then he exhaled and began to brush his thumb to and fro across the back of her hand. Amelia's breath shivered delightfully. "You never submit to anyone," he said.

"Just Professor Ottersock," she amended, despite a swarm of flutters threatening to sweep her voice away, along with whatever intelligence she had remaining after her decision to knock on a gentleman's bedroom door near midnight.

"We're sitting together in bed," Caleb said, as if she needed a reminder. "That doesn't look much like submission to Ottersock."

"Only because he'll never know what we're doing. Should he find out, I'll have no choice but to take that job in Heidelberg, regardless of my mother's prejudice." She sighed as if it were a foregone conclusion. "I'd never see you again."

"Of course you would," he answered at once, lightly scoffing.

"No man could keep me from you, Amelia. And no sea is so vast that I would not cross it to reach you."

Amelia straightened so she could arch an eyebrow at him. "Is that from a poem? Or have you been reading a seduction manual?"

He laughed and choked simultaneously. "Have I— A what?"

"A seduction manual. I've confiscated more than one from my students during class. Actually . . ." She paused, pondering her recollections. "They mentioned submission too."

Caleb appeared to be in immediate danger of perishing from asphyxiation. "Amelia!" he managed to gasp. "You're not supposed to read books like that!"

"There was nothing else to do at the time," she answered with such dignity, her chin lifted of its own accord. "The class was busy with a snap quiz."

"A snap quiz you set so you could read the book," Caleb accused.

His big-brother attitude abruptly annoyed her. "For goodness' sake, Caleb, I'm all grown up—"

"Oh, I'm *very* aware."

The rest of Amelia's sentence devolved into an unblinking look. The atmosphere reeled with shock. Caleb, belatedly having realized what he'd said, went more ghost white than King John. The safety he'd promised now vanished as if it had fallen off the precipice on which their relationship suddenly found itself. Although, to be fair, Amelia knew deep down that they'd been edging toward this point ever since they began fake hating. Caleb might have been the first to make a verbal slip, but she herself was sure to have done so, given a little more time. Evidently there was nothing like forbidding a romance to make one obsess over the attractions of the very person one was not allowed to consider. Poor Ottersock; had he but known, he'd have left well enough alone.

It will be fine, Amelia thought, trying to soothe herself. *If I work quickly, I can fix this situation and get us back to our comfortable normalcy.*

Or . . .

"It's very late," she said with a coolness she absolutely did not feel. "Let's stop talking, all right?"

Caleb nodded, still looking stunned. "All right," he agreed.

"Excellent." She nodded too, unconsciously copying him. "Now kiss me good night."

CHAPTER ELEVEN

Everyone believes they are the hero of their own story.
I, on the Past, Cornelius Ottersock

CALEB WAS ASLEEP and dreaming. He could think of no other explanation for the magic that was unfurling in the strange, gothic heart of this stormy night. First, Amelia had appeared at his door, looking like an angel come to rescue him from his usual nightmares. Second ... Actually, no, he would not count as second the fact that her nightgown was practically transparent in the lantern light, because he did not so much as even glance at it. His eyes merely twitched downward, that was all, due to the lateness of the hour.

Besides, there never was a *second* when it came to Amelia Tarrant.

He might not have peeked at her body (really, trust him on this, he was a completely reliable narrator) but he did notice the way she peeked at his, and he came so perilously close to hardening that he had to hastily don a shirt in case his self-control failed. This hadn't stopped him from folding up its sleeves, though, because he couldn't quite resist making those long, black eyelashes of hers flutter. He'd not spent years in the company of a female best friend without learning just how much women appreciated men's forearms. And he certainly wasn't above exploiting that knowledge.

What he'd most honestly wanted to do was rip off the shirt, and the underwear, and invite her to feast her eyes, or whatever else she chose, on the entirety of his naked body. But he loved that she'd come to his door, trusting him to shelter her in the haunted night, and he'd never betray that trust, not even as every muscle in him strained with the desire to feast on her naked body too.

Then the cruel, cruel woman had climbed into his bed, all warm-bodied and clean and smelling of lilac soap. She'd ruined his every future stroll through a flower garden—for how could he possibly enjoy lilac again without remembering this night, the sight of Amelia where he'd so long dreamed of having her, and the soft comfort of her cuddled up next to him? She'd fussed the way she always did, trying to fix his world into a state of perfection—her efficient hands tucking and smoothing the counterpane and, in the process, ruffling his nerves until they were nigh on threadbare. He'd been forced to stop her, and to raise his knees in an effort to conceal his arousal.

Even then, there had remained hope for some self-control. But the conversation had turned dangerous (he couldn't trace how; one minute he was declaring that not even the sea would keep him from her side, and the next they were discussing seduction—??) and his slightly panic-born efforts to repress it only made matters worse.

"For goodness' sake, Caleb," Amelia had grumbled. *"I'm all grown up—"*

And finally, after *years* of caution, he'd lost his grip and said something so immensely stupid that no doubt the doctorate framed on his office wall went up in flames as a result.

"Oh, I'm *very* aware."

As he heard himself speak, Caleb's heart thumped painfully. *Damn*. What the hell was he thinking?! There was no going back from a statement like that. Amelia stared with a silence that threatened to suffocate him before either of them managed another word. Her eyes were a midnight he'd gotten lost in two decades ago, and from which he'd never found an escape. Not that he'd tried especially hard. He'd loved Amelia Victoria Tarrant from the very first moment he made her smile through her tears, all the way back behind the dormitory when they were little. An innocent love, a friendship, a worshipping, a complete consummation of his soul. She was his light, his life, his grave.

"It's very late," she said in a voice like starched and ironed linen, always so soothing. "Let's stop talking, all right?"

Caleb nodded, heart sinking. He understood her too well. End of conversation—end of the comfort and ease between them. *Bloody wonderful job, you idiot,* he growled at himself internally, but "All right," he said aloud, because what else could he do? Nothing tonight. He'd mucked things up royally with that slip, and it would take weeks, with more hard work than he suspected himself capable of, to reestablish the sanctity of their friendship.

"Excellent," Amelia said. "Now kiss me good night."

What?

Caleb had felt stupid a moment ago, but now he felt like a complete imbecile. Had she just—did it mean—what—*what*??

"Do not friends kiss each other good night?" she asked reasonably.

"Friends." He grasped the word like a rock in a storm.

"*Best* friends," she clarified.

Aha! There was a subtext in that, he was sure of it. Unfortunately, he didn't have the slightest bloody idea what it might be. Was she saying a peck on the cheek would be appropriate? Or was she inviting him to do something more interesting? And was his brain ever going to work properly again?

Thankfully, instinct responded before his ongoing silence could offend her. He'd never been able to deny Amelia anything, and if she wanted a good night kiss, it was his duty as a friend to give it to her.

Heart in his throat, he leaned forward slowly. The calm in Amelia's gaze shattered, revealing what looked like fear and shyness and a longing that seemed to reflect Caleb's own. But he glimpsed it for only a second, and he dared not stop to question her on exactly what she was feeling. Conversation had proven about as safe as an old teaspoon from Hereford. At least he knew what he was doing when it came to kissing.

He pressed his lips gently against hers. Instantly, darts of pleasure like salty magic shot through his body. Shifting back, he attempted a smile.

"Good night," he said.

"Good night," she answered.

And then somehow they were kissing again. Caleb tried to work out how it had happened, but he was a historian, not a physicist, damn it. His eyes closed as he sank helplessly into a desire that was about as far from dutiful as one could get without becoming Benedict Arnold.

The storm outside wept and writhed. Amelia's hand curved around his, and Caleb tightened his grip. Meanwhile, the kiss grew softer, melting into a dream. Amelia lifted her free hand to set it against the side of his face, making Caleb feel treasured. With a tender caution, he coaxed her lips apart, and the silky glide of her tongue meeting his inside her private darkness felt like a wish come true.

"*Merde!*"

AMELIA VERY NEARLY fell out of bed as King John's sword swooped over her head, not so much breaking the kiss with Caleb as wrenching it violently apart. "*Honte à vous!*" the ghost king shouted, raising his weapon for another swing. *Shame on you.* Whether he referred to Caleb and her, or to the barons who had forced him to sign the Magna Carta, Amelia did not know. A more pressing question was ~~when could she return to kissing Caleb?~~ how had the ghost crossed into this room? It suggested that the antique sourcing this spectral incarnation was strongly thaumaturgic indeed.

"That's your ghost?" Caleb asked as he leaned back, watching with mild disconcertment while King John attempted to murder the pillows.

"Yes," Amelia said sourly. "Noisy sod."

"He certainly does vex the dull ear of a drowsy man," Caleb remarked. And when Amelia blinked at him, he sighed with vast exasperation. "Come on, Meely, that was extraordinarily clever. I quoted Shakespeare's *King John* while faced with the actual—"

BOOM!

The sky apparently held the same opinion of Shakespeare as Amelia did. Thunder broke with a bone-rattling blast so close overhead that she instinctively ducked. The ghost flared, filling the room with an eerie blue radiance. It swung its sword with renewed declarations about excrement, and paranormal energy flowed visibly from the blade. Suddenly, Mary Wollstonecraft's biography flew off the bedside table. Amelia straightened, turning to Caleb, and he met her eyes with a flash of emotion that reflected exactly her own.

"Poltergeist!" they chorused excitedly . . . and perhaps a little frenetically; Amelia, for one, being glad to grab an excuse not to discuss what had just happened between them.

"Such intense phasmatic energy may be due to amplification by the electrical storm," she theorized as she climbed out of bed, abandoning all hope of sleep (which admittedly had been slim, considering the kissing). King John roared with Plantagenet ill temper, and the lantern on the bedside table tottered violently. Amelia caught it half a second before it could tip over onto the carpet. "We need to find the ghost's source before it burns down the house," she said.

"Merde!" King John declared in response to that idea.

"Repetitive fellow," Caleb commented. "What is he saying? I can't make out his accent."

"I think he's complaining about fecal matter," Amelia answered. "I'd have Professor Throckmorton in to confirm it, but . . ."

"Yeah," Caleb agreed. The medieval studies professor would immediately telegraph all of Oxford and half of London if he saw Caleb and Amelia only partly dressed in a bedroom together, and then they'd be obliged to murder each other to disprove the gossip. "Go get some clothes on. While you're doing that, I'll start the search in this room for Johnny's source object." He ducked as the king threw a pillow at him in apparent revenge for the nickname. "Bloody hell, I can see why everyone hated this brat."

"Shouldn't you get dressed too?" Amelia suggested. "After all, you're only wearing a shirt and—and nethergarments." She mumbled the last word, for whereas she was imperturbable about such things as deadly teapots, explosive jewelry boxes, and packed lecture schedules, Caleb's trouserless legs evidently embodied her one frailty. Perhaps if they themselves were more frail, less shapely, she would not feel herself now in peril of gawking at them again. And Amelia never gawked. Never mind being a Tarrant—she was an intelligent woman. Yet here she was, blinking hard to keep herself from doing so. Snatching up her lantern, she hastened for the door.

But as she passed Caleb, he caught her by the arm, stopping her. Reluctantly, for she knew what was coming, Amelia turned to face him.

"Yes?" she asked with exquisite nonchalance.

"About the . . ." he began, but trailed off in the obvious hope she'd finish the sentence for him.

"We are friends," she said.

"You keep saying that."

"And we're adults," she added.

"Allegedly," he remarked sardonically.

"It can't be unusual for adult friends to . . ."

"Snog?"

"Experiment with the intricacies of their . . ." Now *she* trailed off, but Caleb remained stubbornly silent. "Friendship," she concluded rather weakly.

Caleb went on considering her for a moment that felt longer than the Plantagenets' entire rule, even while one of its scions raged in the background. Amelia barely heard the ghost's shit-talking. Her hearing was devoted wholly to the anticipation of what Caleb might say next. At last, he shrugged.

"In that case," he said in his gorgeous smooth-and-rough, polished-and-dirty voice. And he bent his head toward her, causing Amelia to promptly abandon all pretensions of breathing. But the confounded man merely whispered near her ear, as if he didn't want King John's phantom to hear, "I look forward to undertaking several analytical trials."

Amelia's nervous system dissolved into hysterics. She'd never heard the word *analytical* spoken in such an erotic manner before, and all she could think of was how she might inspire a further conversation about *sampling*, and *examining*, and *coming to a definitive conclusion*. Caleb moved back just enough that he was able to look at her through a golden lock of hair, and Amelia realized there existed no hope of conversation. For it was impossible to utter any word when her entire body was aflame.

"Merde!" King John yelled.

"No one asked you," they snapped at him in unison. Then Amelia took a step back from Caleb in one final effort to be sensible. "Ottersock—"

"Is in Oxford," Caleb interrupted. "And we are in Cumbria. What happens in Cumbria—"

"Stays in Cumbria."

He shrugged. "Maybe," he said, and the slow, wicked curve of his lips practically deflowered Amelia on the spot. She could only ~~thank~~ blame herself; after all, she'd been the one to request a kiss. And she might just have requested another right then, but King John threw a chamber pot across the room, and in the horrifying second before it was proven to be empty, Amelia concluded that she definitely needed to concentrate on work. With a quick frown at Caleb, she left for her own room and the calm dark it temporarily offered before the ghost and the professor wrought their fascinating chaos upon her again.

FOR THE REMAINDER of the night, Amelia and Caleb searched both bedrooms, evaluating several framed coins of medieval provenance, a badger-haired toothbrush that certainly *looked* as if it had been used in the thirteenth century, and a tin of cocaine cough lozenges that Caleb sampled before Amelia could decipher its faded label. None of these evidenced any thaumaturgic power, although Caleb himself was certainly energized for an hour after eating one (three) of the lozenges: reciting speeches from Shakespeare's *Henry V* just to aggravate King John's ghost, and swatting at hallucinations of flying badgers.

No further kissing occurred, out of fear that someone might suddenly appear at the door. Indeed, they were wholly professional, badgers notwithstanding, and felt rather disappointed that Throckmorton did not turn up. If nothing else, he could have helped with moving the furniture to look for hidden artifacts.

Finally, the first faint stirring of daylight eroded the ghost into silence, and Amelia allowed exhaustion to claim her. Caleb was already asleep on her bed, so she went to his instead. An hour later, upon being awoken by a chambermaid drawing the curtains, she blearily and quite shockingly discovered herself hugging a pillow that smelled of Caleb's aftershave, and turned so red the chambermaid asked if she was unwell.

If having a mad crush on my lifelong best friend might be considered unwell, then indeed, I ought to be in hospital, Amelia thought, giving herself a severe Tarrant-style frown even as outwardly she smiled at the chambermaid.

Returning to her own room, she passed Caleb in the corridor doing the same, and they nodded wordlessly to each other—for no degree of *amor* justifies a conversation at seven thirty a.m., especially after a mostly sleepless night. But as Amelia washed and changed into fresh clothes, her memory of that night awakened; specifically, and in some detail, the kisses she had shared with Caleb. Goosebumps stirred along her bare arms, not just from the morning's chill. The sensation of pulling on her drawers and securing her corset, when layered over with the kisses' soft brushstrokes, made her imagine Caleb taking them back off again.

"*Stop*," she whispered to herself, scandalized.

But then again, why should she? They'd agreed to experiment with their friendship, at least while in Cumbria. In fact, considering they were healthy, intelligent adults with a professionally trained sense of curiosity, it would surely be *strange* if they didn't do so.

Amelia was happy to decide that this made perfect sense, and any rebuttal from a more sensible branch of her intellect need not be entertained. Besides, no one would ever know what went on in the privacy of her own mind.

Now that she finally gave herself permission to imagine, quite *a lot* went on, and quite inventively. After all, one didn't spend years studying history without developing a robust ability to envision things. Furthermore, she would have been a poor scholar indeed had she not attempted to replicate these visions via physical trials. Soon she became so giddy that, had anyone approached her right then to ask the likely provenance of a terra-cotta Zeus figurine, she'd have said "Neolithic England." But work called, so eventually she pulled herself together and finished dressing. With her shoes buttoned and a small book in her skirt pocket as an essential part of the outfit, she felt restored to, if not her usual degree of levelheadedness, then at least an eighty-five-degree angle of sanity.

It was only when she reached for the doorknob upon leaving the room that she discovered she'd put her cardigan on inside out.

But when Caleb entered the corridor just as she did, Amelia was confronted with two rather substantial flaws in her argument. First, every nerve within her began fluttering the moment she set eyes on the man, and her brain shouted *kiss! kiss!* with such enthusiasm that she had to press her lips together in case she spoke it aloud—or, worse, obeyed the command.

Second, she apprehended that her relationship with Caleb really *was* deep; so deep, in fact, that there existed a good chance he'd take one look at her and know exactly what had been going on in the privacy of her mind, let alone her bedchamber. This thought accelerated the flutters to such a degree that she could barely walk straight. Caleb placed a steadying hand on her lower back, and Amelia felt suddenly glad she was dressed in black, considering she was likely to die soon from nervous overexertion.

"Tired?" Caleb asked her, thankfully oblivious to the true cause of her instability.

"Hm," she replied.

"Same," he said with a piteous sigh, rubbing his free hand against his brow. "It was all I could do to get dressed."

"Poor thing," Amelia offered sympathetically, never mind that his black turtleneck jumper and impeccably ironed gray wool trousers suggested that he was planning to abandon their assignment and attend a fashion parade instead. Kohl-rimmed eyes showed no trace of bleariness, and he appeared to have visited a manicurist somewhere between Amelia's bedroom and his own. He was so pretty, she could not resist touching him, even though she knew it was a bad, bad, terrible idea.

"Such fine wool," she murmured, running her fingers down his sleeve and thrilling at the tingles caused in them by the merino's texture. But unexpectedly, Caleb caught her hand.

"You're hurt," he said, and held the hand so that he could inspect it—a necessity, it must be said, for the scratch thereon was so minor he actually would have benefited from a magnifying glass to better view it. A frown creased his brow. "Who did this to you?"

Amelia tried to tug her hand free to no avail. "You, most likely," she said. "Last night you briefly thought I was a badger, and tried to ward me off with a toothbrush."

"Ugh," he said, which she assumed was an apology. And then, far more lyrically, he kissed the tiny scratch.

Amelia's stomach flipped, setting her so off-balance she nearly fell down the stairs. "Caleb," she chided him in a whisper. "Anyone might see you."

"There's no one around to do so," he said, and kissed her hand again. (Two footmen installed at the bottom of the stairs exchanged an amused glance.)

"Really, you mustn't," Amelia told him, and pulled her hand so determinedly, it escaped his grasp. She might *want* him to kiss her, but only in safer circumstances. "Professor Throckmorton is no doubt still here. If he catches you behaving like that, our jobs are forfeit."

"Well, he's leaving this morning. And then we can have all the fun with 'friendship intricacies' that we want."

"Fun," Amelia repeated, her dubiousness born from Tarrant instinct.

"Oh, yes," he promised, grinning so rakishly that Amelia noticed one of the footmen blush. Thankfully, before something caught fire, Caleb jogged down the last three steps into the entrance hall, then turned to watch her follow more sedately. A footman led them toward a half-open door, through which drifted the mingled aromas of bacon and pipe tobacco. "As soon as Throckmorton is gone," Caleb continued, "I'm going to bandage that wound—"

"Tiny scratch," she corrected him.

"Terrible injury. And I'm going to smile at you all I want. And then I'm going to—" He finished the sentence by means of bouncing his eyebrows, and Amelia swatted his arm lightly.

"Stop it, you incorrigible rotter."

"Come on, Meely." He swayed so that their shoulders bumped. "You must agree, last night's kiss was the best in the entire history of—"

"Balderdash!" Throckmorton's bullish voice rocketed out from the parlor, destroying Caleb's playful mood and slamming calm dignity like a barricade across Amelia's face. Pausing in front of the door, they both took a deep breath. *I can do this,* Amelia told herself. *I've sat in faculty meetings full of men like Booming Basil. Just one, just over breakfast, will be tolerable.*

"Nietzsche!" the medieval studies professor shouted. "'There are no facts, only interpretations.'"

"Ah, but if I stab you with this fork, it will cause you pain, and that's a fact," came a second voice. "Empiricism is the sole acceptable method of studying history."

Amelia and Caleb exchanged an appalled look, and not just because of the simplistic argument. As one, they looked behind them to consider possible escape routes. But at that moment the footman grew tired of waiting for them and reached out to push the door fully ajar. Trapped, they turned their heads with grim inevitability, staring into the room.

Professor Throckmorton sat at the end of the white-clothed table, pipe in one hand, heaped spoonful of baked beans in the other, and a squashed bean adrift in his beard. Catty-corner to him, Vanity had her head lowered, focusing intently on a cup of tea. Sir Nigel, in a shabby dressing gown and decidedly un-nerved expression, was gazing at the extensive collection of antique plates displayed on the wall as if counting them. Beside him, with an upraised fork that looked altogether reminiscent of King John's sword (albeit with a piece of bacon affixed), sat a gentleman bedecked in tweed the same brown hue as the large, curved pipe emerging from beneath his bushy mustache.

Amelia's heart dropped. Caleb took a cautious step away from her. Together, they stared in dismay at Mr. Dummersby of the British Museum.

CHAPTER TWELVE

"There are no facts, only interpretations" is itself a statement
of supposed fact, and shows that philosophy is shaky ground
for the wise historian. Objective observation alone can be safe.
A pipe is just a pipe (unless it is enchanted to be a trumpet).

I, on the Past, Cornelius Ottersock

THERE FOLLOWED A period of misery such as Amelia had
not experienced since her earliest days at school. Sorting
through old, dusty bric-a-brac, inspecting each piece so
scrupulously that her eyes watered, noting everything down
with painstaking detail in manila notebooks—it ought to have
been great fun. Usually, the only thing that satisfied her better
was sitting undisturbed on a rainy afternoon, reading a good
book. (Which, alas, speaks poorly for the few young men
who over the years had slipped past Caleb's protective eye in
the hopes of seducing her.) But all too soon Amelia became
doleful.

She'd known things would be bad the moment she saw Mr.
Dummersby at the breakfast table. One thing a historian really
excelled at was predicting the future, and in any case, Dummersby's smirk represented a flashing arrow pointing the way.
Having traveled up to Cumbria to ~~spy on Amelia and Caleb
for gossiping purposes~~ "deliver more packing materials, lest

Miss Tunnicliffe did not bring enough," the museum curator announced that he intended to stay on and "help with the assignment." Not even Amelia's most severely polite look could deter him.

"My presence will streamline things. I can tell you what the museum will most want from Sir Nigel's collection. For example, we're especially keen for anything contemporaneous with—"

Suddenly, he slapped his own face, causing the pipe to drop from his lips and a fleck of bacon to fly across the table, landing in Vanity's porridge bowl. Everyone stared at him bemusedly (except Vanity, who stared at her contaminated breakfast with the particular horror of someone who knows they have to eat it or else risk offending their boss).

"Darned nuisance," Dummersby said, rubbing his cheek. "Been suffering from a magic-induced tic ever since that kerfuffle in the Minervaeum's library." He attempted to frown pointedly at Amelia but was too scared to look her in the eye, so directed the censure over her shoulder, where a footman caught it and almost burst into tears.

"What a shame," Caleb said. "Do you know the trigger? Was it something you said?"

"Hm," Dummersby murmured repressively through his mustache.

"'Keen'?" Caleb guessed with such a brilliant show of innocence he ought to have won an award for it. "'Anything'? 'With'? 'Espec—'"

"Contemporaneous," Dummersby snapped, seemingly helpless to resist the bait, and promptly slapped himself again.

The corner of Caleb's mouth twitched ever so slightly. "Oh dear," he sympathized . . .

And then proceeded throughout the week to maneuver Dummersby into saying *contemporaneous* as often as possible. Which, considering they were historians, proved easier than one might assume.

The museum curator was old-school in his professional approach, which is to say, highly skilled at taking the concept of "streamlining" and tying it up in knots. For example, "That mustache cup would look fabulous in a display of 1830s ephemera," he told Amelia on the Friday morning, even before breakfast was finished, requiring her to explain in diplomatic terms that not only did said cup lack any thaumaturgic charge, but furthermore Sir Nigel was drinking from it at that moment.

"We need more pieces from the Restoration," he informed her on Saturday, as if she could somehow make the Regency-era comb in her hand age one hundred years.

"Are you *sure* you don't want to come work for me, my dear?" he asked her on Sunday, Tuesday, and twice on Wednesday. "You would add such decoration to our team." These inducements stopped only when a portrait of Bloody Queen Mary screamed "Pervert! Pervert!" at him with uncannily helpful timing.

Worse, his presence convinced Throckmorton to stay. The two men, although never having met before, became instant chums on the basis of their mutual preoccupation with Caleb and Amelia's business. They followed the pair through the manor, ostensibly to study medieval architecture and interesting antiques but seeming more interested in trying to spark arguments.

"Heard Sterling say history's an art," Throckmorton remarked with an overtly casual air to Amelia on Saturday afternoon. She was at the time holding steady a ladder upon which Vanity stood to reach a crystal vase on a shelf in the first-floor gallery, and so could not escape a conversation.

"I fear you must have misheard him," she answered politely. "Professor Sterling believes that the study of history is a branch of the sciences."

"Nope." Throckmorton puffed a few ostentatious smoke rings, and the ladder trembled in Amelia's grip. "'Facts? Boring!'" he quoted in a deep, lazy voice that Amelia supposed was meant to impersonate Caleb's. "'Give fun interpretations—stories!—instead.'"

Just then, Caleb himself entered the gallery, and Amelia's attention swiveled instantly to him. "Eep!" Vanity squeaked, clutching at the edge of the shelf as the ladder swayed.

"Excuse me, Professor Sterling."

At Amelia's clipped tone, everyone in the room unconsciously stood up straighter, except Vanity, for whom good posture had become less of a concern, more a future hope, and Caleb, who slanted his head and smiled at her. "Do you think that historical facts are *boring* and we should apply artistic license when teaching them?" she interrogated him.

Caleb looked surprised; then his eyes narrowed as he considered the question. "What facts are we talking about?"

"Eep!" Vanity squealed again pointedly as Amelia abandoned the ladder to set her hands on her hips instead.

"It doesn't matter what facts! Stories are no substitute for documented evidence."

"Oh ho, here we go." Throckmorton chuckled, nudging Dummersby.

Caleb shrugged. "Eh. An interesting poem or legend does enliven—"

"*Legend?!*"

CRASH!

This, fortunately, was not the sound of Vanity falling from the ladder, but of a small dish nearby that spontaneously exploded. Ceramic fragments and sparks of hot blue magic shot through the gallery.

"Oh no!" Sir Nigel cried out. "My seventeenth-century creamware butter dish from Staffordshire!" He ran about gathering the pieces, yelping as they burned him with magic, and in the process almost knocking Vanity once and for all off the ladder.

"Hold on, Miss Tunnicliffe!" Caleb said, and hastened across to grasp the ladder and steady it. Amelia, thus belatedly noticing Vanity's predicament, grabbed hold of the other side also. The two of them looked at each other across the rungs. Caleb winked; Amelia frowned. "Are you all right?" Caleb asked.

"F-fine thank you," Vanity answered as she carefully descended the ladder. Upon reaching the ground's safety, she looked around repeatedly and without any interest in her polite demurrals.

Amelia dragged her attention away from Caleb to the girl. "It must have had psycho-conjunctive properties," she said.

"Psycho-conjunctive," Vanity repeated, sounding out the syllables carefully, as if they might explode too.

"It's a powerful thaumaturgic energy."

Vanity perked up, her near death apparently forgotten. "Ooh! Psycho conjunctivitis, you say?" She giggled, thus making it impossible to know if she was joking or irredeemably stupid. "Is there anything else here like it?"

"Be careful asking Miss Tarrant such questions," Dummersby advised with an unpleasant little laugh. "She'll break your brain with her answer."

Amelia smiled at Vanity with such calm steadiness, she

could have been mistaken for a kindergarten teacher. Before she could summon a dignified remark, however, Caleb spoke.

"Dummersby, old chap, would you mind getting my magnifying glass from the drawing room?"

"Hmph, hmph," Dummersby replied, which was Fuddy-Duddy Academic dialect for *I suppose, if I must*.

"Cheers. And while you're there, would you check if there's a vase that's contempis—contempter—"

"Contemporaneous," Dummersby corrected him automatically.

Slap!

To add to his frustration, Caleb said, and indeed was forced to repeat the little *and steady*—Amelia took silently note in Vanity's direction, doom-laid on the other side of a

THE PRESENCE OF academia's foremost tattletales denied Amelia any opportunity to share a pleasant conversation with Caleb, let alone kiss him senseless (in the name of social science, that is). Instead, she was forced to maintain their pretense of hostility, spurred on by Throckmorton's jibes. This quickly lost its spark, not to mention its store of interesting insults. At the start of the week, she was denouncing Caleb as a "diabolically impertinent miscreant who would make the traitor Simon de Montfort seem like a good friend in comparison." By the end, he was a "brat."

"Okay," he would answer with a careless shrug in any case—which quite honestly almost made Amelia want to fight him for real.

"It is not okay," she replied more than once, driven by tetchiness to use slang. Each time, Vanity would glance sidelong at her and then the surrounding stacks of antiques, expecting another explosion. And Amelia, hating how tense her every muscle had become, tried not to cry with emotional exhaustion. A Tarrant never cried. She herself had not done so since she was eight, and it would be infuriating should two mean-spirited men drive her to it now. Accordingly, she clenched her muscles tighter and set a tranquil smile upon her face, and if there existed a number of puncture holes in her notebook where her pencil tip had stabbed through the pages, that was not, despite appearances, to the point.

Work offered little respite, since she and Caleb were forced into a proximity that might have been thrilling if only not so dusty, so crammed with antiques, and morever occupied by Dummersby, Throckmorton, Vanity, Sir Nigel, Sergeant Sheffield, and several wan ghosts. It was a torment to be in the same room as Caleb, often no farther apart than a few inches, having his permission to stroke him, kiss him, explore his body . . . Amelia paused the thought to fan herself . . . and yet having no opportunity for it. They were watched constantly. Every move they made was accompanied by a chorus.

"Too slow!" Throckmorton scoffed when a soup ladle flew from Amelia's hands on sudden, unexpected wings of magic.

"You are so strong, Professor," Vanity sighed as Caleb moved a chair to evaluate the tapestry behind it.

"*I* would don gloves before I opened an antique book," Dummersby commented tartly, watching Amelia inspect a tattered old copy of Shakespeare's sonnets that she estimated to be worth a penny at most.

"You are so brave, Professor," Vanity exclaimed as Caleb peered into a Ming vase.

Sigh, breathed the ghosts. Amelia knew how they felt.

"Careful, Sterling!" Throckmorton yelled when Caleb lifted a beer stein from a box of assorted drinkware that had been stored in one corner of the sitting room. "Belgian!"

"What's wrong with Belgian?" Vanity asked curiously.

"If you lift the lid of that stein, it plays folk songs," Sir Nigel warned, before Throckmorton could answer. His voice had strengthened through the week as he reveled in having an audience with whom he could share all about his collection (in other words, *every single possible detail of every single antique*, until even Amelia wanted to bash him around the head with a fifteenth-century shoe horn)—but his fingers twined together anxiously as he watched Caleb inspect the silver-lidded ceramic mug, because sharing inevitably led to *sharing*, and he really wanted to keep the antiques entirely for himself.

"I got that stein from a tinker," he said. "Fine fellow, had an extraordinary yellow hat, I asked him who his milliner was and he said—"

"Brussels!" Throckmorton boomed. "Full of magic since the revolution!"

"—A special saffron dye that they make in the—" Sir Nigel pressed on.

"Town hall turned to chocolate!" Throckmorton bellowed.

"Eep!" Vanity clasped her hands against her breast. "Will the mug explode with psycho-conjunctive magic, like the butter dish and the teaspoon from Hereford?"

Amelia's heart skipped a beat. "How do you know about the teaspoon?"

"Oh." Vanity looked flustered, her eyelashes fluttering. "Professor Sterling told me *all* about it."

Something about her emphasis made Amelia's heart not only skip another beat but kick one down into her stomach.

Caleb, however, just laughed. "I did?" Seeing Amelia frown at him, he shrugged. "I don't remember. But no, I don't think this stein is as powerful as the—" He paused fleetingly at Amelia's repressive expression. "The butter dish. If it even has thaumaturgic properties at all." As he tossed it to Amelia for a second opinion, Vanity flinched. Caleb gave her a warm, reassuring smile. "Don't worry. I'd never let anything hurt you."

Vanity fluttered her eyelashes again and sighed dreamily. Meanwhile, Amelia gritted her teeth against a burning pain in her hands as the stein began to prickle with magical energy. Suddenly its silver lid ripped off, speeding across the room to embed itself in the wall opposite. "POUR LA BIÈRE ET LE ROI!" sang out heartily from the mug's interior.

"Seems I was wrong," Caleb said with an apologetic grimace. "Oh dear, are you all right?" The fact that he was asking Vanity, who had jolted with fright, and not Amelia, whose stinging palms had begun turning blue with magic, was of no concern to the latter. She merely blamed the . . . er . . . *the lack of good coffee in Ravenscroft Manor* for feeling at that moment like she'd quite enjoy stabbing something taller and blonder than a notebook.

"Excuse me, please," she said placidly, setting down the beer stein and marching off to count plates in the parlor until she might be allowed to safely use a pencil again.

DINNERS WERE CALMER than the first they had experienced in the manor—which was a polite way of saying they were hideously boring, but at least nothing exploded. Taken in the parlor and shunned by Lady Ruperta (to whom eating dinner in a breakfast zone was akin to King Edward IV marrying a commoner), they might have proven tolerable had not Sir Nigel employed the opportunity to ramble on incessantly about antiques with his "fellow experts." Even Amelia, whose patience was matched only by her interest in collectibles, soon found her mind growing so numb, she couldn't remember which knife she should use for her meat dish, and nearly sprained her wrist trying to cut a steak with a blade made for lettuce.

"You must have traveled extensively, to find so many treasures," Caleb said during a brief pause in a monologue about Peter the Great's pocket watch. "Russian jewelry, French dinnerware, German shields, jugs from Greece." Reaching for the salt to season his meal, he chuckled self-deprecatingly. "I for one get queasy just going from Oxford to London."

"How lucky you and Lady Ruperta are to have visited Russia," Amelia said as she replaced the sugar canister Caleb was about to pick up with the saltcellar he actually wanted. "It's a country I'd love to see."

"Oh, we never travel," Sir Nigel answered with surprise, as if the very idea were preposterous. "Most of my treasures are acquired by agents. Ruperta would like to visit France—she says she wants to drive through Paris in a phaeton, even though I remind her that the wind would ruin her coiffure—but who wouldn't prefer a new piece of Wedgwood Jasperware than a French holiday?" He indicated the plate collection on the wall, among which were seven Jasperware dishes, and Amelia suddenly understood his wife's unpleasant attitude. It was all very fine to love antiques, but one must make room for other interests also, or else risk developing a closed mind. For example, when not working, she herself enjoyed reading (about history), going on strolls (through historical sites), and taking in public lectures (on guess which subject). But she doubted Sir Nigel strolled any greater distance than that between one room and another in the huge cabinet of curiosities that he called his home.

"Now, take this fork, for example," the man said, holding up what appeared to be either a fish fork or seafood fork (the vital difference between these being even more beyond Amelia's tired intelligence than the identification of knives had been). "Fascinating piece, with remarkable—"

Whoosh! The contents of the sauceboat in front of Amelia erupted like a volcano of flaming cream, complete with parsley debris. She threw her linen napkin over the dish, which stopped it spattering but also transformed the napkin into a tiny swan. This flapped overhead in a silent panic for several moments before reverting to its original shape, floating down to land on Grimshaw's head, where it remained, for a butler never undertakes personal grooming during the dinner service.

So much for nothing exploding. "How has anyone survived living in this house?" Vanity remarked grumpily, then caught herself and giggled as if she'd meant it in the cheeriest way.

"It's not usually this hectic," Sir Nigel said, wringing his hands. "True, Ruperta has been turned into a frog once or twice, and there was that time an iron poker belonging to Mac Bethad mac Findláich, the Red King of Scotland—"

"The Scottish Play is a good example of the dangers with interpreting history," Dummersby interrupted. "Shakespeare created a travesty, blackening Macbeth's reputation. He was an honorable king!"

"Mmmpph mm," Throckmorton said through a mouthful, sounding uncannily like he'd said *it's Scottish history, who cares?*

Amelia tried to figure out how they'd got from flaming sauce to Shakespeare, and rather envied Lady Ruperta's having been turned into a frog, which sounded altogether peaceful.

Across the table, Caleb was drinking wine with his eyes closed. She suspected he was asleep, dreaming of Oxford, that cuckoo-echoing, bell-swarmed, towery city . . .

Oh my God, she thought with horror. *I'm quoting poetry.* If anyone needed sleep it was she, most urgently, to restore her good sense.

But night offered no peace. King John's cantankerous ghost rampaged, keeping her awake despite the exhaustion weighing her down. She could not read the biography of Mary Wollstonecraft because she'd left it in Caleb's bedroom, and she dared not visit him to fetch it—or do things more exciting even than reading a good book—for while Professor Throckmorton might be a snoop, Dummersby was a sneak, which represented a greater degree of villainy. On Wednesday night, she finally crept down to the dining room, ignoring mysterious creaks and whispered voices behind the walls along the way (if ghosts wanted her attention, they'd have to seek it during working hours) and she took *The History of the Decline and Fall of the Roman Empire* to read instead. On the way back to her bedroom, she met Vanity tiptoeing along the upstairs corridor by the light of a single candle.

"Professor!" the girl gasped, startled.

"Couldn't sleep either?" Amelia asked her with a smile.

"Uh, er, no," Vanity stammered. "Just going down for hot chocolate."

"You're headed in the wrong direction, I'm afraid. That's my bedroom along there. The stairs are back that way." As she gestured in their direction, she saw an expression on Vanity's face that was so odd, so fleeting, she could not identify it. Her instincts twitched, however. Glancing along the corridor, she remembered that hers wasn't the only bedroom in it.

Oh dear.

"Perhaps you should return to your room," she told the girl kindly. "If you use the bellpull, a servant will attend to you."

Vanity nodded far more vigorously than the suggestion warranted. "Excellent idea, Professor," she said, and dashed away.

Amelia sighed as she watched the girl flee. She couldn't blame her for being attracted to Caleb, but on the other hand was not about to encourage it. Caleb was *hers*. Platonically speaking, of course.

~~As in Plato's theory of each person having another half, a soulmate.~~

As in, *just friends*.

Friends who would have been making good inroads into being less two halves and more one beast with two backs, were there any justice in the world.

On that sober note, Amelia returned to her bed, wrapped a pillow around her head to block out King John's rantings, and delved into *The History of the Decline and Fall of the Roman Empire*. It oddly enough proved less entertaining than kissing a handsome, half-naked man, but did have one benefit—it put her to sleep, even if only for a few hours before a pallid sun rose through the murk like a ghost and the week's history began repeating itself again.

By Thursday, she'd grown frazzled to the extent that her parents, had they seen it, would have disowned her on the spot. She'd also developed a headache from the excessive thaumaturgic energy emitting from so many antiques. (Antiquarians disdained the use of protective equipment, considering it something only "those lunatics in the geography department" needed.) She'd even begun gazing out of windows at the gloomy landscape and sighing forlornly, like a woman in a gothic novel. But matters reached a crisis point over luncheon that Thursday, when she placed jam before clotted cream on her scone.

Upon realizing her error, Amelia reached rather urgently for tea to quell the emotion rising in her throat that just might become a scream. But she stopped, hand suspended in midair, as she noticed Caleb watching her. His eyes were shadowed with concern, and flutters immediately began to dance in her stomach (with scarves, tambourines, and flaming headdresses) as she gazed back at him. Every inch of her skin ached from the deprivation of his casual touch. Never mind erotic possibilities; she missed her chum. Every instinct wanted to smile at him, smooth his hair, and give him a ginger candy that would taste like comfort in his mouth.

Just then, she became aware that the company had fallen into a silence that veritably trembled with fascination. Everyone watched her watch Caleb watching her. It felt as dizzying as it sounded. Luckily, Caleb recognized it too in that moment, and he smirked.

"I didn't take you for having Devonshire manners, Professor Tarrant," he said with a languid disdain that seemed to come worryingly easy to him these days.

"Understandable, since you yourself have no manners at all," Amelia snapped back. Her ire was only partly fake—for the dratted man bore a tiny smear of cream on his upper lip, and he licked it away slowly, purposefully, all the while still staring at her. In that moment, Amelia hated him with a passion that threatened to see her moaning at the table, should she fail to repress it.

"You have stripped me of all civility," Caleb retorted. His eyes flashed, his damp lip glistened in the lamplight, and at the head of the table Sir Nigel grabbed a side plate and began fanning himself with it.

"You certainly are brave, my friend!" Dummersby said to Caleb. "Not many would dare combat such a formidable lady the way you do. We at the museum call her 'Miss Terrifying Tarrant,' ha ha."

Suddenly, the heat in Amelia vanished, leaving her stark white and icy, as though she stood in the pitiless storm that raged outside. Part of her wanted to run out there now, just run and run, fleeing Dummersby's cruelty, and Throckmorton's silent glee as he beheld the scene, and even Vanity's silliness. But she couldn't run; that would only inspire them to gossip more. The only recourse left was to make some barbed comment and suffer the internal consequences. The pain of injured dignity. The loss of self-respect.

She was not a belligerent woman. She was quiet, studious, always willing to help other people so long as they did not try to interrupt her reading. Through her university student days, she'd been a veritable Jane Grey in a court of passionate Tudors. When agreeing to fake hate Caleb, she'd not appreciated just how much doing so would require her to actually be hateful, and how much that would hurt, as if it broke something essential within herself.

As for her reputation: no one called her a trollop anymore, which was good. They called her "terrifying" instead, which was so much worse. She had to wonder: her job and her self . . . were they really equivalent?

And yet, *Caleb*. It always came down to that. Just Caleb. If she left Oxford University to escape gossip and maybe find herself again, she'd lose him. He might say beautiful things about crossing any ocean to be with her, but that was how he talked on a regular basis. The fact was, he loved his job too, and he'd overcome immeasurable obstacles to secure it. Indeed, he'd literally risen from the gutter to become a respectable professor (even if he did sometimes, in a shocking display of bad manners, eat his pudding before his main course). Amelia would not allow him to sacrifice that success.

Which meant sacrificing herself. For who would she even be without her Caleb? Just half a woman, with the ghost of that beloved friendship wandering lost, calling out in anguish for its home.

Looking at him now across the table, she saw that he shared none of her troubled emotions. He was relaxed, even amused, about the situation. In his eyes was the stillness Amelia longed for. He gave her that gift, so that for a few perfect seconds the world became nothing but the two of them, together without words. His gaze was an embrace, gentle and unflinching, better than any kiss (although Amelia would happily take a kiss also—or perhaps several—just to be sure her comparison was accurate). Her stress eased, and even the storm outside seemed to sigh with a wild kind of peace.

Then slowly Caleb blinked, and turning his head, he looked at Dummersby.

"*Professor* Terrifying Tarrant," he corrected the man. Three simple words, a whole threatening monologue within them.

Forget fluttering. Amelia's nether regions outright swooned, and not even the sternest good sense in her brain could revive it.

Dummersby laughed, but it was a tremulous sound, almost

frightened. "Of course. I beg your pardon, Professor Tarrant." He spoke with a skill that so many gentlemen in middle management enjoy: being able to insult someone in the most obvious and yet wholly irreproachable manner possible. Nastiness veritably oozed from the smile he slithered in Amelia's direction. All at once, her stress rushed back. Then, once certain she'd apprehended his intent, Dummersby directed that smile at Vanity. "I'm a great supporter of lady academics, aren't I, Miss Tunnicliffe?"

Vanity immediately nodded, her topknot of hair juddering. "Yes, sir, you certainly are!" she answered with the enthusiasm of a woman who can see Employee of the Month in her near future.

Amelia pushed back her chair so forcefully it scraped against the floor. Ignoring the shot of pain that the awful, ill-mannered noise sent through her nerves, she stood, smiling with a frosty politeness. "If you'll excuse me."

"Going to rest?" Dummersby asked, smugly condescending. "Quite understandable, my dear. Long days of work are hard on feminine delicacy."

Amelia's smile in response was so masterfully serene, it ought to have inaugurated a new annual award category: Women in Academia Restraining Themselves from Slapping Men (gold medals for any and all ladies who achieved it). "To the contrary, Mr. Dummersby," she said. "I am going back to work." The sooner they got it done, the sooner she could return to the serenity of Oxford. Rowdy students would be a balm after the company of these people. "Enjoy your meal."

And she swept from the room before her dignity completely shattered.

———

BUT THE NEXT afternoon, a miracle occurred. Walking from the formal drawing room to the less-formal-but-still-overdecorated sitting room, reading volume two of *The History of the Decline and Fall of the Roman Empire* as she went, Amelia rounded a corner to find Caleb standing in the corridor ahead, inspecting a marble statue of Hephaestus. She halted, he turned, and they stared at each other in silence. They were, for the first time in days, completely alone.

Suddenly, Amelia found herself backed against a wall by almost six feet of impatient (but exquisitely perfumed) male-ness before she realized what was happening. Her book fell from numb fingers to the floor, where it narrowly missed breaking toes with its weight. Caleb loomed over her, one hand on the wall beside her head and a dark heat beneath his long eyelashes. His smile only failed to meet the definition of *caressing* because, alas, it was not actively doing so to her lips.

"Hello, Professor," he said in a low voice.

Amelia swallowed dryly. She'd been greeted thus by hundreds of people over the years, but never before had it ignited such a reaction within her. Indeed, she'd not have been surprised had she fallen pregnant from the words. "Professor Sterling," she managed to reply, her crisp manner concealing the sudden, sparkling chaos inside.

"I've been wanting to get you all to myself for days now," Caleb said, his gaze moving down her body as if he saw that internal chaos and recognized something of himself in it.

"Oh?"

"You've been . . ." He leaned in to whisper against her ear. "Very naughty."

"Nonsense." Amelia's vocal cords supplied this response out of sheer habit, because her brain had abruptly announced it was divorcing her, and was throwing her intelligence out the window like left-behind clothes and toiletries.

"Yes," Caleb said. "You've robbed me of my—"

"Good senses," she inserted.

"Teaspoon," he corrected her.

Amelia blinked as her intelligence snapped back into place. "What? *Nonsense*. You have it. You took it from me that night in the dining room."

"I put it in a safe bag in my suitcase," Caleb told her, "but you've obviously taken it back, considering how that sauceboat erupted yesterday." He began sliding his free hand into her skirt pocket, and she slapped it away.

"I have not," she whispered fiercely, glancing along the corridor to be sure no one was present to witness this scene. "Perhaps it's in one of *your* pockets." She began delving into them, even as he searched all of hers. Their hands rummaged among each other's clothing and brushed against each other's limbs, and so comprehensive was this mutual searching that their breath came fast and their faces began to warm. Only the approaching sound of sharp, tapping footsteps forced them to stop. Caleb stepped back, pushing a rather trembling hand through his hair. Amelia smoothed her skirt.

"Did you actually double-check in your suitcase before deciding to manhandle me?" she asked with a stern look.

"No," Caleb said, and grinned wickedly. Amelia would have gasped, but at that moment Lady Ruperta appeared around a corner, trailed by her housekeeper.

It was like the approach of a royal procession, albeit a very small one. Amelia's dignity yanked her into perfect posture with the speed of someone whose adolescence had been ruled by a ~~pitiless tyrant~~ boarding school headmistress. But Lady Ruperta afforded her only the briefest glance, a mere flicker of generic disgust that consigned Amelia, her dignity, and her doctorate into a bin labeled *Tradesperson*. Garbed in black, Lady Ruperta seemed to sap the light from oil lamps along the corridor walls as she went. Her taffeta dress made a spectral whisper. Her shadow seemed as baleful as the weather outside. The housekeeper, also in black, did not lower herself by even a glance. She was an austere woman named Mrs. Cuddle (pronounced eerily alike to *cudgel*), who wore at her waist a chatelaine of keys that no doubt would have been bones had she lived a thousand years ago. Amelia put her hands behind her back lest she cross herself. Within seconds, the women had departed around another corner, but Amelia knew their image would haunt the night to come.

"I swear, Radcliffe could have written Lady Ruperta's character," Caleb murmured.

"Do you mean Egremont Radcliffe, who took part in the Rising of the North?" Amelia asked confusedly.

Caleb chuckled, and he brushed a strand of hair away from her cheek, even though Amelia was almost certain one did not exist there. "As soon as we're home again I am going to buy you a novel."

She wrinkled her nose. "Why?"

"Because you—*are a termagant who drives me insane!*" he replied, his voice rising as he stepped away from her. Amelia sighed noiselessly before looking around to see a door beginning to open farther down the corridor. Pipe smoke drifted out.

"Fiend!" she snapped, and retrieving her book from the

floor, she stomped off around the same corner Lady Ruperta and Mrs. Cuddle had taken.

Then stopped, astonished, to see a long stretch of corridor ahead of her, not a single door within it, and neither woman anywhere in sight.

"Where did they go?" Amelia asked herself aloud, looking around. But she was entirely alone in the corridor.

Maybe they were ghosts. Disturbed, she hugged her book as she hurried on to the sitting room and the work that awaited her there.

CHAPTER THIRTEEN

Time is not linear, it is a stack of palimpsest pages
that all too often gets shuffled in our minds.
I, on the Past, Cornelius Ottersock

"WE'RE WASTING OUR time," Caleb declared on Saturday morning, rubbing the back of his wrist across his brow as he looked around at stacks of vintage ashtrays chattering with low-grade thaumaturgic energy on the shelves of the drawing room. "We should just transfer the British Museum to here instead."

"You do talk such nonsense, Professor Sterling," Amelia grumbled, although in fact she agreed with his sentiment. Sullen after yet another restless night, and with a headache gnawing at her thoughts, she had reached the conclusion that she'd be trapped in this house forever, counting spoons, shuffling through cigarette cards, too busy to even become a ghost. The rain would fall endlessly, the dust would drift around her relentlessly, and she'd be haunted by echoes of Vanity giggling until she went mad.

"You shouldn't listen to me, then, Professor Tarrant," Caleb snapped. But as he marched across the room to work at a cluttered sideboard, he allowed his smallest finger to brush her hand, electrifying her entire body. Amelia wanted to gasp but instead frowned at him.

"Really, young lady," Dummersby told her with a smirk, "you ought to smile more. Men would like you better if you did."

Suddenly the tar-stained ashtray in her hands flew to the floor near Dummersby's feet, shattering upon impact. "Oh dear, I am so sorry!" Amelia told Sir Nigel, who looked as if he might faint at this tragedy. "It was obviously, and *completely unexpectedly*, a flare of thaumaturgic energy. I assure you that no one in this room, for example, Mr. Dummersby, was in any danger of being hit in the head by it."

At which the museum curator choked on his pipe smoke.

"Where is the gold locket I put here yesterday?" Caleb interrupted tetchily, searching through an array of jewelry on the sideboard. "Oval, etched with roses, gold chain. I set it down right here so I could assess it properly when I had the chance."

"Maybe it's joined the wine goblet I was working on earlier this week," Dummersby said. "Fine Carolingian piece, completely vanished from its cabinet."

Crack! Lightning split the storm-dark sky outside. For one eerie second the drawing room glowed with an eldritch light that dragged everyone's shadows into strange, distorted shapes. The historians all paused, their sudden, troubled silence born from a lifetime of studying narratives and recognizing portents.

Vanity, however, remained innocent of all but her dogged enthusiasm. "A telekinetic goblet!" she exclaimed, clapping her hands with delight.

"I hope not," Dummersby said. "As a museum display, that would be—"

"Worthless!" Throckmorton inserted, and made brisk back-

and-forth gestures by way of explanation. "Zip! Zap! Everywhere!"

"Exactly," Dummersby agreed.

"Oh." Vanity's cheerfulness slumped. "If it's not magical, who cares where it went?"

"It might be interesting in a purely historical sense," Dummersby told her.

"I'm not interested in a goblet," Caleb grumbled. "I want the bloody locket, and then I want to have my bloody luncheon, and then I want to go home."

Another uncomfortable silence followed this declaration. Not only was it remarkable for Caleb to show genuine irritation, but he'd managed to precisely encapsulate the feelings of everyone in the room. Thunder rumbled across the hills as if in agreement.

Then Vanity perked up, reliably. "Maybe someone already packed it. Professor Sterling, you're so efficient, you're probably ahead of yourself." Smiling coyly, she patted his arm.

"Unlikely," Amelia said in a tone so brisk it came close to being a snarl. Snatching up her clipboard, she scanned the attached list of antiques that had been chosen for donation. She and Caleb had thus far identified seven significant thaumaturgic items and nine of lesser value, which was a remarkable haul; sometimes entire years could pass without any new discovery of magic-infused artifacts. It nevertheless made for a very short list, nowhere upon which was a gold locket. "It's not recorded here," she reported.

"Oh, things go missing all the time," Sir Nigel said, and gave a flaccid laugh that soon disintegrated when he noticed everyone was staring at him. "What?"

"You're saying that items with potentially deadly power 'go

missing all the time' from your custody?" Amelia inquired. "Items that unscrupulous people could employ as weapons of considerable destruction, should they get hold of them?"

Sir Nigel blanched at the degree of polite restraint in her voice. "I—I—"

"We had a mad scientist break into the museum last month, trying to steal an enchanted scarab from Egypt," Dummersby said with a chuckle. "Even before our security staff got to him, he'd been thoroughly chewed."

"I," Sir Nigel attempted again, wringing his hands as if he anticipated being devoured at any moment. "I—I—"

Thwack. Amelia set down her clipboard on a small table with such force, not only did the table shake but also Sir Nigel and, over one hundred miles away in Oxford, several third-year students. "Perhaps the locket is merely in a different place than Professor Sterling remembers," she said, and brought forth a thaumometer from her cardigan pocket. The efficiency of her manner both frightened and calmed everyone in the room: she was that most daunting of creatures, a Woman Who Knew What She Was Doing; but on the other hand, who better to solve the problem? With her at the helm, they need not fear England's destruction at the hands of some lunatic wielding a magical necklace—or worse, a delay in getting their luncheon until said necklace was found.

"Hmm," Amelia murmured, frowning at the thaumometer. It's intensity indicator was at seven, and the secondary needle, a direction guide, pointed to where Caleb and Vanity stood at the sideboard.

"It *is* there," she said. "Or, at least, something is." Watching her gauge, she began to cross the room, weaving around furniture. With each step, the intensity needle flicked higher.

"Oh dear!" Vanity exclaimed, backing up until she was against the sideboard. Something fell to the floor, but she ignored it, her expression tightening with anxiety. "Is there going to be another explosion?"

"No," Caleb reassured her.

"Maybe," Amelia said at the same time. "Go and stand on the other side of the—"

Completing this sentence proved unnecessary, for Vanity had dashed across the room to huddle behind Professor Throckmorton even before Amelia was halfway through it. Stepping up to where the girl had been, Amelia set a hand on Caleb's arm to shift him aside. The density of his muscle beneath her fingers sent such a rush of emotion through her that she felt briefly woozy. The man stood right beside her—they were in actual physical contact—and still she missed him quite desperately. She wished she could have just one quiet, private hour with him, chatting about inconsequential things, knocking their feet together in mock battle the way they sometimes did when they forgot they were grown-ups. But this was entirely the wrong moment to indulge in sentimental imaginings. Two of her worst nemeses watched from across the room: Throckmorton, whose gossip had almost ruined her career, let alone her relationship with Caleb, and Dummersby, whose sleazy comments over the years, and whose spite whenever she'd enforced boundaries with him, had at times come close to draining her courage for academia altogether. Together, the men embodied everything a woman of intellect and ambition faced in the world these days, and she would not willingly provide more fuel for their chauvinism. Besides, any moment now Vanity was going to either giggle or say something flirtatious to Caleb, and Amelia feared her headache would flare into an inferno of pain should that happen. So she focused with staid professionalism on the sideboard . . .

Thwomp.

The air seemed to jolt. Lamplight blotted out as if the entire world had blinked, and two seconds later she found herself standing in a small, dirty room, blinking through shadows, inhaling the smell of ashes and old fish.

Amelia raised her brow with a professional degree of surprise (and wrinkled her nose in disgust). Evidently, she was not in Cumbria anymore; the stench alone confirmed that, assisted by noises of traffic and machinery that permeated the thin, stained walls of the hovel. "Hm," she said, and turned to survey her predicament.

Sickly light filtering through broken window shutters illuminated a small, weeping boy huddled on a mattress so filthy, Amelia's skin crawled to see it. A tangle of blond hair obscured the child's face as he hugged himself, but Amelia didn't need to see it to know exactly who he was. The recognition came from her very soul.

"Caleb," she whispered, her pulse staggering. So she was gone not only from Cumbria but from 1890 as well. *Fascinating.* Also possibly irreversible—but Amelia had dealt with magic for so long now, a little thing like being shunted twenty-some years back in time did not immediately alarm her. She checked the thaumometer still in her hand. Its needles were flat.

The boy did not see her, of course. She was less than a ghost; she was a memory of the world to come, a dream of time, beyond his perception. Nevertheless, instinct propelled her forward, drawn as always to be close to him, to touch his head or his tearstained cheek if she could, and so complete her own existence.

"You're dead," he whimpered.

Shock went through Amelia like a thaumaturgic blast, stopping her abruptly in her tracks. But then she realized the child wasn't speaking to her. Across the room, in a pathetically narrow bed, a man lay white-faced, shrunken to the bone by cholera. Caleb's father. Amelia remembered Caleb describing this afternoon to her in terms that had not fully encompassed the stench of the room or the despair he'd felt. An hour later, his mother had come home from her factory job and taken him in her arms, comforting him despite her own grief. A year later, he'd been sponsored to attend boarding school, setting him on the path to becoming a teacher himself. And thirteen years after that, having worked in every spare moment, including summer holidays, he'd finally rescued his mother from the slum, buying her a tiny cottage in beautiful, peaceful Dorset, where she lived yet. He was happy. Amelia knew all this, but even so felt as if her heart might break for the little boy crouching alone with death. She closed her eyes, wishing . . .

"Amelia Tarrant!"

She looked up at the sound of her name being called in a warm, triumphant tone. The scene had changed; time had skittered in a new direction. Before her lay a stage, populated by half a dozen students standing in a tidy row and a teacher at a lectern; it was the latter who had spoken. An audience began to clap politely as a girl stepped from the line—her seventeen-year-old self, Amelia realized. This was the graduation ceremony at boarding school, and she was about to be awarded her second prize of the day, this one for Most Helpful Student. And Caleb . . .

She turned to see an adolescent Caleb standing nearby in the wings, his face a little flushed, his breath panting, suggesting that he'd run to get there. His hair was deplorably tumbled, although somehow it looked perfect on him, as if he'd been interrupted painting a Romantic masterpiece or composing the next great novel. His jacket, shabby and thin, anticipated the shoulder breadth he'd develop in years to come. As for his tie—Amelia winced a little to see its state of disarray.

He'd overslept, she remembered, despite the ceremony taking place in the mid-afternoon. In five minutes' time he'd be named Most Inventive Student, and the audience of their peers would go wild in celebration as he sauntered onto the stage like a fairy prince playing at being human for a while.

Amelia smiled, the recollection providing somewhat of a balm after the misery she'd just witnessed. But then, while she gazed at Caleb, the smile slowly faded into confusion. For his expression was almost sorrowful as he watched her past self accept the award, and Amelia could not understand—did he wish to be Most Helpful Student himself? In that case he ought not have installed the school's milk cow in the headmistress's office overnight.

He pressed a hand against his heart, sighing in a way that indicated more than just breathlessness from having run. It was the sigh of a young man who'd read a lovely, soulful poem and grieved that he could not step into its universe. The sigh of a boy first learning that the age of chivalric knights was long gone. Or, incredibly, the sigh Amelia herself had given too many times through her adolescence—secretly loving this gorgeous, kind friend of hers, desperately wishing they could share more than friendship, and knowing they never would.

As onstage Amelia shook the teacher's hand, Caleb's expression melted into a smile more tender than any Amelia had ever seen. Then the scene swayed dizzyingly. Caleb became a golden shadow; the audience's applause faded into a vague tumult. Amelia blinked, and suddenly she was four years ahead, dancing with Caleb at a university ball. Spangles of lantern light swirled around them, the rest of the world a blur as they waltzed in its heart. Watching, she echoed the sigh she'd just heard from Caleb, remembering this evening and how she had felt comprised of nothing but light and music, held so assuredly in Caleb's hands while he not only danced to perfection but also treated her with exquisite, formal manners . . .

She blinked again, and found herself in shadow.

Every emotion sank to the pit of her stomach. Nearby, crouching on the damp grass behind a boarding school dormitory, a young girl was weeping with such loneliness and hurt that it took Amelia's breath away. Even all these years later, with a degree and a professorship and a pleasant life, she remembered in exact detail the crush of that loneliness, and still felt the hurt some days, as if it had left a scar deep in her soul.

"Are you a lost fairy?"

At the sweet question, she turned, and on the ground her younger self looked up. They both stared at the fair-haired boy gently approaching. He had about him a warmth that seemed to be sourced from pure sunshine, and he smiled as if with sheer happiness at being alive.

"No, I don't think you are," he said musingly as he considered her. *"Fairies don't have drippy noses."*

Amelia laughed. And the little girl she'd been, tears glinting in her dark eyes like dreams while she rubbed her nose with the back of her hand, laughed too. Hearing it, Amelia's emotions rose again in a great, beautiful swell to fill her throat with all the years of delight, good cheer, and love she'd experienced since this moment.

Suddenly, someone clasped her hand, drawing her back into the light.

"Got you," Caleb said.

Amelia looked around dazedly, one last time. Recognizing Ravenscroft Manor's cluttered drawing room, she felt the steady weight of the rain-hushed torpor that had been smothering her all week, and that soothed her racing pulse now. A moment later she was being turned roughly, fingers digging into her arms, blue eyes staring at her with a fear that had defied time to find her and bring her home. Not Oxford home but at his side, where she belonged. *Caleb.* Amelia's heart cried with sorrow and relief. She wanted to take him in her arms, comforting the little boy who had been so cruelly hurt. She wanted to kiss the man who had spent the past two decades making her laugh as if it were his best beloved dream coming true again and again. But their fellow academics were looking on, big-eyed with worry, confusion, and excitement.

"Oh, Professor Tarrant, it was so frightening!" Vanity exclaimed. "You were flashing in and out of visibility! And then Professor Sterling rescued you, like a knight of yore."

"Knight? Hardly!" Throckmorton scoffed.

"He just pulled her out of the spell," Dummersby agreed, grumbling. "He didn't slay a dragon for her."

"It was so heroic," Vanity sighed, nevertheless.

Amelia wanted to sigh herself, although in an entirely different tone from Vanity's, for it was obvious the story of this event was going to be shared all through the antiquarian community. Taking a slow, steadying breath, she returned Caleb's gaze with a temperate one of her own. He on the other hand appeared rather desperate, as if he anticipated her disappearing again at any moment.

I'm safe, she assured him wordlessly. *I'm here with you.*

But aloud she said in a cool, slightly disapproving voice, "You can unhand me now, Professor Sterling. There is no need for such dramatics."

"I am not the one who slipped out of time, Professor Tarrant," he replied, giving her one of his rare, fierce, genuine frowns, the kind he usually reserved for cheating students, conservative politicians, and cold coffee. *Don't leave me again.*

How could a moon ever leave her soul's gravity? she'd have told him, had she been able to speak truly. But even a fleeting smile was impossible, considering their audience.

"Slipped out of time?" Vanity echoed with a disorienting mix of histrionics and glee. "Egad, Mr. Hunt was right! Time's fabric is ripping apart!"

"Not at all," Amelia said, practically yanking herself out of Caleb's grip so as to turn and smile at the girl. "It was only a small pocket of retrospective experience. Time didn't come apart; it drew me in."

"Drew in how?" Throckmorton demanded, the words thick with pipe smoke.

Amelia was not about to share what she'd seen. She wasn't even sure at this point whether she would tell Caleb. Although the visit into his past had been accidental, it still felt like an intrusion, and she feared making him even half as embarrassed by it as she was herself—embarrassed and confused and really quite dizzied by the vision of his eyes filled with such . . . *love* . . . as he'd watched her. And not the genial love of friendship, either, but one that wanted to express itself directly, with hands and lips and other body parts Amelia dared not even think about lest she spontaneously combust, which would be highly unprofessional of her, to say nothing of un-Tarrant-like.

"What caused it?" she mused aloud, looking around at the dozens of antiques cluttering the room. Temporal disruption was a vanishingly rare magic (literally vanishingly, as she'd just experienced), and certainly not one they wanted to introduce to the British Museum's thaumaturgic milieu, unless Dummersby and his associates liked the idea of holding *interactive* presentations of ancient warriors and dinosaur fossils. No, an object with that kind of power needed to go into the Ashmolean's double-locked vault.

If they ever found it, that is, among Sir Nigel's junk.

Just then she noticed that she was standing on a black sock. Shifting her foot off it, she crouched, holding out the thaumometer. Its needle remained flat: no active magic. Picking up the sock, she felt the shape of something small and thin hidden inside, and understood what she had.

The Hereford teaspoon! her brain exclaimed, headache forgotten in its sudden excitement. Although the little antique spoon was emitting no energy now, moments ago its psycho-conjunctive power had actually materialized her wish for more time with Caleb! Such potency was phenomenal. Forget the paper she was planning to write on the teaspoon—this was going to be a whole book! If, that is, Caleb didn't lose it before she could begin work. Struggling to keep her expression unaffected, she stood.

"What's that?" Vanity asked, her voice high-pitched, her face blanching as if she anticipated imminent disaster.

"It's an Italian-milled cashmere sock," Caleb said, frowning at it with a tinge of confusion, while simultaneously Amelia answered, "Nothing important." But the look she gave him told a whole other story. Or, rather, a tract of nonfiction, i.e., the *Thaumaturgic Antiquaries Safety Regulations Manual*, which they were supposed to read once a year to keep its contents fresh in their minds. (Amelia did so every six months. Caleb hadn't picked it up in a decade.) Granted, this manual did not specifically state that dangerous antique teaspoons ought not be stored in hosiery, but surely that went without saying.

"How did it get down here?" Caleb murmured, his confusion deepening from a tinge to a tint that darkened his eyes. "I had it in my suitcase."

"So you *did* double-check it was there?" Amelia asked, recalling their last conversation on the subject.

He paused for the slightest moment, then: "Yes," he said with a tone of outrage that she'd even doubt it. Which meant, obviously, *no*.

Amelia inhaled a breath and held it, along with several sharp words. But the image of the five-year-old he'd been, so small, so impoverished, made her want to cry instead of shout, and hug him, and forgive his appallingly slack work habits. (At least for now. No doubt she'd change her mind next time she had to loan him yet another pen.)

Besides, there was the minor point of her having more than once put that same teaspoon carelessly in her own pocket, even knowing how unstable it could be. But— "Why just a sock?" she asked.

"Look." Caleb pulled back its cuff to reveal another cloth container within.

"Hm," Amelia said, a tiny bit less stern, recognizing that he'd stored the teaspoon inside a safe bag, then covered that with the sock.

"And it's not 'just' a sock," he added. "An *Italian-milled* sock. Using diluted sulfuric acid from a cave in the Apennines."

In other words, one of the most thaumaturgically active

zones in Central Europe. "Hm," Amelia reiterated, but with a tone of approval this time. He'd been quite clever. One might even say "admirably diligent," were one not in earshot of people who believed she hated him.

"I haven't touched it since I stored it away," Caleb told her, and his tone was serious enough for Amelia to believe him. That meant the teaspoon had somehow made its own way downstairs.

Gasp! Could it have telekinetic ability?

Considering it had enchanted her when she stepped on it, even through two extremely strong layers of protection, Amelia was beginning to imagine almost anything of the little spoon.

"When we get home I need to study it more," she said, and desperately wished she was there right now, cozy and alone in her little flat on Norham Road, where a teakettle or book was always in nearby reach and nothing worse disturbed her evenings than Caleb knocking on the door, begging to be let in because he'd lost the key to his own house (again). She clenched the teaspoon, forcing herself quite ruthlessly to focus. "I shall just take it upstairs and lock it in my own suit—"

"No, you won't," Caleb interrupted, snatching the sock from her. "That bloody thing follows you around in the most uncanny way. I'll keep it safe," he insisted.

"Nonsense," Amelia scoffed. "You'll forget to do so halfway up the stairs and toss it onto a side table. I am far more reliable."

She grabbed the sock, trying to pull it free from his grasp. But Caleb stubbornly clenched his fist tightly and pulled back. Amelia clung on with fierce determination (which is far more noble than stubbornness, please note), and a tug-of-war commenced.

"Rapscallion!" Amelia scolded.

"Autocrat!" Caleb retorted.

Their eyes flashed as they glared at each other. Their hearts pounded as they rocked together.

Damn, I adore you, Amelia thought. "Blasted rotter!" she snarled.

"Harridan!" he replied, looking like he might shove her away—or kiss her if she got close enough.

"Are they always like this?" Vanity could be heard asking Dummersby.

"Unfortunately," the curator replied through a disapproving puff of pipe smoke. "Dreadful enemies."

Caleb's glare intensified to the point where Amelia thought she might go up in flames. "Give it back to me!" she demanded. *Take me back into your bed and finish what we started the other night.*

"Never!" Caleb shouted furiously in reply. *I'll never let you go, bella luna.*

"Ahem."

Like the crack of a whip, a woman's voice cut through the scene in the nick of time, just as Amelia feared the teaspoon's magic, or her own wayward passion, would flare uncontrollably and cause havoc. Freezing in mid-wrangle, she and Caleb looked over to see Lady Ruperta standing in the drawing room's doorway.

"Amusing ourselves, are we?" the woman inquired.

At once, Amelia let go of the sock. "Pardon me, ma'am," she said, straightening her sleeve cuffs.

"Sorry for the kerfuffle," Caleb added, taking the opportunity to shove the sock into a pocket, then smoothing back his hair. "Just a slight professional disagreement."

Lady Ruperta sniffed, a sharp little sound reminiscent of a gun cocking. It had them shuffling their feet and reiterating murmured apologies with a demureness Professor Ottersock could never manage to inspire.

"Well," the woman replied, which was clearly meant to be understood as *I do* not *excuse you but have lost interest in this conversation*. She shot a vicious glance at Sir Nigel, who was attempting to hide behind Vanity, then frowned at everyone in general. "Kindly keep the noise down. Some of us are busy and do not wish to be constantly distracted by explosions and fisticuffs."

"Busy?" Sir Nigel queried. Or perhaps he just made a nervous peep; it was difficult to tell which. In any case, his wife had already turned away. Her heels could be heard tapping along the corridor for quite some time afterward, like a heart beating beneath floorboards.

Caleb sighed wearily. "Back to work, friends."

Vanity giggled, heaven only knew why.

"Perhaps Miss Tarrant should go count the parlor plates," Dummersby suggested with a solicitude that barely concealed the snark beneath it. "Since we don't want poor Professor Sterling murdered before this job is done."

Amelia heard Caleb draw breath to reply and almost certainly destroy their ruse of enmity for the sake of defending her. Hastily sacrificing her dignity, she laughed.

"Excellent idea, Mr. Dummersby. The part where you suggest murdering Professor Sterling, that is." And lifting her chin, she snatched up a porcelain ashtray and peered intently but unseeingly at its potter's mark, while her heart spun away back through time, bespelled with lovely remembered dreaming.

Chapter Fourteen

The historian has two primary tools upon which they
must rely: good information sources and the ability
to critically read them. Books require brains
(not in the zombie way).

I, on the Past, Cornelius Ottersock

THE MOOD OVER Sunday's breakfast could have been described most incisively by King John, were he present to
witness it. Amelia, sitting so upright she might as well have
had several books stacked upon her head, applied marmite instead of jam to her toast as an expression of her ennui. Across
the table, Caleb, leaning on his hand, stared bleakly into a cup
of lukewarm coffee. He appeared to be drooping lower and
lower toward the tabletop with every passing minute. Throckmorton and Dummersby issued nasty comments in a dreary,
automatic manner, Sir Nigel sighed dolefully over his kippers,
and even Vanity looked pale and uncomfortable.

"For God's sake," Caleb moaned. "Someone open a window."

The various servants in the room glanced at each other, no
doubt trying to decide how much they could charge for per-
forming this task. Before they reached a conclusion, however,
Sergeant Sheffield rose from the end of the table, where he had
been progressing through his breakfast with the thoroughgoing

equanimity of a soldier who has elevated boredom to the professional level. Striding to the windows, he tugged on one.

It did not move.

Moving to the next, he tried again, with the same result. The servants then joined in the effort, to no avail.

"Trapped!" Caleb laid his arm upon the table and his head atop it. "We're going to be here forever."

"Perhaps you should take a walk, get some fresh air," Dummersby suggested pompously.

"How contemporaneous of you," Caleb snarled.

"That's not what contemporaneous m—"

Slap.

"I might take a walk," Amelia said, rising from her chair. Such was the general gloom, no one even looked her way, let alone stood for her. Relieved, she departed for Sir Nigel's study, some fifty feet along the corridor, which was quite enough perambulation for one day. In the shadowy, book-crammed room, a trestle table had been erected to assist with sorting antiques, since Lady Ruperta was as wearied by the academics' presence in her home as they were, and had decided to contain them in Sir Nigel's zone. Amelia ignored it. Work could wait just a while. With the happy sigh of an introvert who has got herself alone in a room that smells of old paper and book dust, she collapsed into a leather armchair beside the fire.

Then immediately leaped up, yelping, removed the bust of Wellington from said chair, and collapsed again with another sigh, slightly tinged with aggravation but still happy. At last, silen—

"Damn!"

At the sudden voice, Amelia sat upright. Looking around

the room, she saw no one, however. Not even a ghost lurked; not even a broom with malicious magical intent. It must have been a draft, she decided, and was about to slouch in the chair once more when she spied a door slightly ajar in the wall behind her, where previously nothing had existed but dark wood paneling.

Curious, she rose, smoothing her plaid skirt by habit, and crossed the study. As she drew close to the door, it became apparent that it was— "A secret door!" she exclaimed aloud. Her pulse skipped. She hadn't spent years studying history not to appreciate the potential of such a door. Indeed, England wouldn't be the same country today had Edward III not sent men along the secret passageways of Nottingham Castle to take command of his throne . . .

"Oh shut up," she told her brain irritably. It seemed she'd finally done the inconceivable: reached the limit of her interest in historical facts, at least for now. Drawing the door farther ajar, she immediately noticed a scent of floral perfume. Was this how Lady Ruperta had vanished so precipitously from the corridor earlier?

She was about to step inside to investigate further when the actual door of the study began to open, voices sounding behind it. Closing the wood panel hastily, Amelia stepped away from it, setting a tranquil expression on her face just in the nick of time. Throckmorton entered the room, followed by—well, everyone. Amelia's heart, which had risen at the excitement of the hidden passageway, sank again.

"You inspired us to get to work ourselves, Professor!" Vanity announced with a cheerfulness that ought to be illegal so early in the day. "After all, why waste time eating breakfast when there's work to do!" She aimed her wide smile at Dummersby, as if he might promote her on the spot.

"True, that," was all the curator said in reply.

"Mmphum," Throckmorton added through a mouthful, having brought his plate of food with him. Museum staff might be willing to forgo asparagus quiche, but academics knew better which side their bread was buttered on (mainly because that was often all they could afford to eat).

The day did not improve from there. Despite it being a Sunday, everyone was inclined to agree with Throckmorton when he declared, "Soonest done, soonest home." Indeed, the medieval studies professor even began to help with the work, rather than just milling around trying to provoke Caleb and Amelia into gossip-worthy antics. By late afternoon, they had so many antiques organized, and with such singular efficiency, that they could have taken the show on the road to entertain the masses. Caleb and Amelia, standing on opposite sides of the trestle table, went down rows of golden dinnerware and silver cutlery, making assessments at an expert pace. Flipping plates, holding cutlery up to the lamplight, they moved fast . . . faster . . . so fast, it soon became clear they were racing each other.

"You missed a knife," Amelia said, flicking a finger back along Caleb's line as he moved ahead of her.

"Liar," he answered with the flash of a smile. "You just want me to go back and check so that you win."

"I win if the collection is properly searched," Amelia responded snootily.

"No, you win if I do."

She gave a short, baffled laugh. Across the room, Dummersby and Throckmorton stopped what they were doing to glance over, then exchanged a speaking look between them.

"As my colleague, you naturally want to see me succeed in all things," Caleb explained. "Therefore I should be——"

"Wait," Amelia interrupted, holding up her hand. She stared unseeingly into the middle distance.

Immediately, Caleb went still, his expression sober. "What do you hear?"

Amelia snapped her gaze to him with such sharp focus, his own eyes widened. "The sound of my brain breaking under the weight of your nonsense," she said, and without looking away from him, thrust a bread-and-butter plate at Sergeant Sheffield. "Pack."

Certainly there was no love in Caleb's eyes now as he held her gaze. No, it was something hotter, fiercer, and Amelia's stomach fluttered in a way that could not entirely be blamed on the earlier marmite. "Good to know that I shatter you," he said. At his insinuating tone, both Dummersby and Throckmorton blushed scarlet. Caleb flipped the dessert fork he was holding, whereupon it transformed into a long-stemmed silver rose. Holding it out to Amelia across the table, he smiled. "Pack."

They stared at each other for a long, silent moment, the magical rose between them. *Idiot*, Caleb's eyes said. *Totally*, Amelia's agreed. Then Caleb's brow folded slightly: *Wait, which one of us?*

With a sigh that conceded, *both*, Amelia took the rose. It transformed back into a fork as she turned away to wrap it in a safe bag, then pack it into one of the hazelwood boxes made especially for transporting magical objects. Sir Nigel shuffled over, looking as mournful as the sky outside. Amelia realized he'd been weeping, and wondered how much more "donating" of his treasures he'd be able to tolerate.

"Farewell, dear little Hanoverian pistol-handled dessert

fork," he murmured, bending down to pat the box. "You'll be missed. But don't fret; as soon as I find your matching knife, I shall send it on."

"A knife is missing?" Amelia asked worriedly.

"It was here just the other day, I'm sure of it," Sir Nigel told her. He gave a sad little sniff, then dabbed his nose with his cardigan sleeve. "I don't understand where it went."

Amelia frowned with concern but was unable to reassure either Sir Nigel or herself, primarily because the gentleman was now blowing his nose on his sleeve, and to further the conversation would make her quite ill. Turning away, she saw that Caleb was in close discussion with Vanity over an engraved fruit scoop.

A very close discussion, Amelia noted, her eyes narrowing. So close, indeed, Caleb must have been feeling a chill at the fluttering of the girl's eyelashes.

"You are so clever, Professor Sterling," Vanity cooed. Reaching out, she ran a finger along the scoop's handle. "Is this as powerful as your teaspoon that broke the Minervaeum Club's library ceiling?"

Caleb laughed with his usual charm. "Just boring plain silver, I'm afraid. But it is a fine example of the Hanoverian Rattail pattern."

"Oh," Vanity breathed as if he'd just quoted poetry. Caleb took half a step back; she followed him. "What's the most powerful antique you've ever seen?"

"I suppose that would be Dervorguilla of Galloway's sapphire brooch," he said.

"Dervo-who?" Vanity giggled.

"The cofounder of Balliol College. Her husband, John Balliol, was required to fund schooling for the poor at Oxford

Uni. After he died, Dervorguilla established a permanent endowment and formal statutes for the college. A brooch of hers is kept on display in our Hall. Even if it didn't possess extremely potent magic, it's beloved by all Balliol members."

"What kind of magic?"

"The kind I'm not allowed to talk about," Caleb said, and Amelia raised her eyes heavenward (noticing an interesting lightshade but being too distracted to estimate its age and value). Caleb was absolutely allowed to talk about Dervorguilla's brooch; there existed any number of brochures and books describing it, and the only reason she could think of that he wasn't sharing the information with Vanity was that he was trying to be interestingly mysterious.

And apparently this worked, for Vanity gave a pretty little gasp, hands pressing against her heart. "Gosh! Have you touched it?"

Never before had Amelia heard such an active verb. She nearly cleared her throat meaningfully but managed to stop before exposing herself as an eavesdropper.

Caleb's laugh this time sounded uncomfortable. "No, it's kept on display at the college, within a virtually unbreakable enchanted glass dome."

"Gosh." The exclamation practically stripped itself down to silk lingerie and rubbed itself against Caleb. "I would love to have a thorough tête-à-tête with you about it."

"Ha ha," Caleb said through a smile comprised of clenched teeth.

"Ha ha," Vanity answered coyly.

"Ahem." Sergeant Sheffield cleared his throat in a loud, ragged manner that suggested Amelia was not the only one whose nerves were set on edge by the conversation.

Throckmorton, on the other hand, was watching Vanity with a look on his face that Amelia found even more disturbing than the girl's silliness. He seemed *amused*. As if he was about to *chuckle indulgently*. As if Vanity flirting with Caleb was *endearing*.

A muscle in her jaw twitched, and not just because of all the italics. "Excuse me," she announced with smiling calm to the room in general, "I'm going to . . ." Making the vague gesture that is universally translated as *I'm going to the loo but am too embarrassed to say so outright*, she departed.

Walking upstairs with the same smiling calm, she entered her bedroom. Sitting at its small table, still smiling, still calm, she looked out at the surrounding countryside, where hills shrouded in gray drizzle served as a reflection of her mood. Then, with a calm that was beginning to make her facial muscles ache from so much smiling, she tore a page from her notepad and took up a pen to write.

Dear Professor Ottersock . . .

"Imbécile!" King John's ghost shouted, looking over her shoulder, and Amelia jolted, her comma turning into a flourish.

"I don't know if you're referring to me or Ottersock," she told him. "But quite honestly, you're right either way." She ought to have written this letter months ago. Now, without further thought . . . other than to consult her inner thesaurus for the most exact word . . . and to remind herself of a semicolon's proper use . . . she proceeded to inform the faculty head of her intention to resign.

It has been an honor to teach at England's finest university, she wrote as her smile slowly faded. In fact, it had been more than an honor: from childhood, she'd dreamed of being a teacher, thereby having a professional reason to read endlessly about the great people and events from history, and to indulge an imagination that was the very antithesis of a Tarrant's nature. A professorship at Oxford University represented her very most idea of heaven. She could not bear the thought of leaving. *But I must resign*, she wrote, and carefully added a gentle, discreet full stop so that she did not betray her feelings with too heavy a mark.

Watching Throckmorton being entertained by Vanity's flirtation with Caleb confirmed what Amelia had always, deep down, suspected. The man hadn't really cared if she herself and Caleb were in a relationship. He hadn't been motivated by some genuine principle of social rectitude. He obviously, and quite simply, did not like her. And he felt that dislike so strongly, he'd maneuvered to imperil her job by spreading those cursed rumors that she and Caleb hugging was the tip of a far more scandalous iceberg.

The fact that Professor Ottersock had grabbed hold of those rumors with such determination suggested that he disliked her also (except when she was saving the Queen, no doubt, and getting ninety-eight percent pass rates with students).

Dummersby had made it clear the British Museum staff did too.

The Terrifying Scholar. She'd heard people say it . . . well, twice, but that was two times more than her shy, soft heart could bear. It echoed inside her so often, they might as well have been following her around with a bullhorn, repeating it hourly. She was a woman with a sharp brain: that alone was worrisome to her male colleagues. The fact that she did not hesitate to employ said brain without artifice or apology inspired the real terror. How could a man easily dominate such a woman? How could he have command over her realm of knowledge when she was already well educated? It was the academic equivalent of marrying a woman who'd enjoyed sex with other men and knew what she should expect from it.

Then again, Amelia was aware of other women professors in England who succeeded in their role. For example, her brother Gabriel's wife, Elodie, must never have faced prejudice from her male colleagues, considering how confident she was. Amelia admired that tremendously (albeit maintaining a preference for tidier clothing). And recently her cousin Devon married an award-winning young woman professor, Beth Pickering, whom all Oxford celebrated, and who without a doubt had never been demeaned in her position, forced to do such things as washing dishes in the faculty lounge simply because she was female.

With a drooping little sigh, Amelia realized the only logical conclusion could be that *she personally* was the problem.

After all, her family had sent her off to boarding school in an effort to fix her. And no matter how perfect her grades, they'd never brought her home again for longer than a summer holiday. Ergo, she was inherently at fault.

If only she could prove that she wanted nothing more than to do good for others. To please her parents, fix broken things, ensure people had correct information. Not one student finished her course without being educated to an extent where they could easily pass an exam if they only didn't oversleep on the day. Not one waitress at Jabbercoffee was left ignorant of how to make a really good cup of tea. And if there existed in Oxford any student known to be cold or hungry, Amelia hunted them down with sandwiches and a coat.

But apparently she did it all wrong. Or perhaps it just wasn't enough. The one thing she had no idea how to fix was her own self.

Of course, Caleb didn't hate her—there was that. Some nights, the thought of his friendship was all that kept her daring to face the next dawn. And yet, *and yet*, he'd rather pretend to hate her than let the world know she was his dear friend. He fought with her rather than fighting for her. Amelia did not doubt his genuine care. She just wished . . .

Well, it didn't matter. The one thing she definitely got from her Tarrant heritage was practicality. Wishes were a waste of time. Signing the letter, then folding it with a precision that put Ottersock at risk of getting a paper cut when he opened it, Amelia gazed out the window once more, letting the rain do her crying for her. The smile had fallen in sharp pieces to the pit of her stomach, where it dug into the vulnerable, secret dark therein. The letter lay before her like an inevitability.

"I've always considered myself a strong person," she told King John. "I survived negotiating with the curator of Miss Mulberry's Charming Olde Museum over their Regency-era milk jug." (No one in academia was more stubborn, or more disposed to the violent use of a knitting needle, than an elderly woman who volunteered to look after a private museum filled mostly with junk.) "I survive every Christmas with my extended family," (including the world's most obnoxious aunt, who'd never met an accomplishment she couldn't belittle), "but I do believe mailing this letter is going to be the hardest thing I've ever done."

"Merde," King John sympathized, shaking his head gloomily.

Returning downstairs, Amelia placed the letter on the mail tray for delivery, then turned toward Sir Nigel's study. After a dozen steps, however, her brain forced a halt. Apparently, writing out her emotions had created space for good sense to return, and it did so with gusto. Why should she sacrifice her beloved career, for which she'd worked incredibly hard, just because of a few men?! She'd not given up when her parents insisted that she turn to a "proper education" (i.e., science) if she wanted them to fund her tertiary education. She'd applied for a scholarship instead, and they'd backed down before anyone supposed them too poor to pay her way. She'd not surrendered every time a teacher ignored her in class on account of her gender. She'd kept going even in the face of Ottersock's cruel insistence that she choose between friendship and a career.

Unlikable she might be, but Amelia knew that she was also brave. And tenacious. And a damned excellent antiquarian.

Her stomach lurched as she realized how close she'd come to letting those men steal not only her career but her self-esteem. Turning so fast she dizzied herself, she went to recover the letter. But a footman had appeared out of nowhere (in fact, from beside the front door, where he had been standing all along) and had taken up the tray. He was sorting through the letters on it, and Amelia saw a mailbox in his eyes. With a murmured apology, she retrieved her letter from atop the stack and tossed it at once into a nearby hearth fire. As she watched it shrivel within the flames, she released a breath she'd been aware of holding, psychologically speaking, for far too long.

Pretending she'd not noticed the footman pretending not to be amused by her antics, she hastened back to the study. The scene that met her was just as it had been when she left. Throckmorton and Dummersby were discussing the possible cause of King George III's madness ("It was mania!"—"No, it was because he had all those children!"); they gave her a disdainful glance as she entered, then returned to their debate. Sir Nigel was describing the history of a silver dish, indifferent to the fact that no one was listening. Vanity had

Caleb backed into a corner and was quoting at him from Tennyson's *The Princess*, a poem to be lauded for its support of women's higher education, but equally to be despised for how Vanity was not so much reading it as giggling it. Only Sergeant Sheffield stood quietly, hands clasped behind his back, face bearing the blank detachment of a man who doesn't care where he is, so long as his shoes are dry and no one talks to him. Amelia was becoming fonder of the fellow with every day that passed and every conversation they did not have.

Feeling another headache coming on, she trudged over to the table of antiques. But so carefully was she not watching Vanity and Caleb out of the corner of her eye that she knocked against a side table, sending its cargo of clockwork dolls into a tumble. A baby doll with enormous eyes began to wave its arms and emit a high-pitched wailing.

"Bloody hell, Tarrant!" Throckmorton shouted, clasping his ears.

"Mind your damned language with ladies present!" Dummersby shouted in response.

Meanwhile, Vanity was shrieking, for no apparent reason other than taking the opportunity to make noise. Sir Nigel ran over to grasp the doll and ~~stop its wails~~ describe its provenance in detail. Amelia turned in search of an escape from the cacophony, but a servant approached her with a tray of drinks, and someone tossed another log on the hearth fire, and Vanity's shrieks transformed back into giggles that were equally eardrum piercing. And then Sir Nigel said—

"It's going to be okay."

Except Sir Nigel never spoke with those beautifully modulated tones, the result of many years' elocution training. Only one voice was like silk gliding against her skin in that way.

Amelia knew she was being rescued a second before Caleb's hand clasped her wrist, its cool firmness breaking her from the throbbing daze into which she'd fallen. She blinked at the sight of his smile and was horrified when a tear spilled down her cheek. She *never* cried, not even when her mother looked at her in her doctorate graduation attire and said "*Jolly well done, dear, even if it is just a DPhil in history.*" To her relief, Caleb gave no sign of noticing the tear, however. He began tugging her, and she went with him deafly, which required as much trust as if she went blindly. But then, trust in Caleb was one thing she always had to spare.

"'Scuse me," he said as he plowed a track through the room's occupants. "Professor Tarrant is about to vomit. 'Scuse me."

Everyone promptly gave way for them, and within moments Amelia found herself in the cool tranquility of the corridor, with no one around to further trouble her senses (other than servants dusting the light fittings). Introversion breathed a long, pained sigh of relief. Caleb closed the study door, then turned to cup her face in his hands.

"Meely," he said chidingly, or perhaps gently; she could not tell. He swept a thumb across her cheek, erasing its renegade tear. He had noticed after all.

"Caleb," she whispered, and hers was most definitely chiding—for what if someone saw them? Beneath her voice, however, a whole ocean of tears threatened.

And maybe Caleb recognized that, for he kissed her forehead; then, as she feared the ocean might rise in a tsunami to overwhelm her, he stepped back. Taking her hand, he proceeded to tow her along the corridor. Amelia stumbled a little, trying to keep up, but Caleb showed no concern for this. He was clearly prepared to dismiss any excuse or apology she might make. Somehow, it was lovely. At least the flutters in her stomach seemed to think so.

"Did you have to tell them I was going to vomit?" she complained.

"Yes," he said. "Otherwise they'd be out here with us, wanting to know what we're doing."

"What *are* we doing?"

He flashed her a grin. "I'm taking you up to the attic. Come on."

But Amelia stopped, requiring him also to halt or else be ungentlemanly. He looked at her as if preparing an argument.

"Wrong way," she said.

"Oops." Transferring his hold from her wrist to her hand, then setting his own free hand on her waist, he danced her around in a half circle until they were facing the correct direction. Amelia did not even have a moment to recover from sweet, tingly dizziness before he let her go and began to lead her toward the stairs.

"But why the attic?" she asked. "Why not another room in the house? We have so much work to do."

"Not this afternoon we don't," Caleb answered firmly. "You are going to take a break, Professor Tarrant. And you'll be doing it in the attic because, for a start, no one will look for us there. But also because I was exploring the other day and found something I want you to see."

At this, curiosity, the essential trait of all historians, sparked within Amelia's wearied brain. "Ooh. What?"

Caleb waggled his eyebrows at her. She knew all too well what that meant.

They were about to have an adventure.

CHAPTER FIFTEEN

History's most powerful stories of love and sorrows we
can but glimpse like ghosts in jeweled rings, tombs,
and the minutiae of household management records.
I, on the Past, Cornelius Ottersock

THE SHADOWS OF the narrow stairwell smelled hundreds of
years old. Eerie shapes, created by the sway of light from a
lantern Caleb had procured along the way, seemed to reach out
with claws to torment Amelia as she followed him up toward
the attic's door. She wasn't frightened, for her career often led
her into spooky places (haunted houses, museum basements,
and the parlors of elderly ladies who serve lukewarm tea),
but she briefly contemplated acting as if she were, so that
Caleb would hold her hand again. He paused before a door at
the top of the stairs and looked at Amelia with an intensity
made all the more dramatic by deep shadow and the flame of
his lantern. "Prepare yourself," he said in a hushed, solemn
voice.

Unimpressed, Amelia looked back at him steadily. "Are
there ghosts? Spiders? Should I have brought my insect repel-
lent? Or is the roof broken and an enchanted wind blows in
from the fells, keening of the lost summer?"

His expression collapsed. "No," he said rather petulantly. "Just— Well see for yourself."

He pushed the door ajar, its hinges groaning mournfully in the tradition of attic doors everywhere. As he progressed into the chamber, Amelia followed cautiously, for she did not quite trust his assurances on the matter of spiders. But what she saw brought her to a surprised halt.

"Told you so," Caleb said, smiling at the look on her face.

A moderately sized room stood before them, its ceiling angled steeply, its windows narrow and lead lined (*early 1400s*, Amelia guessed, but was not about to ask Professor Throckmorton up for a more accurate estimate). A sense of damp centuries freighted its shadows. So far, so gothic. But the wooden floorboards were well swept and scented with lemon polish. Green checkered curtains adorned the windows. Along one wall stood a rail hung with fluffy, cozy dressing gowns; against another, a scrupulously dust-free sideboard displayed a biscuit jar, an unlit lantern, bottles of whiskey, and tidy stacks of magazines. At the center of the room, two large, faded leather armchairs sat opposite each other, a low table between them.

"Huh," Amelia said, unsure whether to be disappointed (no antiques anywhere to be seen) or relieved (no antiques anywhere to be seen!).

"The servants use it as a private lounge," Caleb said as he set down his lantern on the table and moved to light the other.

Amelia frowned mildly in confusion. "How could you know that?"

"I asked them."

"Good heavens." She was quite astonished by this unconventional means of information gathering.

Caleb shrugged. "It turns out they're . . . well, people."

"You smiled at them," Amelia accused.

He gave her an amused glance over his shoulder. "Maybe."

She watched as he lit the attic's lantern, feeling precarious in a way she could not quite define—almost as if something integral had been slowly peeling away from her over the past week, leaving her not wholly herself. Or worse, *more* herself, the old defenses eroding.

I'm tired, she thought. There had been too much arguing. Too many days of relentless enmity. Even faked, it was agonizing. Amelia felt haunted by the ghost of Caleb, although he stood living and breathing in the same room as her—haunted by the loss of small casual words they usually shared, touches, and knowing looks that made up the better part of her existence. Longing lay on her skin like too much cold air. And not just for kissing (although that too). She felt bereft of him.

But that wasn't the entire truth, and Amelia cursed the analytical efficiency of her brain in admitting it. Part of the trouble had been that the passion required for conducting their arguments made her feel . . . hot. Fluttery. And really so very fluttery hot, she was beginning to feel less English and more like an Italian woman lounging about half-undressed on some beach, with a sea as blue as Caleb's eyes lapping over her bare skin.

While she struggled to recenter herself in what was in fact a damp attic on a gloomy autumn afternoon, Caleb brought a lantern and bottle of whiskey over to the table and set them down. Then turned to her without a word and took her in his arms, hugging her close.

At the feel of his body against hers, Amelia exhaled in deep relief. The embrace filled her with a warm, soft comfort, making her feel complete again, no longer split apart from the other half of her soul. Just as always, Caleb's very presence soothed the sharp little fragments of hurt that had accumulated inside her with every disdainful look from other people, every casual cutting remark. Thank goodness she hadn't sent that letter. With Caleb, she could endure anything.

They stood like that for an uncounted length of time, not speaking, just quietly waiting for the little familiarities to weave together again between them. Finally shifting apart, they shared a smile that was rich with two decades' worth of mutual care.

"I needed that," Caleb said. "My sparkle was quite lost. Indeed, I was beginning to fear that having to obey society's prudish conventions was turning me into that most dreadful of things—"

"Brooding and dark-hearted," Amelia said.

"Boring."

They laughed. "Sit, Meely," Caleb said as he left her, crossing again to the sideboard. "Put your feet up. Have a drink."

"I'm not drinking that," Amelia answered, wrinkling her nose at the bottle, as she sat primly upright in one of the chairs (first checking it for spiders, polished floor notwithstanding). "A lady never consumes drink directly from a bottle. Think of the—"

"—germs. I know. But don't worry, love, I'm getting us some glasses."

"I thought we agreed you wouldn't call me 'love,'" Amelia said severely, even while her heart did a happy little pirouette.

"There's no one to hear it." Opening the sideboard's door, he bent to search for drinkware, and Amelia conscientiously did not ogle his posterior (she just happened to be looking in its direction, that's all).

"They could walk in at any moment," she argued.

"I've locked the door."

"Nevertheless." Then she remembered what he'd told her downstairs. "What did you want to show me?"

"This!" Straightening with an excited grin, he held up a flat, rectangular box.

"Chocolates?" Amelia guessed, her eyes lighting.

Caleb deflated. "No. A chess set."

She gasped, unable to restrain her sudden delight. "Even better!"

He eyed her dubiously. "Better than chocolates?"

"Absolutely!" Had she been able to sit up straighter with excitement, Amelia would have done so. Indeed, she was half tempted to clap her hands, Vanity-style. "But you wish to be punished?" she asked, surprised. "I've won every game of chess we've played."

Caleb shrugged with mild agreement in the middle of that; then his grin returned, tinted with mischief. "Perhaps I let you win."

"Ha!" was the only possible, sensible reply.

"So you'll play with me?"

"Of course." And when he evidenced some trepidation— "It will be restful."

His grin sharpened. "We'll see."

Not bothering to argue, since he would soon enough be proven wrong, Amelia leaned forward to open the bottle and peer inside. "Thirsty after all?" Caleb teased.

"No, I just think that if I'm a little tipsy, it will even the playing field."

"Ha!" He brought over glasses, filled them with what turned out to be rather cheap but tolerable whiskey, and set up the board, placing the white pieces on Amelia's side. Then slouching against one arm of his chair with his head propped in his hand, he smiled at her twinklingly. Amelia suspected this was not a real word but could think of none more appropriate. He was like a trickster god slumming it in the mortal world—all sparkles and just a hint of dark, dark power beneath his smile. Amelia wondered if now was the right moment to tell him that she'd viewed his memories when stepping into the Hereford teaspoon's magic yesterday, but before she could summon the courage to do so, he waved at the chessboard.

"You can start first," he said in a tone either provocative or seductive (Amelia had not yet drunk enough of the whiskey to discern which).

"Hmm," she murmured, rescuing herself from his glamour so she could strategize with a clear mind as she contemplated the board. Its finely carved wooden pieces were old but not enchanted—always a bonus, since being bitten by one's king while trying to escape check was distracting, to say the least. She reached out to move a pawn, then changed her mind and moved another instead.

"Interesting," Caleb said.

Amelia raised her eyebrows at him. "You're just saying that to make it seem like you're good at the game."

"Eh," he said, shrugging in careless admission of the fact. He drank whiskey and then, still holding the glass, nudged forward a pawn seemingly at random. "How's the scratch on your hand, by the way?"

"Fine," Amelia told him while frowning at the board. "You never did bandage it."

"Well, I was just being charming in the moment. Also, it gave me an excuse to kiss your hand."

Amelia ruthlessly ignored her flutters. "Miss Tunnicliffe got scratched yesterday when a figurine of Zeus she was packing took wing."

"Oh?"

Looking up from the board, she aimed her frown at Caleb. He looked back blandly. "I'm not interested in Miss Tunnicliffe," he said.

"Perhaps you should tell her that."

"Honestly, our conversations are quite dull. Mostly she just asks about the value of the antiques and what magic they might do. She wants to quit her job, go to university, and she thinks I can help her, so she's being especially nice toward me."

"She thinks you can help her with *something*."

"I know how to handle a crush. Besides," he muttered a little grumpily, "I don't flirt with mean girls."

"You flirt with everyone," Amelia said, her hand hovering over a knight before withdrawing again. "By the way, have you double-checked that the Hereford teaspoon is secure?"

"Of course," he answered at once. And when she gave him an Amelia Look™, he rolled his eyes and repeated firmly, "Of course."

"Hm." Returning her attention to the chessboard, she trailed her smallest finger back and forth across her lower lip as she debated which piece to employ.

"Fuck." Caleb abruptly straightened, downing the entirety of his drink. Amelia stared at him with surprise. He almost never swore.

"I didn't mean to offend you," she said.

He gave a curt, rather bitter laugh. "I'm not offended."

"Sorry," she said, just in case. "You aren't a flirt, you're just friendly—is that better? And Miss Tunnicliffe is not mean. She's—"

"Excitable. Yes, I remember. So excitable she didn't hesitate to be rude to you."

"That was ages ago, Caleb. It doesn't matter."

"It always matters."

"But—"

"I don't want to talk about Vanity, of all things, when I'm finally alone with you," he interrupted grouchily.

They stared at each other yet again, the air becoming so charged that Amelia wondered if a thaumaturgic antique were inside the room after all. But Caleb was looking a little flushed, almost defensive. He muttered something under his breath.

"I beg your pardon?" Amelia inquired.

"Friendship," he grumbled.

She blinked, unsure how to take this statement. "Yes?"

"It is a serious affection," he explained. "The most sublime of all affections, because—"

"It is founded on principle, and cemented by time," Amelia said, her voice overlapping his, completing the quote. Inside her stomach, the flutters grew stronger. "Mary Wollstonecraft. You've been reading my book."

He shrugged, a silent, insouciant confession that did not quite match the shadows in his eyes as he watched her for a reaction. "Nothing better to do in this blasted house at night."

Amelia swallowed dryly. Somehow it felt deeply intimate that he'd read the same pages she had, touched them, while lying in his bed . . .

"It was most thought-provoking," he said, the way another man might have said, *it made me dream of you in your underwear.* He drank again, apparently not registering that his glass was in fact empty. His gaze remained locked on hers, and Amelia thought that if he did not at least blink soon, she might just faint.

"You're trying to distract me from my strategy," she concluded. Forcing herself to focus once more on the game, she bit her fingertip, thinking . . .

Clunk. Caleb's glass hit the table so hard, the chess pieces trembled. "Let's make a bet," he said, reaching for the bottle.

"Don't bother," Amelia told him. "You won't win it."

"We'll see, clever girl."

"Woman," she corrected him automatically.

"Hm," Caleb murmured with a dark eloquence. He poured whiskey into his glass, then replaced the little Amelia had sipped from hers. "So, since you are indeed a woman—since we are both adults—let's play like it. Here's the bet: whoever wins at chess gets to kiss the loser anywhere on their body."

Amelia felt her eyes grow wide. Caleb smiled, almost belligerent. Now the air was not so much "charged" as "on the verge of nuclear fission." The Ghost of Kissing Past arose to dance a tango with the Ghost of Kissing Future.

"How many times?" she asked.

Caleb shrugged his mouth. "Three? Like in a fairy tale."

"And when you say anywhere, you mean—"

"Anywhere."

Amelia's pulse began to run around madly, throwing off its clothes and hauling on lacy lingerie. Reaching out without looking, she picked up her glass and took a long, slow mouthful of whiskey before setting it down again.

"It's your turn," Caleb prompted her, gesturing with his own glass at the board, then drinking as if he anticipated a tedious wait while she chose between one pawn and another next to it, never mind actually providing an answer to his suggestion.

Not taking her gaze from his, Amelia removed her king from the line of pieces and laid it down in surrender at the center of the board.

CALEB ALMOST SPAT out his mouthful of alcohol. He had expected Amelia to have come to her good senses after their long-ago conversation about experimenting, and to lecture him on the limits of friendship (a good night kiss, albeit lingering) and the sanctity of chess (never to be discounted) and moreover that he should sit up straighter. He'd been half-drunk when he'd spoken—forget the whiskey; to have Amelia all to himself after an interminable week of not being able to smile at her, let alone touch her, was intoxicating. Now he had to hastily assemble a plan to match the wild proposal he'd made.

Swallowing back whiskey and fear, he said rather huskily, "Stand up."

She did so at once, not evidencing even the slightest hesitation. *Oh God.* "Come here," he instructed.

Walking as if she had a book balanced atop her head, Amelia rounded the table to stand before him. Caleb took her left hand in both of his, using all the care he would when handling a porcelain figurine that might explode with deadly magic at any moment. Then he turned it over and gently set a kiss on the pale, blue-threaded skin of her exposed wrist.

Amelia drew in a breath. He did not hear her release it. Looking up through a wayward lock of hair, he smiled.

"One."

It was rather impressive, if he did say so himself, the way he mixed softness and seductive huskiness within that single syllable. All the elocution lessons of his youth were worth it, just for this moment. It must have impressed Amelia too, considering how her face flooded with pink and her breath, finally exhaling, shook just a little. Caleb let go of her hand so he could relax back into the chair, setting his forearms on the wide armrests.

"Sit on my lap."

Now Amelia seemed uncertain, angling this way, then that, apparently at a loss as to how to undertake the maneuver. Caleb couldn't blame her. Dressed as she was in proper, ladylike fashion with petticoats and a long heavy skirt, it was a wonder she could scale anything—a man's lap . . . a ladder to reach some interesting artifact . . . Oxford University's male-dominated professional ranks. Even climbing the steps of the Ashmolean, which he himself ran up in seconds, must have been a trial. Leaning forward again, he placed his hands on her hips and arranged her to face him. He could feel that she was trembling, but it did not seem to be in fear, so he continued.

"Lift up your skirt and sit astride."

She did so. *She did so.* Caleb begged himself not to panic. The soft cotton of her drawers felt like angel wings, even through his trousers' heavier fabric. Did they have an open seam? Should he ask her to move forward, to where his arousal was beginning to strain against his own pants' seam?

No, that was crude, and he wanted every moment of this experience to be exquisite for her, so that later she could remember it like a string of tiny, glimmering stars, each electrifying her in the most delicate and perfect way.

For the sake of friendship, of course.

Looking carefully into her eyes, he checked for any sign of anxiety. But she was all Amelia: calm and composed, despite the unorthodox seating arrangements, and perhaps just the slightest bit impatient. Caleb dissolved into a grin. Mouth, heart, all of him, grinning like an idiot.

"What?" she asked.

"You," he said. Her hair was tied back severely in a knot, as usual, with a few fine strands drifting against her neck. Caleb wanted to play with them, stroking and tickling her bare skin with them, making her shiver. He wanted to kiss the small pearls in each of her earlobes, and follow the trail of her pulse with his lips all the way down her throat. But she was wearing a shirtwaist with a satin bow at its collar, and the temptation of it kept him focused. With a slowness that felt like sweet torment—and that Amelia hopefully felt too—he pulled on the hanging ribbons of the bow until it unraveled, then drew the loose knot apart.

"All right?" he asked as he began unbuttoning the shirt-waist, for she'd stiffened, and while he thought it was antici-pation rather than discomfort, he wanted to be sure.

"Yes," she said in her clipped schoolteacher voice, the one that had always made doing such things as discussing lecture schedules, concentrating in faculty meetings, and unbuttoning a blouse without lustily ripping it off her rather difficult. Caleb willed his fingers not to tremble as he continued with his task. Coming to the last button above her skirt's waistband, he spread open the blouse. What he discovered beneath it nearly stole his breath.

A chemise of the finest white lawn and Irish lace lay be-neath a silk corset embroidered with flowers and decorated with a tiny pink bow that threatened to send Caleb into an outright swoon. He'd never expected such dainty prettiness beneath the solemn practicality of her outerwear. Her skin was so perfect, so creamy, dotted here and there with freckles, that he considered abandoning his plan altogether, since how dare a man such as he despoil her with his touch?

"You're poeticizing, aren't you?" Amelia said dryly.

"A little," he admitted.

"I don't wish to be rude, but this seat is somewhat uncomfortable. Might we progress at a swifter rate?"

He quirked his lips. "You want me to tear your clothes off you, is that it?"

"I'm not saying that," she replied in the haughty manner he knew meant *but I would if I weren't too dignified to utter such a plea*.

As much as Caleb liked the idea, he had no intention of giving her what she wanted so easily. Setting one finger just beneath her throat, he slid it down, watching as her pupils dilated in response. Lowering the trim of her chemise, he set one hand against her back to ensure her safety, then bent to kiss her, right at the border of lace and bareness, above her fast-beating heart.

His own heart ached with happiness. She tasted of lilac. She was warm and soft and, for just that moment, all his. He kissed her tenderly, as one might the heart of an angel. Then straightening, he looked into her beautiful, beloved, slightly stunned face.

"Two."

"Oh, my," Amelia breathed.

Caleb tried not to let smug triumph swagger across his lips (albeit not very hard, it must be said). "We all know I'm an antiquarian genius, but who knew math would also be my forte?"

For once, Amelia did not roll her eyes. They were glimmering like a night strewn with quiet, silvery rain, and Caleb frowned slightly.

"You're going to cry again," he said. "Am I making you unhappy?"

She shook her head and scrunched her eyes closed for a moment, and when she looked at him again, her eyes were—well, a little red, to be honest, and hazy, but she held his gaze with impeccable calm, so he decided to let the subject go.

"What about three?" she asked.

He grinned. "Three will be your most favorite."

And the world turned to sweet, shimmering magic.

Chapter Sixteen

Nature is to be treasured. After all, it is where battles
take place, determining the fate of kingdoms.
I, on the Past, Cornelius Ottersock

"**D**AMN," CALEB SWORE as Amelia climbed off his lap. "Must
we constantly be bloody interrupted by goddamn bloody
magic?"

"*Tsk*." Amelia did not stop to frown at him over the use of
such language, for twinkles of thaumaturgic energy were lur-
ing her attention instead. "It's coming from outside," she said,
crossing to the window (although it must be confessed she
walked a little unsteadily, and inside, her heart—or perhaps
some other organ—was saying *damn, damn* with as much fervor as Caleb had).

"Uh-huh," he answered in a rather pained tone. But he remained in the chair, with an annoying, but not altogether uncharacteristic, reluctance to get up and do work. Now Amelia
did frown, turning back with the intention of chiding him into
joining her in a search for the magic's source. No words escaped her throat, however, for she was struck mute by the sight
that confronted her. Immediately, Caleb leaned forward, ostensibly reaching for the whiskey bottle, but the damage had

been done. The loss forever hereafter of one part of her brain had been achieved. For Amelia knew she'd make a museum room of it, or perhaps even a shrine, so that she could revisit daily the image of Caleb's prodigious arousal.

(Then again, perhaps he'd simply put an antique in his pants for some reason Amelia attempted to construct before her intelligence stepped in and told her to stop being a ninny. Her degree might be in history, but that didn't mean she was ignorant about biology.)

Nevertheless, friends do not think about other friends' stiffened phalluses, she lectured herself.

Sh, her brain replied, busy setting up a display plinth and special lighting.

Perhaps now was a good time to tell Caleb that her feelings for him lately went beyond friendship.

Or, rather, not *now*, considering magic was glinting throughout the attic like a sugar bowl had exploded, but soon. Around the same time that she told him she'd seen his memories. And confessed about the letter she'd almost sent to Ottersock. And asked his opinion of Mary Wollstonecraft too, although that was perhaps less pressing.

Besides, she didn't think she could quite deal with the pain of sharing her heart and having him tell her—kindly, with a smile—that all he felt in return was friendship. Deep, precious, loving friendship, but not the kind of romantic adoration that she was beginning to identify within herself.

Arousal did not count; that was just science. Then again, the way he'd looked at her in that memory she'd experienced . . .

A conversation was definitely in order. Just as soon as she'd fixed this latest problem.

With a remarkable degree of self-discipline, even for a

Tarrant, Amelia turned back to the window. The rain had stopped, the sky was limp and exhausted, and altogether the view resembled nothing so much as a towel that you reach for after your bath only to discover it is damp. One exception to this drabness did exist: a fountain of sparkling white and gold light erupting from a stony field some distance from the manor house.

That's quite the exception, Amelia thought wryly. There being no one in sight, and Guy Fawkes Night still some time away, she presumed it was not a species of firework. Damn. She was going to have to go out in the cold and the wind to investigate.

"No," Caleb said emphatically.

"What do you mean?" Amelia asked, watching the magical fountain shoot stars that spun and flared in the breeze.

"You're doing that standing-straighter thing you do before you plow into action, which means that you'll be wanting me to plow too. But I'm not going out in that cold, Meely, absolutely not. I don't earn enough to justify tramping through farmland."

Amelia turned to give him a crooked smile. He met her gaze—then glanced at her still-unbuttoned shirtwaist—then looked into her eyes once more with an expression that suggested he was not going walking anywhere, but was however willing to undertake a different, more horizontal kind of exercise. The air between them sparkled, and not entirely due to the discharging magic. For one second, Amelia considered abandoning her professional duty, her definition of friendship, her completely reasonable caution, and every last good sense remaining in her, to climb Caleb as if he were a library ladder.

But a thaumaturgic eruption in proximity to a house full of antiques, many of which were magical themselves, was really not to be ignored. Alas. She began to rebutton her shirtwaist.

"I am going out to determine the source and stop it if I can," she informed Caleb coolly. He groaned, collapsing against the arm of his chair in dramatic, seven-year-old fashion, and Amelia clicked her tongue at him. "It's fine, you can stay here. Make yourself nice and cozy, and I'll let you know the results of my investigation when I return."

CALEB LEANED BACK in the armchair as he sipped whiskey. The attic was wonderfully peaceful, and he felt so warm and comfortable that he began to drift toward the restful bliss of a nap.

Or at least he did in his imagination. In actual reality, he trudged through a field that could better be described as a mass of sheep dung, mud, and thistles with some grass strewn among it. His trouser cuffs were soaked, his shoes ruined. "Slow down, Meely," he called out, but Amelia ignored him.

"I'm certain the flash of magic came from over there," she said, pointing to a boulder some distance across the fields. "Or maybe there," she added, indicating now a red-gold oak tree some other distance away. (Yards and feet meant nothing to Caleb; as a historian, the only reason he ever needed to calculate distance was when he wanted a hot drink from Jabbercoffee but was due to lecture across the other side of town in half an hour's time.)

Both boulder and tree formed mere silhouettes in the fading light. A sinister band of red along the western horizon, like the blood of the lost day, warned that soon night would be fully upon them. It was worrying, but not entirely a surprise, considering they had spent *hours* tramping around, looking for magic. The eruption of luminous thaumaturgic energy had disappeared by the time they'd managed to sneak out of the house without being seen by anyone (except two footmen, who had opened the door for them and offered umbrellas, which Amelia, cruel woman, refused on the basis that it "didn't look like it was going to rain," as if they were in some country other than England). Caleb did not know whether to be pleased that the magic hadn't resurged—after all, it was good news for the safety of Ravenscroft Manor's residents—or annoyed, since it was bad, bad news for his shoes.

Hours! he reiterated grumpily, although not verbally, since he'd rather not receive another of Amelia's frowns, even if she did look cute making them. Oh sure, if one wanted to be *pedantic*, it was more like fifty minutes, but even so. Far too much time. And Caleb wasn't the only one to think so. His stomach agreed with him most emphatically.

"We're missing dinner," he told Amelia in dire tones.

"They'll leave us some," she replied, unconcerned.

"We're going to get lost," he tried instead.

"The house is rather hard to miss," she pointed out. "It's that big stone thing behind you."

"Five miles behind me."

"Half a mile at the most."

"Aahhh! A mosquito just bit my hand!"

"Oh dear."

"If I come down with malaria . . . or worse, if I get an unsightly bite on my face . . . the tragedy will be— Ugh, what did I just step in?"

"Sheep shit, probably," Amelia replied complacently, which silenced Caleb for several minutes due to sheer astonishment. And perhaps just a touch of arousal. All right, quite a lot of arousal. Indeed, he'd have pulled her down to the ground and kissed more uncouth language from her mouth if only said ground was dry, clean, and a feather bed.

"It must be around here somewhere," Amelia muttered, pausing in front of a purple flowering shrub. "Hydrangeas are summer blooms, so magic clearly is afoot." She glared at the shrub as if she could frighten its secrets out of it.

Caleb took the opportunity to consider her carefully. She was pale, despite all the exercise, and the way she crossed her arms suggested it wasn't just her usual professorial stance, but an attempt to warm herself. He'd have given her his coat but he'd not brought it. The two of them had gone out in shirt-sleeves like a pair of idiotic city dwellers who would almost certainly develop pneumonia as a result.

He turned his attention to the sky, serious now. It was purpled with age, bruised by dark clouds that threatened more wild weather to come. The wind smelled of mountains and dusky loneliness as it rushed down from the Scottish Highlands like an invading medieval army. It had nigh on defeated Amelia's prim coiffure, and Caleb hated to think about the state of his own.

"'Dreary winds foreboding call the darkness down again,'" he warned.

Amelia gave him a bewildered look. "What?"

"It's going to rain," he clarified in blunt prose. "And we'll—"

"Develop pneumonia," she inserted a little wearily.

"No," he said, offended that she would assume he was thinking such a thing (even though he had been). "I was *going* to say that we'll have to race back to the house."

"I'm sure you'll survive," Amelia told him, although her attention was veering again to the shrub. "I've watched you run across Mayfair to get the Duke of Bedford's clock before Professor Murkle did."

"That was sprinting. I'm not made for going the distance."

"How honest of a man to admit such a thing," she remarked dryly.

Caleb's jaw dropped. He demanded a smart comeback from his brain, but all the fresh air had emptied it of wit. Amelia smiled a little triumphantly, then squatted down to brush at the ground beneath the hydrangea shrub.

"It looks like someone's been digging here," she said.

"Be careful."

"Thaumaturgic minerals aren't usually close to the surface," she assured him. "I'm not going to make anything explode."

"I meant, be careful of breaking a fingernail," he said. Squatting beside her, he peered at the ground. "It was probably just some animal."

"No, listen." She paused, her head tilted to the side. "Can you hear it? Ticking."

Caleb did indeed hear a faint mechanical clicking from within the ground, and his pulse shouted in answer. When Amelia started to dig, he caught her hand, pulling it away from the dirt to set it on her thigh.

"Cale—" she began chidingly.

"Sh," he said, and continued the work himself. Amelia went quiet, watching him, and Caleb felt all tingly at the realization that he'd actually charmed her with his mediocre heroism. Immediately increasing his efforts so as to appear even more impressive, he soon felt something cold and smooth beneath his fingers.

"What the . . . ?" he murmured, and with some tugging, some ruination of an expensive manicure, he pulled a small circular object from the ground. It fit in his palm, ticking with all the contentment of a cat come in from the weather.

"It's a pocket watch," Amelia said, taking it from him.

"I can see that," he said, taking it back. They stood, and Caleb turned the watch over in his hand, brushing dirt from the gold case to reveal an etching of a double-headed eagle inlaid with what appeared to be rubies.

"Didn't Sir Nigel say something about owning Peter the Great's pocket watch?" Amelia asked, running a fingertip over the design. Caleb tingled as if it were his bare skin that she'd stroked.

"God knows. I stopped listening to the man several days ago." He turned the watch over again, noting further details. "I would guess a Russian provenance myself, but Dummersby could probably say better on the subject. I can confirm, though, that it's magical."

"On what evidence?" Amelia asked.

He raised his eyebrows at her. "You mean apart from the summer flowers above its burial site? And the fact the ground is now glowing blue?"

Looking down, Amelia grimaced with alarm. Without further discussion, they beat a cautious retreat to the nearby oak tree. Beneath the shelter of its vibrant autumnal foliage, Amelia once again took the pocket watch from Caleb, opening the case to inspect its interior.

"Gilt champlevé," she reported. "The hands are not moving, despite the tick."

"That'll be thaumaturgic discharge," Caleb said.

"Could this be what caused the temporal disruption the other day, when I got caught in a pocket of memories, rather than the teaspoon?"

"From all the way out here?" Caleb shook his head. "Unlikely. Nevertheless, let's not mess around with it. If there's going to be an explosion, I want it to happen in Throckmorton's vicinity." Retrieving the watch from her and closing its case with a snap, he slipped it into his trouser pocket.

"I wonder how such a valuable piece came to be buried in a field," Amelia mused.

"Maybe it ran away from Sir Nigel to get a little peace and quiet."

Ignoring this brilliant witticism, Amelia frowned at his pocket as if she were still regarding the watch within it. "Do you think it's the cause of all the nature anomalies out here?"

"Uh," was the best Caleb could say, on the grounds that his respiratory system had suspended operations in response to her gaze being focused right *there*. His pulse stepped into the breach by working double time, and for an interesting moment he seriously contemplated fainting, the benefit of which being that Amelia might attempt to resuscitate him. But one glance at the dirty, root-gnarled ground advised against this, and Caleb told himself to man up (*not literally, please,* he added with considerable urgency to his body).

"Let's go back to the house," he said.

Amelia looked at him with mild concern. "Are you all right? Your voice sounds a little rough. I really don't want you to catch a cold, you know. We should have remembered to wear coats." Stepping closer to him, she began fussing with his shirt buttons, intent on closing the upper two as if that would warm him up and protect him from the evening's weather. And as a scheme, it did work, although not for the reasons she supposed.

"Amelia. Sweetheart." Caleb clamped his hands over hers,

which stopped the buttoning up, but at the same time had the effect of pressing her fingers against the base of his throat, where a hard, hot pulse throbbed for her.

"Oh," she said, obviously comprehending the truth, clever woman that she was. Caleb waited, helpless, for her to step away from him and tidy the situation until they were both professional and polite once again. But she did not. She lowered her hands, and his along with them, holding them instead against his heart. Then she bent her head and kissed him so, so gently upon that vulnerable place above his collar, like a fairy bestowing a wish.

Caleb closed his eyes, sinking into the beautiful sensation of her lips against his skin. People asked him sometimes why he'd chosen to become a historian specializing in antiques, and he always answered with a crooked smile, "Because of magic." And it was true. Because of *her*. She was his magic; she had enchanted his life from the moment he first met her. One smile from her and the day brightened. One touch of her finger transported him into a dream. And one slow, soft kiss at his throat sent glitter cascading through his entire body, like the atoms of poems, or the stars that waited just behind Cumbria's sunset and now seemed to light within him instead.

When she eased back, Caleb released one of his hands from her gentle clasp so he could catch her chin gently between his thumb and forefinger, tilting it until she met his silent gaze. They stood like that for a timeless moment, and then somehow, with that strange force that worked between them lately, their own private gravity, they were kissing. Long, warm kissing, while the wind sang through oak leaves and the sky burned with delight. It was as sweet as a fairy tale. At least for a while.

Slowly, it darkened. The warmth became a smoldering heat that made them restless, breaking the kiss, staring a little wild at each other while their hands moved instead. At Caleb's waist, trouser fastenings opened beneath Amelia's nimble fingers. Her skirts rustled as he lifted them. (Then her drawers rustled some more—*good God*, he thought rather impatiently, it was like trying to break into a headmaster's office.) He moaned as she slid her hand beneath his underwear. She gasped as he did the same.

And then they were grinning, like a pair of youths thrilled to find themselves playing a daring new game. Amelia giggled—her eyes widened at the sound—and before her brain could start analyzing the situation and bringing in reinforcements for her good senses, Caleb hurriedly cupped his free hand against the back of her head and kissed her thoroughly, deeply, in the best argument he could make against rational behavior. Meanwhile, his fingers provided extensive supplementary clauses.

And he must have persuaded her, for she drew his own supplementary clause out from his trousers, and she created an irrefutable counterargument with her touch. Caleb felt then the aching joys and dizzy raptures that Wordsworth had experienced too in Cumbria (although almost certainly not for the same reason). They made him want, with all his heart and soul, to ensure Amelia felt them also. He watched her face closely as his fingers experimented, and his heart swelled with every tremor of her eyelashes, every stumbling breath. His pleasure wove through her pleasure and back again, binding them together in new ways, adding texture to the gloss of their friendship. Amelia began to blush redder, her eyes shining brighter, and Caleb desperately controlled himself so that she would

reach the pinnacle before he did. Never before had he attempted an endeavor more difficult. He felt like he would
come just looking at her.

And then—and then—

"Professors!"

At the distant call . . . but nowhere near distant enough . . .
Caleb and Amelia froze, staring at each other in horror. Then
all at once they were moving—hands withdrawing, skirts lowering, things being returned to place. Caleb peered around the
oak's trunk while he buttoned his trousers and saw two figures
out with lanterns, evidently searching for them. He was willing to bet neither was a poet, but also could not believe that
anyone in the house had been so concerned as to dispatch servants to the rescue.

"Did they see us?" Amelia asked tautly.

"Professors!" came the call again.

"Apparently not," Caleb said. He gave her a weary, regretful
look, and she smiled a little sadly in response.

"It's for the best," she told him. "Those clouds look like rain.
We'd have got wet."

"Hm," Caleb murmured darkly. But Amelia was too busy
attacking invisible creases on her skirts to notice the ribald
insinuation, and Caleb had to acknowledge that the mood for
teasing—or for anything interesting at all—had well and truly
passed. "Let's get back, then," he said.

"Let's," she agreed.

Their fingers, warm, damp, met briefly, like a conversation
they otherwise dared not have. Then they relinquished even
that and left the tree's shelter, allowing themselves to be found
by footmen who, surprisingly, had been sent by Lady Ruperta.
Two shillings got them safely back to Ravenscroft Manor,

where the lady herself met them in the entrance hall, looking so formidable Caleb wondered if they were about to be evicted.

"You must not wander around outside!" she remonstrated.

Caleb and Amelia waited for her to explain that doing so was dangerous, or that it distracted her staff, or that she feared they would expire from a chill. But the only thing furthered was her angry frown.

"We apologize," Caleb said with a polite bow of his head.

"Hm," Lady Ruperta replied, which managed to convey in its brusque syllable how much she disliked them and how dearly she wanted them gone, but alas how she was forced to tolerate their presence until they'd rid her house of its junk. For a moment all three stood in grim silence, contemplating the certainty of them being in each other's company for quite some time yet, considering how many trinkets and artworks still awaited assessment in the entrance hall around them. Then Caleb brought out the pocket watch.

"We found this," he said, handing it to Lady Ruperta. She backed away, looking aghast.

"What was that doing outside?" Her voice was so rigid, it sounded like it might crack at any moment. "Sir Nigel is going to be furious." Whipping around, she glared at the nearest footman. "Are you responsible for this?"

"Yes, ma'am," he replied at once. And then his eyes seemed to lose focus, as if he were catching up with his words. "I—I—took it—uh—"

"Dreadful behavior!" Lady Ruperta interrupted him, the very picture of aristocratic outrage (which is the same as everyone else's outrage, except that the clutched pearls are real). "Go at once and make me some tea! As for *you*—" She turned her glare to Caleb and Amelia. "Stay indoors, if you please. One would hope you'll concentrate on your work so it might *eventually* be concluded."

She swept away, and Caleb and Amelia exchanged the same grimace—abashed yet relieved—that they'd expressed after various close calls with authority figures in the past, from Ottersock to the groundskeeper who'd found them behind the dormitory, the first day they met, and had suspected them of that ultimate crime: playing with marbles during school hours. Without further discussion beyond a brush of hands that was more eloquent than a Shakespeare sonnet, they hurried to wash and change for dinner.

At the table, Sir Nigel was delighted to be reunited with his pocket watch, and rambled on from the fish entree to the custard pudding about its various features. Caleb tuned him out. He had more important things to do than listen; namely, glancing repeatedly at Amelia through the thicket of serving dishes and hothouse flowers, no matter how unwise that might be. She, for her part, was more restrained. Nothing existed in her countenance but calm, good manners. Caleb began to question his memory as to whether she really had blushed like wild roses, just one hour earlier, while his fingers glided through her most private place. It was as though magic had never happened, only the purposeless tick of an old watch.

And so things went on, same as before. And perhaps Sir Nigel's antiques had broken time as Vanity feared they might, so that each day echoed the others, trapping Caleb and Amelia interminably in their secrets, until Caleb began to believe he would never see the sunlight of London again, its loveliness a dreamy faint blur of gold behind the city's smog.

Chapter Seventeen

Most important historic decisions were made in the one
place we can never access: the depths of a person's heart.

I, on the Past, Cornelius Ottersock

Thursday afternoon decayed with a sullen, creeping
slowness into grim shadow. A storm that had raged all day
finally dissipated, leaving only a mild breeze like a ghost. The
quiet felt sinister. A few lingering raindrops weeping from the
ancient stone eyes of Ravenscroft's gargoyles sounded like a
countdown when they splashed against the ground below, as if
the atmosphere might soon explode.

Caleb drifted through the manor with a semblance of mel-
ancholia to disguise the fact that he'd managed to get lost
looking for the drawing room. It was there that the company
were to meet for a little pre-dinner gathering Lady Ruperta
had arranged, according to the butler, Grimshaw, who'd announced the fact like one announced the date of a funeral—
lugubriously, but with a promise of drinks and snacks. They
were ostensibly celebrating yet another room of antiques having been assessed and cataloged, and Caleb suspected that
Lady Ruperta was hoping the event would serve as a farewell
for the academics. He hoped the same. Either way, after this

interminable assignment, he was seriously looking forward to a dab of expensive pâté on a minuscule cracker. And several glasses of wine.

Mind you, that would be meager solace in the face of not having been able to touch Amelia these past days. During their first week at the manor, Caleb had feared his health would suffer from not being able to mingle his fingers with hers, brush back her hair, or pretend to remove lint from her shirtwaist. But now, he knew real suffering. The places where she'd stroked him ached with a desperate longing that not even his own hand could assuage. The loneliness of his lips made him want to cry out. Were it not for the volume of Keats's poetry he'd brought with him, he'd probably not have survived.

And now he could not find his way. It was altogether tragic. By the time he eventually reached the drawing room, most of the food and the best subjects of conversation would be taken. And romanticizing the experience of being lost only worked until you accepted that you really *were* lost. Opening a door to reveal yet another unoccupied room, Caleb resigned himself to starvation and wandered in.

Incredibly, the room, although large, was empty but for a dusty velvet chaise lounge and a grand piano that appeared to be made of oak and diaphanous light. Not a single antique blighted the view. Caleb perked up slightly. Walking across just for the pleasure of not having to wind a path through stacked books, boxes of dishware, and statuary, he lifted the piano's fallboard and gazed down at the keys. They were spotless, as if this were the sole item in the house that someone cared to clean.

His hand hovered over the keys, hesitant. It was a strong

hand, pale from a career spent indoors, but somehow in this moment, against the piano's ivory perfection, he could see the ghosts of scratches all over it, black with dirt from the stable filth he'd handled every day as a child, scraping horseshit from corners a broom couldn't easily reach, just to earn a penny.

These days he kept the nails manicured, the hands safe and comfortable in his pockets as often as he could, although good society deplored such a habit. And actually, most of the time he forgot those old grim days. Touching Amelia helped. She was his balm. But the piano keys daunted him just a little. Of course he would not besmirch them if he reached for music, and yet . . .

Laying his right hand so gently on the keys they made no sound, he took a deep breath, then shifted his gaze to the nearby window. Outside, the early evening countryside was more beautiful than a landscape painting in a museum. Trees smoldered with autumn colors against the dimming light. The sky was polluted by nothing worse than a cloud wandering lonely. Looking out at such countryside, a man might suppose he'd never enjoy the comforts of civilization again. He'd become a rustic, with soiled shoes and a dire lack of good-quality starch for his shirt collars. He'd grow so bored, he'd take to chewing books for entertainment. If, that is, he didn't fade away into spectral semi-existence from handling too many thaumaturgic antiques.

Or perish outright from his longing to kiss Amelia just one more time.

But Caleb knew what to do with unpleasant thoughts. He was expert at it, and expended little mental energy in burying them within a coffin of self-mockery. Then donning a pensive smile like a man about to have his portrait taken, he looked down once more to the piano's keys and, with his right hand, played a slow, quiet tune.

"*Oh, my,*" came a woman's voice from behind him. Glancing over his shoulder, expecting to see Amelia, Caleb was disappointed to find instead Lady Ruperta standing beside the chaise lounge. She clutched the rim of its curved mahogany back as if fearing she might faint.

To be fair, Caleb's music tended to do that to people.

How the woman had entered the room and crossed the parquet floor to the chaise without Caleb having heard her, he did not know. She'd added to her usual funereal ensemble a black lace shawl that did little to ease the impression of chill about her, and a ruby brooch was affixed to her throat (or, more precisely—and less painfully—to a black ribbon around her throat) like a drop of blood. But her eyes were oddly bright, and a few strands of hair had gone awry in her coiffure, as if she'd been out in the breeze, or at least standing at an open window frowning with disapproval at the breeze. She directed that frown now at Caleb, and it was plain she still held a grudge about the dining table's destruction, which seemed rather unreasonable considering it had happened more than a week ago.

Unworried, Caleb smiled at her, his charm engaging automatically. "Forgive me for playing your piano," he said. "I can never resist, when I see one."

Lady Ruperta's visage became so arch, it could have served as a war memorial. "But you clearly can," she replied, "since it is evident you've never taken a lesson."

Caleb laughed. "Lessons would be far too tedious. I just enjoy the chance to look sensitive and sentimental."

Amusement tugged at Lady Ruperta's lips, then vanished

again so quickly, it would have given a lesser man whiplash to see it. But Caleb was well used to people annoying themselves by finding him delightful. After all, he'd mastered adorableness when he was a child, it having been an essential survival skill.

Assessing Lady Ruperta thoughtfully—although she'd never have guessed it from the sweetly pleasant look on his face—he perceived very little danger to him, and conversely, a wealth of opportunity to win her over. With an hour and the effort of a few smiles, Caleb felt sure he'd have her willing to subsidize any goal he chose to name.

It was easy to decide what he wanted from her. "Allow me to beg your forgiveness," he said. Lady Ruperta's eyes narrowed—she'd obviously met shysters before and possessed good defenses of mistrust and disdain. But they would be no better than paper against Caleb. Even in just an open-collared shirt and trousers, no expensive gold cuff link or silk tie in sight, he could impress this woman. "You seem like a generous soul," he lied. And sliding his hands into his trouser pockets, he leaned against the piano at an angle that took him a delightful inch past *indolent* into *mellow*.

Lady Ruperta swallowed rather heavily, and Caleb knew he'd hooked her. Now to begin reeling her in until she provided some way to get him and Amelia out of this assignment and on a train back to civilization. He let his smile deepen into one of sympathy and kindness. "Even so, you must be tired of having so many people in your home," he said.

And then she bamboozled him utterly. "I am tired of more than you could ever imagine, young man," she replied.

Caleb was able to do no more than blink at her, his smile frozen. The hauteur had not eased from her face, but he knew enough about pain to see it in the corners of her eyes and in the way her mouth moved with a habit of tightness, of speaking too few joyful words. She gave him a look so penetrating, he felt shaken to a degree he'd not for many years, his own defenses usually being excellent. His smile broke.

"Judging from the look on your face right now, perhaps you *could* imagine it," Lady Ruperta said musingly. "And yet, how fortunate you are, Professor. You can put down history and walk away from it anytime you like."

"Only if you mean antiques," Caleb found himself saying before he could run it through his charm filter.

Lady Ruperta's mouth twisted as if she felt pity but was resisting it. "Are you married?"

He shook his head.

"I didn't think so. Come back to me with your ideas about history, material or otherwise, when you've been wed half as long as I. Now kindly leave the room. Your *associates*"—she said the word in the way someone else would say *plebs*, and Caleb abruptly lost all sympathy for her—"are in the Mauve Drawing Room down the hall."

She did not indicate the way, or indeed move the slightest muscle, and it remained only for Caleb to offer a polite nod and silently make his exit. He felt oddly soiled and wanted to go at once for a bath, to scrub old memories from his skin until he was renewed. Instead, slipping a casual smile onto his face, he stepped out into the corridor.

And collided with a perambulating red-and-white barber's pole. Only upon being thwacked in the face with a topknot of hair did he realize it was in fact Vanity. The young woman gasped so ostentatiously, Caleb suspected she'd not bumped into him but actually pounced.

"Oh, Professor Sterling!" she squeaked and giggled, and Caleb discovered that he was capable of genuine chivalry when he stopped himself from wincing. "Fancy meeting you here!"

"Uh-huh," he said.

"Are you on your way to drinkies? Shall we go together?"

Caleb would rather leap off a cliff than accompany anyone who used the word *drinkies*, but it was too late: Vanity had her arm hooked around his and was practically dragging him down the corridor. *Oh well*, he thought, surrendering to his fate; *at least I won't get lost with her.*

AMELIA HAD TUCKED herself into a corner of the drawing room with her back against the wall, as physically far from the crowd as she could manage, and several hundred years away mentally, musing about how Queen Elizabeth Woodville might have occupied her time in sanctuary during the Wars of the Roses. Amelia rather envied the beleaguered queen that respite from society.

Of course, the four men occupying the drawing room (and an undetermined number of servants) could not really be called a crowd . . . No, *rabble* was a better descriptor. *Throng. MULTITUDE*. And definitely the capital letters were justified. The two academics were debating the Duke of Wellington's scandalous life ("Publish!" Dummersby contended; "Be damned!" Throckmorton rebutted) while Sir Nigel tried to make verbal sallies into the discussion, only to fail each time. His voice was approaching heights that would surely soon render him breathless. Even Sergeant Sheffield's presence added to the sense of overwhelm, for Amelia couldn't help but fret a little about what exactly the man was thinking as he loomed in silence, a glass of sherry looking ridiculously fragile in his grip. One flex of the fingers and he might shatter it.

Vanity had yet to make an appearance, for which Amelia could only be grateful. Such a cheerful young woman, sweetly innocent, and unutterably annoying. If her giggles were added to the present commotion, it would quite possibly break Amelia's sanity. This assignment had been a case study in frustration, but over the past couple of days she'd felt as if everything within her had been pushed right to the edge.

If only Caleb was able to touch her one more time and thus provide the sense of completion for which her body yearned, she might ease back into her usual Tarrant centeredness. Just a single gentle touch, in an interesting place, for an extended period of time. With motion applied. And associated kisses.

But surrounded as they were through the day by company, and with the perils of being caught together at night remaining too great, the impossibility of such a thing happening had left Amelia suffering to a degree not even her imagination could assuage.

Surely soon Lady Ruperta and Sir Nigel would declare that enough antiques had been assessed. Already the wagon in the stables was packed high with items of assorted value, awaiting transport to the Staveley train station and then on to the British Museum. Sir Nigel was in a near-constant state of mournful sniffling. And Dummersby was even beginning to look concerned as to the capacity of the museum's display space. It all suggested that an announcement of their departure might happen at any time. *Such as now,* Amelia thought, holding her breath . . . But the chatter in the room went on. *Or maybe now,* she thought . . . But Lady Ruperta did not enter. Sighing, Amelia lost hope that she would.

Caleb's lack of attendance, however, was another matter.

His tardiness was par for the course, but considering all the dangerous magical antiques and obstreperous ghosts in the manor, Amelia worried that he'd fallen down several centuries or into a cannibalistic bathtub. She tried to deflect her concerns by imagining those of Queen Elizabeth Woodville instead, but with no success. Gripping a tiny plate of hors d'oeuvres that contained far too much sardine matter to actually eat, she kept her eye on the drawing room door.

Where are you, Caleb?

Suddenly, the door opened! But it admitted only Grimshaw, casting a pall over the gathering. "Dinner is served," he announced.

The men began trooping out. But Amelia paused in the doorway, feeling more troubled than she could explain.

"Mr. Grimshaw, have you seen Professor Sterling this evening?" she asked.

"Yes, ma'am," the butler intoned lugubriously. "He and Miss Tunnicliffe went upstairs. Together. Privately."

Oh.

Amelia went from history to geography in one wild leap as memories of Caleb kissing her were crushed by what felt like an enormous boulder dropping into her stomach, their fragments turning to ash in the veritable forest fire blazing across her cheeks.

Half a second later, however, she was rescued by reasonable thinking and her faith in her best friend. Caleb might read poetry, but he wouldn't caress one woman under a tree, then mere days later take another to his bed.

"It was just the pair of them," continued the butler, fitting out a coffin in which to place his murder victim, i.e., Vanity's reputation.

"I'm sure they are involved in academic business," Amelia told him sternly. "I shall go up to let them know dinner is ready."

"I'll have a footman accompany you."

"That is not necessary," Amelia assured him, but Grimshaw had already summoned one of the servants. Thus encumbered, Amelia headed up to Caleb's bedroom, with every step urgently trying to decide how she could fix this situation without causing embarrassment to poor Vanity.

But upon arriving at the bedroom, Amelia took one look at the sight that met her there and discarded any thought of kindness. "Good God!" she exclaimed.

"Mmphm!" Caleb interjected from where he sat bound to a wooden chair, gagged with a handkerchief. All around him was a horrifying mess of clothes, bedding, and—Amelia gasped—her Mary Wollstonecraft biography lying open on the floor, several of its pages folded! At the far side of the room, Vanity was pushing open the window. The young woman turned, raising a furled parasol like a weapon.

"Oh, it's only you," she said with a sharp smile. "Hello, Miss Tarrant."

Ignoring these insults, Amelia crossed her arms and frowned, as if Vanity were one of her students. "What is going on here?" she demanded.

But Vanity just laughed, which no student would ever dare do. Amelia's blood went cold. It was a gritty, confident laugh, the kind that would have stomped on a giggle, turning it to glittery dust. "That's a stupid question from such an educated woman. Obviously, I'm stealing your seventeenth-century thaumaturgic teaspoon."

"Mmmph!" Caleb protested, rocking the chair beneath him as he tried to escape. But Amelia just quirked an eyebrow.

"Stealing, Miss Tunnicliffe? I know the salary of a receptionist must be low, but—"

Vanity interrupted her, scoffing. "I'm richer than you'll ever be. The receptionist job was just a cover."

All at once, Amelia understood. Vanity's crimes were far worse than making everyone play charades. "You're a trafficker for the black market."

"'Facilitator in the covert trade of thaumaturgic antiques,' if you please," Vanity corrected her archly. "When I heard about Sir Nigel's hoard, I decided to hitch a ride on this assignment. But then I saw you with this at the Staveley pub." Producing from a skirt pocket Caleb's Italian-milled sock, stuffed with the enchanted little spoon in its safe bag, she waggled it provokingly. "It took me a while to get hold of it—and when I finally did, I dropped the blasted thing in the drawing room and you stepped on it. You realized what it was before I could retrieve it, and I was stuck in this bloody cursed place for longer. I *had* to resort to robbing the pretty professor or else go crazy. But it was worth it. Forget singing tankards and flaming sauceboats—this one teaspoon is far more valuable than all the treasures in the house."

Amelia managed to remain calm in the face of such an appalling revelation, despite ~~her future bestselling book about the teaspoon~~ Caleb being in harm's way. "It's just an old spoon with a highly unstable thaumaturgic profile," she said. "It won't get you much on the black market."

"Oh, I don't plan to sell *this*," Vanity answered, sneering. "I know it brought down the Minervaeum Club's ceiling. Professor

Sterling has been most informative. A few giggles, a winsome interest in getting an education"—she fluttered her eyelashes, looking so earnest that Amelia, despite everything, felt an instinctual desire to hand her brochures on Oxford University's history courses—"and he told me everything I wanted to know. If it can break a ceiling, it can break through barriers to something *really* valuable."

"You're going to rob a bank using a teaspoon?" Amelia's eyebrow longed to quirk again, but she repressed it with a frown.

"Not a bank," Vanity retorted. "Dervgilly of Glasgow's magic brooch."

"Dervorguilla of Galloway," Amelia corrected her automatically. Then the import of what the woman had said struck her. She became the kind of calm that generally only happens before a storm.

"The most powerful antique in England," Vanity went on. "Never mind the black market—*governments* will pay me for something like that. I know you think I'm stupid, Professor. So did the staff at the British Museum. I meant you all to. But I'm bloody sick of acting like a daft girl."

"You're clearly not daft," Amelia said. "A woman of your intelligence and ambition ought not to waste herself in a life of crime. Get an education instead! Attend university, obtain a master's degree, take on a junior role in a small, local museum, learn the ropes while dusting and making cups of tea, then after a mere seven or eight years you could become a very fine curator."

Vanity laughed. "I feel sorry for you, Professor. You think you're so liberated, but the truth is, although men might have allowed 'the fairer sex' into their universities, the whole education system is misogynistic."

"It is—" Amelia began, but her brain worked faster than her voice, and the intended "not" dissolved in her throat. How could she rebut Vanity when all of Oxford's history courses showcased the lives of men, relegating women to bit parts as their wives? Even the great warrior queens like Isabella of France and Eleanor of Aquitaine earned no more than fifteen minutes in a lecture. Queen Elizabeth alone was highlighted, being impossible to ignore, and the fact that she'd acknowledged herself a weak and feeble woman with the heart of a king went a long way in her favor.

"Besides," Vanity continued as Amelia's sensibilities reeled, "why should I bother with an education when I can just wave a teaspoon and make all my wishes come true?"

And just like that, Amelia returned to solid moral ground. "You must not wield that teaspoon in Balliol College. It's not stable; people could get seriously hurt. Besides, if you don't want an education, there are still so many opportunities for enterprising women these days that don't require breaking the law. I can give you the names of some support organizations that might prove of inter—"

"Don't try to *fix* things for me!" Vanity shouted, her eyes flashing. "I don't want or need it!" Shoving the sock with its dangerous cargo back into her skirt pocket, she climbed onto the windowsill and opened her parasol.

"No!" Amelia cried, holding out her hand as if that might stop the woman. But it was too late. With a witchy cackle, Vanity jumped.

Amelia ran to the window, heart pounding. The ground

was, after all, a considerable distance below, and neither youthful self-confidence nor melodramatic villainy would abbreviate that distance. Vanity did not deserve to die for her various crimes (although tying Caleb up warranted several years in jail).

What she saw made her stomach lurch. Vanity's parasol hadn't slowed her fall. No, it had carried her away across the manor's courtyard and toward the fields in the direction of Staveley, rotor blades spinning above the canopy.

"Helicopter parasol!" Amelia exclaimed. "By Jove! We'll never catch her!"

"Mmmph!" Caleb demanded, rocking so forcefully on the chair that he almost tipped over. With one final scowl at Vanity's departing form, Amelia turned to help him.

The moment he was freed from the rope Vanity had used to bind him, Caleb removed the handkerchief from his mouth and spluttered, grimacing and rubbing the back of his wrist against his lips. "My God, couldn't she have used a linen cloth instead of cheap cotton?" Rising from the chair, he turned to the footman who still lingered in the doorway, looking rather bored. "Why are you just standing there? We need some help!"

"Ahem." The footman coughed discreetly against his fist.

"I don't have any bloody money left!" Caleb shouted at him. "This place has been more expensive than a five-star London hotel!"

"Take this." Snatching up a pair of cuff links from the dressing table, Amelia tossed them to the footman with blithe disregard for Caleb's protesting gasps. "Please go and set up two horses—"

"Saddle two horses?" the footman suggested confusedly.

"Yes. That." She flapped a hand at him in a manner saved

from rudeness by the fact of the cuff links being sterling silver. "We'll be right down."

The man dashed off, leaving Amelia and Caleb staring aghast at each other.

"Well, this is a spot of bother," Amelia said (and which may be translated from British English as *it's a complete disaster!*).

"I'm sorry." Wearily brushing back the hair that had tumbled over his brow, Caleb looked around at the mess in the room. "I wouldn't tell her where the teaspoon was, so she ransacked the place and eventually found it. She had a gun, Meely."

Amelia's pulse thundered. Stepping closer, she wrapped her arms around him, holding him tight against her heart. "You're safe now," she assured them both. "You're safe."

"I'm safe," he agreed. "Everything's okay." But his fingers clutched her blouse as if she were all that kept him from running. He'd sometimes told her stories about gang wars in the rookery, and men shooting each other behind the stables where he worked, and how the fear of it had echoed through his dreams for years afterward. She had her own memories, come to that, although far less awful than his: refusing to attend game-shooting parties with her family and their friends, but still hearing the crack of rifle shots ringing out from the fields, seeing the results served up at dinner, and knowing she could not cry, not for such an ordinary, everyday British thing. Stroking Caleb's hair, murmuring sounds of comfort, she rocked them both gently, and after a little while Caleb tilted his head against hers, sighing.

"Well, it's not *okay* okay," he said, "since Vanity has stolen the teaspoon. The bloody thing is a bomb waiting to happen."

"Not to mention that it seems to have temporal disturbance

powers," Amelia added. "If the girl isn't careful, she'll experience time breaking apart just as she feared."

"Bloody hell. And that's even before she gets her hands on Dervorguilla's brooch. We need to catch her, Amelia."

"We will," Amelia answered, feeling her nervous system clicking into Efficiency Mode as she spoke. Never mind that Vanity was probably halfway to Staveley now, thanks to her helicopter parasol. Such a complication only made the situation more invigorating. They couldn't possibly catch up to her—and yet, somehow, they would. They'd solve the problem, save the world (or, at least, Balliol College, which was almost the same thing), and get her teaspoon back.

For the first time in far too long, Amelia felt like herself again.

A faint ghost of a thought knocked against a window in her mind, begging to be let in, and for just a second she frowned, sensing that she'd forgotten something, or missed an important point. But that seemed unlikely, for if it were *truly* important, her well-trained intelligence would have remembered it. Stepping back from Caleb, she pointed a finger at him, then at the pile of clothing. "Put on a jumper and coat," she instructed. "It's going to be cold outside. Then run downstairs and tell the others what has happened. Dummersby needs to check that the boxes packed for the museum are all still there. She might have stolen more things. I'm going to have Grimshaw send someone to the village with a telegram for the Home Office. I'll meet you at the stables."

"Yes, ma'am," Caleb said with a salute and a crooked grin, and Amelia felt warm little flutters beneath her heart at the sight of him teasing her again, his eyes humor-bright and no longer haunted by memories. She mentally checked that item off her to-do list. Then, giving him a quick, censorious frown like a kiss, she dashed away to her own bedroom.

Exchanging her shoes for a sturdier pair, she donned a cardigan, over which she layered her coat. This wouldn't protect her enough against the chill of the autumn evening, but she anticipated being back indoors soon, with the teaspoon once more in her possession and Vanity Tunnicliffe secured in Staveley's jail. After all, she'd become a liberal arts student in defiance of her family's will, and she'd made several pipe-smoking, tut-tutting senior professors apologize and admit that girls were smart after all. She was a Capable Woman. By the end of this day, Vanity Tunnicliffe would be regretting her poor choices.

Amelia was about to fix things.

CHAPTER EIGHTEEN

Chivalry did not die, it was murdered.
I, on the Past, Cornelius Ottersock

THERE WAS ONLY one horse. Caleb accepted this without complaint, but Amelia worried that the poor creature would be overburdened by having both of them on its back. Moreover, considering that neither she nor Caleb had ridden since high school, when trotting around a yard on ponies a few times was deemed part of their essential education, sharing a horse seemed not only ridiculously clichéd but also a strategy for disaster.

"Sorry, miss," the footman told her when she tried offering money for a second steed. "It's all we've got."

"Thanks," Caleb said, smiling at the horse and patting its neck. "Any idea when the next train goes through Staveley?"

"There's one at seven," the footman said. "You've only got half an hour to catch it, though, and there isn't another until morning."

"We'll gallop," Caleb told him.

The footman shook his head worriedly. "It'll be dark soon. And there's rain coming."

"Then we'll get wet," Caleb said.

"You might develop pneumonia," the footman persisted, apparently dedicated to maintaining Ravenscroft Manor's miserable gothic atmosphere.

"We'll be fine," Caleb assured him—or perhaps disappointed him, judging from his expression—then turned to help Amelia into the saddle. But just at that moment, Sergeant Sheffield jogged up. He was rather more breathless than a professional soldier ought to have been after such brief exercise, and his eyes seemed wild.

"You have to stop!" he urged, holding up a hand like some kind of traffic controller as he staggered to a halt.

Amelia stared in astonishment. This was the first she'd heard him speak, and his reedy, high-pitched voice so contradicted her imagination that she could not summon a word in reply.

"What's the matter?" Caleb asked. "Did something explode again? Please say it was Throckmorton's pipe."

"Caleb," Amelia murmured. They had a thief to apprehend and a college to save; this was no time for jesting. And evidently Sergeant Sheffield agreed with her, for he produced a pistol from beneath his coat and, gripping it in both hands (which was a lot more frightening than with just one), he pointed it directly at Caleb.

"I have urgent business and I need that horse. Stand aside or I'll make it so you can't stand at all."

"Oh God, not again," Caleb groaned. "Why are people being so mean to me today?" He stepped protectively in front of Amelia, which was swooningly gallant of him—but unfortunately she also stepped protectively in front of him at the same time, and they collided. There followed a brief tangle of limbs as they each strove to get ahead of the other, stopping only when Sheffield discharged his pistol into the air. The horse startled, almost tugging its reins from the footman's grip, but Amelia and Caleb immediately froze, clutching each other.

"*Et tu*, Sheffield?" Caleb said with dismay.

"No, I haven't *et*," the sergeant retorted. "And why the bloody hell do you care about my dinner? Stand back, I say!"

Amelia and Caleb (and the footman) obeyed, for there is no wisdom in arguing with a man who doesn't understand basic Latin. Swinging up on the horse, Sheffield galloped away into the deepening twilight—leaving them in, alas, not a cloud of his dust but instead spattered with mud, thanks to all the recent rain.

"Damn that man!" Caleb shouted furiously. "My Savile Row trousers!"

"My *teaspoon*," Amelia countered.

"What kind of urgent business would he have out here, at this hour?"

Amelia shook her head with something very close to frazzlement. "I don't know and there's no time to discuss it." She turned urgently to the footman. "We need another horse."

"We could borrow one from a neighbor," the footman replied with a shrug. "But that would take about an hour. You're doomed, I'm afraid."

"No, we simply must run," Amelia said resolutely. Her brain knew this was a daft idea, considering the distance that must be covered while wearing a long skirt (her) and expensively inadequate shoes (Caleb). Her lungs cowered at the pain they knew was to come. But her heart was full of determination. She taught university students; she could do *anything*!

"Well then, cut across the fields to the road," the footman

advised, pointing the way. "And remember, it's not the thief you're racing but the train. If you get to Staveley before it, you'll have time to catch her."

Amelia marveled at this excellent advice but feared telling him so in case he demanded her pearl earrings in payment. Settling for just a grateful nod, she turned to Caleb.

"Ready?"

Abandoning a futile effort to brush clean his trousers, he met her eyes with the cool professionalism that overtook him in extreme situations like this. "Let's go," he said.

They began to run.

Five minutes later, they slowed to a jog.

Three minutes after that, they were walking. Caleb's pulse beat hard, but he could have continued jogging easily enough (or so he told himself). Amelia, however, was stumbling on every pebble and clump of grass at his side, and he had no intention of leaving her alone out here in the wilds, vulnerable to every passing feral dog or vampire. Eventually she stopped altogether, breathing heavily and clutching her side with a pained expression. "Go ahead without me," she urged. "I'll catch up."

Caleb did not bother answering such brave nonsense. He stopped too, rubbing her back as he frowned through the darkening field to the road, which still seemed an inordinate distance away. "We should have got there by now," he said, turning to judge how far they'd come. His frown deepened, and not only from the stress of trying to do math.

"Amelia," he said with a calm that sounded as cold as the

sensation creeping through his blood. "Look." He pointed behind her.

Amelia glanced over her shoulder, then abruptly stiffened with alarm. She turned slowly to stare back across the field to Ravenscroft Manor. The house wasn't hard to miss, considering it stood no more than one hundred yards away, an ominous bulk looming against the storm-colored evening sky like a troll who had been watching with amusement as they tried to escape its clutches. Several of the lamplit windows winked at them. Smoke fumed from chimneys, and the gargoyles sneered.

"Oh dear," Amelia said.

"That's one way of putting it," Caleb countered grimly. He himself could think of several words that would be more eloquent. "I'm no athlete, but I know it doesn't take me ten minutes to go such a short distance, even in dress shoes. We're magicked."

Without further discussion, Amelia strode toward the house with the attitude of a one-woman army intent on storming it. But after half a dozen steps she abruptly stopped, staggering. Caleb's muscles automatically tensed to catch her if she fell, although she was in fact too far away for him to do so. Steadying herself, she reached out, slapping at the air experimentally.

"Ow!" she yelped, snatching back her hand and shaking it with pain.

Striding to her side at once, Caleb took her hand in both of his, inspecting it for harm. "There's an invisible barrier," she told him. "We're trapped."

"Sh," he said gently, brushing his thumb against a tiny scrape that looked days old. She did not appear in need of soothing, but he wasn't going to let that stop him from doing it anyway. "Everything's going to be all right. But you must take more care with yourself, Meely. No matter how capable and brave you are, you can't just go around slapping the sky."

Amelia scoffed at this, but Caleb noticed with a little flutter in his heart that she did not take her hand from his. So he bent to kiss her fingers once—twice— *What teaspoon? What magic? Why not just stay here, kissing her until his lips tired?*

He couldn't blame himself for the sweet, romantic reverie. It was Amelia's fault, what with the way she emitted such a beautiful moon magic from her very being, magic that tasted like wine, and that would revive his flagging energy if he kissed her just one more . . .

Stop, growled the small part of his brain that bore the burden of professionalism. Sadly, Caleb knew that it was right. Releasing Amelia's hand so he would not be further tempted, he turned abruptly, kicking the air.

A spark of pain flashed through him as his shoe's tip impacted forcefully with a hard surface. "Damn!" he cursed, hopping and clutching his agonized foot. Amelia watched him with little sympathy.

"Now that you have proven in a proper, manly way what I already proved about the air's solidity," she said, "might I dare suggest that we're caught in a thaumaturgic bubble? There must be an active fey line here." Setting her hands on her hips, she frowned at their surroundings as if she could chastise the enchanted minerals out from beneath the earth.

Caleb set his foot down and attempted to look somber, or at least adult. "Perhaps. Or perhaps something else is buried out here, like the pocket watch was."

"Why would someone do that?" Amelia asked.

"Does it matter right now?"

"Hm." She gazed at him unfocusedly, appearing to contemplate his idea. But Caleb could sense the panic rising within her, although she seemed outwardly untroubled, with no more than a twitch at the corner of one eye disturbing her expression. This situation was delaying them from their goal, and Amelia did not do well with being late. One terrible day, when she'd missed the train to a lecture on King Edward Longshanks's enchanted trousers, she'd been so stressed, she'd cut a fringe in her hair. Catching tonight's train was considerably more important than a lecture, but they now had zero chance of achieving it, and Caleb could only be glad there were no scissors nearby—unless someone had buried a pair in this field, that is.

Suddenly, Amelia jolted into action. Striding across to a clump of tall weeds, she scuffed her shoe against the ground. Caleb watched her in wary astonishment.

"What are you doing?"

"If you're right about this bubble being caused by something magical buried out here, we need to find whatever it is and try to break its power." Crouching, she began to dig at the earth. "The pocket watch was under a shrub, so an obvious hypothesis is that anything else would be buried under a similar landmark. We have to work *fast*, Caleb."

"We've probably already missed the train," he pointed out.

"Maybe." Dirt and torn grass flew around her, and Caleb guessed that she wasn't going to surrender her goal of reaching Staveley on time until the very last shred of impossible hope was gone. "Regardless, it's going to be dark soon. And very cold. And there's rain in those clouds." Rising, she began tugging on the weeds. "A thaumaturgic bubble won't save us from hypothermia. We have to work fast before it's too dark to search for . . ."

She paused as she ripped the clump of weeds from the ground, staggering with the force of her effort.

". . . whatever the hell . . ."

She paused again to toss the weeds away, and Caleb hastily reared back, saving himself from being whacked in the face by daisies and grass and brown wheat-like things.

". . . got us stuck here," she concluded, brushing her dirt-stained hands together.

"Good point," Caleb said.

Amelia threw him an exasperated look. "Then why are you just standing there?"

"I'm thinking."

"*Thinking!*" Pivoting sharply, she set her shoe heel against a small rock and pushed, attempting to lever it out of the ground. Caleb retreated farther in case it would be the next thing thrown at him. Amelia was the most sedate person he'd ever known . . . until she wasn't. But he himself had no intention of breaking a fingernail digging up half the field, not when he had two decades of quality education at his disposal. Scanning the area, he noticed a nearby patch of daffodils. Spring flowers at this time of year certainly suggested a leak of thaumaturgic energy from the ground beneath them. The fact that they were *blue* daffodils reinforced this idea. Wandering over, Caleb put his hands in his trouser pockets as he contemplated the flowers.

"What is it?" Amelia asked, hurrying across. Her hair had begun slipping from its knot, and her face was flushed with exercise. She would have looked like a wild-hearted Catherine Earnshaw were it not for the intelligence sparking in her dark eyes.

"All right, so pausing to think might have been a moderately good idea," she conceded, frowning at the daffodils. A few seconds later, she turned the frown on him. Somehow it made her even more fiercely beautiful. Never mind being like a book character; she was like Shakespeare's fairy queen Titania, or the heroine of an opera. Then her eyes narrowed with suspicion. "I suppose you're waiting for me to do the digging?"

No, I'm falling even deeper in love with you, Caleb thought. But aloud he said, "There doesn't seem any sense to us both dirtying our hands."

With a scoffing laugh, Amelia crouched down. "I think someone's dug here recently," she said as she worked. Clumps of dirt smashed against Caleb's shoes, but he dared not complain, not with Amelia in this mood.

"Aha!" she declared seconds later. Standing, she held up a gold locket dangling from a chain.

"Well done," Caleb said. Then his pulse tripped as he recognized it. "That's the locket I was looking for the other day."

Taking it in her hand, Amelia made a small, interested sound. "Tingles."

"Come now, Professor, don't you mean 'nerve stimulation due to thaumaturgic discharge'?" Caleb asked, grinning.

"'Tingles' is more efficient," Amelia said. She weighed the locket thoughtfully. "What does it do?"

"I don't know. I hadn't gotten around to assessing it."

Both glanced at the enchanted air surrounding them, then exchanged a shrug.

"Seems obvious?" they said in unison.

"Does rather," they answered together.

"Open it," Caleb suggested, gesturing at the locket.

"It might explode," Amelia said.

"Eh. It's been a good life."

Amelia paused, contemplating the risk, then went ahead

anyway. After all, *risk* was practically a nickname for material history studies (in fact, most MH students called it "Bric-a-Brac-a-Boom Studies," but Amelia did try to elevate her language now that she was a professor). She'd never get anything done in her job if she worried all the time about things blowing up in her face.

Pressing the locket's latch, she carefully levered open the case. "Huh," she said with surprise. "There's a tooth inside. I wasn't expecting that."

Caleb did not reply. He was watching the air shimmer like molten rainbows behind her as the thaumaturgic bubble dissolved. They were right, the locket had been responsible; opening it had immediately unraveled the magic. The sight was beautiful, illuminating Amelia's hair, crowning her with tiny white stars until she seemed indeed like a fairy queen . . . a heavenly queen . . . the goddess of his heart. Caleb knew that, from now on, every time he reread *A Midsummer Night's Dream*, he would envision Titania with dark hair, a plaid skirt, and dirt-packed fingernails.

If, that is, he remained capable of reading at all, considering how his brain also seemed to be dissolving into gossamer dreams while he gazed spellbound at Amelia. Then she looked up from the locket at the eroding magic, and her eyes widened.

"Oh my," she said rather breathlessly. "What a pretty manifestation of unconstrained thaumaturgic discharge." She looked at him again, lucent, lovely, and completely Amelia with her dry humor and endless practicality. Caleb felt so enchanted, it was as though the magic had pooled in his heart. "I am compelled to admit," she said, "that you were very clever to have found the burial spot so quickly."

"No, no," Caleb said, shaking his head. He lowered his eyelashes and glanced up through them at her, offering his sweet-est smile. "I was a bloody genius."

"Language!"

At the sharp voice, they both spun about in fright. Two el-derly women emerged from behind a nearby bush where they must have been hiding all along. They looked like grandmoth-ers from a children's tale of country life, with floral cotton dresses, aprons, and gum boots, but their menacing expres-sions and the alarmingly sharp farm implements they held made it evident that this was very much an adult horror story instead. The spade propped against one woman's shoulder was exactly the kind Caleb imagined gravediggers used, and the pitchfork grasped by the other could well have been what re-quired a grave to be dug in the first place. He stepped back nervously just as Amelia stepped toward him. Their hands reached for each other and clung tight.

"Good evening," Amelia said in a serenely polite voice, as if they were standing outside a High Street shop, making small talk. "I believe we've met before? In the Staveley pub?"

"We have," answered one woman. "I'm Hilda, and this here's Mavis. And *you* are the antiquarians." She made it sound like a crime—which, to be fair, Caleb was beginning to think it was, considering this blasted assignment. He summoned a charming smile, the one he employed specifically with older ladies, and that had over the years gained him all the antique brooches (and all the cake) he wanted.

"We're in a hurry to reach Staveley but seem to have got turned around," he explained. "What are two ladies such as yourselves doing out . . . here . . ." His voice trailed off as his brain finally leaped back into action, taking note first of the dirty spade, then of the ground from which Amelia had just retrieved the locket. *Well, that was interesting.* "Miss—" he said gorgeously.

"That's *ma'am* to you," Hilda snapped, glaring at him so fiercely his smile vanished with all the speed of a suffragette printing an edifying brochure. He clutched Amelia's hand even harder. "There's no point trying your masculine wiles on me, lad. You professors are a pain in the—"

She paused.

"Rear end?" Mavis suggested.

Hilda shook her head. "I was going to say 'proverbial,' but you know how I feel about alliteration, Mavis."

"I do, Hilda," Mavis replied sympathetically.

"Pain in the *bum*," Hilda amended, scowling, and everyone blushed.

"We heard about you finding the Russian pocket watch and taking it back to that darned villain, Nigel Harroway," Hilda said, jabbing her spade toward Ravenscroft Manor in such a violent gesture that Caleb wondered if, inside the house, Sir Nigel shuddered as though someone had just walked over his grave. "And now here you are with another antique in your hands, like you've got some kind of map to them all."

"All?" Amelia echoed. "Do you mean there are *more* buried out here?" She drew in a deep breath, clearly intending to lecture the women about safety practices when dealing with thaumaturgic antiques. Just then, Mavis jammed the pronged end of her pitchfork into the ground, causing the handle to shudder, and Caleb watched Amelia change plans between breathing in and breathing out again. "That explains the seasonal anomalies," she said instead.

Caleb tried smiling at the women again. "I hope we didn't intrude upon some treasure-hunting game?"

"That's not for us to say," Hilda snarled, and he gave up the smile as a waste of effort. "We're going to take you to someone who'll decide what to tell you . . . and what to do with you."

"We are?" Mavis said with some surprise. "Who, Hilda?"

The other woman gave her a sharp look. "You know, Mavis."

"No, I— Oh wait, you mean—"

"Yes. Do try to keep up, dear." She pointed the spade at Caleb and Amelia. "Let's go."

"We can't!" Amelia exclaimed, caution disintegrating in her urgency. "We have to recover a dangerous—"

"Dangerous?" Hilda scoffed. "Pft! What could a little girl like you know about danger? You're running around out here in the half dark, getting tangled up in magic when a storm's about to break."

"We should show them real danger," Mavis said. Yanking the pitchfork out of the ground, she lifted it and, grinning, touched a finger to one of the sharp points.

"Are you going to kill us?" Amelia gasped.

"What?!" Mavis stared at her with alarm. "Of course not! I'm saying, farm implements are really dangerous. What is it with the younger generation these days, Hilda? So dramatic!"

"It's probably all that education," Hilda answered with a shrug. "It bloats the brain." She shook her head. "Enough talking. Move, Professors. *Now.*"

Caleb rapidly considered his options. If it came to a physical altercation, fortune almost certainly would not bet on him. He might be a man who kept himself fit by playing rugby and running away from university bursars, but these two elderly ladies clearly had spent their lives breathing fresh air, drinking milk still warm from the cow, and going on hikes through the countryside *because they wanted to*. Caleb knew his match when he saw it. He wasn't even sure he and Amelia could outrace them, no matter how close the shelter of Ravenscroft Manor seemed. He'd thought the road close too. The magical bubble caused by the locket had dissolved, but there might be any number of thaumaturgic objects hidden out here to stop them in one manner or another.

No, all things considered, and with the expertise of someone who'd been in trouble more times in his life than he could count, he decided to surrender for now, and await a better opportunity for escape. "Lead the way," he said.

"How kind of you to approve your kidnapping," Hilda remarked dryly, then gestured for them to get moving. Amelia gave Caleb an anxious frown, and he smiled reassuringly at her in response. Without a word, they allowed themselves to be herded across the field toward the rear of Ravenscroft Manor.

As the shadow of the great house reached out to engulf them, a distant horn could be faintly heard, blistering the evening's quiet. Caleb realized what it was when Amelia exhaled a shuddering breath: the train leaving Staveley, taking Vanity Tunnicliffe and the perilous Hereford teaspoon south to disaster.

♡

CHAPTER NINETEEN

When it comes to history, we only know
what we've been told.

I, on the Past, Cornelius Ottersock

A MELIA REMAINED CALM as the two women took her and
Caleb across the field and through a small kitchen garden
toward the back of the manor house. With every step, she
evaluated possibilities for escape but ultimately overthought
each one so much that they had gone deep in the apple orchard
behind the house before she reached any decision. Night thick-
ened as the heavy rain clouds loomed steadily closer, and although Hilda had taken a lantern that hung from one of the
trees and lit it to illuminate their way, this provided barely
more than a pallid ghost of light in the eerie, whispering darkness beneath the orchard's canopy.

Amelia felt like a blighted Tudor queen entering the Tower
of London, unsure of her fate but anticipating something unpleasant. Her calm intensified until she had to acknowledge it
was in fact dissociation, wrought of fear. Beside her, still
clutching her hand, Caleb breathed with a spikiness that suggested the carpet of fallen leaves and rotting apples beneath

them was ruining any lingering hope he might have had to save his shoes.

Stopping abruptly between two trees, Mavis dragged the leaf litter with her pitchfork until she located a loop of rope. When she pulled on this, the ground levered up in the form of a hatch, dirt and leaves scattering off its wooden surface. Hilda's lantern revealed a ladder descending into a tunnel beneath the earth.

"Down we go," the woman said with a cheerfulness that gave Amelia goosebumps. Mavis climbed down; then Hilda jerked her head at Amelia and Caleb.

"Your turn. Inside."

"Look, we're just historians," Caleb told her anxiously. "We're not interested in anything that's less than a century old, and of course you're *much* younger than that." He smiled, but both the night and Hilda's mood were too dark for it to have any effect, so he pressed on with increasing desperation. "We don't care about you burying treasure, and I promise we won't tell any—"

"In. Side." Hilda's punctuation made an inarguable point.

"We aren't going to hurt you," Mavis called out from below.

"So long as you do what we say," Hilda added.

Caleb squeezed Amelia's hand, then released it. He began to climb slowly down the ladder. "Oh God!" his voice arose from the darkness, and Amelia gasped at the horrified sound, fear shooting through her. "There are *spiderwebs*!"

"*Tsk*," Hilda said contemptuously. She gestured to Amelia. "In you go. Sounds like he needs someone to hold his hand."

Hoisting her skirts, Amelia began the descent with all the Tarrant courage she could muster. *Spiders are more scared of me than I am of them*, she silently chanted. This helped her about as much as it always had—which is to say, *aaaahhhhh, arachnids!*—and when she made it to the tunnel floor she could not restrain herself from reaching through the darkness to hug Caleb, both assuring herself of his safety and steadying her own nerves.

"There, there," he said, patting her back. But his voice was more high-pitched than usual, and he felt softer than she recalled, and two seconds later she realized she was in fact hugging Mavis. Pulling away, blushing so fiercely it was a wonder she didn't light up the whole tunnel, she murmured a hasty apology.

"It's fine," the woman assured her, wryly amused. "Being kidnapped is harrowing, I'm sure."

Hilda came down the ladder, pulling the hatch shut behind her, and the group moved into the tunnel. Packed dirt lay beneath their feet, but wooden buttresses had been established to keep the walls and roof from crumbling, and there was enough space to walk comfortably upright. Indeed, other than the mustiness, the spiderwebs, and the whole fact of it being a secret underground tunnel leading possibly to their doom, Amelia found it really quite interesting, historically speaking. Before long they arrived at a second ladder, at the top of which a hatch opened to another tunnel, only this one featured wooden floorboards, and wooden walls, and the musty smell was somehow more civilized. Amelia concluded that they were inside the manor.

"Secret passageways!" she exclaimed with the delight of one who had solved a mystery. She recollected not only the door that had suddenly opened in Sir Nigel's study but also how Lady Ruperta and her housekeeper had disappeared in a corridor without exits, and her mind started running ahead of her, even while she inched carefully, slowly through the dark between Caleb and Mavis.

"Keep quiet!" Hilda ordered in a severe whisper. Muted household sounds could be heard through the walls, suggesting the servants' realm was within hearing—and possibly rescuing—distance. Amelia considered shouting for help, but that seemed more likely to get her a spade applied forcefully against her head than a rescue.

And so they trudged on along passageways and up a crooked flight of stairs. Amelia could not help but feel rather thrilled, despite the circumstances, to be experiencing a secret escape route that might have been created long ago in case of war, or for Catholics needing to evade religious persecution. *Throckmorton would love this,* she thought, and a welter of emotions tumbled through her—fear and fascination and, most confusing of all, a kind of melancholy fondness for the medieval studies professor that suggested she was suffering from oxygen deprivation in such an enclosed space.

At last, Mavis halted beside a blank wall. From its other side came the sound of a voice speaking in an unusual cadence, as if chanting. Amelia's stomach clenched.

Tap-tap, tap-tap, tap, Mavis knocked against the wall.

Nothing happened.

"It's supposed to be *tap-tap-tap, tap-tap,*" Hilda whispered from the rear.

"I don't think so," Mavis said, and reproduced her knock. Still, nothing happened.

"I'm telling you—" Hilda's whisper increased in volume.

"And I'm telling *you,* I know what the secret knock is," Mavis snapped.

"Obviously not," Hilda answered snarkily.

Mavis glared at her through the dim lantern light with such a ferocity that Amelia and Caleb prudently shifted back, pressing themselves against the wall.

"Shall I knock the code against your head, to remind you of it?" Mavis suggested.

"You can *try*," Hilda said, raising her spade. "Alternatively, you can try *tap-tap-tap, tap-tap* against the wall, like a sensible person would do, it being the CORRECT secret code."

Wincing at Hilda's choleric tone and obvious capital letters, Amelia groped for Caleb's hand in the darkness. He caught hers in a strong, reassuring grip, and she knew that, with him at her side, she could survive belligerent lady farmers, claustrophobic dark passages, and whatever existed behind the wall (although perhaps not spiders).

"I'll do it just to prove you wrong," Mavis said. Without shifting her gaze, she reached out and knocked as Hilda had suggested.

Nothing happened.

"Ha!" Mavis declared triumphantly. The sound echoed like desperate ghosts through the passageway. "Wrong!"

"You were wrong too!" Hilda pointed out, whisper abandoned in favor of bluster as she took a step toward Mavis. Glancing at each other nervously, Amelia and Caleb attempted to lean even farther backward, despite the solid wood behind them—

CREAK.

Suddenly, the wall at their backs disappeared as someone yanked open what was evidently a secret door. *"Stop being so nois—"* began an irate demand that was cut off when Amelia and Caleb stumbled backward, colliding with the speaker. A tumult of voices and limbs ensued, ending horizontally on the floor. Dazed, Amelia looked up through streaks of her hair to see Mavis's embarrassed face.

"Oops, sorry, knocked in the wrong place," the woman said.

"We need to mark it better," Hilda added.

"Then it wouldn't be a secret door," pointed out the woman currently lying beneath Amelia. She shoved and wriggled, and Amelia hastily clambered up as Caleb did the same beside her.

"Are you all right?" he asked, touching her face, tidying her hair. Amelia did not have time to answer before a familiar voice whipped sharply between them.

"What are you doing here?!"

Turning, clutching hands again automatically, Amelia and Caleb faced the dramatic and rather bewildering sight of Lady Ruperta enthroned like the Queen of the Dead upon an elegant and overtly expensive mahogany chair (*Chippendale, cabriole legs, eighteenth century,* Amelia estimated) at the center of some five other senior ladies, all of whom were seated on velveteen chaise lounges of lesser value. Amelia thought back to the murmured voices she'd heard at various times inside the house walls and realized they were not ghosts after all but a secret society of women lurking in the darkness.

Although it wasn't actually darkness. The chamber they occupied was in fact a cozy, chintz-papered salon, warmly illuminated by lamplight. Potted ferns, gilded mirrors, and several portraits of female nudes decorated the space. Delicate melodies drifted through the exotically scented air from a music box in one corner. On a side table, plush iced cakes, doughnuts, and biscuits quickly became the focus of Amelia's interest, considering the last thing she'd eaten was half a sardine hors d'oeuvre, more than an hour ago.

Altogether the scene seemed vaguely risqué, despite the fact that the women were not only dressed in sturdy woolens and gum boots but also busily working on knitting projects. The only exception to this was Lady Ruperta, in whose hands rested a small gilded book.

"We caught these two in the field," Mavis announced.

"We were organizing the combustibles when they appeared," Hilda said. "Magic was triggered somehow, and they got caught in it."

"Then they found a necklace," Hilda added. "We couldn't risk them giving it back to *him*."

"So we brought them here," Mavis concluded.

Lady Ruperta slammed shut her book. Amelia glimpsed the title, *Poems of Sappho*, and felt a belated curiosity about her hostess.

"I told you to not go outside, Professors," Lady Ruperta growled. "You could have been killed." Judging from the tone of her voice, this option remained on the table.

"It was all my fault," Caleb said, as he always did when the two of them were brought up in front of authority for some misdeed or another. Then he paused, shrugged, and gave Lady Ruperta a look so *real* that Amelia's nerves tingled. For a moment, he stopped being her Caleb and became instead a mystery, a man with connections to other people that didn't include her. She couldn't decide if she felt intrigued or upset by it. Lady Ruperta, on the other hand, watched him with narrowed eyes, seeing whatever it was that Amelia could not.

"Actually, no, it wasn't my fault," he contradicted himself suddenly, all the endearing charm stripped from his voice. "Vanity Tunnicliffe stole something belonging to us. We were

trying to get it back when the locket's enchantment caught us."
He angled his head to regard Lady Ruperta thoughtfully. "Why
have you buried your husband's treasures outside?"

A gasp went through the salon at this question, followed by
taut silence as everyone waited for Lady Ruperta to inflict some
violent punishment on Caleb for his impertinence. It was not
so much his words that had been bold, but the sense beneath
them that he understood something about her on a more personal level than a stranger—a man—ought to.

Then Lady Ruperta huffed a dry laugh. "Because I could
not bury my husband there," she said in simple response.

Clack clack. Knitting needles began operating at speed, like
a Greek chorus that utilized yarn instead of words.

"He is a villain of the most dangerous kind," Lady Ruperta
continued.

"What has he done?" Caleb asked.

"He has been dull, and stodgy, without the slightest portion
of humor."

Caleb's expression wavered between confusion and amusement. "That is unpleasant indeed," he agreed, "but not what I
would call dangerous."

Nine pairs of female eyes raised heavenward in despair at
this ignorance, including Amelia's. Had the man not listened
during secondary school lectures about the English Civil War
and the Puritans who murdered the king, despite being so
dull and stodgy they even banned Christmas? (Actually, no, he
hadn't.)

"Sure, I wouldn't want to be married to him," he amended,
"but . . . ?"

"Nigel was considered an excellent husband for me," Lady
Ruperta said. "Wealthy, titled, unlikely to take mistresses. I

disliked him from the start, but that was of no consequence. My family needed money, and he wanted someone to manage his house. So he acquired me like an antique."

"You could leave him," Caleb said.

Clack clack clack.

"Caleb," Amelia murmured repressively. Surely he comprehended that being trapped in a hidden room with several women bearing sharply pointed objects was not the best circumstance in which to be provoking?

As the thought came to her, she almost laughed. *Of course* he didn't comprehend, unless he'd undergone an entire personality transformation in the past thirty seconds. Provocation was practically his astrological sign. She squeezed his hand, and he was good enough not to get them killed with some further comment.

Lady Ruperta straightened in her chair, clutching the book of poetry so tightly her knuckles grew even whiter than they had been. "Leave him? And lose everything, including my reputation? Besides, if I do, who will restrain the man from hoarding so much junk that the house eventually collapses? I cannot leave."

"Lady Ruperta is a true heroine," Mavis interposed from behind Amelia. The loyalty in her voice was heartwarming—as in, Amelia's heart grew warm with anxiety that the woman would stab both her and Caleb with her pitchfork should she consider them a risk to her friend.

"I am indeed," Lady Ruperta agreed. "Bitter and long have been the years of pretending that I tolerate my husband. Of smiling when people tell me about their travels to Paris, or show me their fashionable dresses. As for the particulars of wedlock: closing one's eyes and thinking about England only goes so far, I can tell you. Thankfully our daughter was able to escape this mausoleum, although *bitter* is the least I can say about one's child running away to Australia.

"But I have my special friends to console me. Granted, we must hide our gatherings, in case our husbands want to join them"—a general groan of distaste arose from the company—"but we still have a gay time." She smiled at those around her, and for the first time Amelia spied a genuine warmth in the woman.

But then the smile soured, withering away. "Nigel is the very last person who ought to possess dangerous enchanted objects," she said. "He's too dull to consider the consequences of their magic, and too humorless to care. Our estate manager was turned into a frog not one hour after besting Nigel at a card game, and I'll never believe that was accidental. This is why I cannot divorce the man, you see? I must stand guard."

"Why didn't you alert the Home Office?" Amelia asked. "They would have sent someone here immediately."

Lady Ruperta scoffed. "I did approach them. Useless lot. A fellow in a cheap suit told me not to worry my little head about it, just focus on taking care of my husband like a good wife should. I do declare, I've had enough of mediocre men thinking they are so clever!"

General murmurs of agreement followed this statement. Caleb remarked wryly, "I've heard a few lady academics express the same sentiment. I'm starting to wonder if all women feel that way."

There followed a long, eloquent silence as every female gaze in the room directed itself at him. "Ah," Caleb said. "Right. Well, I'm certainly glad that *I'm* not mediocre."

Lady Ruperta scoffed. "We'll be the judge of that, young man."

"What about calling the police?" Amelia asked.

"Oh, I'm sure they'd also say Professor Sterling was mediocre," Lady Ruperta answered, and Amelia choked on a traitorous laugh.

"No, I mean call them about Sir Nigel," she clarified.

Lady Ruperta shook her head. "Nigel bought all his treasures legally. And he's never posed a threat. Apparently 'driving people into a stupor with his prattling' and 'setting fire to the piano with an enchanted vase' are not crimes. We're talking about *England* here, Miss Tarrant: the country that gave us bread pudding and the House of Lords (two things I would not call interchangeable, but only because I am very fond of Mrs. Cuddle's bread pud with custard). As a baronet, Nigel would have to assassinate the Queen—"

"God save Her Majesty," everyone murmured.

"—before anyone helped me restrain him. The best I've been able to manage is hiding his more dangerous pieces, even burying some outside, before finally convincing him to donate to the British Museum."

"But you did convince him," Caleb said, "and we're here now. So why are antiques still going missing? And why were these two"—he half turned to indicate Hilda and Mavis, and swallowed heavily at the ferocity of their expressions—"these two excellent ladies burying things even tonight?"

"Because I don't trust you," Lady Ruperta replied simply.

Amelia considered this, then nodded in acceptance, but Caleb blinked at the woman with dazed astonishment. "But—but—we're experts."

"Ha!" Lady Ruperta's curt laugh was echoed by the other woman. Even Amelia winced slightly. "You broke my dining room furniture on your first day here. Since then, there have been exploding mugs, ruined bedding, constant arguments, and who the hell keeps *giggling*? I'm not confident that you will keep Nigel's most powerful antiques safe."

"That's understandable," Amelia said. And when Caleb gave her an outraged look, she added, "But only from your perspective. Antiquing is seldom a quiet practice. Ghost rampages or object explosions tend to be par for the course. Usually we require people to sign a liability acceptance form, but perhaps Miss Tunnicliffe did not provide you with one—?"

"She did have some papers," Lady Ruperta said, sniffing imperiously, "but it would be plebian of me to read what I sign."

Amelia smiled, which seemed more advisable under the circumstances than shouting with frustration. The Material History degree course included a module on Dealing with People, and she had aced it (although only because her final essay was so good that the flaws with her practicum were overlooked). "I do beg your pardon for any misunderstandings," she said politely. "I hope you will reconsider unearthing the buried items and handing them over to Mr. Dummersby."

Although this sentence was outfitted with a full stop, the existence of an unspoken extra clause detailing what would happen should Lady Ruperta not reconsider was plain for all to perceive. The government, if properly informed by an expert (more specifically, by *Mr.* Sterling, Amelia had to admit), would never tolerate such powerful magical objects being amassed without security on private property. Nor would the British Museum, for that matter—not when an excellent profit could be made from putting them on public display. The gold locket alone warranted a full team of antiquarians, curators, and lawyers descending upon Ravenscroft Manor, every one of them accompanied by a soldier.

"I do not wish to speak with Mr. Dummersby," Lady Ruperta said, her lips flattening as if Amelia had demanded that she shake hands with a plague-ridden beggar with fleas. "Speaking with the two of you has been quite enough of an endurance test."

"But unfortunately Professor Sterling and I must leave at once," Amelia said before Caleb could reply instead, considering that he'd managed to slither out of the Dealing with People module altogether. "We have a matter of urgency to deal with in Oxford. Indeed, we were leaving when your ladies intercepted us."

"Very well, I suppose," Lady Ruperta relented ungraciously. "But for God's sake, leave by the actual road, will you? And lest anyone accuse me of being a poor hostess, I shall procure raincoats for your comfort, despite how you destroyed my dining table."

Nods of farewell were then exchanged, which was all either of the parties could bear to offer each other at this point, and Hilda gestured that Amelia and Caleb should follow her out.

"Thank heavens, we're finally getting out of this place," Caleb whispered to Amelia as they headed back through the secret passageway. "Even if I catch pneumonia doing so, raincoat notwithstanding."

CHAPTER TWENTY

> Ghosts are just the manifestation
> of thaumaturgic energy. You should not
> be afraid of them. You should be bloody terrified.
>> *I, on the Past*, Cornelius Ottersock

HILDA LED THEM to another door some distance from the ladies' salon, but upon cracking it open and peering through, she closed it again immediately.

"Sir Nigel is in his study," she whispered to Amelia and Caleb. "You'll need to go through the servants' domain instead. Just keep your heads down and move quickly. Don't let Grimshaw catch you, for God's sake, or you'll be sorry." A few minutes later she tried another door, opening it warily. "All clear," she whispered. "Good luck!"

"Thank you so—" Amelia began, only for her words to stumble, along with her feet, as Caleb pulled her across the threshold.

Once Hilda had closed the door behind them, he grumbled, "Please tell me that, next time you're kidnapped, you won't thank the person."

"There is no circumstance in which one should surrender one's dignity," Amelia replied archly as she looked around the corridor in which they found themselves. It was not much wider than the one they had left, but bore the dignity of radiant wall lamps, lemon-scented polish, and a well-swept floor. The noise of clattered dishes and jostling voices came from nearby. To their right was a door marked *Linen*; to their left, at the end of the corridor, a door stood half-open to what Amelia believed was the manor's central hallway. She looked questioningly at Caleb—he shrugged—and with this discussion concluded, they proceeded toward the exit.

Suddenly, a footman appeared through an opening in the wall ahead of them, swinging an empty silver tray in his hand as he made for that same door. Amelia and Caleb stopped, holding their breath, but he had not noticed them. However, it had become clear that they would be forced to pass by the kitchen. Without a doubt, they were going to be seen.

There was nothing to do except keep moving. With a pace that tried to balance between *a casual stroll* and *running like hell*, they walked past the entrance to the kitchen, not daring anything more than a glance inside. A half dozen servants were sitting or standing casually around a long table, laughing as they watched one footman perform a scathing impression of Professor Throckmorton—"Brain? None!"—while employing a salt grinder as a pipe.

Amelia hastily clapped a hand over her mouth to repress a laugh of her own. But the movement attracted the attention of a chambermaid, and two seconds later everyone was staring at them, including a man at the head of the table who bore an uncanny resemblance to the butler, Grimshaw. He could surely not be Grimshaw, however, considering the way he slouched comfortably in his chair, wineglass in hand, face reddened from excessive laughter.

"Oi!" he shouted, proving his identity—for although the

voice lacked its usual funereal timbre, it still managed to send a chill through Amelia and Caleb. They immediately came to a halt, Amelia feeling half inclined to salute. After all, in England's hierarchy of authority, only the Queen is superior to a butler (and even then, not to her own).

"What are you doing here?" Grimshaw demanded.

Caleb pointed first to himself then to Amelia. "Us?" he asked innocently.

"No, the horde of barbarians behind you," Grimshaw quipped, then laughed again. It was the loose guffaw of a man well pleased with his own intelligence, despite not really having much of it. In response, the rest of the servants chuckled, but their expressions had tightened with what looked rather disconcertingly like nervous anticipation.

"We were looking for the drawing room and got lost," Amelia said. "So sorry for interrupting your evening. We'll just be on our—"

"Come in, join us!" Grimshaw urged with a sweeping gesture that almost had Amelia flinching before she understood that he was welcoming them. "We've got the good coffee in here! Sit down, sit down. I'll tell you all about the history of Ravenscroft Manor. When I was a young man, things sure were different around this place!"

Perhaps he is Grimshaw's twin, Amelia thought, bemused. Behind his back, two footmen with rictus smiles were shaking their heads urgently in warning. Several others peeled away from the group and began making themselves busy stacking dishes, dusting furniture, or moving candlesticks back and forth as if a difference of three inches were of vital importance. Grimshaw, noticing none of this, gestured again.

"Come on, you'll be fascinated by some of the things I can

tell you," he enthused. "There was this time the prize ram got free from his paddock . . ."

Someone groaned. The two footmen were grimacing like they were in pain. Amelia now understood why Hilda had warned against getting caught by the butler. His dolorous manner was patently just an act, the truth of his character being something far worse: *jocular*. Indeed, as he prattled on about the absconding ram, a twinkle in his eye suggested that, at any moment, he might suddenly leap to the heights of old-man humor; i.e., removing his false teeth.

"Terribly sorry," Amelia interrupted him, even as Caleb grasped her elbow and began tugging her along the corridor. "We are in a dreadful hurry. But we shall return with pen and paper as soon as we can, to take proper note of all your—" At which point, they were through the doorway, and Caleb shut the door firmly behind them.

"Right," Amelia said briskly. She began to stride down the hallway with such a rapid pace that Caleb had to half jog to catch up. "We've missed apprehending Vanity in Staveley, but that's no excuse to slack off. If we leave at once, we might be able to get a ride on a late-night freight train."

"A freight train from Windermere," Caleb said dubiously. "What will it be bringing, container loads of poetry books? Maybe we should hold off until morning."

"No," Amelia said, not so much an argument as a command. "Look, there's the front door right ahead of us. I am leaving this house *now*, while I have the chance."

"Wait—Lady Ruperta mentioned raincoats."

Amelia considered this, accepted it as an excellent point, but did not slow down. She had her momentum back and it would take more than raincoats to stop it.

"Also, we haven't had any dinner," Caleb added. "We should pack some food to take with us."

Another worthwhile point, reinforced by the fact that they were approaching the parlor, from wherein came delicious aromas—although also the sound of conversation, which was almost enough to spoil her appetite. Apparently, Dummersby and Throckmorton had taken the news of Vanity's thievery with a grain of salt—and a dollop of gravy on their roast chicken, from the smell of it. Amelia considered entering the room, did a rapid cost-benefit analysis of the kind her parents taught her when she was still in the nursery, then pivoted so sharply that Caleb almost collided with her.

"We shall go back to the kitchen for supplies," she said, taking his arm to turn him. "And then we shall start walking to the village. We can eat as we go."

"Amelia, wait," Caleb urged as she towed him along with her. When she ignored this, he stopped, requiring her to either stop also or else release him. He knew her too well, damn the man. She was constitutionally incapable of letting him go.

With a little flash of impatience, she halted. "What?"

Caleb stepped forward until he was at her side, sliding his arm around her back and drawing her closer to him. "Meely, sweetheart, take a breath. Let's go upstairs and pack our suitcases. We can call a servant to bring us what we need."

"Suitcases? You're willing to carry your luggage all the way down to Staveley?" She gave him a wry look.

"And yours also," he said, smiling with a sweetness she knew perfectly well was in fact him being cheeky. "And I'll carry you on my back too," he added winningly. "Might as well make use of this magnificent physique. I'll be your hero, Professor Amelia Tarrant."

She huffed. "You'll grizzle the whole way."

"Of course. I have a soulful nature. How can I not, when I am met with beauty in the mirror every day?"

Amelia couldn't help herself; she laughed. "You are ridiculous."

"And you love me for it," he replied, grinning.

"I—" she began automatically, and closed her mouth before she exposed too much truth. She did love him, *ridiculous* man that he was. Lovely, kind, generous man. But kisses in Cumbria did not equate to anything real in Oxford, and should Throckmorton appear in the corridor at that moment, they'd need to step apart and snarl at each other. Amelia knew herself to be brave, but not even she possessed enough courage to place her truth in such a position.

"I agree that your plan is a good one," she said instead, and allowed him to turn her to again face the entrance hall and its stairs leading upward.

Abruptly, they stopped, eyes widening at the sight that met them.

"Uh . . ." was all Amelia could manage to say.

"What the . . ." Caleb said, equally dumbstruck.

They stared in utter bemusement at a dark, narrow passageway leading to the mudroom.

"I must be more tired than I realized," Caleb said eventually. "I could have sworn we were heading for the entrance hall."

"We were." Taking a step forward, Amelia set her hands on her hips and turned in a slow circle to comprehensively frown at the passageway. Had it been an undergraduate student rather than a piece of architecture, it would have transformed immediately, with apologies, into the entrance hall. But not even Amelia's strictest look could perform such magic. *Something had, though.*

"We must have gone past an active thaumaturgic antique," she said.

"The hallway was empty," Caleb argued.

"Then something under the floorboards."

Caleb shook his head. "We'd have experienced effects before, were that the case."

"Then it must be this," Amelia said, taking the locket out from where she'd stashed it in her skirt pocket. "It created a temporal bubble to prevent us from leaving the property. Perhaps it's doing something similar now."

"A binding magic?" Caleb said. "Well, opening it broke the enchantment before. Let's try that."

Amelia unlatched the case and opened it to reveal the tooth within. Caleb grimaced. "That's disgusting."

"It's just a tooth, Caleb. You have several of your own in your mouth."

"Yes, but that looks ancient, and not in an exciting, I-want-to-study-it way."

"Let's try again for the exit," Amelia said.

They headed once more toward the entrance hall but were a few yards from reaching it when suddenly a door ahead flung open. Caleb stopped abruptly, catching Amelia's arm to keep her still, and they waited for someone to leap out and accuse them of shenanigans. No one appeared, however, and after a minute the door swung shut again without any human intervention, its latch clicking back into place with a contemptuous *tsk*.

"Well, that's not spooky," Caleb murmured. They turned back to the entrance hall, and he sighed. "But *that* is."

With some frustration, they considered the drawing room in which they now stood. Maniacally floral wallpaper in shades of mauve and pink would have disoriented them had not the sudden relocation already done so. Candlelight drifted with grief-colored ghosts that reached out indistinct hands toward them, gasping, weeping, starved for humanity.

"This is nonsense," Amelia declared in strident tones. "I cannot be wasting my time in such fashion. Students are in peril from Vanity Tunnicliffe and need me to save them."

"Us," Caleb corrected her.

"That's what I said." Snapping the locket shut, she jammed it into her skirt pocket, then marched for the door. Throwing it ajar, she stepped through.

Darkness swallowed her whole.

"DAMN," AMELIA MUTTERED, since there was no one around to hear her bad language. The darkness pressed against her like an old eiderdown quilt, hot, suffocating, and smelling faintly of mold. Reaching through it, she discovered bare wooden walls close by on either side of her.

"Secret passageway!" she spoke aloud, trying to diminish the oppressive pitch-black silence with her voice. She did not know whether to prioritize aggravation or a relief that she was still inside the living world. Panic, however, made a vociferous argument that it should take precedence. *You're going to be trapped in this house forever,* it screamed along her nerves. *You'll become one of the nameless ghosts, begging to be heard, eternally misunderstood.*

"Rubbish," Amelia chided herself coolly. Did panic not appreciate that she was Professor Amelia Tarrant? Certainly, this current snafu was a challenge—how exactly did one find a concealed exit in complete darkness?—but she'd faced worse over the years. She'd been dragged by magic into a funereal urn; stuck in a haunted castle tower when its ancient stairs collapsed; and forced to search the basement of Miss Honeychurch's Kitchenware Museum for an enchanted egg cup. This now represented nothing more than a time-consuming diversion.

"Amelia!" Caleb's voice, faint but heartwarming, echoed from a distance. Immediately, panic breathed a sigh of relief. Amelia's perception of the world reoriented until Caleb became its north, and she turned, making her way slowly toward him.

"Caleb!" she called, her fingers trailing over the walls as she went, feeling for any suggestion of an exit. *The spiders will all be above me,* she assured herself.

The spiders will all be above me! her brain echoed, but in the opposite tone. She picked up speed.

"Amelia!" Caleb shouted again. A rhythmic knocking followed, like a heartbeat, calm and steady, to guide her. Closing her eyes, Amelia focused on it, her own heartbeat in synchronicity. Closer and closer . . .

"Meely," Caleb seemed to murmur into her ear. She felt him near, his smiling golden spirit encompassing her. The now-familiar flutters stirred within her stomach in recognition and welcome.

"Caleb!"

"I can hear you," he replied from behind layers of magic. "Sing something, and I'll find you."

She laughed. "Certainly not!"

"Frère Jacques, Frère Jacques," he chanted, and Amelia rolled her eyes. It was a nursery rhyme they'd used like private code

throughout their childhood, and which she'd abandoned for the sake of dignity in adolescence. Still, every now and again Caleb would sing a line or two just to tease her—for example, from the audience while she was trying to give a serious presentation. He was a nuisance, a pest.

"Dormez-vous? Dormez-vous?" she sang in response.

"Stop there!" His tone was so serious, Amelia halted at once. "Don't move!"

"Caleb . . ." she began warily.

CRASH!

Alarmed, Amelia leaped back as one of the walls shuddered. What the—

CRASH! Suddenly a section of the wall slammed open, sending light bursting into the passageway. Dust rained down like shattered darkness. The house groaned so dreadfully that it felt for a moment like it might collapse entirely. Amelia cowered, hands over her head to protect her from the terrifying possibility of falling arachnids. Caleb walked through the space where a secret door had stood before he'd kicked it open so forcefully that its latch had broken and its edge splintered. He looked like an angel: radiant with golden lamplight, furious at the darkness in which he'd found her. Without a word, he picked her up like a sack of flour, sparing no consideration whatsoever for her self-locomotive capabilities, and carried her out to a painfully bright room. Amelia squinted, her eyes burning as they tried to adjust to the sudden change.

"Did you have to break open the door?" she asked.

"Yes." Caleb set her on her feet, and half a second later she was being hugged to within an inch of her life. Sighing, she relaxed against his body, allowing him the comfort of comforting her.

"*Din, din, don. Din, din, don,*" he whispered, completing the rhyme. Amelia lifted her face toward him, this man who was her sun, and he smiled. Unthinkingly, instinctively, she kissed that smile. He welcomed her without hesitation or complication, just a deep need to reconnect. The kiss was soft, warm. It went on for a few seconds or forever . . . In some ways, Amelia felt they had been kissing like this since the moment they met. Finally, with her calm restored, she laid her head against his shoulder again.

"Please stop disappearing on me," he said in a conversational tone. "It does uncomfortable things to my blood pressure."

"Lady Ruperta is going to make you more than uncomfortable when she sees what you've done to her secret door. Why didn't you just push it open gently?"

"I did."

"Um," Amelia disputed.

"I *wanted* to use an ax," he said, "but the servants probably would have charged me a year's worth of salary to borrow one." His embrace tightened. "I'd have broken down the entire house to get to you."

She laughed. "Please quit your job as a teacher and become a poet instead."

"Terrible idea. All my poems would be titled 'Amelia,' and I'd be disparaged as a one-trick pony."

The flutters beneath her heart perked up, wondering if they should take action, but Amelia assured them this was nothing compared to how Caleb usually spoke to her. *Ooh*, they answered dreamily, and shook themselves so that a velvety gold feeling billowed through her. She smiled against the privacy of Caleb's shoulder.

"Were you hurt?" he asked, his voice low with concern.

"Not at all. Where are we?" The room in which they stood appeared to be empty of all but a chaise lounge and piano, and its lack of old clutter made her instantly worried that they'd stepped out of time or into a whole other house.

"We're just down from the Mauve Drawing Room."

This answer, along with the manner in which his hand was stroking her back, soothed Amelia completely. She could have stood for hours, resting against him, being petted. "You didn't go far," he said. "I'd suspected this room had a hidden door, so once I figured out that you were inside the walls, I came to look for it. Only a few minutes have—"

"A few minutes!" Amelia interjected with a horrified gasp. She pulled away from him, scowling around the room as if she could locate the lost time and reclaim it, along with a few extra seconds in compensation for her trouble. "We'll never catch Vanity now."

"But we know where she's heading," Caleb reminded her. "And it's unlikely that she knows her way around the uni. We'll take a morning train and be back in Oxford before she even finds her way to Balliol College, let alone to Dervorguilla's brooch."

"If we manage to escape this house," Amelia added grimly. "Right now, that feels impossible."

"I don't know if the locket is to blame or not," Caleb said, "but why don't we just put it down somewhere and leave without it?"

Amelia shook her head. "No, that doesn't feel wise. Such an incredibly strong binding power . . . Lady Ruperta was right, Sir Nigel is a terrible person to have power like that anywhere within his reach."

"True. He might use it to trap someone in a room and talk

at them for hours. Let's at least put it in a safe bag. That should repress the magic."

They went up a back stairwell to the first floor and within a few minutes were in Caleb's bedroom, evidently with the locket's approval. Caleb found a safe bag among the mess Vanity had created, while Amelia restrained herself with some difficulty from tidying up. "Right, put it in," Caleb said, holding open the little black bag.

Bringing out the locket, Amelia opened it to check that the strange dental cargo was still inside. "You're right," she told Caleb as she contemplated the rotten lump. "It is disgusting."

"I wonder who it belonged to," Caleb mused.

Amelia wrinkled her nose. "I don't c—"

"Merde!"

King John's ghost suddenly materialized in the room, screaming with such force that Amelia and Caleb staggered backward. He raised his sword in both hands, slicing the air as if trying to cut through heaven in order to slaughter them. It created a whirling maelstrom of supernatural wind, ice-cold with antiquity, howling with grief for long-lost time. Clothes took wild flight. Books, candles, toiletries shot across the room, smashing against walls before bursting into vivid blue flames. Sheets arose from the bed like ghosts.

Amelia and Caleb exchanged a mild look.

"Merde!" King John cried again, his voice breaking with desperation.

Amelia blinked, struck by a sudden realization. "Oh! I've been mistaking his accent. He's not saying *merde*. He's saying *ma dent*!"

"Ma dent?" Caleb echoed dubiously. "I don't know, they sound quite different."

"It's been almost seven hundred years since he was alive. Accents change."

"I suppose. We could ask Throck— Okay, no need to kill me with that eyebrow, thank you. I studied Latin, not French; what does *ma dent* even mean?"

"This," Amelia said, and taking the tooth from the locket, she threw it at King John.

Seven centuries imploded. An abrupt, stunning peace fell over the bedroom—literally. Clothes dropped to the floor, sheets sank onto the bed, and the air, with a weary exhale, settled once more into calm. King John had vanished. No poignant look, no last word; just gone, and not at all mourned.

"Whew," Caleb said, smoothing his wind-tossed hair. "That explains how we couldn't find the ghost's source before. But why was he haunting our bedrooms when his tooth was nowhere in them?"

"Maybe he ranged through the entire house and we simply weren't aware of the fact because no one mentioned it," Amelia said.

Taking the locket from her hand, Caleb regarded it, serious-eyed and thoughtfully silent. Then he said, "Question: if I was to put a strand of Ottersock's hair in this locket, then toss the whole thing into the Thames River . . ."

"Caleb," Amelia chided, even while her imagination giggled at a vision of grimy river fish burrowing for insects among the professor's sideburns. "However, I do want to conduct some real experiments on it. This kind of binding magic is rare." Retrieving the locket before Caleb could spontaneously misplace it, she slipped it into the safe bag, then into her skirt pocket. "We should be able to leave now that the binding is broken and the ghost released. Let's pack quickly and go."

"Or . . ." Caleb countered. Glancing at the bed, he offered Amelia a smile so wickedly hot, her entire body ignited in a flaming blush. "Everyone thinks we've left. The next train won't be until morning. We could . . . play a game."

Amelia wavered. She fluttered. She very nearly made a running leap onto the bed. But despite all this internal motion, Caleb was the one who moved first. He stepped toward her, slowly and quite specifically: a step like a question.

Amelia stepped toward him in reply. It would have been impossible not to. Years of secret wishing were like a combustion engine, driving her body forward. Never mind leaving; she would have given up all the world and every teaspoon in it if Caleb asked her to stay with him, even for only the duration of one kiss—a few minutes; a beautiful eternity.

They came together in a silence that rang loud with the discussions they'd not yet had, but as their foreheads touched, their noses brushing, their breath shivering from open mouths, Amelia could not remember a single word of all the things she ought to say. They did not kiss, but only because the not-kissing was like a kiss in itself, hot with anticipation, shooting sparks along their nerves—a kiss very different from the one they had shared downstairs. It spoke now of tongues, and the removal of clothes. Their lips met, featherlight, then parted again. They sent a burning look to each other in potent silence. Anticipation grew to the point where it felt as if their next breath would ignite a bonfire . . . Then, slowly, their lips met again and—

Knock knock knock!

With a mutual groan that was far less erotic than the one Amelia had expected to be making in the near future, they reluctantly pulled away from each other. Amelia fanned herself while Caleb crossed to open the door. Mrs. Cuddle stood there with two raincoats and a look that plainly said, *I know what I just interrupted and am duly scandalized.*

Their last chance for romance having been thus snatched away, Amelia and Caleb turned instead to packing (which was not quite as much fun as sex would have been) and reunited in the corridor with wry smiles and regret-filled eyes. Clad in oversized raincoats more effective than any prophylactic, and encumbered with luggage that had somehow managed to become heavier during their stay, they trudged downstairs. The moment they reached the ground floor, Grimshaw appeared with uncanny timing, his countenance professionally doleful, his voice suggesting dread portents as he handed them umbrellas and wished them the unlikely event of a safe journey.

Amelia smiled with a weary politeness. "Thank—"

Thwomp. Her umbrella flung open.

Caleb and Grimshaw gasped in unison. Laughing at their horrified expressions, Amelia closed the umbrella again. "It was an accident," she said. "I know people say it's bad luck to open an umbrella indoors, but I don't believe in luck."

"Do you believe in magic?" Caleb asked mildly. He was staring behind her, his eyes heavy with a mix of tiredness and alarm. Turning to see what the problem was, Amelia sighed.

"Well that's just ridiculous," she said as a coat rack lurched to attack, glowing with cold cobalt fire that had been emitted from the tip of her apparently thaumaturgic umbrella.

"Stand back, Meely!" Caleb urged. Raising his own, as-yet-unopened umbrella in the manner of a sword, he dashed forward to meet the coat rack in battle. Its arms flailed to defend itself from his assault, its three feet clattering back and forth with the speedy grace of magic.

"Be careful," Amelia told Caleb, as if this would materially assist his fight.

"I'll be fine," Caleb assured her, thrusting and parrying with ease. "I've taken fencing lessons."

Thwack. The coat rack flung a bowler hat at his head.

A pair of footmen came running. Diving upon the coat rack, they wrestled it away across the hall. Amelia dropped her umbrella (not noticing how it caught fire as it struck the ground) and grasped Caleb's hand. "Let's go. Now."

Flinging his umbrella aside, Caleb blew a strand of hair from his eyes. "I swear, not even Bethnal Green was as bad as this bloody house. No offense," he added to Grimshaw.

"None taken, sir," Grimshaw replied in a professional monotone. But the speed with which he turned to open the door suggested offense had not only been taken but painted on a banner and illuminated with floodlights.

"Just think," Caleb murmured cheerfully to Amelia. "Tomorrow we'll be breathing smog again."

"Checking in on our students," she added.

"Drinking real coffee."

"Aaargggh!" a footman shouted as the coat rack kicked him to the ground.

Boom! Throckmorton's brash laugh burst from the parlor.

Clutching each other's hands tighter, Amelia and Caleb turned to face the night and their freedom.

Then stopped, their jaws dropping.

Professor Ottersock stood on the other side of the threshold, his arms crossed, his scowl blurred by pipe smoke as he demanded, "What on earth is going on here?!"

CHAPTER TWENTY-ONE

> History teaches us that discord doesn't happen
> because people speak different languages, but because
> they simply don't want to listen.
>
> *I, on the Past*, Cornelius Ottersock

PROFESSOR OTTERSOCK'S WORDS chilled Amelia so thoroughly, she felt as though she'd been turned to stone. In the gloom, with his pipe smoke and the large black umbrella he held overhead, he gave the impression of being more a dragon than a faculty—

Thud.

Yanking the door from Grimshaw's hold, Caleb had slammed it shut before Amelia could realize what he was doing, let alone stop him. The sound of Ottersock's shocked exclamation was heard through the wood, and Amelia pressed a finger against her brow, where the low-grade headache she'd been feeling all week now threatened a migraine.

"There is a small chance you probably shouldn't have done that," she told Caleb wearily.

"There is an even greater chance you're right," he agreed. "I don't know what came over me."

"Fright?" Amelia suggested. "Anxiety?"

"Horror at his triple tweed outfit." Releasing her hand from his grasp, he donned a rueful expression, straightened his shoulders with the air of Hector preparing to meet Achilles outside Troy, then reached for the door handle.

Grimshaw got there before him. With a scowl that had Caleb figuratively hung, drawn, and quartered for the crime of usurping a butler's door-operation privileges, he opened the door once again.

"Good evening, sir," he intoned to Professor Ottersock, although it was clear what he meant was, *My apologies, I am in no way associated with these idiots.* Ottersock, pipe bobbing and sideburns trembling, muttered something dour that sounded in turn like, "Apologies accepted, since I *am* associated with these idiots." He bustled through the doorway before he might be shut out again, his umbrella dripping rain and bad luck all over the flagstones. As he closed it, Amelia and Caleb retreated several steps to avoid being "accidentally" smacked with said umbrella.

"You look like you're about to leave," he remarked as he scanned them and their luggage from beneath a hairy frown, proving why he was paid the big money (eighty pounds a year) to head a university faculty.

"Miss Tunnicliffe has stolen the teaspoon I st—er, discovered in Hereford Cathedral," Amelia informed him. "She intends to use it to access Dervorguilla of Galloway's brooch. We are about to undertake hot pursuit."

"Cold pursuit, more like it," Ottersock rebutted, "considering the weather. And I see magic is afoot," he added, watching the footmen trying to shove the coat rack into a closet. "Why am I not surprised to find chaos happening in your vicinity? You're not going anywhere tonight, Professor Tarrant."

That, apparently, was that: his pipe smoke gave an autocratic billow, and Grimshaw took this as a signal to close the door.

"No!" Amelia said, forestalling the butler. "We must leave at once."

"At once," Caleb agreed.

"At once," Grimshaw practically pleaded.

"You can't just go running off into the night," Ottersock said. "Especially since I have come all the way here to talk to you. Close the damn door and point me in the direction of the nearest teakettle."

Grimshaw began swinging the door shut with an even more doleful expression than usual.

"Wait!" Amelia interjected. The butler froze once again. "We must stop Vanity before she steals the brooch!"

"*Pff,*" Ottersock scoffed. "Miss Tunnicliffe is just a girl with a mediocre education. She's no danger to anyone."

"She has a gun," Caleb said tersely.

"And contacts in the black market," Amelia added.

"And she's smarter than she acts," they concluded in unison.

Ottersock hesitated at last, his eyes sharp as he regarded them. Amelia suspected, however, that it was not their arguments he was considering but their physical proximity to each other. She moved a discreet step away from Caleb, then realized with an internal wince that doing so had only served to highlight just how close to him she'd actually been. Ottersock's regard grew so sharp he could have outright stabbed her with it.

"The only place you two are going is into a private room with me," he declared. "I want to know why I received a bill for one hundred pounds from the Black Boar pub in Staveley. One. Hundred. 'For damages incurred.' And why Lady Ruperta

Harroway sent a testy letter demanding the university replace her dining room set. And I don't want to even ask about that coat rack. I sent you to Cumbria to *stop* the damages, for God's sake! Now this excellent gentleman butler is going to close the door and direct us to the warmest room in the house, with no further arguments."

"The parlor," Amelia suggested in weary surrender. "That's where Professor Throckmorton and Mr. Dummersby from the British Museum are. I'm sure they'll be glad to see you."

Instantly, Ottersock went pale. Snatching the pipe from his lips, he jabbed it at Grimshaw, who almost had the door shut. "What are you *doing*, man?! Open that at once! We're leaving! Sterling!" Now he directed the pipe at Caleb, who appeared entirely confused at this extreme change of attitude. "Help Tarrant get her luggage into my carriage. And hurry! We have to go before they find out that I'm here."

Within minutes the three antiquarians were crowded into Ottersock's rented carriage and being driven toward Lancaster by a villager who'd been offered a small fortune (six pounds and a signed copy of the professor's memoirs) to do so. "Forget waiting for a train at Staveley; we'll travel on through the night," Ottersock said, relighting his pipe while Amelia and Caleb, side by side on the bench seat opposite him, tried to get comfortable beneath armloads of their luggage. They regarded the faculty head with bemusement, for although this haste was (a) excellent, it was also (b) uncharacteristic of the man and (c-d) inexplicable, if not outright weird.

Seeing their expressions, Ottersock finally explained in a redolent puff of tobacco smoke: "I can't risk Dummersby knowing I'm anywhere in Cumbria. Last time I happened upon him at the Minervaeum, he trapped me in a corner for an hour, prattling on about his latest display of Egyptian jewelry. *It wasn't even enchanted jewelry!* And as for Basil Throckmorton— if he tells me one more time that the history department needs to start putting on plays to educate students by way of entertainment, I will be tempted to violence. Learning should not be *fun*, or else every Tom, Dick, and Harry will want to do it, and experts will become ten a penny. God knows a professor's salary is low enough as it is!" Furious, he pursed his lips so tight, his pipe jutted upward. "Besides," he added, with the pipe bobbing, "you said Miss Tunnicliffe was in trouble."

"*Causing* trouble," Caleb corrected him, but Ottersock wasn't interested in becoming informed.

"Can't imagine it of the girl, frankly. Sweet, good-humored, ladylike creature she was. No, you must have gotten the wrong idea. Trust me, I have an excellent nose for sniffing out lies."

Puffing his pipe aggressively, he scrutinized first Amelia, then Caleb, then the two of them together. "You both look done in. Let me guess: still dire enemies, fighting each other at every turn? *Tsk.* I was at a meeting of faculty heads the other day and you two were quite the topic of discussion. The consensus was that, if you can't come to an accord, Professor Tarrant will have to be transferred to a curator role at the British Museum. Dummersby's been offering a plum role for you, dear."

It was as if he'd punched her in the stomach. Amelia blinked with a calm that forestalled the sobs she could quite easily (and probably hysterically) have wept in that moment. After all she'd done over these past few months to protect her job, it remained at risk. She comprehended at last, with a dreary kind of surrender, that no matter what she did, Ottersock would persist in keeping her teetering on the edge of demotion or outright unemployment, just to show her that he was the one with power, no matter how successful and professional a woman she might be.

Caleb shifted a little beside her, his edges becoming sharper, his jaw tightening in a way that warned Amelia two seconds before he spoke. "You said the same thing when we were deemed too friendly," he reminded Ottersock.

Judging from the rapidity with which Ottersock's face reddened, Caleb's gender alone saved him from being evicted from the carriage on the basis of impertinence. "There must be moderation in all things, Sterling. If history teaches us nothing else, it is this."

Amelia would have laughed were circumstances different. History had taught her that you only got what you wanted if you were immoderate, intense, and preferably had an army at your back. But perhaps the lesson was different for women. She wondered what Isabella, the She-Wolf of France, would do in this situation.

And then, since murdering Ottersock with his pipe was not really an option, she gave a silent sigh and turned her focus to the carriage window. The world outside was a weeping darkness, not even one single light to be seen for hope's sake. It felt like she was still inside Ravenscroft Manor, only in concentrated form.

"I notice," Caleb said to Ottersock, "that no one is forcing Throckmorton out of his job because he has an enmity with Professor Tarrant . . . and with me . . . and with *you*, for that matter."

Ottersock sniffed. "Throckmorton is a tenured professor. The only way we'll get rid of him is if someone accidentally hands him an explosive medieval antique."

"But you can get rid of me," Caleb pointed out. "I'm the one who should take the curator job."

"Don't be ridiculous, Sterling," Ottersock snapped. Then his facial expression shifted. "I don't suppose Sir Nigel had any explosive medieval antiques . . . ?" When Amelia and Caleb shook their heads, he sighed with regret. Leaning back, he closed his eyes and puffed malodorous smoke into a silence that haunted the carriage as they drove on through the night.

STOPPING IN OXENHOLME to change the horses, they ate dinner at a plump, whitewashed coaching inn that had survived the railway network's dominance by offering a hearty stew, a cozy atmosphere, and several bedrooms possessing only one bed. Ottersock considered resting here until morning, since it was a safe distance from Dummersby, but the place was so crammed with travelers that people were having to share rooms. (Luckily, they all just happened to be married.) Alas, a glass of whiskey to ease the discomforts of the journey was deemed impossible, since the university's reputation would be jeopardized by them taking alcohol, even in moderation, and despite the fact that they were two hundred miles from Oxford with nothing but Ottersock's pipe to suggest they were professors. Tea was the only decent thing under the circumstances. Caleb loaded his cup with sugar just to feel alive.

As soon as their carriage was ready, they continued southward. Ottersock fell asleep, his snores gusting like a breeze through his whiskers and the odor of mutton stew wafting from him every now and again. Amelia and Caleb could neither converse nor relax against each other, however, for fear of him waking at any moment and catching them at it. Consequently, Caleb's back began to ache with a vile intensity for which he could find no relief; ditto his heart.

Stopping again in Burton-in-Kendal sometime near midnight, they used the bathroom facilities at the Kings Arms coaching inn; then Caleb and Amelia stood together on the footpath outside, waiting for the carriage to arrive with its new horses. Ottersock lingered indoors, reversing the meal he'd had during their last stop.

The village was brightly moonlit, its skies a marvel of cloudlessness that Caleb could not quite believe. The stone buildings lining each side of the street held a restful silence that dragged on his exhausted body until he yearned to simply lie down right where he was and sleep. Remaining upright felt heroic, and the fact that Amelia was more interested in their surroundings than in him was grievous. He stretched his back, rubbed his face wearily, and sighed with such fervor that she finally looked at him.

At once, he forgot all his aches. She was a moon goddess, all pearly white and haunting dark, with eyes that were ancient shadow-seas. She was beauty exemplified. She was also frowning, and Caleb winced both anxiously and apologetically—offering her two options, since he had no idea what he'd done wrong. Usually he could tell from the angle of her mouth, or the way she held her smallest finger. But increasingly these days she was a mystery to him. He could sense her feeling things she didn't tell him about, and it worried him—enthralled him—made him want to unwrap her and find the secret inside.

At least one thing he knew for sure: "Ottersock is an ass." Saying this, he took her nearest hand and chafed it gently between both of his to warm her fingers and console her spirit if he could. "But even given that, he won't fire you, no matter how often he threatens and blusters."

"I know," Amelia answered calmly.

Ah. Caleb had become an expert in her calm over the years, and this particular gradient of it communicated quite clearly that she was pissed off. Or, as Amelia herself would no doubt put it, *a little vexed, but not to the extent that anyone need concern themselves.* When she was in this mood, Caleb absolutely did concern himself with it. Kissing her hand, he tucked it into her skirt pocket, alongside the little book that was in there, then took the other hand to begin warming that one too.

"Everything will be all right," he told her, smiling. "We've obviously been getting a little too much into the spirit of fake hating. We'll tone it down to mild annoyance instead, and Ottersock is sure to leave us alone."

Amelia abruptly snatched her hand from his and looked away, staring so intently at a chimney that Caleb was amazed it did not topple. Moonlight limned her profile, and the cold air became a ghost within her breath. Gazing at her, Caleb had to quite honestly admit that he was amazed *he* didn't topple. She wasn't just a moon goddess; she was a whole pantheon in single form. Indeed, she reminded him of the marble bust of Aphrodite he'd seen in the V&A Museum that whispered fragments of Hesiod's poetry when touched. Not that Amelia was poetic, of course—except in her bones and her breath and the sweep of her extraordinary eyelashes.

I love you. The old, bittersweet thought arose from the mental safe bag Caleb kept it in, deep beneath his heart. Now he was the one who looked away. The two of them stared in opposite directions.

"There's no fixing this, Caleb," Amelia said in a low voice that had grown so calm it was practically the doldrums.

Of course there is, he wanted to reply. *I'll take care of you, and you'll take care of me, just as we've always done.* But in truth, she was right. There was no fixing it, because it no longer was "just as always." A new vulnerability had come upon them these days, one that expressed itself as kisses, whereas before it had been only smiles and touches that pretended an innocent friendship.

"You're right," he said. "I wish I could give Ottersock a real piece of my mind. Actually, I wish I could punch him in the nose, and Throckmorton too. Let me, Meely. It won't fix anything, but it will make me feel better."

He turned to give her an imploring look and found her gazing at him with big, soft eyes, just as she had when they were eight years old and he'd won her eternal devotion by presenting his handkerchief. He'd treasured that moment ever since. Remembering it now, he felt all grandiloquent sentiment and poetry fall away, leaving only profound silence in his heart.

"Thank you for offering to fight for me," Amelia said in barely more than a whisper. "That means so much. But . . ." She smiled. "Prison would be terrible for your complexion."

"True," he said, and sighed. "Are you going to take the job in Germany?"

"No." Such a small and simple word, but it saved Caleb from utter heartbreak (since he would of course have gone with her, and he hated bratwurst). "I don't want to leave Oxford, and yet I'm not sure if I can bear continuing on as we have been."

"Understandable," Caleb said. "We can invent a new scheme. Fake rivalry, perhaps. Fake—"

Amelia closed her eyes, and he stopped immediately. He

waited, feeling anxiously that they were on a precipice and one step in the wrong direction would prove fatal.

"I don't mean how other people see us," she told him, the words seeming to tiptoe as if she sensed the precipice too, "but how we see ourselves. I want to be your friend." And before Caleb could answer with something inane, such as *you are*, she added quickly, "I would say 'more than a friend,' but that's not right. It's not about more, it's about . . . deeper. I want to be . . . do . . . all the things that the very best friends can."

"You mean like eating from the same bowl of ice cream?" Caleb asked, because he knew what she really meant and his stupid, stupid brain tripped over itself in an excess of nerves. He winced. *Damn it.* There was only one thing to do now. But bare, solemn sincerity always frightened him. He'd spent so long being charming, cheerful, and pretty, hoping that people would like him enough to give him what he needed to survive in the rookery—in boarding school—in adult life with all its perils. But he didn't want to just survive when it came to his relationship with Amelia. His pulse skittered as he took a deep breath and spoke.

"I want to take you into my bed," he said, quiet and serious and oh God so brave, "and show you just how much of a friend you are to me."

Amelia's eyes grew wide, brimming over with such sorrow, such longing, that Caleb felt rocked by it. She said nothing, but words would have been superfluous anyway, considering the lyricism in her gaze. Caleb could not restrain himself from reaching out to cup her beloved face with one hand, stroking his thumb across the moon-soaked skin.

"My soul is friends with yours," he said. "I want no more limits on expressing that."

She swallowed heavily. "That's what I was trying to say too."

Triumph rushed through him, conquering all fear. He sent a quick glance over her shoulder, checking that they were alone, before he stepped closer to her. "I want not even clothes between us. I want to be inside of you."

"Yes," she whispered in return, gazing up at him adoringly and making him harden with just that look. "I want to open myself to take you in."

"Slowly at first," he said, his thumb stroking her lips now. They parted for him, her softly gasping breath warming his skin. "So slow . . . in and then gliding out a little before inching forward again, teasing you, indulging in you, until at last I can go no deeper."

"And then?" she asked so softly the words were just a dream. But Caleb heard them; he knew her so well. He bent his head so that the universe shrank to the heated little space between them.

"And then faster," he whispered. "And faster, my beautiful moon, my darling friend, until I bring you to such pleasure, you scream my name, not caring who might hear you."

"Oh God," she breathed.

"You can just call me Caleb."

They were so close now that their smiles felt like the same smile reflected back and forth; like kisses without quite touching. Caleb no longer remembered the name of the village they stood in. It could have been a wilderness for all he knew. It could have been a windowless, hidden room deep inside Ravenscroft Manor, and the whole journey south with Ottersock just a fever dream. Nowhere mattered, nothing in the world mattered, except this woman.

"Amelia Victoria Tarrant," he said. "I lov—"

"You cannot be serious!"

Ottersock's appalled shout struck them like a shock wave, pushing them apart with such speed that Amelia almost fell. Caleb reached out to steady her, but she avoided his hand, frowning so darkly he had to choke back a wounded sound, even knowing that she was faking. Girding everything that could possibly be girded, he turned to face the faculty head.

But Ottersock was not even looking their way. He stood by the door of the coaching inn, arguing with the proprietor.

"It's not my fault your plumbing system is inadequate!"

Caleb dared not glance at Amelia, for fear he'd start laughing or possibly crying. But he nudged her with the back of his hand, and she tapped her fingers against his in reply, and it was as much a conversation as words would have been. *I love you. I love you. It's us, always.*

Just then, the rented carriage arrived, its driver yawning widely. Caleb held Amelia's hand as she climbed in, and she brushed his thigh as he sat beside her. The air trembled. The silence between them was so lush with secret understanding that even Ottersock, dropping onto the seat opposite them, fanned himself with his gloved hand.

"Whew, is it hot in here, or is it just me?" he asked.

"It's not you," Caleb said. And setting his bag atop his lap for safety's sake, he leaned back, closed his eyes, and dreamed his way through the long, aching night in the hope of a new day to come.

Chapter Twenty-Two

If you want to be remembered,
you must be memorable.

I, on the Past, Cornelius Ottersock

THE SUN WAS rising among the still-dreaming towers of Oxford when the historians finally reached the city. It being Friday, the train station was packed with students heading off for weekend jaunts with a blithe disregard for the day's lectures. Amelia, beyond exhausted from the drive to Lancaster and the consequent train journey to London, then Oxford, abandoned both Caleb and Ottersock to bustle at speed through the crowd before all the noise and smells and general peopling induced in her a nervous breakdown. Indeed, such a hurry was she in that she did not even see the man exiting the turnstile beside her until she crashed into him.

"Careful there, Professor," he said as Amelia swayed from the impact. His voice sent a shock through her nervous system. She'd heard it only once before but would never forget it.

"Sergeant Sheffield!"

Suddenly, Caleb catapulted over the turnstile to reach her side, placing a hand against her back as he pointed threateningly at

Sheffield, who stared back with a detachment that did not entirely conceal glints of amusement.

"Don't even think of touching her!" Caleb growled.

"What are you—" Amelia began, but the throng of passengers exiting the station was jostling around them with an impatience that neared violence.

"Come with me if you want Miss Tunnicliffe to live," Sheffield ordered, and on that thrilling but perplexing note the three of them sidled hastily out of the traffic's flow. Once in a quieter space, Amelia scowled at the sergeant.

"What are you talking about? And what are you doing here?"

"And did you just get off the same train as us?" Caleb added, looking confusedly back at the turnstile through which they'd all come. Sheffield gave a brusque nod.

"Missed the train from Staveley," he answered with a Throckmorton degree of scorn for pronouns. "Galloped to Manchester, caught one from there." Reaching into his jacket, he drew out a leather wallet, which he unfolded to display a small metal plate. "Home Office."

"You're joking." Caleb tipped forward to peer more closely at the badge, then straightened with a look of surprise. "You're not joking."

"We got a tip-off that the Harroway house contained a number of dangerous items and that a team of historians was going to check them out. It sounded like the setup for a heist, so I was sent to investigate. Our suspicions were confirmed when Sir Nigel reported various objects missing. At first I thought you were the likely suspect . . ." He eyed Caleb, and the air seemed to ring with a laugh that was not uttered. "I considered Throckmorton next, but that man is nothing more than a buffoon. As for Dummersby—he didn't need to steal

anything, since it was all going to his museum in the first place."
Sighing, he shook his head. "I've seen battle, but this has been
the most exhausting assignment I've ever known. The rain. The
boredom. I was beginning to think that some doodad in the
house had killed me without my realizing, and that I was a ghost.
Then Miss Tunnicliffe brought me back to life by snatching
your teaspoon."

"You didn't suspect me?" Amelia could not help but ask,
feeling oddly put out.

Sheffield turned to her, solemn. "Ma'am, you could do no
wrong even if you tried."

"Oh." She blinked at such an unexpected compliment, her
face heating with delight. "Oh."

Caleb grinned, nudging her. "See? You're an angel. Even
Sheffield thinks so."

"Professor Tarrant is a woman of excellent quality," Sheffield agreed.

Amelia pressed a hand to the base of her throat in hopes
that doing so might repress the warm tears that suddenly
threatened. "You're very kind, but—"

"An exemplar of female grace and intelligence," Sheffield
continued, speaking right over her.

"True," Caleb said, although he took hold of Amelia's hand
in a way that made it very clear to any man in the vicinity, and
Sergeant Sheffield particularly, that she belonged with *him*.

"Decent, dignified, gracious, and elegant," the sergeant continued nonetheless.

"Right, we get the idea." Caleb maneuvered Amelia back
several inches lest the man attempt a marriage proposal. "So
when you took the horse from us at the manor, it was to chase
Vanity?"

"Yes. My source in the Harroways' staff informed me of Miss Tunnicliffe stealing your teaspoon and fleeing the premises. I hoped I could save her from harm—"

"You mean from *doing* harm," Caleb interjected.

Sheffield frowned. "The young lady is refined, tenderhearted, and innocent of true malice—"

"Excuse me, we are talking about Miss *Vanity* Tunnicliffe?" Caleb interjected again. "The woman who flirted with me for days, no doubt trying to get information, then kidnapped me and threatened to shoot me?"

"She is perhaps a little misguided in her ways."

Amelia did not roll her eyes, but it must be said that her pleasure in the compliments the sergeant had given her disintegrated as it now became clear what a lousy judge of character he was.

"Actually, Vanity has a very definite guide," Caleb retorted in a bitter tone, "and it's aimed right at Dervorguilla of Galloway's brooch, in Balliol College."

Sheffield's frown shifted to a more professional angle. "Brooch?"

"An extremely dangerous brooch," Amelia told him. "Vanity doesn't appreciate just how dangerous—"

"Of course she doesn't," Sheffield interjected solemnly. "Such a sweet and pretty lass, she's clearly been corrupted by some fiend."

"I'm beginning to see what Lady Ruperta meant about the Home Office being useless," Caleb murmured to Amelia.

"Hm," she replied dourly. She considered demanding whether Sheffield would be so forgiving about a male thief but decided there was no point. The man had obviously fallen under the thrall of the wicked teaspoon thief at some stage during their time at Ravenscroft Manor. No doubt all that giggling had done the trick. Amelia couldn't help but wonder if she herself could get Ottersock and Throckmorton to like her more if she tried the same thing. The thought was so dreadful, it brought her back to her senses within half a second.

"We need to stop Vanity from using my teaspoon to break through the brooch's protective case and steal it," she told Sheffield. "A collision of two such intense magical energy sources could cause tremendous damage . . . and hurt poor Miss Tunnicliffe," she added cleverly, causing Sheffield's eyes to widen.

Just then, Ottersock appeared, panting from exertion. "There you are! Why did you disappear in the crowd like that? And why are you just standing around chatting now? Didn't you drag me through the night across half of England so you could protect Balliol from some girl?"

"Professors Tarrant and Sterling have been acting in the interests of national security," Sheffield intoned sternly.

"Who are you, the police?" Ottersock jeered.

"Home Office," Sheffield snapped, holding up his wallet.

Blanching, Ottersock came to attention at once. The fact of the Material History faculty being authorized by said Home Office to deal in thaumaturgic objects was pretty much all that elevated his staff from being a bunch of weird people who fussed over old knickknacks, like Sir Nigel was, into estimable academics. "Lead on," he said, gesturing with deference to the sergeant.

"No, after you," the sergeant replied, gesturing in turn.

"No, no, I insist."

"No, *I* insist," Sheffield, er, insisted. "I don't know the bloody way."

THEY ELECTED TO catch a tram to Broad Street, thereby halving the journey's time. However, this also placed the fate of Balliol College in the hands of Oxford's public transport schedule, and after several achingly long minutes of waiting at the tram stop . . . double-checking the timetable . . . fidgeting . . . pacing . . . frowning along the road as if doing so would magically make the tram appear, it became clear that they had made the wrong choice. And yet there also existed the terrible possibility that, the very minute they gave up and started to walk, the tram would arrive. As a result, they dared not move.

When at last the tram did come, pulled by a horse whose miserable expression suggested that it had given up all dreams of frolicking in green pastures, there was The Queue to be endured. No British person worth their tea and crumpets was going to let anyone jump ahead of them, Home Office badge or not. Consequently, by the time they arrived at last on Broad Street, they could have run there in far shorter time. Nerves were stretched so tight that even Amelia was on the verge of losing her calm.

"The brooch is kept on display in the Hall," Caleb told Sergeant Sheffield as they ran into the college's Front Quadrangle. "That's where the members dine."

"Thankfully, breakfast will be finished by now," Amelia said.

"You go ahead," Ottersock urged breathlessly, waving them on. "I'll let the proctors know what's happening."

He turned away, and the others ran through to the Garden Quadrangle. There, students were milling about, chatting, dozing on the grass, and generally doing all they could to avoid being educated. They watched with only vague interest as the historians and Sergeant Sheffield raced along the path, for this was Oxford: if they were to be agog every time someone had to save the city from an impending magical explosion, they'd soon develop eye strain.

At the far end of the Quad stood the Hall, a magnificent building of pale silver-and-gold-hued stone, with tall arched windows and a gabled roof that sported a single ornate steeple at its center. Although it had been built just fourteen years earlier, Amelia usually felt like she was entering a grand old church as she climbed its wide granite stairs, passing beneath the archway halfway up, inhaling the dusty shadows. But this morning her only sense was aggravation at having to run up those stairs in a long skirt.

Arriving at the upper landing, they discovered the dining chamber's double-sided door was closed. Screaming and crashes could be heard through the wooden panels. "Open it, hurry!" Sheffield urged Caleb, who was rattling and tugging at the door's handle without effect.

"It's locked," Caleb told him.

"Stand back." Pushing Caleb aside, Sheffield grabbed hold of the door handle with his massive hand and rattled and tugged without effect.

"Gosh, I'd never have thought of trying that," Caleb muttered.

Amelia stepped forward. "Let me."

"I don't think you'll have better luck, ma'am," Sheffield said kindly (in other words, condescendingly, but with a well-meaning smile).

"Nevertheless," Amelia replied in the tone every man

recognizes as A Woman at the End of Her Patience. Wisely, Sheffield retreated. Amelia pulled a delicate brass hairpin from her coiffure and, with some careful manipulation, inserted it into the door's keyhole.

"That won't work, ma'am," Sheffield advised her. "It's a myth that hairpins can open a lock. You'd best step aside so that I—"

Click.

Amelia glanced with a forgivably smug smile at Sheffield, whose own expression had gone blank. Behind him, Caleb was trying not to laugh.

"I was head girl at secondary school," she explained. "I spent half my days unlocking things." Sliding the clip once more into her coiffure, she opened the door and entered the dining hall.

"Oh, dear," she said in dismay.

"What is it?" Sheffield demanded, hurrying in behind her, Caleb at his heels. Both men stopped abruptly, staring.

A long chamber stood before them, its portrait-laden walls gleaming as morning sunlight shone through several arched windows on either side. Four narrow tables stretched toward a low dais at the far end where the masters' table stood. A few bench seats had toppled over, and a few table lamps lay broken among them. But the glass-domed plinth that held Dervorguilla's sapphire brooch stood untouched at one corner of the dais, and altogether the chamber's state appeared not much worse than the aftermath of a rowdy dinner. With one exception: an eerie blue tint stained the air, sparkling with dust motes.

"Magic," Caleb said.

"Miss Tunnicliffe is not here," Sheffield noted.

Amelia pointed to the vaulted wooden beams overhead. "Look again."

Vanity floated high above them. Arms sprawling, purple-and-red lace dress hanging like the flag of an especially enthusiastic country, she was endeavoring to turn herself toward the door, but moving with all the grace and efficiency of a swimmer in a mud pool. *"Help!"* she screamed. *"Help me!"*

"Stay calm," Amelia called to her in the perfectly unruffled tone that only a teacher who daily faces anxious students (to say nothing of exploding antiques) can achieve. "We'll get you down in no time at all."

"Aaahhhh!" Vanity replied (much as the students tended to do, especially when the antiques exploded).

"What happened to her?" Sheffield asked, his voice unsteady, his eyes straining as if he could will the girl into a safe descent.

"She got her comeuppance," Caleb said, and Amelia whacked him with the back of her hand.

"The teaspoon has psycho-conjunctive powers," she explained more sensibly. "And a rather twisted sense of humor. Perhaps Miss Tunnicliffe was thinking highly of herself when she tried to use it to break the brooch's security dome."

"How will we get her down?" Sheffield demanded, not taking his gaze from the levitating girl. "A ladder won't reach that far. What if the magic stops? She'll never survive the fall!"

"I have a plan," Amelia said, although it was only now taking shape in her mind. "It's a little risky—"

"Risky?!" Sheffield and Vanity squealed in unison.

"—but you are correct about the possibility of the magic stopping. Most thaumaturgic effects are short-lived."

"Perhaps that's not the best phrasing to use in Vanity's presence, under the circumstances," Caleb murmured.

"Sh," Amelia whispered to him. She gave Vanity the reassuring smile that never failed to work on students whose academic prospects were almost as dire as the girl's current situation. "Never fear, Miss Tunnicliffe! You can count on me to save you. Now, if you please, where is my teaspoon?"

"I dropped the horrid thing over there!" Vanity said, gesturing in a way that encompassed half the Hall. "All I did was touch it to the glass dome and everything went—"

"Boom?" Amelia suggested.

"More like zoom," Caleb said, pointing upward.

"Aaaahhh!" Vanity screamed, and not just in response to their wit. She had suddenly dropped several inches before coming to an abrupt, juddering halt. "Aaaahhh!" she added, grabbing at the air.

"Aaaahh!" Sheffield screamed, gesticulating wildly.

Amelia sighed. "Caleb, would you please fetch the teaspoon?"

At once he took off running down the Hall, leaping over fallen benches with a casual athleticism that Amelia would have liked to admire, if only she had time. She returned her attention to Vanity.

"Those earrings you're wearing—are they gold? Real gold?" Vanity nodded, her topknot bouncing. "Perfect. Take one out and throw it down to me, please."

Weeping and bemoaning fate's cruelty, Vanity removed an earring and dropped it. Amelia caught the little bob in her cupped palm.

"Aaaaahhhh!" Vanity resumed.

"Miss Tunnicliffe!" Sheffield called up to her. "Be brave!"

"I really could do with a nice quiet ghost hunt just now,"

Amelia muttered to herself. "Right," she said briskly to the sergeant. "I'm going to bring her down by magical means. Hopefully the descent will be slow, but—"

"I'll catch her," Sheffield interrupted with a determination that brooked no consideration of physics. He strode to position himself beneath Vanity, crouching with his feet apart and arms spread—a pose that was certain to have no effect whatsoever if the girl dropped as rapidly as her earring had done. There was no way to predict with absolute certainty what might happen, but Amelia consoled herself that she was giving Vanity the best chance she could, and that Balliol had an excellent janitorial team should it go badly.

"Found the teaspoon," Caleb announced, crawling out from beneath the dais's table. Getting to his feet, he blew strands of hair away from his eyes as he looked along the Hall to Amelia. He clearly had no idea what she was planning but trusted her nevertheless. Excitement glinted in his expression. Amelia couldn't help but feel the same lovely, tingly sense of fun. This was the best part of antiquarianism—not finding magical antiques, but using them!

Reaching into her skirt pocket, she drew out the safe bag containing Sir Nigel's thaumaturgic locket. With sedate professionalism—disguising the fact that she'd forgotten to store the dangerous magical antique in a proper manner, and suggesting instead that she'd purposefully kept it to hand for an occasion such as this very one—she removed the locket and cast aside the bag (which is to say, set it neatly on a nearby table).

"Ready?" she asked Sheffield.

"Ready," he affirmed.

"Ready?" she called up to Vanity.

"*No!*" the girl cried.

Without further ado, Amelia opened the locket's case and placed Vanity's gold earring inside.

Nothing happened.

Holding her breath, Amelia angled the lid slowly downward . . .

"Uhh." The nervous sound shook from Vanity's throat as she began to descend at a gentle pace . . . "Aaaahhh!" It suddenly swooped up in pitch as the woman herself swooped up—then shot toward the door—then spun around—and began flying first one way, then another, like a purple-and-red bee that had drunk too much fermented nectar.

"Aaaahhh!" Sheffield hollered, running hither and yon to remain beneath her, arms still outstretched, face a study in panic. "What's happening?!"

"I'd say the teaspoon's metaphysical energy is interacting with that of the locket in a decidedly nonconstructive manner," Amelia said, frowning a little.

"What?" Sheffield stared at her with frazzled bewilderment.

"The streams have crossed," Amelia explained again. She looked along the chamber to Caleb, and he looked back in silence, his expression steady. They both knew what had to happen now.

"Must I?" she asked him.

He shrugged. "It's your decision."

Her frown deepened. "Bother." With a glance at Vanity, who was on a dizzy spiral up toward the high apex of the ceiling, she turned back to Caleb and sighed. "Fine. Do it."

He smiled at her like a blown kiss. It was lovely, beautiful—and did not help at all. Amelia watched with dark eyes as he grabbed a chair and proceeded to employ it in smashing a window.

"You needn't look so enthused," Amelia grumbled.

"Come on, Meely!" he replied, eyes bright. "Every Balliol student would love to do this!"

CRASH. Glass shattered.

"Get ready, Sergeant," Amelia warned Sheffield with automatic professionalism, even while she continued to watch Caleb. He cast the chair aside, and with a force that spoke of all those weekends playing rugby, he threw the Hereford teaspoon through the broken window.

"Eeee!" Vanity fell like a stone.

CHAPTER TWENTY-THREE

History might have no beginning points,
but it certainly has endings.

I, on the Past, Cornelius Ottersock

SO, YOU SEE, because the locket's magic creates a bonding effect, my placing Miss Tunnicliffe's earring inside it allowed me to bind her to its vicinity—close to the ground—and so counteract the teaspoon's effects, bringing her down from the ceiling."

Amelia paused following this explanation, looking at Ottersock's desk rather than directly at the faculty head himself. Caleb suspected that she was arguing with herself over whether she should apologize for the Hall's broken window and also Sheffield's cracked knee, caused when the man fell after catching Vanity. So he quickly spoke before she could.

"It was all my fault."

"Actually, it's my fault," Ottersock said as he poured willow-bark powder into his tea. "I should have sent you both on assignment to Greenland and left you there. Although you'd probably have caused a fire on the glaciers, knowing you two. As it is, you were damned lucky that poor Miss Tunnicliffe didn't plunge to her death."

He stirred his tea like exclamation points in action, the teaspoon clinking sharply against the cup. On his desk lay another teaspoon: the little Hereford antique that had started all of this. After Caleb had tossed it through the Hall's window, it landed by sheer misfortune in front of Balliol's second-best student, who knew how to recognize not only a thaumaturgic antique but an opportunity to become first-best. As Ottersock strode past him toward the Hall with proctors in tow, the enterprising young fellow had handed the teaspoon over. Caleb doubted that Ottersock would ever relinquish it to Amelia again. And judging from the rigidity of her posture, she believed the same.

"We were not lucky, Professor," she said, her voice so steady and polite that the contradiction sounded practically like an agreement. "I closed the locket's lid at a slow pace, which I was certain would be reflected in Miss Tunnicliffe's rate of descent. I was correct."

Ottersock halted in raising his teacup to pin her with a dictatorial stare. "You were *lucky*, Tarrant."

"Yes, sir," Amelia said, and Caleb bit back a curse word.

"It seems all's well that end's well, however," Ottersock relented. He sipped tea, his face contorting with disgust at its taste. "Miss Tunnicliffe was unable to get hold of Dervorguilla's brooch."

All three of them shivered at the thought of her coming close to doing so.

"I might just have a word with Balliol's master about putting that brooch in a restricted area," Ottersock said. "Such power is simply too dangerous for public viewing, even with special protection."

"The power of truth," Caleb mused soberly.

"Can you imagine if just anyone was able to get their hands on it?" Ottersock added more willow bark to his tea and stirred with a troubled vigor. "Truth is not something that should be bandied about freely!"

Caleb did not argue. He also refrained from pointing out that Ottersock had inadvertently picked up the Hereford teaspoon instead of his own.

"Thank goodness poor Miss Tunnicliffe is unharmed by her ordeal," the professor said.

"Indeed," Caleb drawled. "Aggravated robbery is such a wearying task."

Ottersock scowled at him. "Sergeant Sheffield has taken the girl into his custody and will make sure she gets what she deserves."

"A wedding ring, no doubt," Caleb said, thinking of Sheffield's red face and foolish grin when Vanity had clung to him after her rescue. From the corner of his eye, he glimpsed Amelia's lips twitch in the world's smallest, briefest smile.

Ottersock tried scowling again but then gave it up with a tired sigh. He dropped the teaspoon haphazardly onto his desk, causing milky droplets to sprinkle across the mail strewn there, then drank the medicine through a grimace. "Ugh," he said, setting down the cup. "Sometimes I think the migraine would be more pleasant than the cure. I—"

He stopped, his eyes growing wide, as a slip of paper began drifting up from his desk. Hastily snatching it, he looked around the room in bemusement. "Strange, I didn't feel a breeze." Amelia shot Caleb a fleeting, darkly amused glance, and he found himself struck with a desire to kiss her, deeply and passionately, right there in front of their faculty head. Fortunately, a ripe snort of derisive laughter from Ottersock squelched the impulse.

"It's a telegram from that fool Dummersby," the professor said, flapping the slip of paper. "He says it's taking longer than expected to assess the Harroway collection, and he wants some students sent up to help him. As if one man's antiques require so much work! I'm guessing you all spent your time hiking and picnicking and playing parlor games."

"No, Professor," Amelia answered primly, but Ottersock just scoffed at this.

"You are hardly a trustworthy source, Tarrant. Professor Throckmorton telegraphed me days ago to say you'd been flirting with Sir Nigel. I know you can't help yourself, being female, but I confess myself disappointed."

Caleb's jaw dropped, preventing him from coming to Amelia's immediate defense. She, however, just gazed beyond Ottersock's shoulder with a calm that made her appear like marble, pure and untouched by human concerns.

"At least we have the locket," Ottersock continued, huffing through his bushy whiskers. "I'll send it over to the museum just as soon as I . . ."

His voice drifted off, and his eyes grew so dreamy it was obvious he was enjoying a vision in which he placed strands of their hair inside the locket and threw the whole thing into the Thames River. Then another piece of mail floated up from the desk, fluttering imperatively, and he snatched it.

"Huh, it's from you, Tarrant. Postmarked 'Staveley.'" He looked questioningly at Amelia, even as Caleb did the same, but she continued to stare into the middle distance. Her face had turned white—and yet in every other respect she retained that cold, inhuman calm. For the first time in all the years he'd known her, Caleb finally understood that it was not a defense but a prison. It kept her from being herself in a way that might incur the disapproval of her parents and teachers.

"I thought I had destroyed that letter," she said impassively. "I must have burned another by accident."

"What does it say?" Caleb and Ottersock asked together, although with different tones of wariness.

"By all means, open it," Amelia told them.

Caleb watched with a growing sense of dread as Ottersock tore the envelope and withdrew its contents. No doubt Amelia had merely sent a dutiful report about their work's progress at Ravenscroft Manor . . .

But his instincts knew that she had not.

Ottersock's eyebrows lowered in a preemptive frown as he unfolded the letter, then suddenly shot up like a pair of electrified sheep. "You resign?!" he shouted.

"You resign?!" Caleb echoed, staring at Amelia in astonishment.

"I do," she replied tranquilly.

Caleb opened his mouth . . . then closed it again. He was beyond words. He could not even see words on the farthest horizon. Amelia resigning did not in itself surprise him; she'd talked about it before, after all, and had a job offer from a German university, should she wish to take it. The timing was also understandable, since she'd written that letter sometime during the past week, on an assignment that would have made even the steadiest person want to quit—obviously, considering the most steady person in England had just done so. What he failed to comprehend was that she'd written it without telling him.

"Why?" Ottersock demanded, shaking the letter at Amelia. She did not flinch, but she did blink rather heavily, and it was all Caleb could do not to grab Ottersock's hand to stop him. "Why? Why would you do this?"

Amelia smiled. But it was a faint, poignant smile, and Caleb's heart plunged into the very pit of his being, a darkness wherein he'd buried memories of his father's death, and hungry nights, and the day he was almost expelled from school because a teacher caught him reading her volume of Charles Baudelaire's erotic poetry. He recognized a pivotal moment when he saw one.

"I'm resigning," Amelia said, "because I love—"

"Stop," Caleb said, clutching her arm before he knew what he was doing. It was hardly the action of a man who supposedly hated her, and yet he found himself unable to let her go, even as Ottersock looked on with a rapidly darkening glower.

Amelia turned her smile to him. She was beautiful, beautiful; she was everything to him. Just the sight of her transformed a world with slums and rotting stables into an absolute paradise. Caleb wondered dimly, rather desperately, if he should go down on his knees to her right then and there—the same thing he wondered every single time he looked into those midnight eyes, that face like moonlight. But Amelia took his hand gently and eased it away from her arm.

"I'm resigning," she said, "because I love me."

Then just like that, she turned and walked away.

AMELIA WENT HOME. Two students and a fellow professor attempted to waylay her, each of them in possession of some urgent problem only she could solve, but Amelia just smiled, shook her head, and kept going.

In her cozy, book-lined flat on Norham Road, she dropped her suitcase without another glance at it and, shedding clothes as she walked through the lounge into the tiny bathroom, she drew herself a bath. Sinking into its warm, rose-perfumed water, sighing wearily, she closed her eyes. The darkness behind them felt dusty, cloying, with a ghostlike memory of Ravenscroft Manor. Only after it finally cleared into fresh, unstained peace did she emerge from the water. Drying herself, she dressed in her favorite lace negligee, then made a cup of tea.

Dark, fragrant tea in her best mug, with no one watching her drink it. And a biscuit on the side just to complete the experience of heaven.

Leaning against the kitchen bench, she watched sunlight venture over her books, listened to dim sounds from the city, and tried to ignore two students arguing on the street outside. Slowly, warily, her mind began to emerge from the haze that had been ensconcing it ever since she left Ottersock's office.

I just quit being a professor! The memory hit her like a punch to the stomach.

Yes, I really did, she answered herself, smiling into her tea.

No more nasty gossip from male colleagues.

No more scorn from her faculty head.

She might even consider wearing a pretty floral dress, now that she didn't need to present a scrupulously professional front at all times in an effort to deter gossip and scorn. Granted, she probably wouldn't be able to afford such a dress, considering she'd just relinquished her income. Indeed, she'd have to leave this dear little flat . . . leave Oxford entirely . . . perhaps even return home to her parents . . . get a job as a receptionist . . . and learn by necessity how to giggle just to survive . . .

She was on the verge of a marriage of convenience and significant hyperventilation when the doorbell rang. She literally ran to answer it. Caleb stood on the doorstep, of course, all smiles and the merest hint of a swagger. He smelled of fine cologne, and his suit must have cost an entire year's salary— although the tie was crooked, like an invitation. Amelia's nerves began to hum excitedly.

"Um," Caleb said, his eyes widening as he imbibed the sight of her lace negligee (which did not take him long, since it was very skimpy), her bare feet, and her loose, still-damp hair. Amelia considered slamming the door shut and running away to hide inside a high-necked, heavy black gown, but clutched all her courage to her, along with clutching the edge of the door, and did not move.

"Hello, Caleb," she said calmly.

"Um . . . I have something for you." He looked up into her face with some effort.

"If it's a written apology from Professor Ottersock . . ." Amelia began, but stopped as Caleb reached into his jacket pocket, for she wasn't exactly sure how she would finish that sentence. The question proved moot, however, when he brought out a small black safe bag and handed it to her.

Amelia gasped as she felt the contents' shape through the material. "My teaspoon!" she exclaimed delightedly. Then she frowned. "You stole a valuable thaumaturgic artifact from Professor Ottersock."

Caleb shrugged and nodded.

"He'll fire you!"

"No, he won't," Caleb answered lazily. "I quit."

Amelia's mouth fell open. She hastily closed it, but not before an incredulous laugh escaped. "You—what—*why*?"

Caleb tilted his upper body toward her so as to answer in a low, deep voice that transformed the humming of Amelia's nerves into a full operatic chorus and sent a blush over her cheeks. "Where you go, I go too."

"But your career is so important to you," she argued. "Please tell Ottersock that you've changed your mind."

"No." He smiled as if abandoning the dream that had guided him all through his youth were a matter of little consequence. His eyes lit with that smile, turning them into the most enchanted summer. "Don't look so disconcerted, Meely. I only studied history so I could stay with my best friend. If you'd chosen to study geography instead, we'd currently be knee-deep in a muddy tidal pool somewhere."

"Oh," Amelia said blankly. If her blush grew any hotter, the negligee would burn right off her (which, she suspected, might have been part of his plan). "Um."

Caleb's eyes twinkled, for he knew that he was charming, and he loved it. "I'm seriously proud of you for resigning. And even more so that you did so for the sake of self-love. You *should* love yourself—you are very, very lovable, Amelia." His smile deepened, and the twinkles became sparks that sent thrilling little electric shocks through Amelia's body. "Besides," he added, "I've been *so bored*. If it weren't for you, I'd have quit months ago."

"But what will you do? Caleb, my dear friend, I admire you in so many ways, but you're not the best at planning."

He leaned against the doorframe, hands in his trouser pockets, wholly unoffended by this criticism. "I have a plan. The first thing on it . . . well, the second thing . . . is to buy two typewriters. I'm going to write a novel, Meely. I know a publisher, Bernard McDonald, who is keen to buy one from me."

Amelia's eyes narrowed. "Bang-Bang McDonald? Didn't he put the dean's carriage upside down in the middle of the lacrosse field and blame you for it?"

"Yes, and now he owes me."

"Hm. Well, that is a good plan. You'll make a marvelous novelist, and publishing surely pays better than teaching. But why do you need two typewriters?"

"One's for you, so you can write your future bestselling book about the teaspoon."

"Oh." Amelia looked down at the safe bag in her hand, then up again at Caleb, and somehow within that one and a half seconds her love for him grew a thousandfold. "Oh," she said again, which was oddly more eloquent than real words would have been.

"Is that not a genius idea?" Caleb asked, a little cocky, a little shy.

Amelia nodded. "Mm-hm," she managed to say. Inside her brain, several thoughts were already coming up with chapter headings, while several more were designing various experiments she could perform. Caleb watched her with a fond smile, no doubt all too well aware of this mental activity. Amelia forced herself back into the conversation and frowned at him with a teacherly habit that would probably take years to break. "If this was second on your list, what's first?"

Caleb's smile vanished. He straightened away from the doorframe. "Er, well, yes, well, I'm not quite prepared for that yet," he admitted, rubbing his hands up and down the expensive cloth of his trousers. "I need to rent a marquee, you see, and get together a string quartet, and then there's the difficulty of finding three dozen roses at this time of year."

"Right," Amelia said, blinking bemusedly. "That sounds very . . . extravagant."

He bristled. "Of course it is. A man can't just propose marriage while standing on a doorst—"

He was abruptly silenced due to Amelia leaping on him. She threw her arms around his neck in a manner that her mother would vehemently denounce as contradictory to Tarrant dignity. But Amelia did not think of her mother in that moment. Her feet left the ground, and Caleb, with a joyous laugh, wrapped his arms around her so that she was safe against him. He walked them both inside, kicking the door shut behind him.

"Sorry," Amelia began. But she proceeded no further before he was kissing her. The flutters fluttered, and sparkles sparked, and Amelia wrapped her legs around him as he strode across the room at a speed that felt wildly thrilling after all the years of waiting and wishing. Pressing her back against a random wall, he kissed her so thoroughly, her bones seemed to melt.

Amelia could have stayed there all day, kissing the time away. But Caleb soon advanced the conversation, setting her on her feet, extending his kisses along her jaw and against the shy, sensitive place behind her ear. Amelia's only contribution now was a moan of pleasure, but this seemed sufficient for Caleb, and she felt him smile against her skin. By the time he had kissed down the length of her neck, she'd made her second monumental decision of the day.

Stepping back, she looked at Caleb with all the love and longing that had been archived in the secret recesses of her heart for so many years. His eyes darkened in response. Cupping her face with one hand, he stroked a thumb across her cheek, as if she were a priceless antique whose magic he yearned to experience. He said nothing; but then, words never had proved capable of encapsulating the depth of friendship between them. Taking his hand, Amelia silently led him into her bedroom.

Two weeks ago, she'd have derided this as an unwise decision. Before Ravenscroft Manor, she'd have suggested taking their time. Had the Hereford teaspoon never come into her life, she'd still be standing with him on the doorstep right now, discussing publishing schedules and the cost of typewriters. Or worse, continuing to listen in demure silence as Professor Ottersock berated her.

Furthermore, a small, well-trained part of her mind began fretting that she'd not yet offered him a cup of tea, but she ignored it. Instead, the minute they entered the bedroom, she pulled Caleb against her and resumed kissing him. He tasted better than tea, even the Earl Grey variety. And judging from the passion of his response, he did not regret her lack of proper hostessing.

Their hands, which had been playing together for two decades, got down to business at once. Buttons were released, shirts removed, shoes heedlessly thrown across the room. Nakedness being achieved in short order, the hands then drifted in an enchanted dream, causing a thousand little flares of sensation that had Amelia gasping. She stepped backward, drawing Caleb with her, until she met the edge of her bed. But then he stopped, holding her still. He looked over her shoulder, and a confused, uncertain frown tumbled across his brow.

"Only one bed," he said.

Amelia laughed. "Of course only one. Did you think I'd have bunks?"

"I mean, a bed for only one person. It's awfully narrow, Meely."

She glanced back at it, taking in the neat brown counterpane, the patchwork quilt folded at the end, the single heavy pillow, and she frowned too. Her bed had always been just a place to sleep—she seldom even read there, for that was deleterious to healthful sleep patterns—but now she appreciated that it could fairly be described as the most unenticing bed in existence.

"It's all I've needed," she said.

"You're going to need something a lot larger before I'm through with you," Caleb told her in a husky whisper.

To which there was only one reasonable reply. Turning away from him, Amelia began yanking the counterpane from the bed.

"What are you doing?" Caleb asked, laughing.

Amelia gave him a hot, fierce look. "You told me that you'd never shared a bed with anyone before. Show me what you do instead." And throwing the counterpane, quilt, and pillow onto the carpeted floor, she presented him with a ~~mess~~ cozy opportunity.

"Oh, Amelia," he said in such adoring tones, it was fortunate there was now soft bedding on the floor, for she veritably swooned. They went down together in a sweetness of tangling limbs and tangling tongues. "I love you," Amelia whispered. Or perhaps it was Caleb who did. At that point, there felt little difference.

All the promises he'd made the night before, while standing on a moonlit path in the middle of England, arousing her to pleasure with simple descriptions and tempting smiles, he kept now. But the experience of it was so much more intense than Amelia had imagined. (And she'd done quite a lot of imagining during the train journey back to Oxford.) She'd never guessed how her very soul would stretch even as her body did to accommodate him. She'd not thought that "slow" would involve long, luxurious moments of just gazing at each other as they reveled in the experience of being united. And while she had anticipated Caleb's joyful tears, she'd not believed herself capable of them also. Together they wept, and smiled, and whispered compliments, all jumbled up in an intimate treasuring that was so lovely it almost hurt.

By the time they reached the "fast" part, Amelia was in such a haze of soft delight that every sensation felt like an electrical storm, scorching, exhilarating. And when they climaxed, she cried out Caleb's name just as he'd promised she would, regardless of any neighbors who might be trying to enjoy the peace of their gardens at that moment. Amelia had never known such perfect freedom. Sagging into the quilts, laughing in delight, she closed her eyes to relish the fluttering aftermath.

"Oh my God," she breathed.

"I suppose that, since you continue to insist on the nickname, I won't complain," Caleb told her, grinning. And then he kissed his way down her body, settling between her legs, where he employed his tongue to show her just how good a friend he could be.

♡

CHAPTER TWENTY-FOUR

Nothing anticipates the future more
than the past does.

I, on the Past, Cornelius Ottersock

Six months later

THE MINERVAEUM CLUB's duty manager stood near the library door with a fire extinguisher at his side. Water buckets had been stationed in every corner of the room, and staff carrying thaumometers along with trays of hors d'oeuvres patrolled warily. Antiquarians had gathered in the library to celebrate the opening of the *Harroway's Household Wonders!* exhibition at the British Museum, and frankly, no amount of precautions could be enough.

Tweedy scholars and curators milled about in the dusty lamplight, slowly killing themselves with pipe smoke and arguing in mild, professional tones as to whether the exclamation point on the exhibition's title was undignified or not. Sir Nigel Harroway himself had been invited as a special guest, and every few minutes someone approached him with congratulations, only to discover that the man was the academic version of sticky fly paper. From a safe zone just beyond Sir Nigel's line of sight, Mr. Dummersby watched his horrified peers endeavor to escape becoming acquainted with the minute details surrounding each thaumaturgic item in the exhibit. At the start of the evening, Oxford's head of Material History, Professor Ottersock, had floated the idea of bestowing upon Sir Nigel an honorary degree. Less than an hour later, the professor was consulting train schedules for when he could soonest send the dreadful fellow back to Cumbria.

(Lady Ruperta Harroway had also been invited to the soiree. She gave her regrets, being unfortunately too busy taking in an opera show, shopping at Harrods, touring royal sites, and making an overnight trip to Paris, where she met a fascinating and beautiful artist who offered her a life of thrilling romance and adventure, which Lady Ruperta declined on account of said artist being middle-class.)

At a table in one corner of the library, beside a window that glinted with rain, a young woman in white lace sat drinking tea. Every now and again she looked out at the crowd with an expression of vague amusement. None of the gentlemen dared to meet her eye.

"Who is that lovely creature?" a graduate student from America whispered to Dummersby, his eyes alight with fascinated curiosity.

"That is Mrs. Sterling," Dummersby informed him. "She is an eminent scholar of material history. It's her public lecture, 'On the Dental Thaumaturgic Manifestation of a Simulacrum Poltergeistic King John' that you will be attending tomorrow."

"Snappy title," the student remarked.

"Hm."

"And who's that sitting beside her? The scowling fellow."

Dummersby's eye twitched nervously. "Professor Gabriel Tarrant from Oxford's geography department," he said, and clutched his pipe a little tighter. "He's Mrs. Sterling's brother. Don't approach him, whatever you do."

"*That's* Professor Tyrant?" The student whispered the name, taking a cautious half step backward. "We know about him even in Stanford."

Dummersby sniffed with the apparent disdain of a man who himself wasn't even known in Cambridge, let alone another country. "The woman beside him, who appears to be wearing two different earrings, is his wife, Professor Elodie Tarrant. Try to ignore the way they look at each other—such unseemly behavior in public, even if they are geographers!"

"Hm," said the student in a carefully neutral tone.

"You probably know the others at the table."

"They're Professors Pickering and Lockley, aren't they? The famous orthi—orithno—birders! I wonder if I could get their autographs."

Before Dummersby could advise him against such a course of action, the library door swung open with an ominous creak. Silence clamped down on the entire company. Standing tiptoed for a better view, the student saw a man enter. This newcomer did not wear proper tweed but instead was clad in a suit so expensive it looked plain. His hair shone like heavenly gold in the lamplight, as if he were the god Apollo, come for sherry and a chat at the club. He read a book while walking, and when he turned a page, a bejeweled wedding band glinted on his ring finger. At the sight of it the student, despite having a fiancée back home, felt an inexplicable regret.

"Sterling!" the crowd chorused.

Looking up, the man blinked in surprise. "Goodness, is it that time of night already? Uh, nice to see you all again, I suppose!"

This was spoken with a good cheer that only barely concealed his obvious dislike, but the majority of the crowd did not seem to realize. They shuffled forward in the hopes of shaking the hand of the fellow who'd done what each of them secretly dreamed for themselves: leaving academia to become a full-time novelist. But before any could manage it, he slammed shut his book, staring across the room.

Silence clamped down again. As one, every head in the crowd turned.

The woman at the table stared back at Mr. Sterling, her eyes darker than the night outside.

"Oh dear, here we go again," Dummersby muttered, and puffed his pipe disconcertedly.

AMELIA WATCHED WITH trepidation as Caleb approached her. He was grinning . . . Indeed, his entire walk was like a grin, and the lamplight seemed to glitter around him out of sheer delight for his existence. She began to flutter internally.

"Close your eyes, Gabriel," she murmured from the corner of her mouth.

"What?" Her brother looked at her with a bemused frown. "Why?"

There was no opportunity for Amelia to provide a further warning, however. Caleb arrived, and without even so much as a glance at the others around the table, let alone a polite greeting, he cupped Amelia's chin in one hand. Tilting her face up, he afforded her one hot, electric second to prepare before he bent and kissed her.

"*Ahem.*" Gabriel cleared his throat disapprovingly. Everyone else at the table chuckled, and Amelia thought she heard a charmed *"Aww"* that was no doubt from Elodie, who tended to see romanticism in a mere handshake and could be relied upon to melt dreamily when anyone in her vicinity actually kissed. Which was of course a rare occurrence, since this was England, where the general consensus was that expressions of marital affection ought to take place in private. With the curtains closed. And the doors locked for good measure.

Caleb seemed to be on a one-man crusade to overturn that.

Thankfully, he released Amelia before she (and Mr. Dummersby as well) needed to be checked by a cardiologist. "Hello, wife," he said, and Amelia blushed as if he'd not taken every opportunity to say that in the past three months since their wedding. Then he tossed himself into the empty chair beside her and grinned at the others present. "Hello, you lot."

"Hello," they replied (except for Gabriel, who said a proper "Good evening").

"Sorry I'm late, I was chatting to my publisher upstairs in the Shakespeare Lounge."

"Is that it?" Beth asked excitedly, indicating the book Caleb had placed on the table. *"A Regal Love?"*

Caleb patted the plain white cover with the kind of wry fondness that comes from having spent months in a complicated relationship with some eighty thousand words. "Yes. Well, it's an early copy that I'm editing. Turns out I'm unconsciously obsessed with the word *realize*; and you'd think King Edward the First had a nervous tic, considering how often I describe him blinking." He gave Beth a warm smile. "It's nice to see you, sweetheart. Congratulations on being awarded High Flyer for your presentation on the giant carnivorous moa."

"Thank you," Beth said demurely, although she became luminous with his kindness. "Devon did most of the work, though."

Her husband scoffed genially. "I just held your parasol—"

"And used it to beat off the smugglers who were trying to capture the moa," Beth added, with a chiding look in which Amelia could practically see lovehearts. It made her feel like crying happy tears that her cousin Devon was so adored.

Then again, she cried happy tears at breakfast this morning when her first spoonful of porridge was the perfect temperature. And she cried them yesterday too, upon seeing a child skipping on the steps of the British Museum.

It was all Caleb's fault. And Amelia smiled privately to herself at the thought of telling him so, once she had a doctor confirm what she herself had only recently begun to suspect was the cause of all these wayward emotions. Laying one hand in an entirely casual, nonsignificant manner on her belly, she reached with her other for the teacup . . .

And stopped as it trembled in its saucer.

Thud. A book fell off one of the library's shelves. The floor shook. Looking around with some alarm, academics murmured worriedly to each other through mouthfuls of sardine pâté and pipe smoke.

"Earthquake," Gabriel said with the utmost Tarrant calm. "Interesting."

Elodie, however, was already on her feet, causing her chair to totter. Gabriel reached out without looking to place a steadying hand on her back. "That's no normal tremor," she declared. "Do you see the tint of blue in the air? Magic! I need to get my thaumometer."

"Wait," Caleb interjected before she could dash off. "This is all too familiar." He turned to Amelia with a look of suspicion. "Dearest, would you do me a favor?"

"No," she answered at once, for she knew what he was going to suggest. The air between them began crackling, and only partly due to the buildup of thaumaturgic energy. At the end of the table, Beth and Devon glanced at each other nervously. Elodie sank back into her chair, but slowly, suggesting that she'd rather run for the door. Gabriel drank tea with the peace that being oblivious to other people's emotional dramas granted him.

"Meely, really?" Caleb shook his head, the very picture of tragic disappointment. "You promised you'd stop carrying that teaspoon around with you."

Amelia held herself even more primly erect. "I'm worried Ottersock will try to steal it back," she explained.

"Ottersock is too busy trying to keep his job as faculty head after losing his two best professors. Hand it over."

"Certainly not," Amelia declared with an outrage that, under more private circumstances, would have been a passionate kiss instead.

"Do you mean that teaspoon?" Gabriel asked, pointing to where one lay on the floor beside Amelia's chair.

Gasping, she reached down to retrieve it. "It must have slipped out of my pocket," she said, wincing apologetically. In all honesty, she ought not to have brought the blasted little Utensil of Chaos (as Caleb had dubbed it) with her tonight—but despite what she'd just said, she'd actually forgotten it was in her pocket. As she straightened, clutching the silver handle tight in case it slipped away again, she wondered if her constantly forgetting it was part of the magic.

She also had to secretly admit that this was not the first time lately that the teaspoon had fallen to the floor. Or flown across the room. Or tapped playfully against her desktop for no apparent reason. The episodes did not appear connected to her own emotional state at the time, and more than once Caleb hadn't even been in the house. It was a mystery, for her studies thus far had proven the psycho-conjunctive magic interacted solely with human emotions. Furthermore, its range did not extend far enough to include neighbors, and no other living soul had been in the house . . .

Oh dear, she thought, placing an instinctively protective hand on her belly. Had the dratted teaspoon enchanted the baby she suspected she was carrying? Had it created a witch child?

Oops. Caleb was going to be so—well, delighted, probably.

She held out the teaspoon. "I think you should keep hold of this," she told him soberly. "At least for the next seven months."

Caleb, reaching to take it, stopped, staring at her with an utterly blank expression. Amelia looked back at him nervously, heart in her throat. If in that moment any other person existed in the entire world, let alone the Minervaeum's library, neither she nor Caleb knew it. A deeply intimate silence encompassed them, filled with worry—and wonderment—and love, always love. Slowly, Caleb's expression transformed like magic into the most beautiful Amelia had ever seen. He reached for her hand.

She remembered him in the shadows so long ago, bringing her sunlight, giving her his handkerchief. She'd sworn in that moment never to cry again. Now, as she took his hand and heard the tiny, sweet sound of their wedding rings kissing together, Amelia felt tears once again fill her eyes. They made the whole world seem filled with silvery magic.

Whoosh!

All of a sudden, the teaspoon flew out of her other hand.

"Aaagghh!" The crowd of academics screamed as flames leaped up from their pipes, instantly setting fire to the ceiling.

Boom! A case of books erupted, toppling large volumes of historic household records onto Dummersby's head.

With a sigh, the Minervaeum staff rushed for their water buckets (again).

♥

ACKNOWLEDGMENTS

As BEFITS HISTORIANS, Amelia and Caleb have been with me for years, loitering at the back of my imagination, waiting for their turn to be written. Perhaps that's why I had so much fun with them during the creation of this book, and why I cried sentimental tears in parts too! They are both deeply special to me, and writing "the end" was bittersweet. I wish I could talk with Amelia for hours about the history we both love.

This book is a fantasy rom-com, which means that although it's ostensibly set in late Victorian-era England, it's an alternate universe that contains such fantastical things as magical teaspoons, comfortably sized train compartments, and young women working as professors long before that was allowed in real life. For example, Dervorguilla of Galloway was a real person, but Balliol College possesses no brooch of hers, enchanted or otherwise.

My sincere appreciation as always to Kristine Swartz, Mary Baker, and the whole publishing team at Berkley Romance.

Thanks also to my wonderful audiobook narrator, Elizabeth Knowelden. I'm hugely grateful to Katie Anderson, and Margot Reverdy, who blessed me with yet another stunning cover. Heartfelt hugs to my agent, Taylor Haggerty, along with Gabrielle Greenstein, Jasmine Brown, and Holly Root, to whom I am more grateful than I can say. Thanks also to Stacy Jenson and Heather Baror-Shapiro. All my love to Amaya, Julie, Simon, Anya, and Myla. And of course a big hug to my readers! I appreciate you so very much!